HELEN MOORHOUSE

THE DARK WATER

POOLBEG

This novel is entirely a work of fiction. The names, characters and incidents portrayed in it are the work of the author's imagination. Any resemblance to actual persons, living or dead, events or localities is entirely coincidental.

Published 2013
by Poolbeg Press Ltd
123 Grange Hill, Baldoyle
Dublin 13, Ireland
E-mail: poolbeg@poolbeg.com
www.poolbeg.com

1

A catalogue record for this book is available from the British Library.

ISBN 978-1-84223-542-3

Typeset by Patricia Hope in Sabon 11/15

Printed and bound by CPI Group (UK) Ltd, Croydon, CR0 4YY

www.poolbeg.com

Praise for Helen Moorhouse

Book Trade reviews

"*The Woman In Black* has met her match! Deep within this terrifying and sinister tale lies a sad story of loss and regret. I could not put *The Dead Summer* down" – Eason reviewer

"I would recommend to anyone who enjoys gothic, ghostly and atmospheric stories. It has a similar feel to that of *The Lovely Bones* by Alice Sebold, *The Little Stranger* by Sarah Waters, *The Place of Secrets* by Rachel Hore and *House of Echoes* by Barbara Erskine. I look forward to more from this author and more of this type of book from Poolbeg"

– Waterstone's Drogheda reviewer

Author reviews

"An exhilarating, enthralling and spooky read. A great debut novel that leaves you eagerly awaiting the next one" – Linda Kavanagh

"A poignant historical thread is woven through this story of a haunting" – Martina Devlin

ABOUT THE AUTHOR

Originally from Mountmellick, Co Laois, Helen Moorhouse lives in Drumcondra, Dublin, and is a wife, mum, daughter, sister, aunt and great-aunt. After many years spent behind the scenes in radio, Helen now works as a freelance writer. Her interests include TV, movies, eating and things that go bump in the night. Her debut novel, *The Dead Summer*, was published by Poolbeg in 2011.

For more, see www.helenmoorhouse.weebly.com

ACKNOWLEDGEMENTS

The Dark Water has been a long time coming.

My huge thanks go first and foremost again to the team at Poolbeg, especially Paula Campbell, who was with me every step of the way on that long journey, taking care of me with long conversations, fresh ideas and endless patience. Thank you.

To my editor, Gaye Shortland, the invaluable Third Eye – thank you for your dedication and patience, yet again!

Thanks to my family: Seán & Claire Keenan – here's another footprint, Dad; Margaret & John Laidlaw; John, Mary, Hugh and Rory Keenan; Tony, Bríd, David, Neil and Meadbh Keenan; Rose, Ray, Rachel and Brendan Comerford (and little Kit!); Angela, Donal, James and Kevin O'Neill; Avril & Alan Moorhouse; Adele, George, Maitiu & Jake Reid; Colin and Andrea Moorhouse. Thank you all for your love, support, help and encouragement.

A special thanks is reserved for two extraordinary ladies who undertook solo transatlantic flights to take care of me and my girls, and give me free hours to bury myself in this story. Avril and Rose – thank you so much.

To Suzy – who did for me what all the king's horses and all the king's men could not.

To the Heads. As always.

The Dark Water runs parallel to an extraordinary period of my life. To the extraordinary teams of people that I have encountered since this process began – you are too many to name but each and every one of you know who you are and that you have touched me and my family immeasurably. The team at OLHSC Crumlin; the team at Florida Proton in Jacksonville; the team at Bandon

Hyperbaric – everyone who has cared and helped. Never doubt that we are forever in your debt.

To all of my friends, former colleagues, acquaintances and well-wishers – your kindness and support have been a harness on this rollercoaster and will never be forgotten. You have no idea how grateful we are.

To Daryl, Daisy and Florence. A million hundred dollars.

And to my readers – to everyone who bought, borrowed and enjoyed *The Dead Summer*. Your response has been overwhelming. Thanks to everyone who took the time to mail and message, to recommend, to review, to simply read. I hope this is another step on a long journey together.

There is one reader, however, who is much missed. Thanks to Louise Jesson for being a fan, a boss, a friend and an inspiration. Wish you were here.

For Florence, who puts the joy into every day

CHAPTER 1

October 29th

Silently, the intruder slipped into the apartment and stayed a while in the hallway, listening, contemplating his next move.

He was drawn to the living room – had been since the first time he'd come here, unnoticed and silent. He moved so stealthily that it was hard to tell if he walked or floated down the corridor. Once there, he moved the living-room door at the very end of the passage and it squeaked defiantly, causing him to pause a moment, to listen for sounds of movement from the room on his left – the one he hadn't dared visit yet. There was only stillness. He proceeded, entering the room and beginning the familiar walk-around.

He walked by the first window, a shadow crossing past the amber glow from the streetlight outside. Next, to the writing desk which fitted into the space between the two long sash windows. He riffled through a book open on the desk – *The True History of Edinburgh's Vaults* – losing the page that had been left open. Beside it, a notepad – should he try to leave another message? The last one had been so difficult. And it had taken so much of his energy. He decided against it tonight.

The intruder moved to the mantelpiece of the tall fireplace, grasping its edge momentarily, leaving four fingerprints behind in the dust. He then ran a forefinger along the mantel, leaving a trail,

1

pausing at the end. At the picture. Gently, he turned the frame toward him, to see it better – the black-and-white photograph of a boy in swimming trunks – nine or ten years of age – he couldn't remember precisely. The boy stared back at him, a familiar broad, proud grin across his face, holding a brick, of all things, under his left arm and in his right hand, thrust toward the camera, was a medal on a piece of ribbon.

The intruder stared at it a long time, lost in the face of the beaming child, thoughts and memories rushing through his head, so many that they hurt. He turned away, unable to sustain the energy that they needed. He wanted to go, but knew that he couldn't leave yet. He had a job to do and he was determined that tonight he was finally going to do it.

He glanced around the rest of the room, at the belongings of the man. Empty teacups, a half-drunk bottle of Bell's, a glass left with a sticky stain on its base where the last drains of a drink had congealed. A long black coat was slung over an armchair, the pocket pulled inside out. Dirty dishes were scattered throughout.

The intruder moved toward the door again.

This time, he didn't pull it toward him to open it, or pull it behind him to close it. Instead, he stepped silently around it, despite the fact that he seemed too big, even for a small person, to negotiate the space. In a second, he stood outside the next door to the right. In yet another second, having summoned all of his energy, and as quietly as he possibly could, he stood on the other side of it, taking in his surroundings: the wardrobe and tallboy, the bedside lockers, the vast bed. And in it, the man he desperately needed to see. The one person who could maybe help him. The one person that he needed to know.

In his sleep, Gabriel McKenzie dreamed that someone had entered his room. They hadn't used the door – he hadn't heard the handle turn – but they were in there with him all the same. Gradually, he found himself swimming up from deep, deep sleep, to something verging on consciousness. Half-awake, he became gradually more aware, his heart starting to beat faster, his breathing audible as he surfaced from his slumber. There was someone in his room, someone standing at the end of his bed, watching him.

Gabriel didn't want to, but he knew he had to. He gasped with fear and expectation, forced himself to sit upright, ready to confront who was there. He subconsciously sought words – a 'who the hell are you?' or 'get out' or 'don't hurt me' – he wouldn't know until they came out of his mouth.

But there was no one there.

Gabriel's heart raced as he scanned the room, his eyes darting from right to left and back again to the end of the bed where he'd felt – no, known – that someone was watching him, but the room was empty, the only sound his own ragged breathing. Not again, he thought.

CHAPTER 2

October 31st

"Come *on*, Martha, it's starting!"

Martha Armstrong glanced impatiently at the clock in her kitchen, two empty glasses in one hand and a chilled bottle of wine in the other. She had to resist shouting back to Sue in the next room, to let her know that she was on her way. She jigged a little from foot to foot and forced herself to look at the screen that Will was studying intently, his elbows resting on the granite-topped island where they both stood, staring at his laptop.

"There!" he said, pointing at the screen. "What do you think?"

Martha stared at the screen. It showed a large room in darkness, visible only in the green tinge of night-vision cameras. The shot was focused closely on a grand piano to the left of a marble fireplace. Suddenly, what seemed like a small, flickering ball of light rose directly up from the closed lid of the piano, hovered for a second or two and then appeared to double – a second, identical ball of light appearing to imitate exactly what the first did – before they zoomed off the screen and disappeared.

"Orb?" asked Will, leaning on his elbows and turning toward Martha, his face intent and hopeful. Martha couldn't help but smile and resisted the urge to lean forward and kiss him. "Moth, my sweet," she grinned and put the glasses and the wine bottle down on the kitchen island before reaching for the computer mouse.

Will sighed. "Are you sure?" he said, frustrated. "The Leith Street Group sent this to me, positive that there was something in this particular piece of footage."

Martha shook her head. "Watch'" she said, returning to the beginning of the segment of video and playing it again. "The movement is fluttery, I suppose you'd call it, exactly the same as a moth or a butterfly, and the hovering is just too similar to the movement of a flying insect to conclusively prove that it's paranormal – you're always saying yourself that it can only be paranormal if you can't in any way, shape or form prove that it's *normal* – and this is just too normal for me."

She reached again and picked up the wineglasses, intending to move away.

"But it splits in two!" Will said, exasperated.

Martha sighed and put the glasses down again with a clink. "Seriously, Will – you don't even believe in orbs being the first stage of a spirit manifestation. *You* told *me* that you thought they were only ever insects or dust or reflections of passing lights or whatever – I didn't pick my cynicism up off the side of the road." She was growing increasingly impatient. So many conversations with Will were like this these days.

"The footage is very grainy but, look, there's a mirror on the mantel up above the fireplace, and my guess is that the edges are bevelled – hence our moth, or insect or whatever, fluttering about, looking for a way out, reflected in the light from the camera, suddenly doubles up, one becomes two – its own reflection – and then zips off about its business. The mirror is unframed, and the angle of the shot, up that close, makes it difficult to get a clear view of the scene as a whole. It's a simple mistake to make though, especially for believers in orbs. Which you're not, right?"

Will knew she was correct but Martha could tell it didn't make him happy. He so desperately wanted evidence these days to prove absolutely that there was something out there. He knew it, and she of all people knew it but proving it was the elusive dream for people like him, and hundreds of thousands of people before him. When he'd had Gabriel to bounce off, he'd been less disheartened every time something proved inconclusive but now he relied more and more on her, and his own desperation. Obviously his age didn't help – approaching his late thirties might well have catapulted him into a mid-life crisis and a need to make a significant mark in his field before it was too late.

For that matter, at the age of thirty-seven, perhaps she was in premature mid-life crisis too.

"Shit," he said simply.

Martha tried to avoid eye contact with him and continued to stare at the laptop. She knew it was ridiculous but sometimes she felt that he almost wanted to blame her when something could be explained rationally and she was the one doing the explaining.

Will went and picked up his waxed jacket from a nearby chair and slid his arms into it. "Shit, shit, *shit!*" he said, and ran a hand through his hair. "Of course it's a moth!" He rolled his eyes upward. "It's so stupid of me to think otherwise but you're right – I need to get a grip and get back to using my head when it comes to these things. It's just so frustrating sometimes . . ."

"Here, Will, what's this?" Martha suddenly interjected.

"What?" He was back at her side in a single step, as she leaned closer toward the screen, dragging the mouse across to take the footage back a few moments.

"Watch this." she said, leaning back to allow him a closer look.

They stared as the camera automatically pulled back – it was a static night-vision camera, fixed on a tripod but with the facility to focus automatically if it sensed movement or needed to expand its view to allow a shift in light or mass to fit the frame. The shot was much the same as before – the grand piano, the fireplace, the mirror now clearly visible, reflecting the wall just above the camera, faintly lit with the glow of the infrared light from the piece of equipment. The movement was so fast that had they not been staring intently at the screen, they might never have seen it but, as they did, Will gasped, and grabbed the mouse in his right hand to watch it again.

It was definitely the shape of a person. It moved in a flash across the wall, as though walking quickly from left to right. What thrilled Will most was that, as the shot took in the mirror, they could quite clearly see that it wasn't a shadow caused by a reflection. There was nothing to reflect.

Will watched it several times in a row, each time his face becoming more animated and the beginnings of a smile creeping across his features.

"Good?" asked Martha tentatively.

He turned to her and beamed. "You bloody genius!" he exclaimed and straightened, grabbing her in a bear hug.

It wasn't comfortable – he squeezed too hard, and his jacket smelled musty, the wax slimy – but Martha allowed herself to be crushed in the embrace and smiled at his enthusiasm, closing her eyes for a moment.

"It's clear that the shadow isn't caused by a person – we'd be able to see anyone crossing the room in the mirror! How did I miss this before?" he said, breathless, releasing Martha and turning back to the screen to watch it again.

Martha glanced at the clock – eight fifteen. "You were looking too hard?" she offered, smiling. "C'mere, didn't you say you'd meet the guys at half eight?"

"Hmm?" he asked, preoccupied.

"Only it's a quarter past now," she continued, "and you've got to get all the gear set up and it's Hallowe'en and there's a caretaker waiting at the house for you . . ." She allowed her voice to tail off as Will glanced at the time at the bottom of the computer screen.

"Oh Christ, you're right," he said, and hurriedly snapped the laptop shut.

He was going on an investigation he'd been excited about for weeks – a recently renovated former tenement house in Edinburgh's Old Town. Will and his group from the university were to be the first to investigate it for signs of ghostly activity and they were hopeful of concrete evidence, based on the reports they'd received from the new owners and their workmen – a ghostly apparition of a priest coupled with odd noises and knockings in the dead of night.

Martha picked his keys up from the table and held them on her forefinger, clinking them gently from side to side to make it obvious, as he searched around the kitchen frantically for them,

patting the many pockets on his jacket as he did so. Will smiled as
he finally turned and saw them dangling there. He grabbed them
with a grin, leaning in to kiss her softly as he did.

"You know I love you to absolute bits?" he said quietly so that
Sue, waiting in the living room, wouldn't hear.

"And so you should," she grinned and kissed him back. "Now
please be careful tonight, don't bring anything back with you, and
don't trip over stuff. And drive safely."

"I promise," he said and pocketed the keys before tucking the
laptop under his arm and leaning in for another kiss. "Seeya, Sue!"
he called into the living room as he strode out of the kitchen,
turning briefly to give Martha a warm smile of parting.

She followed him out to the hall to watch him head out into the
dark evening, feeling the blast of cold air that gusted in through the
front door before he closed it softly behind him.

"Is he bloody well gone?" called Sue from the couch.

Martha grinned before retreating to the kitchen to pick up the
wine and glasses. "Finally!" she answered and flicked off the
kitchen light before joining her friend in the cosy living room and
closing the door behind her.

"My God, I thought he'd never leave!" said Sue, reaching out to
grab some cashews from a dish on the coffee table. A fire crackled
in the grate and the TV hummed low in the corner. "I set it to
record so we didn't miss a millisecond – the Hallowe'en special is
going to be too bad to be true!"

Martha smiled as she settled herself in an armchair and began to
pour the wine. She felt guilty at being so excited about what they
were going to watch, but Sue was right – it was terrifically bad TV.
If Will caught the two of them about to gorge on a two-hour
special, he'd go into one of his sulks. "Right then," she said, "Hit
it!"

Sue jabbed her forefinger dramatically at the remote control on
her knee and immediately green footage, much like that which
Martha had been watching moments before on Will's laptop, filled
the screen.

A theremin played a 70's science-fiction-style theme tune, just
audible under a deep voiceover which announced that the next two

hours would most likely change the lives of those who watched, and prove without a shadow of a doubt that life after death existed.

Sue mouthed aloud along with the final few sentences which were part of the credits each week: "*'They're young, they're ready for anything, and they* believe. *We are ghosts . . . ghosts are them . . .* Ghosts R Us!'"

The theme tune grew louder and the 'cast' of the newest ghost-hunting show on TV flashed up one by one on screen, all in their early twenties and equipped with various cameras, thermal imagers – the sort of equipment that Will used on his investigations – all captured in various states of what seemed to be terrible fear. And at the end, one last 'character': the resident psychic medium who accompanied the team every week. Gabriel McKenzie.

CHAPTER 3

November 1st

Martha buttered a third piece of toast for Ruby who was perched on a kitchen chair and wiggling from side to side while cramming as much of a crust into her mouth as she could manage.

"Now say 'Ruby Doo'," instructed Sue earnestly.

"Dooby Doo," replied the almost-eighteen-month-old, as clearly as she could.

"Excellent," said Sue, taking a drink from her coffee mug. "Now say 'Stinky Poo'."

"Dinky Poo," came the response, accompanied by a broad grin which revealed most of the contents of the little girl's mouth.

Martha burst out laughing at Sue's face which registered complete disgust.

"Ruby!" Sue cried, outraged. "What have I told you about speaking with your mouth full? Now say 'Sorry, Sue'!"

This only served for Ruby to open her mouth wider to repeat the phrase and as a cue for Sue to tickle her. Bits of soggy toast sprayed over the table and Sue's dressing-gown sleeve as the two of them giggled.

Martha smiled and moved Ruby's plate a safe distance from her wriggling form as the little girl writhed out of Sue's grip and almost fell off the chair.

"*Beebies*!" Ruby demanded suddenly.

Patiently, Martha helped her get down from her chair and watched as she waddled toward the living room, toast in hand, to watch the TV which Sue had left blaring before they sat down to breakfast. She was glad of some peace and quiet to chat with her friend.

"So," she said, "on a scale of one to ten, how would you rate the pain and anguish of deprivation at the moment?" She mimed smoking a cigarette and looked at Sue, eyebrows raised.

"Oh, don't talk to me – I'm bloody dying for one!" came the response, as Sue took herself another slice of toast and began to butter it roughly. She smeared it with honey and took a huge bite. "I'm going to be the size of a house at the rate I'm going but Simon says that smoking's the one thing about me that he'd just prefer I didn't do around him so I'm taking that as an incentive. Been on the fags way too long, I guess. And before you say anything it's not that I feel he's trying to change me or anything – he just does that thing where he looks so damned *disappointed* every time I excuse myself to go and light up that I just can't enjoy them anyway!" She took a second and third bite of the toast and polished off the slice, immediately picking up another.

"Simon says . . ." mimicked Martha in a playful voice and grinned at her friend. "You'll have to bring him up next time you're coming – I'm very curious to meet the man who can turn you off ol' Mr Smoke."

Sue rolled her eyes and grinned back. "He *is* rather dishy!" she said, shrugging her shoulders demurely, fluttering her eyelids and feigning ladylike shyness.

She finished the second piece of toast, put a hand out for another and checked herself, clasping her coffee cup instead. "And your new house will be just about good enough for him to be brought to as well!" she said, her eyes scanning the large kitchen around her. "I love coming to stay since you moved onto millionaire's row."

Martha nodded and took in a breath through her teeth. "Don't mention the war," she replied. She, too, loved the big house with its huge garden, which she and Will had fallen in love with the previous spring. They were finally settled there now after the move, but she sometimes caught herself wondering if they hadn't been happier in Will's flat in the centre of the city.

11

"Oh?" asked Sue, concerned.

Martha made a dismissive movement with her hand "Oh, it's fine, but the mortgage is a bit of a killer."

Sue poured herself another coffee from the pot on the table and made a '*whoo*' noise as she exhaled, her eyes wide. "Do you guys still have Will's place in Barcelona?"

Martha nodded, although it was a lie. The Barcelona apartment had had to be sold to pull together the funds for the deposit on the house but she didn't want to tell Sue that just yet – it seemed so much like putting all of their eggs into one basket prematurely. She didn't want to tell her either that she had gone back to work part-time because she needed to, rather than wanted to. Or that Dan hadn't paid maintenance for three months in a row. Martha hadn't even told Will that yet.

She was glad of the distraction as Ruby waddled back into the kitchen, tugging ineffectively at the waist of her pyjama bottoms which had slipped down and made them dangerously long around her feet.

"Toast! Toast!" Ruby demanded, pointing at the table.

Sue obliged, picking up a knife and proceeding to butter while Martha pulled up the pyjamas and rolled them halfway up Ruby's legs to prevent her from tripping. It was timely, as the scrape of the key in the front door led the toddler to whip her head around and almost trip in the process of getting to the hallway.

"*Wull!*" she shouted at the top of her voice, toast forgotten, as she bolted to greet her adored Will, returning from his night's investigation.

Martha could just about see the front door from her seat and smiled as she saw Will whisk the child up into his arms, giving her a kiss and squeezing her to him in a hug.

"Wull!" repeated Ruby, patting his stubble-covered chin before wriggling to get back down again as she heard something of interest from the TV.

Will placed her safely on the floor and she ran off again in the direction of the living room.

"Morning, Sue!" said Will and kissed Martha on the cheek.

Sue raised her mug of coffee in salute.

"You look pooped," observed Martha, standing to take a mug from the cupboard behind her.

Will gave a tired smile and accepted it gratefully, pouring himself the last of the coffee from the pot on the worktop.

Martha began to spoon fresh grounds into the pot.

"Not for me, ta," he said, shaking his head. "I'm going to have this and get an hour's kip or so if that's okay with the ladies?"

"You actually look like absolute shit," observed Sue, a smile playing on her lips as she began their usual insulting banter.

Will gave a tired grin. "And you're still fat," he replied, leaning against the breakfast bar.

"Oh, I dunno," replied Sue, glancing down at her eight-stone frame. "Weight can be lost – but looking like you do – that's not possible to change. What on earth were your parents thinking? Doing . . . what do you call it? . . . *reproducing*!"

"How did the investigation go?" interrupted Martha who had sat through hours of such duels when her partner and friend were together.

Will looked at her and smiled. "Absolutely bloody brilliant. Wish you'd been there – I can't wait for you to have a look through the material. We had a trigger object move and I'm almost sure we've got it in a clear shot – and as for the audio – fantastic stuff! And I haven't even had a chance to listen to all the EVP's yet."

Sue observed them, understanding only in part what they were talking about.

"And what did Big Mr McPsychic think of it all?" she asked.

Will frowned and looked at her, then back at Martha, annoyed.

Martha shook her head at him and then turned to Sue. "Oh, Gabriel couldn't make it last night 'cos of the – thing – the show," she said.

Will rolled his eyes and pushed himself upward from where he was leaning on the counter top to cross to the sink and pour away the last of the coffee. "I'll see you in a couple of hours," he said and strode from the room without a second glance.

Martha watched his back as he left the room, a sight that she saw too often lately. "See you then," she replied quietly and took a deep breath. She was going to need more coffee.

CHAPTER 4

November 1st

In a central Edinburgh apartment, a tall, well-built man sat forward on his expensive leather sofa, his head in his hands, rubbing his eyes with exhaustion. He had barely slept again, in anticipation of visitors that had ultimately never arrived.

In all his forty-odd years, it was the first time ever Gabriel had been alone at Hallowe'en. Normally he couldn't think for spirits coming through, trying to get messages across, all shouting together. It was his Boxing Day sales, he always joked – people crammed up against the glass trying to get to the other side and, there, keeping an eye on letting them through as best he could, was his brother Laurence – his spirit guide. But not this year. This October 31st he had been totally alone, unable to bring himself to watch that stupid TV show, which was being shown as 'live', when it had been recorded two weeks previously. It was all that he could do to actually get the TV crew to physically *go* to the location they were meant to be investigating and, even then, certain segments were always touched up afterwards in the TV studios.

Right now, however, that was the least of his worries. Where the hell had his gift gone? Why was there no contact from spirits any more? And where was Laurence? Since he'd been twenty-eight years of age his brother had been his constant companion –

presenting himself as a nine-year-old boy physically – but able to communicate with Gabriel as an adult. Was Laurence angry with him for the same reasons as Will? Had he seriously managed to annoy the living *and* the dead by trying to earn himself the few extra quid that the TV show paid?

Gabriel ran his hands down his face and inhaled deeply, surveying the scene before him in the George Street apartment where he had moved the previous spring. It covered an entire floor of the Georgian building, painted and decorated in a modern fashion but respectful of the original style. He loved it. It was his dream home, the kind of place where he had always wanted to live. At the moment, however, it resembled a student flat share rather than the elegant and stylish home to which he had always aspired. The coffee table was piled high with newspapers, half-filled coffee cups, an empty bottle of whisky and a couple of empty bottles of wine.

His black coat, his work 'uniform' as he liked to think of it, was flung across an armchair where he'd left it days before. At least three pairs of shoes were strewn across the un-vacuumed carpet. At his feet a bed of crumbs and crusts from his staple diet of toasted sandwiches lay, causing a crunch when he stood up and sticking to his bare feet. Over everything in the room was a layer of dust and it was this that he longed to get rid of most, except he couldn't. Not yet. Because that's where he kept finding the fingerprints. And even though he hadn't dared to yet, he needed to have them checked in some way – or at the very least have someone else witness them to prove that he wasn't going mad.

And he also needed someone to read the message on his desktop pad. The one that terrified him. He had found it over a week ago now, maybe more, and covered it with a newspaper so that he didn't have to keep looking at it every time he passed. Or turned that way. Or even thought about it.

He hadn't written it himself and there had been no one else in the apartment, not even the cleaner because he'd phoned her to say he was unwell and that he'd call again when he needed her. He couldn't get the image of the message out of his mind – a long squiggle as if the pen was being dragged across the page first, leading into the distinct shape of two words written like a child might if their hand were held by an adult's, or by a drunk person, or someone writing with the wrong hand very badly . . . Gabriel had been rolling the message around his mind, around his mouth, since he had seen it there. 'Do it' it said simply, before the words faded into another long squiggle.

Do what, he wondered. What should he do? And who had put it there in the first place and why?

Gabriel rubbed his face again and shook his head almost to clear the vision of the words from it. He couldn't do this again today – sit here all day in his boxers and a T-shirt. Nor could he bring himself to start cleaning up just yet – he just wouldn't know where to begin.

Gabriel made a sudden growling noise aloud as if to motivate himself and stood up, inhaling sharply as he did. shaking out his hands. It was a beautiful sunny day. That was it. He'd just go – get dressed, and have a stroll in Princes Street Gardens. Just get out of here for a while – away from the dust and the dirt and the puzzlement and the loneliness. The loneliness he felt, despite the fact that he felt quite sure he wasn't completely alone.

CHAPTER 5

November 1st

"You're telling me they haven't spoken in six months?" Sue said incredulously.

"Not since last May. Around about the time Gabriel moved to his apartment in George Street."

Sue shook her head as the two friends turned from the coffee stand and walked toward the nearest bench to sit down.

Martha rested her coffee on the bench between them and undid Ruby's straps, lifting her out of the pushchair and readjusting her woollen hat before allowing her to toddle off a little way by herself to follow a pigeon that she had spotted pecking at the ground.

"*Buhdie!*" Ruby shouted gleefully and screamed in delight as the bird took fright and flapped its wings to take off.

"Oh God, why didn't you *say*?" groaned Sue, running a gloved hand over her face in embarrassment. "No wonder Will was pissed off earlier with me burbling on about Gabriel like that. I thought they always came as a matching pair? What the hell happened?"

Martha removed the lid from her cup and blew on the coffee to cool it down before attempting to take a mouthful. Then, with a sigh, she turned to Sue.

"It all kicked off around the time Gabriel signed up for *Ghosts R Us* as the resident medium," she said. "We went round to his for drinks because he had a big announcement to make and we had just popped the cork on a bottle of champagne when Gabriel told us all about the TV show and next thing I knew himself and Will were in a massive shouting match with Will going on about integrity and Gabriel going on about not wanting to be a bloody tour-bus guide all his life and it ended up with Will storming out and me having to go after him. There's been no contact between them ever since."

They sat in silence in the early winter sunshine. Martha turned her face toward it, trying to absorb as much of the last rays of heat as she could before winter set in. She felt Ruby press against her leg and rubbed a hand across the blonde curls as the child searched, oblivious, for the packet of raisins that she knew she might find in her mother's handbag, beaming to suddenly discover instead a small chocolate bar. Ruby held up the spoils of her search to her mother expectantly and Martha relented, pulling open the wrapping and handing it back to the child.

"Oh, you jammy thing, Ruby!" exclaimed Sue. "I'm bloody starving!"

Martha laughed aloud. "We finished breakfast an hour ago!" she observed, grinning at her friend. "Oh, shut up," replied Sue grumpily. "Don't you even remember giving up cigarettes? Give us a bite, Roobs – there's a good girl!"

The toddler obliged and Sue pretended to take a bite, rewarding Ruby with a grin and a kiss on the cheek. She sat back and sighed deeply, taking in her surroundings.

"Seriously, Martha, don't you ever look at your life and think how weird it is?" she enquired, looking at her friend side on, trying to gauge the response to the forward question.

Martha shifted in her seat and closed her eyes to the sun again. "What do you mean weird?" she asked. "I'm divorced – one beautiful, if chocolatey, daughter – living with my partner who I love very much in a beautiful house – with my second children's book being published in the spring and a part-time job that I actually enjoy . . ." She opened her eyes and tilted her head to one side. "When I put it like that, I think I'm pretty bloody lucky!"

"Actually you're right," agreed Sue. "But the whole . . . *ghosty* bit? Will out all night videotaping *nothing* in the dark and then you spending hours going through the *nothing* trying to find *something* that might not exist? And the fact that his former best friend actually makes a living on TV talking to alleged ghosts, in possibly the *worst* TV show I have ever watched in my life? I mean, come on – you saw it last night – you could clearly see that pebble was thrown by the sound guy. And when that '*whooo*' sound happened, everyone looked in the direction of the doorway, except Gabriel who looked directly at the actual source of the sound . . ."

"You mean the cameraman!" Martha giggled at the memory.

"Exactly! The cameraman! And as for it being live – I mean the editing was just horrific! What about that bit where they flicked away from the presenter and then flicked back and she had a slightly different jacket on!"

Martha laughed and then cringed inwardly at the thought that Gabriel was a part of the wretched thing. It was such a sham – she could understand why Will was angry with his friend for being part of it when they had both worked so hard, for so long, to establish themselves as reputable – Will as an investigator, and Gabriel as a medium.

"It's no weirder than spending a weekend at a convention of bog-snorkellers," retorted Martha, referring to one of Sue's favourite assignments of recent years. "Or hanging out with white supremacists, or greengrocers –"

"Oh, come off it, Martha – all of those things are *real*!" laughed Sue. "And don't diss the bog-snorkellers – I've befriended one or two online!'

Martha laughed even harder. "You talk about things being real and then you make friends on the internet? I'm going to be ousted as your *actual* friend because you have *virtual* bog-snorkeller buddies now?" Her laughter stopped as she saw Sue suddenly sit up and grow serious, staring into the distance across Princes Street Gardens. "What's up?" she asked, looking frantically around for Ruby who, smeared with fudge and chocolate, was playing with the hood on her pushchair. Momentarily reassured, she followed Sue's gaze across the park and finally saw what had made her friend sit up. It was a familiar figure standing on the path a short distance way, dressed in a long black coat, a bright red scarf knotted at the neck.

"Speak of the devil and all that, but isn't that Gabriel?" asked Sue.

Martha leaned forward for a closer look but there was no mistaking him, even behind the sunglasses. Beside him, on the ground, lay a spilled cup of some hot drink, the contents draining away toward the edge of the path and into the grass.

Gabriel seemed to be focused on something straight in front of him. He looked tense, poised as if trying to catch better sight of something or someone in the distance. Suddenly they saw him shout and raise a hand, as if trying to catch someone's attention. And then he broke into a run, in pursuit of something or someone that he was intent on catching. Except to Martha's eyes, and Sue's, there was no one there. They watched as a couple of passers-by stared after Gabriel as he pursued his imagined quarry, the long black coat flying behind him.

Martha stood, suddenly, and thought about calling to him, but he was too far away now so she simply watched as he ran after something that wasn't there or that only Gabriel could see.

Sue looked at Martha in confusion. "What's he running after?" she asked, puzzled. "Can you see anything?" She looked again in Gabriel's direction, shielding her eyes from the sun.

Martha sighed as he vanished from view. She shook her head and sat back down. "I don't know, Susie," she said, staring at where he had been. "But I have a funny feeling it wasn't someone that's been breathing any time recently."

Silence fell between the girls as they watched the park, curious to see if Gabriel might reappear, but there was no sign. A touch on her shoulder made Martha jump suddenly and she shrieked, grabbing her coffee cup tighter in her hand as she turned. Instant relief washed over her as she saw Will's face smiling at her, his expression sheepish, his eyes ringed with tiredness.

"Will!" she exclaimed. "You frightened the life out of me. What the hell are you doing here?"

Will wrestled Ruby upwards so that she could wrap her arms tightly around his neck.

"Wull," she said, snuggling into him, a sure sign that nap time was looming.

Will rubbed Martha's arm apologetically and smiled. "Got your text to say you were coming here and I had to follow. I couldn't sleep." He lowered his voice. "I'm really sorry for being a grumpy so-and-so earlier."

Sue, politely, continued to stare in the direction where they had seen Gabriel, pretending not to listen, though overhearing them was unavoidable.

"Sorry to you too, Sue!" called Will in an exaggeratedly loud voice, acknowledging this.

She didn't turn, just raised a hand, the movement also exaggerated for humour – a gracious wave. Will smiled. "I was just really tired and – well – you know that certain subjects set me off."

Martha smiled back and rubbed a hand gently across his cheek, taking in his boyish face underneath the small black woollen cap he wore. She tugged the end of his striped scarf, knotted at his throat. "Forgiven," she grinned.

"Excellent," he replied. "Now I'm starving, so who's for an apology brunch? Sue?"

Sue turned and replied almost as quickly as Will asked the question. "Yes, please!" she barked. "Where do I go to sign up for that?"

They laughed as Will indicated that she should link his arm. "This way, please!"

Martha protested, half-heartedly. "Seriously guys, we've only just had breakfast!" but was ignored completely by the others who set off laughing back across the park in the direction of Princes Street. She didn't care that they didn't answer her. With the hand that wasn't holding the coffee cup, she took the handle of the pushchair and began to follow them . . . but not before, burning with curiosity and concern, she took one final look back in the direction where she had seen Gabriel run.

CHAPTER 6

November 2nd

A train pulled slowly out underneath her as Martha crossed Waverley Bridge on her way back to work at lunchtime. She'd needed to pop over to a bookshop on Rose Street to pick something up for Will and the walk had been brisk and enjoyable on yet another sunny winter's day. A few of the shops on the way along Princes Street had already been decked out for Christmas, and even though she knew it was very early – too early in fact – Martha couldn't help but feel excited at the prospect of her first actual festive season in Edinburgh. The previous year, Will had visited his parents in Cornwall and she and Ruby had gone to her dad's in Oxfordshire but this year they were having Christmas, just the three of them, in their own house and then having Sue and Simon and Will's sister Lucy to stay for Hogmanay.

As she strolled past the majestic facade of the Scotsman Hotel, she thought about how she proposed to decorate the huge house and enjoyed mental images of the fire crackling in the living room, of Ruby opening gifts on Christmas morning, of Will and her relaxing, enjoying old movies and mulled wine. She was lucky that she worked only three days a week and had plenty of time to get herself organised for her fairytale Christmas. And who knew, maybe Dan would cough up his missing maintenance money between now and then and that would make things a little more comfortable.

As she walked, Martha allowed her mind to drift back to the previous year when she and Will had celebrated Christmas a week early with Gabriel at Will's apartment. Martha smiled as she remembered how she swore she'd never move to Edinburgh but as the weekend commutes grew more and more arduous on her own with a demanding toddler, and she grew more certain about a future with Will, she had relented and promised to move on a temporary basis the previous February. She had never left. They had purchased Calderwood in the autumn, needing what Will called a proper family home.

The previous Christmas had been the precursor to all of that and they had shared champagne and smoked salmon with Gabriel, sitting up until the wee hours, playing board games and laughing. Martha sighed and wondered if somehow this year might be the same – if something could ever be done that would bring the two men back together?

She glanced upward at the buildings on the Royal Mile and realised that she was back at her workplace without realising it. She chastised herself for not taking more note of her surroundings. She had grown to love Edinburgh city centre, adored working right in the heart of the Old Town, a stone's throw from the Castle, from St Giles' and from tourist haunts such as the Grassmarket. She loved this time of year with the brown leaves crunchy underfoot and the trees taking on their bare appearance for winter. In two or three months she would be filled with a longing for sunshine as the weather grew colder and any Christmas snows became either a dirty sludge or a worsening hazard but for now she loved to take it all in as the air grew cold and crispy and first frosts formed.

She mounted the stairs to the office over the tiny gift shop selling tartan and shortbread and pushed open the glass panelled door at the top, revealing the cramped and dingy office where she spent her days. It was a million miles away from her previous life in a glitzy advertising office but she loved it. Loved the electric fan heater that she had to keep under her desk to stave off the early morning chill in the air before the central heating kicked in, loved the tiny kitchen area where there was barely room to make tea but which was always stocked with biscuits, and loved the smell of must and old books that filled the room as a whole.

Her work partner, Maisie Gordon, looked up as Martha entered the room and hung her trench coat and scarf on the wooden coat-rack just inside the door. "Hello there," she said in her soft Scottish accent and returned to reading *Heat* magazine, incongruous in the current setting, against shelf after shelf and pile after pile of books which were hundreds of years old, covered in pigskin and some barely readable after years of bad storage.

"Did I miss anything?" asked Martha, the stock question when returning from anywhere outside the Old Edinburgh Data Preservation Project as her workplace was known, the clunky title disguising the fascinating nature of the work that they did, taking ancient record books from historic buildings, institutions, clubs – record of attendance, minutes, family trees, diaries – and transferring the data to computer before the books were sent to be preserved. Some of the books that they dealt with went as far back as the 1400's and Martha every day revelled in the living history that she held in her hands, Scotland's heritage right there under her fingertips.

She was aware that some might find the work mind-numbingly boring, pointless even, but she adored it – handling the past and learning about real people – how they lived, how they died, what they called their children, their professions. She would sometimes come across a death record for someone whose birth she had discovered weeks before and occasionally took it upon herself to try to find records in between – marriages, children being christened, appointments – all the elements that went together to paint a picture of real lives from the past. Martha loved touching history itself and was slowly gathering enough experience to think about her next writing project – a historical novel but based on real facts and real people.

Martha and Maisie worked as a team with the records – one reading the handwritten information out, the other transferring it to the computer database, both of them often working together to try to figure out a word or identify a strange name for a job or even a disease that might have killed someone. It had taken them a while to find that 'Bad Blood', for example, was another name for syphilis – the taker of an entire family of eight infants and then the father and mother after many years, and that a 'bule' was in fact a tumour that had killed an elderly man in the Tolbooth parish. There were many more like these and many instances, of course, of the plague that had taken so many lives in the 1600's.

Maisie glanced up from her magazine, took a chocolate biscuit from the pack in front of her and thought for a moment. "Well, it's been crazy in here as always," she observed without a hint of a smile.

Martha grinned. The office was usually so quiet that if the phone rang both of them jumped.

"Like the stock exchange, if the truth be known," continued Maisie drily. "Actually there *was* a phone call – put my heart crossways in me!"

Martha sat back at her desk, fishing a pre-packed sandwich from her handbag. "Really?" she asked.

Maisie nodded and continued to munch the chocolate digestive. "*Mm-hmm*," she continued. "It was for you as well – some fellah – not Will – I know his voice."

Martha furrowed her brow as she unwrapped her lunch. "Did he leave a name?" she asked.

Maisie shook her head. "No – said he'd call again over the next few days. Posh English accent he had but no other clues I'm afraid."

Martha shrugged. "Can't have been too urgent then," she said, tucking into her sandwich and looking at the clock. "Bloody hell – two already! Where does lunch hour go?"

Maisie closed over the packet of biscuits and flung her magazine into the recycling bin. "Well, when you're as busy as we are . . ." she said, finally cracking a smile. "Right then, for the afternoon what do you fancy – Old Greyfriars or, wait for it – *New* Greyfriars?" She held up two ancient-looking books bound in leather.

Martha crumpled her nose – one of the books looked fire-damaged and she wasn't in the humour for trying to identify information on charred paper on such a lovely afternoon. "Left hand," she said, pointing at the undamaged book.

Maisie smiled. "A very good answer, missus," she said, "In fact, the only correct answer! Now, let's see . . . Mhairi Abernethy's diary is first up this afternoon. Hello, Mhairi, can you tell us your vital statistics, please?"

Martha grinned again. It was a game that they took in turns, pretending to interview the subject in the book for an imaginary and irreverent magazine they'd invented called *Plagueboy*. Ready to become absorbed in the game, Martha giggled as 'Mhairi' started to reply to her interviewer.

CHAPTER 7

1963

It was Sunday. A sunny and warm summer's afternoon as the girl sat nursing the mug of now-cold tea at a table as far away from the window as she could manage. She'd been there for a couple of hours now, watching the comings and goings of people having hot and cold drinks and cakes; families coming in for ice-cream sundaes and treats. She knew that soon she'd have to finish up and get back on the road if she wasn't to draw attention to herself. The travelling was harder than she'd imagined, but she knew she had to keep going. She didn't know where to, but she absolutely had to keep going.

She was tired, however. Her feet ached and her back and ribs were so sore. Thinking of the pain, she was reminded to pull her lank greasy hair down over the left side of her face for the hundredth time and she lowered her head again to look out from under it. The bruise was the sort of thing to definitely get her noticed. But five more minutes here wouldn't hurt, would it?

The girl tried to focus her thoughts. Where should she go next, she wondered? The past week had been a blur – leaving the island for the weekly trip to the mainland and not returning. And then the interminable running and then walking along roads she didn't know, to places she didn't recognise, gripped with fear at the thought of pursuit. She couldn't trust anyone enough to take a lift, even though many cars had slowed down for her. And she'd only felt safe on the roads – there was no point in coming this far to fall into a bog or a pothole. But when could she stop? She was filthy, she knew that. She could even smell herself a little, another reason why she distanced herself as far from other people as possible. She was ashamed of her appearance. And of the markings on her face which had calmed from angry red and purple to dirty brown and yellow.

The few hours' sleep that she had caught here and there had been of no benefit to her but she had to keep going and she could rest when she was far enough away to be safe. She didn't know where that was, or when it would be, but she felt compelled to get further and further away. As far away as she could.

She tried to block out everything that had happened to her. Funnily enough, it wasn't one of the worst beatings that had finally made her run – if it had been, then she'd never have been fit enough to get this far. It was odd too that her mother hadn't come with her to the mainland that day – normally the two of them travelled together, but that day she had insisted that the girl go alone. It was almost as if she knew.

The girl was startled again by the bell ringing over the door of the shop as another customer entered. She jumped in her seat. I must stop doing that, she thought to herself. It was the kind of thing that would get her spotted. She watched from under the protective curtain of hair as a skinny young man entered, about the same age as herself, she reckoned. He was dressed in a brown tweed suit, too heavy for the warm day and a little too big for him. In fact, it looked completely out of place on his young frame, as though it belonged to a much older man. From where she sat, she could clearly see the counter where a middle-aged woman served her customers. She watched as he reached it in a couple of long strides and casually leaned over it, resting on his elbows, the position forcing him to look upwards into the face of the proprietor, who smiled.

"'Allo, Duchess," he said with a grin and smiled back.

At least that's what the girl thought he had said. She had never heard anyone speak like that before.

"Good afternoon, Martin," replied the woman, smiling at him. "How are you this fine day?"

"I am absolutely wonderful, Mrs Fairlie," he replied and righted himself, standing up to peruse the counter, examining in close detail the trays of cakes under their domed glass covers.

"Shame to be indoors on a day like today," the woman offered, watching him.

"That is why, Mrs F," he replied, "I am merely here to purchase, as always, on this day of rest, six of your finest cream buns to take back up to that greedy lot and, while I am on the premises, it would be rude not to 'ave a cup of my usual. And then, when Mrs T is finished visiting 'er uncle I shall be forcibly carryin' her to my automobile and getting back to that fine lake for a spot of fishing." He tapped the counter with a flourish.

Mrs Fairlie smiled again and began to pour a mug of hot, brown liquid from a metal urn behind her.

"I'm sure Mrs Turnbull will be delighted with that plan, Martin," she remarked drily. "And an Eccles cake, did you say?"

It was the young man's turn to grin. "Go on then." He pointed at one of the cake trays and tapped the glass dome that covered them. "And box up some custard slices – the usual half a dozen. Teatime treat and all that."

"I'll drop them over to you," replied Mrs Fairlie, picking up an Eccles cake with a tongs and placing it atop a doily which she had already deftly slid on to a plate with her other hand.

The girl watched as the young man picked up the cake and mug and turned away from the counter.

"Martin!" snapped Mrs Fairlie and a broad grin spread across his features.

He turned back to the counter and placed his spoils back down. "Ah, Mrs F!" he exclaimed. "You're too clever for me!" He rummaged in his pocket for some change and carefully counted it while the woman held out her hand in expectation.

"And you do this every time you come in here!" she chided, but with a warmth to her voice, as she took the coin and checked it carefully with one eye, while keeping the other on the skinny young man as he turned again and surveyed the scene before him.

He took in the family at the window first – the two small girls whose faces were smeared with the ice creams that they were devouring while their parents looked on proudly. He moved his gaze to the couple sitting by the window, a pot of tea between them, untouched, as they held hands across the table and gazed at each other.

The girl saw the young man grimace and then he looked in her direction and caught her eye. She looked down into her tea as quickly as she could, her fingers again straying to the hair on the left-hand side of her face, pulling it forward and smoothing it down. She prayed that he wouldn't come her way. There was no reason he should. She didn't know him and, besides which, she was no one. She'd been told that often enough.

"Wotcher," he said as he slid into the seat across from her at the table.

Her instinct was to look around suddenly, her heart starting to beat faster and faster. Watch what? she wondered. Who was there? What was there to see?

"Calm down," he said again. "I'm only saying 'ello while I'm waiting for me friend. Ain't seen you round 'ere before?"

The statement was posed as a question, an answer expected. The girl shrank back on her seat, trying to make herself as small as possible, glancing at the other customers to see if they, too, had spotted her. She could barely understand a word he was saying. 'Round' came out as 'rahnd' and 'before' like 'befoah'. She'd never met anyone who wasn't from the island or the village where they went to market. He might as well have been speaking a foreign language.

"I'm Martin," he continued – 'Mah-in'. He thrust a skinny arm across the table at her, long bony fingers extended to shake her hand.

The girl shrank back further into her seat and didn't reciprocate. "Please leave me alone," she said, so quietly that she almost whispered it. It didn't have the desired affect.

The skinny boy grew still for a moment, surprised, and then sat back in the chair, perusing her carefully. He said nothing, just sipped his drink and stared.

The girl squirmed in her seat. Should she say it again, she wondered? Just leave? But she didn't want everyone looking at her, didn't want to create a scene. Why had he come over? Why couldn't he have just left her alone, like everyone else had?

He responded by suddenly sliding his cup across the table toward her.

"Do you know what?" he said, abruptly. "I fancy a cup of tea instead all of a sudden."

The Eccles cake on the plate was next to skate across.

The girl watched these unexpected actions with caution.

"And I'm really full after me Sunday lunch. Why don't you 'ave this lot? I'd just be greedy if I ate that cake. Didn't even ask for it," he lied nonchalantly.

He looked up as a shadow fell across the table. The girl looked no further than the flower-patterned apron that she could see beside her from the corner of her eye. This was it, she thought. The woman was going to start to ask questions, to ring the police. Her heart began to pound and she rubbed the tips of her fingers across her palms where she could feel the sweat starting to build. She was hit for a moment with the uncomfortable smell of herself, and shifted in her seat, making it more pungent to her own nostrils by doing so. Could everyone else smell that, she wondered, and felt ashamed.

"Here's your cakes, Martin," said the woman, placing a white cardboard box tied up with string on the table.

The girl could feel both sets of eyes burning into her as she stared helplessly at the steaming drink and the Eccles cake on the plate that the boy had given her.

"Thanks, Mrs F," she heard him say as he placed the box on one of the spare chairs. "I was just sayin' to me mate 'ere that I actually fancy a cuppa tea today for a change. Think you could do the honours, Duchess?" 'Think' came out as 'fink'.

There was a pause for a moment before Mrs Fairlie agreed to the request. "Not like you to have tea, Martin, but it's your money," she said and the light flooded back over the table as she retreated toward the counter.

The girl looked up at the face in front of her. Why on earth was he doing this, she wondered.

"Go on, it'll go cold. Waste not, want not," he urged, pointing at the hot drink and smiling. He flopped back in the chair and wedged both hands firmly in his suit pockets, tipping the chair back on its two back legs until he was swinging gently back and forth.

The girl's hands slowly rose from her lap, where they she had been holding them clenched tight. She glanced up at the counter and saw Mrs Fairlie completely focused on spooning tea into a steaming metal pot, paying her no attention. Her fingers snaked then around the cup, absorbing warmth from the pottery, and she lifted it to her lips, taking a generous mouthful. This was another new experience. It looked like tea but wasn't. It was at once bitter and sweet, milky and sharp. She pulled it away from herself and looked down into it in surprise.

The young man laughed across from her and the chair clunked as it landed back on all four legs. "Ain't you never 'ad a cup of coffee before?" he giggled childishly, and in surprise she looked at him full on, regretting it almost instantly.

It was always the same when people saw her for the first time. That was why she tended to keep herself to herself, to wear her hat low over her face, to pull her hair across her features in a veil. Her mother had told her that her eye hadn't always been like that – that when she'd been born, both of them looked in the one direction but as time had gone on, one of them had got stuck somehow. Her father said it was the wind changing that had made it stay that way. That it made her such an ugly little girl that no one would ever want her. That it made her stupid and ungrateful and lazy too. Her brothers liked to say that the fairies had done it. She had begun, lately, to suspect that it had gone that way when she had been hit across the head perhaps, with a fist, or the broom, or whatever was to hand . . .

At least the boy would make his excuses and go away now, she reckoned. No one wanted to stay and talk to someone whose eyes didn't look in the one direction.

It was much to her surprise that his eyes stayed fixed on her face and, for a few seconds longer than she should have, she looked back. At his shock of wild curly hair, unkempt and unruly. At his huge blue eyes with their girlish lashes. At his full lips, pointed nose and chin. A face that looked, she thought, like its owner hadn't grown into it yet.

"Don't tell me," he said, pointing in the direction of the left-hand side of her face, at her palsied eye, she was sure. "You're a stunt driver for the movies, ain't ya? And you've 'ad a crash . . ."

The bruise, she thought suddenly. He's looking at the bruise. And he's going to laugh at me, call me clumsy . . . or he's going to know . . .

To her surprise, the boy was smiling, showing a full set of teeth. She found unexpectedly that she couldn't help herself and all of a sudden smiled back. And then he started to giggle and she felt laughter rise within herself too.

"Car flipped right over, did it? Blimey, you were lucky to escape with your 'ead, I reckon. Do you know Sean Connery?"

She didn't. Didn't even know what he was saying, much less the subject matter. But his smile, his ridiculous chatter, the easy way in which he leaned his elbows on the table and rolled himself a cigarette from tobacco he'd taken from his pocket – she couldn't stop herself being infected by his good nature. For a few moments, the girl relaxed without being aware of it.

Afterwards, she realised it was probably the first time in her life she had ever felt at ease with another human being apart from her mother.

She took another swig of the coffee, smiling still when Mrs Fairlie brought down the mug of tea to Martin and they played their game again where he acted like he wasn't expected to pay her, and then feigned surprise when she held out her hand. The girl was amazed to see the woman ruffle the thick mop of hair on Martin's head as she walked away, and even more so when she caught the smile that was meant for her before the lady turned back to her work.

The girl broke a little off the Eccles cake and nibbled it, laughing again when the boy slid the plate roughly back across the table, toward himself.

"Give it 'ere," he said. "I'm not that full after all," and they shared it between them.

The girl realised that she was famished – she'd eaten nothing but what she'd managed to forage in fields and farmhouses for the past *few days. She'd never tasted anything as sweet as this, however. To her, the coffee and cake was the most glorious meal she'd ever eaten, and she consumed her half carefully, and in silence, to make it last. She didn't know after all, when she'd eat again.*

"So, where you stayin' then?" the boy asked suddenly.

He wasn't looking at her – his eyes were fixed on the match that he held to his hastily assembled roll-up cigarette. He pulled deeply on it to ignite the end, and inhaled, looking again at her once he breathed out a great cloud of smoke.

The girl's hand froze as she reached for the last of the Eccles cake, and she withdrew it sharply, clamping her fingers together under the table and looking down again. The questions were starting now, of course. He was going to find out, he had to know something . . . or he'd guess and her father would come and find her . . .

"While you're in Dubhglas?" he continued, chewing absent-mindedly on another piece of cake, unaware of her discomfort. "Only like I said, I ain't seen you round before."

The girl wasn't sure how to answer. She twisted her fingers together. She had to get around this and get away before he uncovered anything and told the police.

"I'm . . . I'm just passing through," she whispered in response, eyes darting from side to side, checking if anyone else could hear. In case suddenly the door should spring open with a 'ding' and there would be her father and her brothers . . .

The boy continued to eat, and slurp his tea, all the while a thin plume of smoke from his cigarette snaking into the air. "How you doin' that then?" he quizzed further. "'Ave you actually got a motor?" He stared at her wide-eyed for a second and then rolled his eyes. "Wot am I sayin', you ain't old enough to 'ave a motor. Where you off to?"

The girl squirmed in her seat and didn't answer.

This made him stop and regard her carefully again.

"Nowhere," she whispered, keeping her head down.

"Nowhere, is it?" he answered but this time in a low voice of his own. He put down the piece of cake that he had been about to eat, and raised the roll-up in his other hand to his lips. Another pungent cloud of smoke formed as he took a drag and then exhaled slowly, raising middle finger and thumb to his lips to remove a piece of

tobacco stuck there. His eyes narrowed against the trail of smoke that came from the cigarette. "Only I 'eard they closed up shop in Nowhere last week and there's not much 'appenin' there."

There was silence for a moment. He took another drag and this time the smoke puffed out of his mouth in time with the words as he spoke.

"Where you really off to?"

He wasn't going to let this drop, she realised. She could tell by the tone of his voice. The girl thought hard, her brain a blank underneath the pressure of his stare. What should she say?

"Glasgow," she blurted suddenly. It was the first place she thought of. She had no idea about Glasgow, of course. No idea where it was, even, or how to get there, or if she was near to it or on the right route. But she'd said it now and couldn't take it back.

There was silence again, a long pause between them. The girl jumped as the door suddenly made its 'ding' again and her eyes flicked toward it, sure this time . . .

It was a lady who had entered. The girl felt the relief flood her body. This was all too much, she thought. She had to get going.

"Thanks very much for the coffee and –" she began, but he had his head turned toward the doorway and was speaking over her. He hadn't even heard her in fact.

"All right, Mrs T?" he said loudly, motioning for the lady to come over to the table.

The girl sat still, her moment of escape gone, and now there was someone else to deal with. Why hadn't she left when he sat down, she wondered, silently kicking herself for staying so long.

"There you are, Martin," the lady replied in a soft voice.

She was pretty, thought the girl. In her thirties, maybe, a little thick around the waist, wearing a beautiful cotton summer dress – a coral colour, patterned with small cream flowers, the skirt flaring out from the hips. The girl couldn't stop staring at it, conscious of her own grey tunic and the old brown blouse underneath. She had patched the seam under the sleeve as best she could, but she was aware of a slight tear that had reappeared, defying her basic needlework. The navy-blue winter coat – her mother's cast-off – was slung across the chair. It was far too hot outside to wear it, of *course, but the nights had been cold enough and she'd been glad of it. How she longed to wear something like that dress! How she'd love to just twirl round in it, just once, to see how it felt.*

"Hello!" said the lady.

The girl realised she was addressing her. She started to panic again, wished the ground would swallow her. She sat in the seat, helpless.

"This is my new friend," she heard Martin say. "She's going to Glasgow, Mrs T, imagine that!"

There was a tone to his voice – something forceful and pointed that the girl didn't recognise. She stared back again at the table, taking in only what she could see at eye level. The lady's white belt, for example, and some red nail polish – imagine – a plain gold wedding ring and a small gold watch on her left wrist.

"Glasgow," repeated the woman. "Oh my, that's quite far, isn't it?"

A scent of lavender filled the air as she sat down gently on a third chair. "Glasgow. Goodness – oh, hello, Margaret. I won't be staying, thanks – just collecting young Martin here."

At that moment, the girl dared to allow her eyes flicker upwards for a second. She caught the woman's eyes. They were kind.

"Have you a car, or a lift, dear?" the lady asked gently, bending her head to try to catch the girl's eyes.

The response was a shake of the head.

"Oh dear!" The lady's voice was grave. "Well then, you'll have a long way to go."

Martin spoke again then. "Didn't you say, Mrs T, that Mr T was heading Glasgow direction tomorrow though?" he said loudly.

The girl's eyes flickered up toward him. She felt helpless in the face of these people.

"Did I? Oh, I did. That's right, dear – my husband, Mr Turnbull, is driving to Glasgow tomorrow – or the day after perhaps – and if you like I could see if he'd give you a lift?"

Panic. "No, it's fine, really, I can make my own way," she mumbled, praying that they would just leave. She'd stayed too long now. She had to get back on the road. A wave of exhaustion washed over her and she closed her eyes for a second.

There was another pause. Mrs Turnbull again looked at Martin and back at the girl who didn't see the expression of alarm that crossed their faces.

"It would be no trouble," Mrs Turnbull said. "In fact, the company would be good for Mr Turnbull, wouldn't it, Martin? We live up at the castle, dear. Dubhglas Castle – we work there. If you like, you could come up with us now. I was planning on some cold cuts for tea – Mr McAllister has been growing tomatoes in the greenhouse and they're lovely with the cold ham, aren't they, Martin?"

The boy grunted in affirmative response, exhaled a thick cloud of smoke and bent the stub of the roll-up into the ashtray, squashing it down with his forefinger.

"You're more than welcome to join us," the lady went on, "and come to think of it you could spend the night – heaven knows there are enough bedrooms there. And then Mr Turnbull would have you to Glasgow in no time in the morning. Dubhglas is very far from anywhere actually so it's easy to get lost round here . . ."

She left the sentence hanging.

The girl knew that she shouldn't say yes but the idea of it all was so tempting. A bed, and some food. And maybe Glasgow was a good place to go after all? She was so tired . . .

"And do you know, that silly Esther has left the stove burning all day – in this heat, imagine, Martin! So we have so much hot water I don't know what to do with it. So much of it we could all have hot baths tonight if we fancied . . ." She let her voice trail off again.

The thought of it. The girl didn't think that she'd ever had a fully hot bath in her life. There was always her father first, then her brothers, then her mother before her.

There was a silence. The girl could feel herself wanting to give in. It was just for one night . . .

"You'd be perfectly safe with us," the lady said suddenly.

It was such a simple thing but in an instant the girl felt safe too. She forced herself to raise her eyes to the lady, who was smiling kindly at her, and nodded. It was barely perceptible but the lady nodded back, breathing a sigh that seemed strangely like relief.

"Right then," she said brusquely. "That's settled. Martin – did you get the cakes for tea by the way?"

"Six custard slices, just like you asked!" He grinned as he stood up sharply and slid his chair in to the table with a flourish, then picked the cake box up by its string with one finger.

Mrs Turnbull tutted and stood up herself, looking at the girl with a glance that indicated she should follow. "You know very well that I asked for five cream-and-jam puffs, Martin, and that Esther doesn't like custard."

The girl stood as quietly as she could. She was used to doing that, trying to stay in the background, to move as noiselessly as she could, to never draw attention to herself in case she did something wrong. And she always did something wrong . . .

She gathered the ancient coat to her, and the small hemp bag which carried her purse with its few shillings, her bible and a comb. All she had in this world. For a moment she hesitated, a thrill of panic running through her. What if it was a trap? She should run, now, keep moving . . .

But somehow she found herself pulled along gently by the warmth from the lady and the boy with the curly hair and the big smile. They were bickering now over the change for the cakes, the boy saying that he'd been tricked by a circus clown who'd happened to pass while he was enjoying his tea, and the woman was cuffing him gently over the ear as she laughed.

Mrs Turnbull bade Mrs Fairlie goodbye with a friendly wave as they left the shop and stepped out into the warmth of the small village street.

"You're a rogue, Martin Pine," she said as they sauntered toward a parked car further along the street.

And the boy was grinning, swinging himself in a circle around a lamppost that they passed along the way, "But you love me, Mrs T, isn't that right?" he said in his strange accent.

The girl watched it all as if in a dream, warmed by the sunlight on her bones.

"What's your name by the way?" he demanded suddenly, turning his attention to her.

She flinched, recoiled a little, and raised a hand to smooth her hair down again. She'd vowed that she wouldn't tell anyone, she reminded herself. But that felt so long ago . . .

"I'm Claire," she offered timidly, in her habitual whisper. "Claire Drummond."

CHAPTER 8

Martha jumped as her mobile phone vibrated against the desk unexpectedly and started to ring. She groaned inwardly. All morning she had sat at the kitchen table at Calderwood, doing everything in her power to avoid doing some work – she had spent hours on internet forums and reading online newspapers, made five cups of coffee, plucked her eyebrows – she simply couldn't think of a single thing to write. And now that she had a sentence in her mind – a single sentence – the phone had to ring. She would have killed for a phone call in the last three hours. If she made one, then that was actively avoiding work. If she *received* one, however – well, that was totally out of her control.

Martha was well aware of how ridiculous her logic was as she clicked out of *coffeebreaktimes.com* and leaned across the desk to pick up the ringing phone, clicking also out of her online banking and *scotgossip.com* which had also been open simultaneously. Her eyes remained focused on the computer as she did so and when she finally turned her attention to the phone it went immediately silent, its screen blank.

"Dammit," she whispered and placed it back down, opening a new blank document and taking a deep breath before typing:
Sometimes, in her dreams, Mhairi Abernethy still saw the beaked mask

40

of the plague doctor and thought about the man she had lost back in Mary King's Close. Martha knew that a draft of the third in her series of children's books was due soon, but today she had promised herself a start on the novel which was rolling around in her mind for so long, inspired by the characters that she encountered through the ancient books with which she worked.

This sentence was all that she could think of, however, and was glad when her phone gave a 'ding' to indicate that a message had been left and she could check it as yet another distraction. As she dialled the mailbox number and waited for the commands to be called out, she inwardly chastised herself. Nothing was going to get done at this stage of the morning. Plus, she should be concentrating on earning money, not setting off on some flight of fancy that might take her nowhere. *Lonely Pony* had been a moderate success and her first royalty cheque had been a pleasant surprise but certainly not enough to live on. That hadn't been a concern when she still had some of her nest-egg, before Calderwood, back when Dan still paid his way . . . Martha blocked the subject of money from her mind.

She suddenly sat bolt upright, all other thoughts banished, as she heard the voice on the other end of the line. It was a shock after so long, such familiar tones. Once the message was done, she hung up and looked at the phone, contemplating what to say when returning the call, because return it she must. She made to press 'redial', but then thought better of it and stood up suddenly. At the door of the room she hesitated for a moment and then carried on, picking up her bag and keys from the hall table and putting on her winter coat as she left the house.

She parked in the Niddry Street Car Park and made her way across to the Grassmarket through a blustery wind which whipped brown leaves off trees and almost blew an empty crisp packet right up into her face. From now until the end of November, the wind served to make sure that all of the old, dead leaves were blown from the trees – nature's clearout, leaving the branches bare until the spring.

The man who had phoned was sitting just inside the front door of an old-fashioned tea room. Martha pushed open the door and smiled as he turned his head. The cafe was cosy in contrast with the day outside. Steam came from the coffeemaker behind the counter and a smell of baking filled the air as an almost empty tray of scones was replenished in a display case where it sat alongside brownies, shortbread and an array of cakes – chocolate, carrot and lemon, each cut enticingly open to display creamy fillings. Martha was glad of the cosy atmosphere as she pushed the door shut behind her and weaved between two tables to take her place opposite her friend.

"Gabriel," she said aloud, unsure whether she should have hugged or kissed the big Scotsman before she sat down.

The moment was awkward – Martha hadn't seen Gabriel since the night in his flat when he and Will had fallen out. She had picked up her phone to text or call at least ten times since then but, never knowing what to say, had always put it down with a promise to do it later. She felt guilty looking at the man who had done so much for her and Ruby the previous year, hundreds of miles away in that godforsaken cottage. And yet she hadn't sent as much as a text since the spring. She had no clue how to acknowledge the enormity of her omission, the length of time spent apart and the fact that by her silence she must be seen as condoning Will's opinion when, in reality, she felt he was being unreasonably harsh about the whole thing.

"Gabriel, I –" she began, but the medium cut her off, ignoring her completely as she tried to speak. "My *God*, woman, what the hell took you so long to get here? You can pay for a hot pot of tea!" he barked, picking up his fork and shovelling a huge piece of chocolate cake into his mouth.

Martha smiled. It was all right then. He wasn't mad at her. Things could go back to the way they used to be. "I'm sorry, Gabriel, but the traffic was terrible coming in the road and then I had to drive round for ages in the car park . . ." Martha's voice trailed off as she realised that Gabriel was staring at something out of the bay window in which they sat.

"There!" he barked. "There, do you see him?" He pointed out of the window to the square outside, the area where public hangings had once taken place.

Martha's eyes followed where his finger was pointing and she craned her neck to see what Gabriel was looking at. There were a number of passers-by outside – groups of tourists taking pictures, local business owners going about their daily affairs – one man sweeping the pavement clear of dead leaves outside a pub opposite. Martha didn't know what she was supposed to be looking at.

"Who, Gabriel?" she asked, again trying to follow the line of his finger as it began to move.

"Oh, he's on the move!" announced Gabriel and shoved his chair back, standing up as if he was about to run out after whatever it was Martha was supposed to be looking at.

"*Who?*" she asked again, beginning to feel a shiver down her spine.

"The skinny chap in the brown suit," Gabriel said, annoyed. "He was over there in that pub doorway – didn't you see him? And now he's . . . oh, bloody hell, where's he gone?" He sank down again onto his seat, searching the market area outside but now clearly unable to see what he had so desperately wanted Martha to observe.

Martha was unnerved – and more than a little confused. This is exactly what he had seemed to do in the park the previous weekend and then, too, there was nothing to be seen – at least not by her. It had to be one of Gabriel's spirits – as a medium, he'd confessed to her once that he saw them everywhere in all of their various incarnations. But why did he think this one was any different? Why should she be able to see this one when she couldn't see all of the others? Most of them anyhow . . .

Martha had a clear view of the pub doorway where Gabriel claimed to have spotted the man, and she was fairly sure that there had been no one there at any time in the last few moments. Now, the man who had been sweeping the leaves was walking back through the doorway but he sported dreadlocks and wore a parka.

"Gabriel, what's going on?" she asked.

Gabriel turned away from the window, an exasperated look on his face. Martha actually thought he was about to burst into tears and reached out to touch his arm as he covered his face with his hands. She withdrew suddenly as Gabriel took a deep breath and looked her in the eye for the first time since she had arrived.

"He's bloody *everywhere*, Martha. I can't go to the shops or for a drink or go to work but he's somewhere, just waiting for me to see him. All he does is stare at me – I've tried calling him, following him, shouting at him – I'm going out of my mind because he's quite clearly there – he's so *solid* – but I can't seem to get him to communicate and I want to know what the bloody hell he wants! Are you *sure* you didn't see him?"

Martha sat back in the chair, silenced. She was taken aback by this. She had seen Gabriel upset in the past, but never this desperate. She knew also that he saw spirits all the time – beings just going about their business or trying to make contact with him – but he almost never remarked on them. There were so many that he probably wouldn't have made it through a single conversation at any time without indicating that he could see at least one soul who had passed over somewhere in the vicinity. Sometimes he might flinch if the spirit presented in some visually unappealing way – like when they had walked into a shop on the ground floor of an old building once and he had immediately turned to leave again because all he could see was a body hanging from a stairway that was no longer there, blue and buzzing with flies. She didn't know how he coped with it all, but she had never seen him once respond like this. Maybe this was it and he was finally having a breakdown brought on by years of seeing dead people? Martha recalled Sue's words that previous week, about how her life was weird, and it struck her now that Sue was absolutely correct.

Martha shook her head. "I swear, Gabriel, I didn't see anyone who looked like that. Are you okay? I saw you in the gardens last week . . ."

Gabriel rubbed his eyes, not listening to what Martha was saying, and it struck her how tired he looked. He sniffed loudly and again looked out the window, checking to see if the man had returned.

They sat in silence for a moment, Martha unsure of what to say. It was eventually Gabriel who broke the silence.

Still with his eyes firmly fixed out the window, his cake and tea untouched before him, he spoke.

"I didn't think I'd ever say these words, Martha, but I think I'm being haunted."

CHAPTER 9

They walked, against the wind, to Gabriel's apartment. Martha had offered to drive but he refused, saying that the fresh air would do him good. Martha was inclined to agree. With a sideways glance, she noted a greyish tinge to his pallor. He looked exhausted, like a man who had barely slept for weeks.

Gabriel talked while they walked, explaining things to Martha. How he had first noticed the young man, popping up now and again, never quite within reach. Around the same time that Laurence had vanished.

"I don't know what to do with myself with Laurence gone. I mean he's been with me for *years*," said Gabriel, looking at his feet as he walked. "He's my brother – and my spirit guide – and without a spirit guide I'm finding it really hard to get in touch with spirits and since I took that stupid TV job it's my bread and butter to talk to people who have passed over. Luckily, the production team for that show are so *dense* that they haven't noticed yet that I'm having to bluff. Too bloody busy throwing spoons and pulling chairs round with bits of string. I feel such a bloody sham though." Martha remained silent about this, aware of a growing level of bitterness in Gabriel's voice as he talked about the TV show.

"I mean, Laurence was there one day as usual and the next – poof! – totally gone. Now there are no spirits coming through to

45

me at all. Makes me feel like I've imagined the last seventeen years or so, like my gift has never existed. All except this skinny guy – I mean, I've been convincing myself that he's a real person, that I'm being followed for some reason. I've tried to convince myself he's someone I must owe money to or a creepy fan of the show or else it's a case of mistaken identity but I'm just kidding myself. So you saw me in Princes Street Gardens?"

Martha nodded. "Myself and Sue. She was staying with us for the weekend."

Gabriel nodded slightly. "There was no one there, was there? He frightened the life out of me –made me drop my cappuccino and then scarpered and I chased him like a mug. Must have looked like a total moron." He made a tutting noise and rolled his eyes in embarrassment. "And me on the telly and all now! What must folk be thinking when I suddenly take off after nothing at all? Talk about attention seeking!"

Martha grinned. "And that wouldn't be like you at all, Gabriel, now would it?" she asked softly and was rewarded with a smile from her companion.

"Less of your smartness, young lady," he replied.

They walked a further few steps in silence before Martha felt a huge arm go round her shoulders as Gabriel hugged her to him. He left his arm around her as they walked.

"Loath as I am to be nice, thanks for coming to meet me today," he said into the wind, but Martha knew it was sincere.

"Gabriel, it's the least I could do after the last six months," she replied quietly, still ashamed of her reluctance to contact Gabriel for so long.

"I didn't know who else to contact," he continued. "I mean it's Will, really, I should be speaking to but I just cannot summon up the courage to ring him. I mean he's *furious* with me and I thought you would be too but you're not quite as scary as him so I went for the soft option."

Martha made a face of mock outrage and looked up at Gabriel who made an exaggerated face of embarrassment in return.

"Well, I could take you in a fight is what I mean," he said, by way of explanation and then grinned. Martha smiled back. "I'm sorry I haven't been in touch. I'm not furious with anyone – and for what it's worth, I don't know what's got into Will other than the fact that he's a bit . . . driven, I suppose."

Gabriel squeezed Martha's shoulders and then released her before putting his hands back in his pockets as they made the turn onto George Street. "Drivin' me crazy, more like. He's a bit scary when he's cross, isn't he?"

Martha nodded and then giggled. "I guess so," she replied.

They continued in silence until eventually they reached Gabriel's front door. Immediately a sense of dread filled Martha as he rooted for his keys.

"Gabriel, why do you want me to go in? Are you sure I'm not going to see something I don't want to see?" she asked nervously. "Only I don't really do this sort of thing . . . live action, as it were. I mean, I still look at some of Will's evidence and stuff but I don't go actively seeking things out." She peered nervously into the hallway, which was surprisingly bright, as Gabriel held the door open for her to enter.

"I think you'll be fine – I mean, I haven't seen anything too scary myself," he sighed. "But I do want a second opinion on a couple of things and you're the best person for the job in my mind. You're still rational enough not to believe everything straight away – aren't you?"

Martha stepped into the hallway and looked nervously around her. "I think so," she lied.

"Then please help me," said Gabriel.

It wasn't a question, or a demand. It was a plea. His face looked almost desperate as he asked and glanced up the stairs in the direction of his apartment.

"I just need to know I'm not going mad, and then I need to take action – I need to find out what the hell is going on before I lose my reason."

Martha glanced up the stairs herself and with another look at Gabriel's pleading face – his greying skin, his tired and bloodshot eyes – sighed deeply and placed her foot on the bottom step of the stairs and silently began to climb. She heard Gabriel close the front door behind them and flinched a little as the sound of the heavy door echoed around her. What on earth was she getting herself into again? He was the one who should have known what he was doing, who should have been protecting her, who should know exactly what was going on – and instead here she was, leading the way to a room where events had been taking place that he didn't seem to understand. That said, she owed him.

Martha summoned all the courage she could find as she reached the front door of Gabriel's apartment, thinking of the last time she had been here, armed with flowers and champagne. Her heart sank as Gabriel put his key in the door but she smiled bravely at him as he opened it and stood aside to let her in. Here we go, she thought. Again.

Minutes later, Martha was sitting on the couch in Gabriel's apartment, surveying the mess around her as he made tea in the kitchen. The disorder made her feel uncomfortable. However, there was something in the room which made her feel even more uneasy than the mess. It was a feeling with which she was familiar but hadn't experienced in over a year. Her eyes were suddenly, inexplicably, drawn to a corner above the fireplace and she stared intently at it. There was nothing there. She shuddered as a chill ran down her spine. She felt as though she wasn't alone, as though someone else was watching her.

She looked around her, terrified in case she saw something or someone that she didn't want to see.

The room seemed empty and much the same as she remembered it from before – tastefully decorated to reflect a modern take on the Georgian era. The burgundy walls were dark, but the cream upholstery on the suite of furniture lifted the room and the two long sash windows filled it with the fading light of a winter's afternoon. The furniture – Gabriel's desk, covered in books and notepads, the coffee table, numerous side tables and a large bookcase – were all in a dark wood. Everything was covered with a layer of dust and they had already joked that Miss Havisham had taken up residence with Gabriel.

The fireplace was a beautiful feature. It was tall, Martha noted. The mantel and outer surround was the same dark wood as the furniture while the inner surround was made of cast iron decorated with fluted columns, the panelled frieze dotted with urns and Grecian figures. The side panels were cream with ornate tiles depicting small figures and the hearth was also tiled but in plain red. She noted that the mantel was covered with bric-à-brac – an authentic Georgian table clock, small figurines, ornamental boxes – and at one end stood a photograph which she didn't remember from her previous visit, incongruous because of the simple wooden frame amongst all of the elaborate and somewhat gaudy curios. Martha stood up to get a better look.

The photo was thick with dust but she could tell it had been moved recently by the fresh thumbprint on its right-hand side and the clear swoop on the mantel underneath where it had slid along. From it, a fresh-faced boy beamed back at her and as she studied his features she could see a similarity to Gabriel in the grin and around the eyes.

"Oh you've found Little Laurence then," came a voice from behind.

Martha jumped and turned suddenly to see Gabriel closing the door with his foot as he carried two steaming mugs and a packet of digestive biscuits. She exhaled with relief and took one of the proffered mugs, declining the offer of the plain biscuit. Judging by Gabriel's current standards of hygiene, she didn't really feel that eating and drinking was a good idea in the flat, today at least.

Martha turned back to the photograph and studied it again. "I thought it was you actually – you're so similar around the eyes and mouth." She chuckled aloud. "Why on earth is he holding a building brick, Gabriel?" she asked, peering closer at the boy in his swimming trunks, with his medal held proudly aloft.

Gabriel made a tutting noise. "Did no one else but us have swimming lessons through school in the Dark Ages?" he asked, outraged. "It's a lifesaving medal he's holding – part of their forward thinking in the olden days was to chuck a brick in the water and then send children in to get it – sometimes in their pyjamas even. I suppose if they made it out they got a medal for surviving." Martha turned, even more confused. "They had to rescue a *brick* from the water?"

Gabriel nodded and sipped his tea, grimacing as he did so. The small white floaters on the surface hadn't passed Martha's eye unnoticed and she reckoned that Gabriel had just discovered the hard way that he needed some fresh milk.

"Don't ask me what the logic behind it being a brick was, but our Laurence was apparently the wee man from Atlantis according to Ma. She never talks about him really but the one thing she told me is that he used to win medals all over the place, spent his life in the local baths splashing about from dawn till dusk and that he was a whizz at brick-saving. I found that photo at home and there's something about his face that just . . . I dunno . . . reinforces the bond I have with him . . . probably because we look so alike in it. That picture was taken a few weeks before he died."

Martha turned again to face Gabriel and was met with an expression of sincere sadness in his face. She was taken aback – he was usually so pragmatic about his brother's death, as brutal as it all sounded.

Gabriel went to take another mouthful of tea and thought better of it, placing the mug on the already overcrowded coffee table. "I suppose I miss him – as my spirit guide, I've felt like he's always at my shoulder, if that doesn't sound too strange," he said simply.

Martha nodded and turned back again to the photo of the boy. "You've been looking at this a lot recently, haven't you?" she said, kindly.

"What makes you think that?" asked Gabriel.

She knew by his tone that the question was a leading one. "Well, not to cast aspersions on your housekeeping skills but we've already commented on the fact that your home looks like Miss Havisham lives here too. Therefore it's easy, my dear Watson, to detect what one might call *movement of things* on account of the tracks left in the dust, and this picture has been moved very recently, am I right?"

Martha saw Gabriel's face turn to a frown and he stood up quickly and crossed over to stand beside her. When the medium saw the marks in the dust, he blanched and stepped back.

"I missed these earlier. He's been here again," he said simply.

The words chilled Martha to her bones. She shivered.

Gabriel pointed to a section of the mantelpiece to Martha's right and she moved over to see what he wanted to show her.

"There's more fingerprints here – the ones he left before," he said, pointing at barely discernible shapes in the dust. "And on the coffee table." He crossed back to the table in a single stride and searched the four corners until he found what he was looking for. He looked at Martha, almost breathless. "I keep finding them in the mornings when I come in – please tell me you can see these?"

Martha peered down to where Gabriel was pointing, feeling increasingly uncomfortable as she did so. There was no mistaking the prints that she saw before her, as if the fingers of a hand – a right hand, she could tell – had been placed on the surface. She looked at Gabriel.

"And you're sure that you didn't leave these?" she asked.

Gabriel shook his head. Martha had known the answer already but had felt compelled to ask anyway. Gabriel held his own fingers over the prints as further proof of the contrast. They had been made by a much smaller hand – but not a child's.

Gabriel was eagerly studying Martha's face. Her apparent discomfort at what she was witnessing made him almost tremble with relief as he realised that he wasn't alone.

"You think that this man you keep seeing is getting in here and doing this?" she asked, with a tone of incredulity to her voice. Always look for a rational explanation, she thought to herself, calming herself down as she did so, remembering what Will always told her to ask herself when spooked or scared.

Gabriel sat down on the couch and reached to take Martha's hands, drawing her into a sitting position beside him. She found it unlike him to do so, and felt slightly uncomfortable as he gripped her fingers.

"I've felt him, Martha. He comes in at night-time when I'm asleep. I can sense him with me, but I can't see him – can't communicate with him. Then I get up and there are fingerprints, and the door to the living room is left ajar, even though I make sure it's closed before I go to bed. And whoever it is isn't getting in through the front door because firstly it's alarmed and secondly I've left little booby traps in the hallway – just things like shoes or balled-up socks – and they're completely undisturbed which wouldn't be possible if the front door was pushed in." Gabriel's eyes were growing wilder as he blurted out what he had been experiencing. "And then there's this . . ." he announced, dropping Martha's hands and standing up suddenly, striding around the back of the sofa to his desk.

As he passed the window, Martha became aware that the room had grown gloomy as darkness approached. She glanced at her watch – it was almost four o'clock on Bonfire Night and it would be dark soon. Her sense of unease grew as she watched Gabriel pick up a notepad from the desk and charge back to sit down beside her.

"What do you make of this?" he demanded, breathlessly, thrusting the notepad at her.

Martha took it, and held it toward the window to get the most of the light in the ever-darkening room. What she saw sent a shiver down her back. She knew that Gabriel hadn't written this. In fact, she knew that no one alive had written this and it scared her more than anything else. On the page, she saw the long squiggle leading into two words and then the pattern of the pen trailing off the page. Below it, she saw the same again and again all the way down the page, the letters curling and looping until the page was completely covered with the same message over and over again.

Martha threw the notepad on the coffee table as if she had been burned and pulled her hands back in toward her chest, as if to distance herself from what she had been holding.

"When did that happen?" she asked nervously, turning back to Gabriel, who looked positively excited now that someone else was sharing in his experiences.

"Och, a couple of weeks ago," he said. "And then there's been more of them most mornings since – I've slept on the couch a few times and even then it happens. I don't hear anyone doing it – it's just there in the morning."

Martha glanced back at the message gingerly, as though hoping it might disappear, or possibly might never have been there in the first place. It was still there, however, the writing veering between hard against the paper and the pen softly held, covering the page with the message to 'do it' over and over again, squiggles drawn over words, attempt after attempt to write the message over and over again. Spirit writing. She had heard Will talk about this phenomenon but had thought it a load of nonsense, until now, until confronted with the handwriting of a dead person.

Martha shook her head, squeezed her eyes shut and stood up. "Gabriel – you're a bloody spirit medium," she said, suddenly annoyed. "How can you be telling me that all of this is going on without you having a clue what's happening?"

Gabriel looked at her as she walked around the coffee table and paced up and down in front of the fireplace, creating a physical distance between herself and the writing. There was silence for a while as she tried to take it all in. A silence broken by a strangled sob and she looked back at the sofa to see the imperturbable Scotsman crying openly, his face in a grimace and huge tears rolling down his cheeks.

"I don't *knoow* . . ." he wailed, prolonging the words like a crying child trying to make a point. He started to shake his head and held his hands in the air in a helpless gesture of defeat before gulping in air and starting to sob again. The tears ran down his cheeks, rolling down his chin and plopping onto his knees. Snot bubbled from his nose.

"Gabriel!" gasped Martha. She had never seen him this upset before.

She rushed to his side and threw her arms about his neck, allowing him to weep silently. They sat like that for a number of minutes before Gabriel sniffed and spoke in a broken voice through his tears.

"I'm scared, Martha," he confessed. "I try to talk to him but I can't get through. I mean, spiders are scary. Clowns are scary – I even find something unsettling about *moths* –"

Martha had to stifle a chuckle.

"But what I don't find scary are ghosts," he said. "Except right now. You can see that all this stuff is going on round me and I don't know what to do and I am not proud to say it but I am absolutely *shitting* myself at what's going on here."

Martha nodded. "I'm sorry, Gabriel," she said softly. "I didn't mean to sound like I didn't appreciate what's going on – I just don't understand it."

Gabriel rooted in his pocket for a tissue and blew loudly into the small crumb of paper that he found. He wiped his cheeks with the back of his hand. "You and me both, kid," he observed. "Can you help me, though?"

Martha looked up into his bloodshot eyes, puzzled. "How?" she asked simply. "I haven't the first clue how to go about helping you with this."

Gabriel sniffed again, thinking carefully about what he was about to say. "Can you talk to Will for me?" he said in a tiny, pleading voice.

Martha sat back from him and rolled her eyes. Of all the impossible requests!

"He'll know what to do but he won't listen to me! He still likes you – he'll hear you out – *please*, Martha!" he begged, a note of panic in his voice.

Martha took a deep breath and closed her eyes before consulting her watch. It was fully dark outside now and, if she wanted to get back to her car and then pick Ruby up from the childminder, she'd need to make a move. She sighed, gathering herself together.

"I'll try, Gabriel, but I can't guarantee anything," she finally said.

"Thanks for that," he whispered, and gave a half smile. "There's one more thing that might help – that might pique his interest," he added, raising his forefinger in the air.

Martha shifted in the seat. She was unsettled enough as it was – what was Gabriel going to produce now? She watched again as he reached under a pile of papers on the coffee table and withdrew a small envelope with which he fumbled, eventually withdrawing a card and a folded-up sheet of paper, the same thick, expensive quality as the envelope. Gabriel held up the card first for Martha to see. It was an invitation.

Martha leaned closer to see the wording which was in gold on a simple white card and read aloud: "'*You and a guest are cordially invited to attend 'The First Day of Christmas' party at Dubhglas Castle, Scotland, on the evening of Saturday, December 1st. A banquet will be served, dress formal, RSVP.*'"

She sat back again and looked at Gabriel for an explanation but he was deeply intent on unfolding the sheet of paper from the envelope.

"And now this," he said, handing the letter over to Martha and looking around him as if finally he was taken by surprise at the fading light. He stood and strode efficiently across the room to switch on the wall lamps before walking back to plonk himself down heavily on the sofa beside her again. "That's better," she said. She held the letter closer to her, noting the use of a fountain pen, the curling script neat and precise, and began to read.

Dear Gabriel,

I do hope that this letter finds you in good health and looking forward to the annual Christmas party here at the Castle. It is, of course, quite some time since we have seen you at Dubhglas but Mr Calvert understands that you are busy with your television career.

I am writing to you personally on this occasion, not on behalf of your godfather. The staff and I at the Castle have spoken and we hope that this year you plan to join us for certain at the party. There is a problem here, with which you might be able to help, we feel. I am not entirely sure how to put this, but it is a delicate issue of a supernatural nature and we are unsure where else to turn. We hope that your knowledge of and love for the Castle will encourage you to attend on December 1st. I don't wish to go into the matter any further at present, but we can talk in more detail – and privately – then.

Yours sincerely,
Donald Gifford

Martha lowered the letter and looked at Gabriel who held out his hand for it to be returned.

"What is this all about?" she asked as she handed it back to him.

Gabriel took a deep breath. "I've told you about Dubhglas, right?"

Martha nodded. He'd spoken about it in that casual way of his – a castle where he'd spent his summers as a child. The story had prompted Will to remind her that Gabriel was a gift that just kept on giving.

"Your grandfather –"

"Godfather," Gabriel corrected, indicating the letter in his hand where a reference had been made.

Martha saw a familiar flash of impatience cross his features at her mistake.

"My godfather lives there. I used to spend my summers there as a kid – lots of history. Anyway, he throws this annual shindig before Christmas every year and I normally try to get out of it but then I get this letter stuffed into this year's invitation, from Gifford –"

It was Martha's turn to interrupt as Gabriel's explanation gathered speed and threatened to run away with itself before she was in full possession of the facts.

"Who's Gifford?" she said, resisting again the urge to glance at her watch as the evening grew late. "In the olden days he'd have been a valet, maybe," mused Gabriel, "or a butler – buttling about the place, I suppose. Nowadays he's sort of an estate manager, I guess. Mainly the house – sort of a housekeeper, except there's also an actual housekeeper but her role is to cook and order food and –"

"I get it," said Martha, suppressing another grin as Gabriel's face contorted with the effort of trying to figure out this man Gifford's job description.

Gabriel took another deep breath. "He's the head servant, I suppose," he said in a low voice, as if somehow he could be heard and didn't want to insult the staff.

"And this . . ." he pointed a finger to the letter which he had refolded in his hand, "this is *very* unusual." He stared at Martha, almost as if he felt she should understand that.

"In what way?" she asked tentatively, nervous in case she should somehow prod Gabriel's already tried patience any further.

"Very unusual," he repeated, "for Gifford to contact me directly. He's a lovely man – super-efficient – but I'd swear that he learned his modern-day worldview from *Upstairs Downstairs*. He's incredibly subservient – in a nice way, you know. He doesn't bow and scrape but he sort of *knows his place*, do you understand?"

Martha wasn't sure she did but she nodded regardless.

"To approach me directly about this must have taken him out of his comfort zone," he continued. "I'm completely mystified about what he could want but if he's taken the trouble to contact me, then, whatever it is, he really needs my help."

"He said it's of a supernatural nature, didn't he?"

Gabriel looked slightly aghast. "I *know*," he replied. "That's the weirdest thing of all. My gift has never been acknowledged at Dubhglas. It's pretty much a spook-free zone. Godfather doesn't believe it – he's aware of it but he pretends it doesn't exist. I'm sure the staff have all had a wee gossip about it – but for Gifford to ask for my help in something like this? That's downright freaky in itself."

Martha thought for a moment. "Are you going to go? And help?"

Gabriel leaned in close to her face. "And how can I propose to do that nowadays – in 'The Great Supernatural Silence', I suppose you'd call it?"

Martha nodded. "I see. So that's something else that you want me to talk to Will about?"

Gabriel sat back, sighed, and laced his fingers together, nodding as he did so. "I don't know where else to turn," he said helplessly. "First of all there's all this . . ." He waved his hand to indicate the space around him, his own supernatural problem. "And now this . . ."

This time, the hand pointed to the letter. "And me of no use to anyone . . . and no one to turn to . . ."

"Except Will," finished Martha.

Gabriel nodded again, and shrugged. "Who you gonna call?" he wisecracked lamely.

Martha studied his face again in the light from the wall-lamps and felt again the comfort from him, the security she felt in being back in his company.

"I'll talk to him," she responded, seeing relief flood his face. She stood up to leave, adding, "I can't guarantee anything, mind."

Gabriel nodded, standing to join her, towering over her small frame. "I know. But I'd really appreciate it, Martha, really I would."

Martha nodded in agreement and made her way toward the door. "I'll call you, okay?" she said, carrying on out to the hallway.

Gabriel didn't follow. "I'll wait by the phone, honey," he piped cheerily but as she pulled the heavy front door open to leave, Martha knew that the faux cheeriness in his voice was born of relief and that Gabriel was a man in desperate need of assistance.

CHAPTER 10

1963

Claire jumped slightly as a shape shifted in the shadows before her but relaxed against the wall of the corridor.

"Well, 'ow did it go?" he demanded in a hushed voice while pushing himself upright using the foot that he had been tapping on the wall behind him.

"Ooh, Martin, you startled me," said Claire in her habitual hushed tones.

She had the quietest speaking voice that Martin had ever heard, used as he was to the sounds of London markets and nightclubs. He often laughed that they were like two people speaking different languages – he with his loud cockney accent that Claire still found difficult to understand and she with her hushed whisper and the thick tones of the island to the north from where she came.

He fell into step beside her as she scurried along, back toward the kitchens, trying his best to peer into her face, but the passageway was dark and he couldn't make out her expression.

"Well?" demanded Martin again.

Claire glanced at him. "He says I can stay as long as Mrs Turnbull is happy with me," she replied. Martin detected a hint of pleasure in her voice that he hadn't really heard before.

"That's bloody fantastic!" he roared in response, his words bouncing off the high ceilings.

"Shhh, Martin!" giggled Claire. *"I don't want him to hear me telling you – he'd probably tell me to leave again."*

"Nonsense!" he replied as they reached the door which led to the stairs down to the kitchen.

He held the door open and Claire looked at him awkwardly, as if unsure what to do, and nodded in gratitude as she took timid steps toward the thick stone stairs.

"Does Mrs T know?" he asked.

Claire shook her head.

"Then we'd better tell her, and get the kettle on fast. This calls for a celebration cuppa."

"Martin!"

A voice boomed down the corridor behind them. Claire recognised it immediately, as did Martin. As low as her own heart sank on hearing the gravelly tones, she could sense that Martin's had sunk further.

"Martin!" came the roar again. Impatient. Vicious. Cruel.

"Oops!" grinned Martin, a little too jovially, pausing and taking a step backward up the stairs. *"Maybe keep that cuppa warm for me. I've a feeling I've some errands to run."*

He turned and scampered back up the few steps down which he had come and disappeared back into the passageway above. Claire watched him go, unable to stop the feeling of concern that grew every time that man called any of them, particularly Martin. He had it in for poor Martin, it seemed. Turning and blocking the summons from her mind, she continued her descent to the kitchens, a skip growing in every step as she went back to work. To her job. Her very first one. I have a job, she said quietly but aloud, and hugged herself with glee.

It had been a full month since the day she had met Martin and Mrs Turnbull in the coffee shop. Since she had returned with them in the car to Dubhglas Castle.

They had been so kind that day, Mrs Turnbull and Martin. And there had been others coming and going, saying hello as they passed. She had jumped every time someone new appeared, but they seemed to almost take her as part of things, greeting her and carrying on about their business. No one remarked on her face – her eye or the bruise. She didn't think she'd been anywhere so strange in her life.

And then the bath that Mrs Turnbull had run with real bubbles. And the loan of the brushed cotton nightie. Mrs Turnbull had apologised because it was old, but Claire had never worn anything so warm or so clean in her life. And the sleep. In a bed with clean sheets, in a room at the top of the castle which was little more than a cell but to Claire, had she ever heard of the Ritz, she would have felt that this was better.

It was noon the following day when she woke, confused, afraid and embarrassed. Woken with a cup of tea brought to her by Mrs Turnbull in her bed. It turned out that Mr Turnbull couldn't go to Glasgow that day after all, she'd told Claire, but if she cared to wait a couple of days then he'd definitely be making a run to the city and he'd take Claire with him.

But of course that had never happened. And here she was, a month later, giving Mrs Turnbull a hand in the kitchens, still waiting for the lift to Glasgow which she knew deep down was never going to come. At first, it had made her feel terrified. Were they keeping her here, some sort of prisoner, until her father and brothers arrived to take her home? But as the days went on, and the kindness grew, so did Claire's inner strength and she began to feel that these people had no motive other than to be generous and kind and she was happy to clean the floor in return and blacken the stove and make cups of tea for the gardeners when they came indoors for a break, sweating in the summer sunshine.

And then today she had been granted a formal interview with Mr Calvert for a proper job. It had been Martin's idea, she knew. They'd dressed her in more of Mrs Turnbull's cast-offs that morning and clipped her hair up and she'd taken a rare foray into the main body of the castle with its fancy furniture and stags' heads and heavy fabrics. Into the library full of books and the small fire lit, even in summer. She'd been surprised at how young he was at first.

He'd looked at her eye of course. She'd expected that. Any prospective employer might. She'd thought that would be it then.

That he'd know from her eye that she was slow and stupid and tell her to leave straight away and maybe that was for the best. Get back on the road. Keep running, keep moving. But would she ever be truly safe? Any safer than here anyhow? Behind these thick castle walls, with passages and doorways through which to run and hide?

Instead, he was kind, like the others. He didn't ask her much about herself but asked if she was hardworking – she'd never known anything but hard work in her life – and if she was punctual, which she was, of course. Being late would mean a beating with the belt so she had learned at a young age to be early for everything. He'd looked her up and down then, asked if she liked to read and if she liked the library and then told her that he was happy to put her on the payroll as long as Mrs Turnbull was satisfied. And then he'd dismissed her. No cruel words, no warnings of punishment. And payment? For this? To be warm and sheltered, and given clothes and food and kindness? A part of Claire felt that it had to be too good to be true. But another part wanted to knuckle down, to start work and stay working as long and as hard as Mr Calvert wanted so that she might never have to leave. For this reason, she was eager to get back to the kitchen to see what task Mrs Turnbull might give her next.

There was always such a buzz about the castle. She had been taken on a tour by Mr Turnbull when Mr Calvert was away once, shortly after she had arrived. It had been purchased some years before by a Mr Ball of London but Mr Calvert, his nephew, lived there permanently and was in charge of the day-to-day running and the restoration of the castle.

As it had been unoccupied for years, the last of the original owners having died out a decade before, there was much to be done. So far, the kitchen, the library, the entrance hall and the servants' rooms, along with a bedroom for Mr Calvert had all been finished, she knew. But he was in the process of modernising the whole place – guest rooms were being repaired and redecorated, new bathrooms were being installed next to every room. Claire was at first overwhelmed by the great hubbub of so many builders and workmen. She was mainly confined to downstairs of course, but she knew from her visits above that there were scaffolds erected throughout the house, sheets covering surfaces as ceilings were painted and restored, floors repaired in many of the rooms. It was so exciting, she thought.

And it wasn't just the house that Mr Calvert was turning on its head. Mr Turnbull explained how much all of this was of benefit to the small village of Dubhglas. How Mr Calvert was creating jobs – staff, workmen, people to work in Mr Calvert's business. "He's a very good man," Mr Turnbull had stressed. "We're very lucky he's the one in charge."

Claire listened carefully to what he had to say about her new boss and the respect he commanded. She was even more stunned to find out that Christopher Calvert was doing all of this in his early thirties. Not all that much older than she was, when you thought about it, and all this to show.

When the sun shone the surroundings of the castle could be glorious but the area was susceptible to thick mists sometimes which made the days grey and dull. Claire didn't care about the weather. In her experience bad things could happen on nice days as much as on wet and cold ones, so every day was the same to her. She had only ever known life as a hard drudge, with fear at every corner, not knowing where the next punishment would come from.

When she was smaller, she had thought the beatings were the worst. A belt here, a blunt instrument there. Her father had used the head of a garden rake once which had left her with gashes all over her body. It had taken months for that to heal up. But it hadn't stopped him.

It was when she grew older that she realised, however, that there was so much worse out there than being hit. To get by, get through it, as it grew more frequent, she learned to leave herself. To lift herself out of her body, despite the pain and the shame.

She knew that her mother knew, of course. And sometimes she saw the scars on her mother's arms and legs too and knew that she had been through the same things as Claire. But she never did anything to stop it. Until the day that she had insisted that Claire go to the mainland alone . . .

Claire tried not to think about all that too much. She didn't trust anyone of course. After all, everyone got beaten. Or did they? As she looked around the faces of the staff at Dubhglas Castle – Martin, Mrs Turnbull, the ghillies, the gardeners, the maids Sheila, Esther and Dots – they didn't seem to ever expect a beating in punishment. And they were all very kind to her. Claire knew that she had done things wrong since she had got here – Mrs Turnbull had told her as much – but there was never a hand raised to strike her. She had heard the ghillies fighting once as well, voices raised so high that they echoed up the stone staircase, and Mr Turnbull had rushed in to intervene. The noise had made her want to run and hide, and she had cowered in a corner of the kitchen while they banged the long wooden table with their fists and pointed at each other in rage, their faces red, spittle flying from their mouths. But they hadn't raised a hand to each other, and soon they shook hands and gave each other a grudging apology. Claire had watched in fascination. Had it been her brothers then one of them would have been lying on the floor bleeding before long. And the kitchen would have been left in complete disarray with pots overturned and furniture broken. And it some way it would have warranted another punishment for her, she knew.

And another thing – no one made her stay on her knees on the stone floor for hours praying for repentance. Instead, Mr Turnbull gathered all of the staff who lived in at the kitchen table each night and they bowed their heads for a few moments while he read to them the briefest of passages from the Bible. There was church on Sunday but only if you wanted to go.

"I ain't never gone to church since I was a little 'un," Martin observed cockily. "Me old ma used to bring me when I was a nipper but I ain't got time for that now."

Claire eyed him in shy wonder as he lounged at the kitchen table, swinging back on the rear two legs of the chair where he sat, a cold cup of tea before him.

It was a Friday morning, a fortnight after Claire had become a member of staff, and she was engaged in her weekly task of blackening the top of the stove. She had paused long enough to turn and watch Martin as he lazily examined his fingernails, his shirtsleeves rolled up, slightly too long for him as always. As Claire wore Mrs Turnbull's cast-offs, Martin wore her husband's. Claire thought again of asking Martin where he had come from, with his strange accent and wardrobe of hand-me-downs. Her hand slowed in the application of the black polish with the special brush and she stared at him for a moment, jumping back to the task suddenly as the far door creaked and Mrs Turnbull bustled in from the cottage where she and Mr. Turnbull lived, across a cobbled courtyard to the rear of the castle. Claire began to apply the polish vigorously. She couldn't help but grin as she heard a smacking sound and an exclamation from Martin, along with the legs of the chair landing back on the floor with a bang.

"Ow! Mrs T! What was that for?"

"Where would you like me to start, Martin," replied the housekeeper, sternly, but still with a hint of mirth to her voice. "For weakening the legs of our kitchen chairs? For idling when there's fuel to be brought in and the post collected from the village? For distracting my kitchen maid?"

With that, Claire looked up long enough to see Mrs Turnbull smile warmly and wink at her as she placed a basket filled with vegetables and herbs from the kitchen garden on the big wooden table.

"Plus, the car needs a bit of spit and polish, I think you'll find. The McKenzies are arriving this evening and the lad will be staying for the rest of the summer so you'd better get ready for full-on nannying for the next month or so."

Martin shrugged. "I like the lad," he said simply, standing up with a jump and re-rolling his sleeves. They insisted on rolling back down his arms.

"And if he's here then it gets me out of the house for a while. A bit of fishing and climbing and running and jumping with young Larry there. This is great news in fact! And with that, I will bid you ladies good day. I think the young master might like himself a new catapult in case of any dangers while in the countryside so I must commence a'whittlin' post haste!"

Martin swept dramatically toward the kitchen door, doffing an imaginary cap as he did so.

"*Post office post haste!*" *shouted Mrs Turnbull after him with a warning tone to her voice but he was gone, the door swinging behind him.*

Mrs Turnbull tutted as she began to lay bunches of herbs from the basket on the table.

"*That boy,*" *she said with a sigh.* "*No wonder he's such good company for Laurence – he's barely more than a kid himself. And worse than that, he's a city kid let loose in the countryside. It's like letting a wee monkey out of a cage.*"

Claire slowed again, partly to watch with interest what Mrs Turnbull was doing with the herbs, partly to finally ask the question that had bothered her since she had first met Martin.

"*Where is Martin from, Mrs Turnbull?*" *she said in her usual quiet, hesitant way.*

"*London, dear,*" *replied the older woman, preoccupied with sorting the rosemary from the thyme.* "*Near enough to where Mr Calvert and Mr Ball come from, I think – it was Mr Ball who brought Martin here in the first place, if you understand . . .*"

Claire didn't, but at that moment Mrs Turnbull changed the conversation to a description of what she planned for dinner and the subject was lost.

"*Now, I'm going to do roast pork this evening so I'll be adding this – rosemary – to the meat and then popping some of this – thyme – into the stuffing, along with some parsley and onions. It's Laurence's favourite. He's Mr Calvert's godson, Claire, and the apple of his eye so you'll need to be very attentive to him while he's here for the summer. Not that he'll be indoors much, of course. He's always outdoors, and if he's not then he's down in the garage pestering Martin to teach him about cars and engines. I think we'll find that for the rest of the summer we'll have two young boys to put up with!*" *Mrs Turnbull smiled again.* "*He's a lovely lad, though. And his mother is an absolute gentlewoman. She doesn't come as often as she used to, of course, but she may come and I never know if Captain McKenzie is arriving with her so I always cook a bit extra just in case. Heaven knows it never goes to waste with Mr Turnbull on the premises!*"

And with that, she turned back again to her task, shuttling between the pantry and the kitchen table, setting about preparing that evening's meal. And all the time Claire watched her, learning as she did. More new arrivals, she thought to herself. She hoped the boy wouldn't make fun of her eye – the boys at school had, of course, calling her all sorts of names and teasing her by running up just behind her and tapping her shoulder roughly, just where she couldn't see them with her poor peripheral vision.

"Can you give me a hand with the stuffing, Claire?" said Mrs Turnbull suddenly and Claire found herself busy once again, washing her hands thoroughly with pungent carbolic soap and then enjoying the delicious soft feel of crumbing a stale loaf. She took a deep breath and inhaled the aromas of the herbs and the onion that Mrs Turnbull was chopping beside her. They worked in companionable silence as they prepared the meal and, when they were finished, shared a cup of tea and Mrs Turnbull told Claire of the boy's exploits on previous visits. And as always, Claire sat in silence and absorbed it all until it was time to move on to the next task.

Claire Drummond was busy and satisfied, she realised. In fact, she verged on happiness.

CHAPTER 11

November 11th

Martha pressed the 'off' switch on her PC with a flourish, simultaneously reaching behind her for her scarf. She glanced at the clock. Officially she wasn't supposed to leave the office until after five but Maisie was gone since three to a dentist's appointment and she didn't think that leaving half an hour early would cause any problems, especially on a dark, miserable day. The phone hadn't rung for three days straight – apart from another message for Martha where the caller had refused to leave a name and had politely said they'd call back. She had assumed it was just a random sales call – for stationery or something similar – and had put it to the back of her mind.

Martha hurriedly stood up and pulled her coat on, rummaging in her pockets for her knitted gloves. She leaned over to pick up her umbrella but a glance out of the window proved that it was completely unnecessary. A gust of wind lashed the rain against the ancient panes and Martha reckoned that she wouldn't even get the umbrella above her head before it needed to go in a bin. She decided to just pull on a woolly hat she kept in her bag and make a run for it as best she could.

She still had a couple of things to pick up, but the majority of her purchases had fitted into the backpack she had brought today, with the intention of walking home. She was keen to get home early, to get out of the weather firstly, but also to get started on cooking dinner. It had been a week since she had visited Gabriel's flat and she still hadn't found the right time to talk to Will. He had been completely tied up with two investigations and writing up the subsequent papers for the college – in fact she had barely seen him over the entire weekend and he had stayed late at the university the past two nights. She had insisted that he be home early tonight because she wanted to cook a special dinner, to sit down and relax together, have some wine and a proper conversation. And she wanted to tell him all about Gabriel and see if she couldn't get him to help.

Martha stood at the door to the office and glanced back to make sure that everything was in place for the following day. Blinds closed, check – petty cash locked away, check . . . Martha's eyes were drawn back to her own desk where she let them rest for a moment on the bizarre gift she had received that day. Puzzled again by who could have sent them, and what they meant, she stared at the small bunch of blue thistles that had been delivered to the office that morning. Tied beautifully with a blue bow, they had been dropped up by a lady Martha recognised from the flower stall across the Royal Mile. She sold all the usual sorts of flowers but the thistles were a huge draw for tourists, being the emblem of Scotland. Martha thought them beautiful with their dusty shades of blue and purple – she had included thistles in her wedding bouquet actually, when she had married Dan. Roses and thistles and hypericum berries. It was no reference to Scotland. She had no idea then that one day she'd end up living there.

The bunch contained just five or six of the spiky flowering plants. There had been no card, no wishes, just a message delivered by the stallholder that they were to be given to Martha Armstrong and that was it. Martha and Maisie had puzzled over them until Martha had decided enough was enough and popped them into a vase and left them to one side of her desk. Perhaps they were from Gabriel – a thank-you for listening the previous week, or a spiky reminder to talk to Will for him more likely. But thistles of all things? People sending flowers normally didn't select thistles as top of their wish lists. Martha was stumped. She decided to leave them on her desk – they'd still be there on the following Monday when she came back in and maybe some inspiration as to their source might hit her over the weekend. Besides which, she had too much to carry as it was, without lugging them home and damaging them in the process.

Another gust of wind lashing the raindrops against the window roused her from her thoughts and she shuddered. Best get going then. She disliked being in the office alone late in the evening, once it had grown dark, and hurriedly opened the door, pulling it shut behind her and locking it before hurtling down the dark stairs with its blown bulb. The offices overhead were vacant in the old and badly maintained building and the sounds of wood settling, the creaks and groans of the old structure reminded Martha too much of past experiences to warrant her staying around for long in the dark.

She turned right and made her way toward the castle. Her destination was a small coffee and cake shop hidden down one of the closes off the Royal Mile. She intended picking up a lemon cheesecake, Will's favourite, and then making a run for the nearest taxi rank – she had no intention of walking home in this weather. A gust of wind slowed her progress and she battled against it, holding tight to her hat and the strap of the backpack for ballast. She stepped closer to the buildings on her right as she approached the tiny archway entrance with its steps down to the cobbled close which was her destination.

The archway provided shelter for a moment and she held tight to the metal railings, knowing that the ancient steps were uneven and slippery. The wind howled down the Royal Mile behind her and her back was pelted with heavy rain. She knew she mustn't slip – the backpack contained two expensive bottles of wine and she had no intention of landing on her back and having them not only break but in the process ruin the fresh ingredients for the casserole that she planned.

So intent was Martha on staying upright and safe that she didn't see the figure step out and stop dead in front of her as she reached the bottom step. Even if she had wanted to, by the time she looked up and registered the black shadow in the darkness of the archway, she couldn't have turned to run because it had reached out an arm and grabbed hers tightly in a vicelike grip. As Martha felt the fingers close around her arm, a chill ran through her entire body, her mind growing blank with a fear overload and she screamed, unconsciously, as loudly as she could.

"Martha, Martha! Jesus! Easy, woman!" The figure spoke in a voice that she recognised but in her panic couldn't place.

Suddenly the grip on her arm was released and the shape stepped backwards, away from her, making a rustling sound in the darkness. Martha whipped her head around – partly to check that there were no other assailants blocking her in from behind, partly to see if there were any passers-by who could help. She half-turned, prepared to run back up the steps but at the same time fearful of slipping. As she took a look back at whoever – whatever – it was that was standing in her way, she suddenly registered that, yes, she did know who it was. And that it was the last person she expected to see in a dark alleyway, in Edinburgh, on a stormy winter's evening.

The figure took another step backward, the light from a streetlamp further down the close illuminating its features. Raising a palm toward her in a conciliatory gesture, was Dan Smith. She hadn't seen her husband in almost two years and here he was, in the dark and the cold and the wet. With a huge bunch of roses and thistles now visible in the hand that wasn't raised in peace.

"Hallo, love," he said. "Sorry if I gave you a fright."

Martha stared at him, unable to think straight, unable to even fully remember his name for a second until the adrenalin coursing through her body had calmed a little. She looked him up and down, in his long, black trench coat, collar turned up and hair soaked against his head.

"What the *fuck* are you doing here?" she snarled, at last able to form words, fury rising in her gut.

"Are you okay?" he asked, genuine concern in his voice.

Martha couldn't take it all in. "What are you *doing* here?" she demanded again. "Hanging out in alleyways, frightening the life out of me? How did you even know I'd be here? Are you bloody following me? 'Cos if you are Dan, I swear . . ."

Again he placed a hand on her arm gently. "I'm not, Martha, I promise," he said calmly as she shrugged his hand away and pulled her backpack up further on her shoulders. "I knew that you'd be finishing work soon so I was heading up to your office to meet you when you finished. And to give you these . . ." He held out the bunch of flowers to his ex-wife.

Martha couldn't believe what he was doing, and couldn't believe how much rage she felt. She impulsively smacked the bouquet away as hard as she could, knocking it out of Dan's hands and onto the wet cobbles. He glanced forlornly at the bunch as it fell to the ground but made no effort to pick it up.

"You've finished earlier than office hours, have you?" he asked softly.

Martha wanted to scream.

"How the hell do you know where I work? And what time I finish? And what are you doing in Edinburgh? I don't bloody well want you here, Dan. It's been two years . . ." Her voice trailed off. This was too huge, too complicated, and she just did not want it to be happening.

She stared at the face once so familiar to her. She often dreamed about Dan, even though she'd never tell Will that she did. They weren't affectionate dreams – they were troubled ones where he'd try to take Ruby away from her or, worse still, ones where she was sharing romantic and happy moments with someone she thought was Will and who would then turn into Dan. His betrayal of her with their colleague, Paula, for years before Martha had found out, still hurt her deeply, even though her life with Will was happy and settled. Dan had lived two lives – one with Martha, expecting Ruby, living in their home in the London suburbs and being the devoted husband – one with Paula in their luxurious apartment at Canary Wharf, where Dan eventually settled once Martha discovered the deception and kicked him out shortly before Ruby was born. He had never known his daughter, had chosen to leave regardless, leaving Martha alone and Ruby fatherless – until she had met Will.

Dan was soaked and looked dishevelled, but she could see that he was still attractive in a distinguished way. His blonde hair, parted to one side, gave him an aristocratic look – Brideshead, Sue had liked to call him. He had pale skin and distinctive cheekbones, his light-blue eyes a little bloodshot. Dan did very well for himself by painting a picture of a gentle English aristocrat with an old-fashioned charm. In reality, he was a ruthless advertising man who had reinvented himself when he first moved to London in his late teens. That was the key to Dan: things were never quite the same underneath as they seemed on the genteel surface.

"Look, Martha, can we talk? Maybe sit down and grab a coffee or a bite to eat maybe?" he said softly.

Martha recognised the tone – it was one he used on clients to take them in, become their friend, and it worked very well in his career. It was also the tone that he had used on her too many times as he tried to lie his way yet again out of another situation. It reminded her that she had believed him for so long with his untruths, his whole other life, while she stayed at home, excitedly awaiting the birth of their baby, yet another start for the two of them, or so she had thought. The softly put request didn't calm Martha at all – in fact it had the complete opposite effect and she tried to push past him to get down the alleyway back into the open air and make her way home.

"I think we've done all the talking that we ever need to do, Dan," she said through gritted teeth as he once again grabbed her arm, this time succeeding in stopping her in her tracks.

Martha looked up at him – at six feet tall, Dan towered over her five-foot-three frame, but their faces were close. Martha knew that she could barely conceal the contempt in her eyes but couldn't fathom Dan's expression as he seemed to look at her as if he was seeing her for the first time. She stared at him defiantly while he blinked and shook his head slightly, as if trying to clear his thoughts.

"We need to talk Martha – about Ruby, about . . . us," he said. "There are things I need to say to you – that I've come a long way to say. I haven't been stalking you, but I did find out where you worked – I'm staying in the hotel at the bottom of the steps there . . ." He looked behind him, indicating the path downwards where Martha knew there was a chain hotel although she couldn't remember the name. "I was taking this short cut up to your work.

The flowers were stupid – I'm sorry about those, and the ones I sent to you earlier – but I didn't want to just appear empty-handed and a box of chocs just didn't seem right." He smiled a little, continuing to stare at her. "I'm sorry if I scared you – I just saw you on the steps in front of me and I thought you were going to slip so I grabbed your arm. Old habits, I guess." He hung his head a little, as if to indicate shame.

Martha didn't know if he was acting or genuine. Typical.

She wrenched her arm free and took a step backwards. This was massive. She'd have to think about it but she had so many other things to worry about at the moment. She didn't want to talk to him, but he was right – he'd obviously travelled a long way here to talk to her about something and she at least owed him the courtesy of a few moments of her time. Martha sighed. This was just an added bother that she could do without.

"Look, Dan. You've given me an awful fright and you should have called before just . . . turning up like this," she said, looking at the ground.

"I tried," he said, "I rang your office a couple of times but you're never in and I didn't want to leave a message – it just felt – weak, I guess."

So that was who had been leaving the mystery messages.

"I work part-time," said Martha, by means of explanation. She glanced at the time which was already heading toward five thirty. "I can't talk now. Give me your mobile number and I'll phone you over the next day or so and we can have a coffee or something. I really don't have a huge amount to say to you, Dan." She looked up and caught his eye, her own expression hard and steely. She had been so upset for so long – how dare he turn up like this just as she was finally moving on to a new phase?

Dan nodded, again with the shameful expression on his face. His wet hair flopped onto his forehead and he swept it back with a damp hand. "That would be great," he said. "I'm in town for a while. The number's the same as it used to be."

Martha almost snarled at him. "You think I kept it after everything?" she said through gritted teeth. "Have you got a card or something?"

Dan nodded and reached inside the breast pocket of his trench coat for a business card. Martha flinched as she saw the familiar logo of her old company where they had worked together – he as an account director and she as a copywriter – for so long. She associated that logo with feeling miserable. It wasn't the fault of Anderson and McKeith that she'd grown to hate it there, she knew, but she could never shake the feeling of dread when she saw the familiar A and M entwined.

Martha grabbed the card from her ex-husband and slid it into her pocket.

"I have to go," she said simply.

Dan nodded again and stood to one side, letting her pass. "Shall I walk you down?" he suggested as she stepped in the direction from which he had just come. Martha shook her head. Too much, she thought. Tonight she needed to block this from her mind, concentrate on her present, not her past. "No, Dan," she said. "You shan't."

She didn't even look at Dan as she walked past him, back out of the shelter of the small alleyway and down the dimly lit cobbled lane.

CHAPTER 12

Martha glanced across the table at Will as he mopped up the last of the casserole on his plate with the roughly cut crusty bread. He popped it in his mouth with relish and smiled across the table at her. "That was absolutely delicious, as usual," he said enthusiastically and Martha couldn't help but beam back at him. She stared across the table at him as he reached out for another slice, taking in his dark hair, cut a lot shorter now than when she had first met him, and starting to show signs of grey over the ears. He also had a slight stubble, she noticed. It suited him better than Dan, she thought to herself and immediately banished the comparison from her mind. There was no space tonight to even think about her ex. That was for another day.

It had been a lovely evening. The casserole was a recipe at which she was well-practised and she had put it together very quickly while Ruby, fresh from her childminder, devoured an evening snack at the kitchen table. The little girl watched her mum as she cooked and they chatted, mainly Ruby reciting words that she knew repeatedly until Martha said them back to her and they'd share a smile. Much as she tried to keep Dan from her mind, Martha couldn't help but notice previously unacknowledged similarities between her daughter and the child's father. The pale blue eyes, for instance. The blonde hair. Martha shook her head to banish the thoughts. Her baby was *hers* and always had been. After all, Dan had only seen her once . . . Martha had tried her best to focus on pouring cream and wine into the pan, pushing to one side the niggling realisation that Ruby had been made by both of them, however weak the link between child and father.

Will had arrived home, bringing a gust of wind into the hallway with him, just as Martha was preparing Ruby for bed and she felt a brief moment of cosiness as she heard the front door slam against the wind and heard him take off his coat and shoes and pad up the stairs in search of her and the little girl. They had bathed her together, Will taking charge of hair-washing and games and Martha busying herself closing curtains and blinds and lighting lamps, selecting Ruby's clothes for the following day and pulling back the covers on her bed to make it more inviting.

By eight o'clock, Ruby was drifting off under Will's supervision and Martha poured two glasses of wine in the kitchen. She had a brief moment of annoyance as he arrived downstairs and accepted the glass without an acknowledgement and then moved aside her careful place setting to open the laptop that he kept at home and proceed to check emails, but she said nothing. He tended to get annoyed if she commented on him working at the dinner table and she decided to leave it. Pick your battles tonight, she thought.

They had chatted warmly throughout the meal – the wind gusted outside the kitchen window, the rain pelted the panes, and Martha felt warm and safe inside. This is how it should be, she thought, laughing with Will as he described how a colleague had spent the entire day with his sweater inside out, lecturing students. She said nothing of her own day, other than that Maisie had finished early and that she had found an interesting link between two families she had encountered in her research. They laughed together at Ruby's latest trick which was to point behind people and shout "*Bee!*" at the top of her voice, laughing hysterically when they'd turn around. Yes, thought Martha. This is how it should be all the time.

Martha leaned across the table and picked up the bottle of wine, aiming to pour another glass for Will and frowned as he blocked her by covering the top of the glass with his hand. "Oh, no more for me, thanks," he said. "I have a load of work to do and I want to keep my head clear."

Martha's heart sank as he pushed back his chair and stood up, picking up his empty plate, ignoring the fact that she was still eating. She put down her fork.

"I was hoping we might just have tonight for ourselves?" she said quietly, afraid almost that he might take offence at this. This was happening a little too often for her liking these days – more and more of his time spent deep in his work, trying so hard to prove an impossible point, or so it seemed to her.

"I'm afraid we'll have to do that another time," he said, leaving his plate on the draining board and turning back toward the table, talking over the kitchen island. "I'm just so busy at the moment –"

"You're *always* busy," snapped Martha. She hadn't meant to, but she couldn't hold back. "We never spend much time together any more, Will."

Will's face darkened. "That's not true, Martha," he snapped back.

Martha sighed. Here it goes again, she thought. "I don't want to fight, Will, but did you know that it's been three weeks since we sat down together in the one room after Ruby's gone to bed?"

Will snorted. "That's rubbish, Martha, and anyway there's more to life than just plonking down in front of the TV every night."

"Plonking down in front of the PC every night, you mean?" snapped Martha, her temper growing, much as she didn't want this conversation to disintegrate into an argument.

Will snorted and shook his head. "I don't want to get into this now," he said, picking up the laptop from the counter top where Martha had placed it before she served up dinner.

"Neither do I, Will," she replied as calmly as she could. "But if we don't get into this now, then when do we?" She paused. "Will, there's actually something I need to talk to you about, seriously."

Will, only half-listening, already preoccupied with whatever task lay ahead of him, began to walk away. "Can it wait till later?" he muttered, and kept going out the door.

He doesn't mean it, Martha reassured herself, at the same time marvelling at his total focus. "Not this time," she replied. She got up and strode to the doorway, stopping him in his tracks as he crossed the hall to the stairs, as she said: "Will, I've seen Gabriel. He needs your help."

They stood like that in silence for a few moments – Martha in the kitchen doorframe and Will in the middle of the hallway.

Eventually he turned his head slightly in her direction and spoke over his shoulder. "What do you mean you've seen Gabriel?" he asked, stony-voiced.

"He really needs to talk to you," said Martha, eager not to get into a 'who saw who', 'who instigated what' type of conversation, hoping to appeal to the side of Will that must surely still feel something for his friend.

"He called me, out of the blue. I met him and went to his flat and –"

"You went to his *flat*?" asked Will in disbelief, finally turning back to face her. "When did all this happen?"

"Jesus, Will, calm down," said Martha. "It was last week – I –"

"Last *week*?" he repeated, a furious tone entering his voice. "And you're choosing only to tell me about it now?"

Martha bit her lip for a moment, wishing that this conversation wasn't happening this way. She took a deep breath.

"Yes, last week. He rang me really upset and asked me to help him. It sounds bizarre, but he's being haunted."

A flicker of something other than anger crossed Will's features. Could it be curiosity, wondered Martha.

"There's a man – a spirit – who's following him, and fingerprints in the dust in his flat, and a feeling that there's someone with him all the time. And someone's been leaving him messages – spirit writing."

Will continued to stare at Martha as she explained what Gabriel had told her.

"That's why he wanted me to go there with him, so I could see all this for myself. Plus, on top of that, he's had a request to help out with something at Dubhglas Castle – you remember he told us about that before? He's got some childhood link with the place. Help out with something paranormal." Surely that would hook his interest?

Instead, he turned and began to climb the stairs.

"There's one more thing," added Martha, stepping into the hallway after him. "Laurence is gone." Will stiffened and turned.

"That's nonsense," he said, bluntly.

It wasn't the response that Martha had expected. "What do you mean?" she said, uncomprehending. "Rubbish, all of it," repeated Will, his tone growing angrier. "There's no way that could have happened. He's just making this up to get attention because his bloody television show is a heap of rubbish and he wants to get back in my good books. Well, he sold me out and decided which side he wanted to be on so he can bloody well stay there, as far as I'm concerned!" His face was red and the laptop slipped from under his arm. He just about managed to catch it on time and the action made him even more furious. He swore under his breath.

Martha took a step back. "My God, Will, why are you so bloody *angry*?" she snapped. "You and Gabriel were the best of friends for years and now he's asked for your help – you're being completely irrational."

"And he's a social climber who left me high and dry, so let his new buddies in TV sort him out this time. I haven't got time for his hysterical carry-on! And as for you sneaking around behind my back –"

"Me? Sneaking around behind your back?" Martha could feel fury rise inside her. "Do you think you *own* me, Will? I'm entitled to meet and be friends with whoever I bloody well like and not be governed by whether you've got some irrational rage going on at the time. I swear it's like living with a nest of wasps sometimes!"

Will turned and continued to climb the stairs.

"Typical!" hissed Martha. "Don't worry, Will, I'll just wait until you're finished all your highly important work, to feature in your life again. I don't mind one little bit!"

He kept going and then she heard the door to the office room click shut.

She stood silently, bubbling with rage and dissatisfied with the conclusion of the conversation. Where had *that* one gone wrong, she wondered helplessly as she retraced her steps to the kitchen and picked up the wineglass left beside her unfinished meal. So much effort spent on making things perfect and yet here she was, feeling alone and shut out when all she had wanted to do was to take the first step at reconciling two friends. She picked up the glass, and then the bottle, and headed to the living room where she closed the door behind her and flicked on the TV, too angry and exhausted even to cry.

CHAPTER 13

Martha roused from the dream and blinked, trying to figure out where she was. Her room looked unfamiliar. The dream had been so unsettling. Dan had been supposed to take care of Ruby, but he'd lost her and what was worse, he didn't seem to care . . .

Her mouth was sandpaper dry. She longed for a drink of water and the longing woke her further. She was relieved to find that she was in her own bed and could hear Ruby's little snores through the monitor handset on her bedside table.

She propped herself up on her elbows and glanced across at the digital alarm-clock on Will's side of the bed. Unsurprisingly, she thought, she was alone, and it was almost four o'clock. Will had either fallen asleep at his desk or was crashed out in one of the spare bedrooms. He had taken to doing this lately after working late so as not to disturb her by coming into the room when she was asleep. Or after an argument which they seemed to have more often these days. The difficulty with Will, Martha realised, was that he couldn't just be interested in something – he had to be completely fixated. And these days – without Gabriel – it was as if he had decided to take on the whole world of paranormal investigation solo, become the only individual on the planet to prove that there was life after death. It was becoming a complete obsession.

Martha swung her legs over the side of the bed and sat there for a moment before turning on her bedside lamp. She yawned, contemplated lying down again and trying to sleep but with her thirst unquenched she knew that was impossible and wearily stood up, sliding her feet into her slippers.

The house was in complete silence. She opened their bedroom door quietly and padded on her toes out to the hallway in the dark. She didn't want to disturb Ruby by turning on the light. Or Will, wherever he was. She couldn't bear the thought of another round of argument. The door to the study was open and she glanced in as she passed, the room lit by the glow of the computer screen where Will had been working, but there was no sign of him. The door to the other spare room was closed so Martha reckoned he must be asleep in there and sneaked past carefully.

She knew the house so well in the darkness that she didn't fumble or slip en route to the kitchen where she filled a pint glass with water and took a deep draught before refilling the glass and turning to leave again. The living-room door was ajar, she noticed, and the sound of breathing coming from within indicated Will's whereabouts for certain. She glanced in and saw him slumped on the couch, asleep, a troubled expression on the features lit by the soft glow of the dying fire. Martha stared at him for a few moments, longing to just rub a hand across his brow and urge him to go to bed. Why were things so strained between them? And what could she do to make it better?

She sighed and pulled the door gently shut behind her. Will's back would hurt in the morning but she just couldn't face him now, not when there was just no reasoning with him. She padded back up the stairs and toward her own room at the end of the landing, pausing for a moment at the door of the office before taking a step inside.

She never snooped in Will's things, particularly his work, but now she felt wide awake, and a compulsion rose in her to see exactly what he was working on right now. What had distanced him from the family life that he had professed to have wanted so much when they moved in together? She had been the reluctant one. Ruby had been just starting to toddle and was demanding of time and patience from adults. Martha had clearly said that she hadn't wanted to burden Will with this, especially when Ruby wasn't his child, but he had looked at her like she was mad and said that he couldn't wait to make a proper family of the three of them, that he didn't care that Ruby wasn't his. Martha smiled at the memory. Will used to say things like that all the time and while she knew they couldn't stay in a bubble of love forever, surely it wasn't right either that they were so distant and so argumentative such a short time since making the decision to build a life together?

Maybe Will hadn't realised what it took to be a parent to a toddler, she mused, crossing over slowly to the desk, glancing around the room as she went. She'd thought so long and hard about them being together all the time, and eventually reassured herself that of all the men she'd met he was mature enough to take them both on. Maybe she'd judged him wrongly and now he was missing his bachelor lifestyle and throwing himself into his work to get away from domestic drudgery?

Martha felt a huge weight on her shoulders as she sank into his swivel-chair at the desk. Was it time to start making serious decisions about what to do for her and Ruby? Surely they could work it out? She couldn't just move on again. Mostly, she just didn't want to.

She glanced around at the computer screen on the desk and out of habit shook the mouse to clear the screensaver. She was surprised at the document that she found herself reading. "McKenzie is a true enigma," was the first sentence. "His work with what he knows as the world of spirit is entirely altruistic and he asks those he helps for nothing apart from updates from time to time as to whether they are still troubled. He is a modest man, with a modest lifestyle and a day job as a guide on one of Edinburgh's many tour buses, showing tourists the city that he loves as much for its strong paranormal connections as well as the amazing architecture and genuine warmth . . ." It was Will's unfinished book, provisionally titled *Ghost Interpreter: The Works of Gabriel McKenzie,* the main thrust of his work prior to his and Gabriel's falling-out.

Martha glanced down the page, at lines highlighted in red.

"McKenzie can be accused of being a fake, as are many, if not all, men and women who work in this area . . . The word 'charlatan' has been bandied about more often than not and he takes it all in his stride ... His strength is his integrity and the genuine urge to help people that he shows in his own inimitable style ... Gabriel McKenzie is, above all, not about making money from those in need."

Martha sighed. There was the problem, she knew. Gabriel genuinely believed in what he did, had a sincere respect for the spirit world and would never have compromised himself for cash but since he'd signed up with *Ghosts R Us*, thereby earning more of it, Will didn't agree with it. Will had very strong principles, Martha knew. It was one of his qualities that she admired most, but she couldn't agree with his belief that Gabriel had completely sold out by taking the TV job and that it was only a matter of time before his integrity and reputation were compromised and, by association, Will's.

Will felt that the paranormal was an undiscovered science and, like any scientist, was desperate to prove his theories correct. Gabriel had been such a huge part of his research, and integral to that was Gabriel's complete faith in what he believed and the fact that he received no monetary gain for it. Will – and Gabriel for that matter – had no belief whatsoever in mediums who performed on stage, or put themselves up for hire.

They had visited a number of these 'roadshows' during the course of their work and enjoyed regaling Martha with their tales. Once, Gabriel swore blind that the medium on stage was accompanied by a spirit guide but chose to actively ignore him throughout the entire event, using only the names and basic information given to him to invent creative and emotive messages to pass on to the loved ones in the audience who lapped it all up. Gabriel particularly loved to tell the story of one elderly lady from the audience. It was true that her sister was called Margaret and she had worked as a dinner lady for many years in a particular school. However, the message from the so-called medium that 'the money was in the carriage clock' seemed to leave the lady stumped and she left the auditorium more puzzled and less reassured than when she went in. Until, of course, she bumped into Gabriel in the foyer who just couldn't bring himself to let her leave without clearing things up. He had tapped her on the arm and when she turned to him, had whispered the words "Celery salt!"

in her ear. Her delight was instant. That was the only secret she had needed to know from the other side. Margaret's hidden ingredient for gravy. There was no money, Gabriel knew – there wasn't even a carriage clock – the message was about what had been missing from Sunday lunch since Margaret had passed on. It was moments like this – the pure joy and gratitude on that old lady's face – that convinced Will that Gabriel was genuine about his skill, as he liked to call it. The next step was convincing the rest of the world.

Until, of course, *Ghosts R Us*. Big pay meant big compromises as far as Will was concerned and he couldn't see how Gabriel could preserve his integrity and be part of this show at the same time. Will felt bitterly betrayed and had closed his files and his notes on the book immediately, telling Gabriel that he might consider speaking to him again once he'd left that awful TV show and had a long think about what really mattered. Martha knew, however, why Gabriel had taken the contract with the production company. The modest lifestyle to which Will referred in the book was just a little bit too modest and Gabriel simply wanted a mortgage, some nice clothes, creature comforts – all the things that his day job couldn't afford him. He'd never had any intention of selling out or of suddenly becoming a showman – or a conman – like others they had seen. He'd been unable to convince Will of this however and now here they were, separated and unable to resolve the massive chasm that had grown between them, worsening with time.

Martha noticed another tab open on the computer screen behind the manuscript which she knew Will hadn't looked at for a very long time. She clicked the second tab and was immediately interested to see that Will had been reading a newspaper article from a Sunday magazine written by a reputable journalist whose name she recognised.

The headline read "The Other Side: How Ghost Hunting TV Might Not Have the Proof that There's Something Out There" and the article went on to analyse various TV shows, amongst them *Ghosts R Us*. It was the only show where the reporter hadn't been able to tag along with the team on an investigation – all the others had welcomed her with open arms, keen to prove that they were genuine. The article suggested that they weren't, necessarily, although some fared better than others, but *Ghosts R Us* had cited 'tight production schedules' as their reason for leaving her out and then had refused to take any more of her calls and emails. It seemed, however, she had spoken to a show insider, who was keen to remain nameless but pointed out various features of the show that differed from others. And seemed to suggest that it wasn't as genuine as it liked to make out.

> "The external locations were filmed by a small crew who headed off in a van last winter and did them all in the one go," the whistleblower alleged. "Much of the other stuff – the actual supposed investigations – is filmed in a studio in night vision. It's easy to fudge it with grainy night-vision cameras, and the style of the show means that there are frequent cuts to close-ups of the crew – who were really hired for, shall we say, their looks – doing pieces to camera so there's never a sustained requirement for a camera to point at one thing. The crew aren't averse to sometimes creating their own drama as well, if you know what I mean."

Martha continued to read. This was all information that Gabriel had given her but under warning that it must remain strictly confidential or he could run the risk of getting the sack.

The article continued with an observation from the journalist:

> "The only genuine thing about Ghosts R Us seems, oddly, to be the so-called 'spirit medium', a Gabriel McKenzie who claims to have had second sight since leaving the army a number of years ago. McKenzie often looks clueless on set when things 'kick off' as the team like to call it, and is never included as one of the talking heads recounting the increasingly breathless adventures. This could be down to the fact that he's in his forties, tubby and balding – a father figure, if you will, to the team who have clearly been selected for the job at hand on the basis that their combined age wouldn't even make for a good whiskey and each is more beautiful or more buff than the last. It could also be

down to the fact that McKenzie has managed to maintain an unsullied reputation as actually genuine within the paranormal community and it has been queried more than once just what the hell he's doing on the show."

Martha grinned, wondering if Gabriel had read this. 'Tubby' and 'balding' were certainly not words that would make him happy, she reckoned, but the reference to his reputation and the respect held for him amongst his peers would. She wondered if it had done anything to reassure Will.

She glanced down at the remainder of the article which outlined two shows. *Ghosts Wanted* and *Britain from the Other Side* as seemingly the most reputable on air but ultimately put the success of these shows down to the appetites of "housewives and the unemployed whose lives are so humdrum that they become fascinated by the prospect that there has to be more out there – other than the prospect of cooking another plate of turkey twizzlers or having to go get a job." The conclusion was that the paranormal was all escapism. Martha shuddered. She knew this not to be true but put the proof that she had witnessed to the back of her mind.

She stared at the screen for a while, and then around her at the reams of paper, the files, the DVDs and the other paraphernalia of Will's work. What was the point, she began to wonder, and then allowed her mind to go blank, merely tracing the familiar shapes of his handwriting scribbled in margins and the doodles of flowers and trees that he insisted on drawing on everything.

She was roused by a whimper from Ruby's room, only audible because the house was so quiet. Martha breathed in sharply, and glanced at the time on the bottom right-hand side of the computer screen. It was after five and she realised that she really had better get back to bed. She had a heavy day ahead taking care of the toddler. And some heavy thinking, she reckoned, as she pushed herself up from the swivel-chair. The room in darkness, she picked up her glass of water and returned to her bed, after satisfying herself that Ruby had merely turned over in her sleep.

There was much to be done, thought Martha, and closed her tired eyes against it all.

CHAPTER 14

November 18th

Dan had wanted to meet at Martha's home. His text messages had requested her address and her working days, but Martha had refused, instead insisting that they meet at five thirty for a drink at the Scotsman Hotel, near to her work. Neutral territory was essential, she felt, for her first proper conversation with her ex-husband in over two years.

He was there, waiting for her, when she arrived. She saw him sitting in a corner, his mobile held to his ear, looking around almost nervously. A half-drunk pint of Guinness sat before him.

Since bumping into him in the alley off the Royal Mile she had wondered endlessly what he wanted. Why was he back? What if there was something wrong with him? Something genetic, for example, and he needed her to know for Ruby's sake? Martha had stewed and fretted for a week. It had been so long since he'd been around that she'd almost allowed herself to believe that he didn't exist and she had grown to like it that way. His presence now was an intrusion.

She had dressed carefully that morning, avoiding looking too businesslike – she didn't for one second want him to think that she was dressing to impress him. Nor, however, did she want him to think that she didn't care. She wanted to look her best, but look herself.

She had settled on a simple pair of skinny black jeans and expensive leather riding boots with a cashmere polo-neck sweater in royal blue. She accessorised with a short, military-style jacket and a tan leather knapsack which Will had bought her in Barcelona on their last trip there. She had kept her jewellery simple – a pair of diamond stud earrings which had been a gift from her father on her twenty-first birthday and a ruby ring which Will had given to her when they moved in together.

Martha studied her reflection with satisfaction. It looked like *her*. It would show him that she had regained herself and grown to be so much more than the mousy housewife he used to see in her. She had wanted domesticity in their marriage, to stay together and have a family. Dan had wanted someone to spar with, to enjoy the cut and thrust of business – someone entirely different from her. Their difference made him view her as weak. A view that she had begun to share after a while.

She took a deep breath before striding as confidently as she could toward him. She noticed his Guinness was flat, leading her to believe he'd been there a while.

He saw her as she made her way across the bar and stood to greet her with a wide smile. Martha glanced around her as she reached the table and hesitantly sat down. It was foolish, she knew – she was unlikely to meet anyone who knew her – but she didn't want to appear eager to be sitting down with this man in case somehow it got back to Will. She still hadn't mentioned the fact that Dan was in town to him – partly because she wanted to figure it out in her own head, to find out exactly what Dan wanted first. Partly because Will's humour had grown no better since she had confessed to seeing Gabriel. If suddenly she piped up that her ex-husband was appearing to her in alleyways, she felt that Will might just go over the edge.

"Thanks so much for coming," said Dan, taking his own seat again once Martha was in hers.

His accent was cut crystal, as always, she noticed.

"I haven't got long," she said sharply. "I have to pick up –" She paused. She didn't want to mention Ruby for some reason, to bring her to the table with her long-absent father on the other side of it.

Martha's stomach jolted as the realisation came to the forefront of her mind that it was possible that Dan might be looking for her daughter and the one thing that Martha did not want, above all else, was to share her precious little girl.

"I have to get home," she finished. "I've only got about half an hour, so . . ." She let the words trail off. She wanted to tell him to spit it out, to say what he had to say and then get back on the next train or plane to London and out of her life, but she also wanted to be civilised and polite. With the way she felt about Dan she reckoned that the best way of doing that was to say as little as possible in case the wrong thing was blurted out.

Dan nodded. "Absolutely," he said, raising his hand to attract the attention of the waiter who headed straight for their table. "Let me get you a drink. I really appreciate you coming. Eh, white wine, please," he said to the waiter. "Still Sauvignon Blanc?" he asked Martha with a smile.

Martha felt cold and her expression remained fixed as she turned slightly to the waiter standing just behind her. "A glass of Merlot, please," she requested. She didn't normally drink red but it galled her that Dan had taken the liberty of ordering for her, literally over her head. Assuming that she was the same person he'd known once, when she wasn't.

Dan was aware that he was being corrected and, having ordered a second Guinness for himself, he shifted uncomfortably in his seat. A silence fell over the table. If he thinks I'm going to jump in with chitchat, thought Martha, he's got another think coming.

Martha looked at his face and noticed that he had lost weight – though that was a perfectly reasonable thing for a human to do in two years. The silence was broken by the arrival of the waiter and Martha leaned back a little to allow him place the glass of wine in front of her and the stout in front of Dan.

"What's this about, Dan?" she asked once the waiter had left them alone.

Dan ignored her – another habit she realised had driven her nuts when they were together. His face suddenly growing animated, he leaned over to study her right hand.

"Nice ring," he offered.

Martha was unsettled. "Thank you," she replied. "It was a gift from Will." Dammit. She hadn't wanted to mention Will. Not yet anyway. She didn't want to keep him a secret but she also didn't want to seem like a schoolgirl, dropping her new boyfriend's name into the conversation within minutes.

Dan's eyes flickered, but he carried on with his line of questioning. "Will's your new partner, right? What does he do for a living?" He licked off his Guinness moustache.

Martha stared back at him, uncomfortable, seeing that he was genuinely waiting for an answer. "He used to be in property," she replied, and sipped her glass of Merlot, longing to pick it up and gulp it back in one go before asking for another.

"Used to be?" said Dan, sitting back in his chair. "What does he do now?"

Martha squirmed slightly, thought about lying, and then thought better of it. "He's a student of parapsychology," she said. If she didn't look ashamed, then Dan might leave the subject. Saying it out loud, however, made it suddenly seem flaky and a waste of time, when it had never bothered her before.

Dan's eyes widened slightly and a slight smirk formed on his face, a familiar grin of derision. At once, Martha recognised it and her anxiety shifted up a gear. It was exactly the sort of thing that Dan liked to make fun of.

"So he studies *ghosts*? Am I correct?" he asked, the smirk growing wider.

"The paranormal," clarified Martha, growing furious. "Not just 'ghosts' as you put it. And at least he isn't a cheating shit who lives a double life with his mistress. Now why am I here, Dan?"

There it was. She'd said it, it was out there. Two years of communicating carefully through solicitors and she'd managed to lose it within five minutes of meeting him. Who did Dan think he was? She sat there, stony-faced, her eyes fixed on Dan, almost daring him to respond.

Experience led her to expect a sharp retort, or at the very least to have him snap at her to calm down. What she didn't expect was for him to suddenly lower his head and nod in chastened agreement.

"You're right," he said. "I am a total shit and I want to apologise."

Martha was shocked. She again reached for her wineglass and this time took the big gulp that she had wanted. Of all things that she had expected Dan Smith to say, 'I'm sorry' wasn't one of them.

Dan looked at her suddenly, with his blue eyes, and again she saw Ruby in them and felt irked.

"I screwed up big time, Martha. I can see that now with the benefit of hindsight. I had a really good thing with you and our marriage, and our home, and I blew it all in a really bad way and I hurt you very much. It wasn't right for me at the time but I truly am very sorry."

Martha had waited a long time to hear those words, but instead of giving her satisfaction they almost made her feel even angrier than she had before. If they'd been insincere then it might have been easier to deal with – she expected nothing better from the man who had set up a second home with his girlfriend while she was pregnant – but what galled her most was that, judging by his expression, he seemed to actually *mean* it.

"You can't have it back, Dan," she said.

"I don't want it back," he replied quickly, leaning over the table toward her. "I mean, yes, I'd love it back but I know if I did . . . I'd just cock it all up again. You and I weren't meant to be together and we both know that."

Martha knew he was right, but his reasoning made her realise something. That she wanted him to demand to have her back and she wanted the power to refuse him, to deny him what he most wanted, like he had with her two years previously. She wanted the control, the revenge, and here he was taking that away from her. It had been a bad idea to come here, she thought.

"How *is* Paula?" she asked coldly, taking another swig of wine, realising that her hands were starting to tremble. In saying the other woman's name, it was as if the rest of the room went dark around her and Dan was illuminated in a single spotlight. She knew she didn't want him back, but she wanted him to say that Paula had left him. Or better still that he had left Paula, or that Paula had cheated on him. Anything to indicate that they weren't still together, happy and solid as they had been throughout the marriage break-up, the relationship that was meant to be – Dan and Paula, not Dan and Mousy Martha. More than anything, she wanted him to be unhappy. And she hated herself for that.

"Paula's fine," said Dan quietly, and Martha's heart sank. "She's in London, still working with AM. We're moving to a house in Hampstead and she's doing it up at the moment. It's all go actually."

Hampstead, thought Martha. He might as well have smacked her in the face. That's where she had wanted them to live, to bring up a family and grow old together. She'd thought she was over all this but here he was, replacing her with Paula again, digging up all the pain that she thought had passed. Martha longed for Will suddenly and twisted the ring on her finger, as if it could magically summon him.

"So you and Will live here, in Edinburgh?" continued Dan.

It took Martha a moment to realise that he was looking at her, waiting for an answer "Yes, we do," she said, coughing nervously. "We've bought a house here actually."

Dan perked up and made an 'impressed' face. "Must be good money in ghost hunting?" he grinned. "Only kidding," he added, and smiled softly, raising his hand in mock defence. "Seriously though, I'm glad that you've done so well for yourself and that you're happy."

Martha forced a grin back.

Dan's face suddenly became serious. "I'm happy for both of you," he said.

Martha was confused. He didn't know Will from Adam – wasn't he really overdoing the patronising bit by being happy for him?

Dan registered her furrowed brow and clarified his point. "For you and Ruby," he said, and Martha's blood ran suddenly cold.

"How is she?" he asked, almost shyly. "How is my daughter?"

Martha's brain suddenly felt under attack. No, she thought. No, he cannot ask about her. He cannot even mention her name. She's not his, at least not now she's not. She's mine and only mine. She scrambled for an answer desperately, or more precisely scrambled not to answer him, to take Ruby's name out of the air, to make him forget her and leave them alone.

"Why do you want to know all of a sudden?" she asked coldly. "You've no right, Dan, not after what you did."

Again, he nodded. Martha didn't feel curious this time as to why, however. She didn't want to know why, just knew that she wanted to go home and pick Ruby up in her arms and hold the back of her soft little neck and never let her go. Never let him get her. Every hair stood on end, her maternal instinct to protect her child in overdrive.

"I know you feel that way and I know why," he said, again in his soft voice. "But the truth is that I've been doing a lot of thinking and . . ."

Martha didn't want to hear what was coming next, wondered if there was still time to run away. She sat bolted to her chair instead.

"I'd like to . . . review . . . our custody situation, Martha. I want to see more of Ruby, to be her dad.". He looked directly at Martha with what could only be described as pleading in his eyes.

"No," said Martha, without a second thought, and scrabbled at her feet to find her handbag. She had to go, couldn't be around him, had to get home and lock the doors and hide under the bed. This was worse than any bloody ghosts. He was going to try to take Ruby away – take her to bloody Paula, after everything that he'd already put her through. "*No!*" she said again and made to stand up.

Suddenly, Dan reached across the table and laid his hand across her hand, covering the beautiful ring that seemed so irrelevant now. "Martha, I'm sorry," he said, in such a way that it stopped her in her tracks. There was something in his tone that brought her back to the very start, to before Paula, before Ruby, back to the beginning.

She sank back into her chair, trembling.

"I'm *so so* sorry for fucking things up," he continued, speaking softly but quickly, as if to cram in all the words he wanted to say before she ran away. "So sorry for leaving you – I'm sorry for marrying you, truth be known, because if I hadn't then none of this would ever have happened . . ."

And Ruby wouldn't have happened, thought Martha.

"But it has and I want to make up for it. I'm older now, and wiser, and I've realised that I have a daughter." He stared at Martha for a moment. "A beautiful *daughter*," he stressed.

It struck Martha as strange – did he think she didn't get the concept?

"And I want to see her, and spend time with her and get to know her. And I know that deep down you know that if I do it right, then that's the right thing to do for her future. I know this is a shock for you, and a lot to take in, but I really want to do this the right way. I want to make sure we're all happy with everything – I'll do whatever it takes, Martha, but I don't want to suddenly grow old and know that Ruby's grown up and that I missed the greatest chance of my life."

Martha was stunned to see a tear form in the corner of his right eye and suddenly release itself down his cheek. He made no effort to wipe it away, and continued to rest his hand on hers, grasping it. "Please let me do this," he said. "I know it's the last thing you want, but I know I have rights and responsibilities and I want to live up to them, to make it up to you both and be a good dad." He released his grip on her hand.

Martha stared at him for a long time, his words flying around her head, crammed in there, fighting with each other for reason and sense. She couldn't take it in, wanted to refuse him point blank, but at the same time it dawned on her that what he said was true. Rights and responsibilities. As much as it killed her, she knew he was correct. He had the right to see Ruby and now all of a sudden he wanted to. But what if he took her away? What if Ruby preferred him? Or preferred *Paula?* The thought horrified her.

"I have to go, Dan," she said abruptly and stood, pulling her bag over her shoulder, her face filled with shock and disbelief.

Dan nodded, a lock of blonde hair falling past his eye. "I want to do this right," he said again. Martha stared at him and then found herself nodding, before turning and walking away, unsteady on her feet as she went, desperate to get to the door of the hotel and out into the misty evening.

"You know where I'm staying," she heard him say after her. "Just call me and we can set it up. I'm in town for as long as it takes. And Martha, I'm sorry."

CHAPTER 15

Martha released the child carefully from the restraint of the car seat and lifted her gently into her arms. The tiny blonde head lolled onto her shoulder and, once there, snuggled itself closer into Martha's neck. The sensation was overwhelming and Martha thought that her knees might buckle and was overcome with a feeling of tearfulness. She inhaled deeply, the smell filling her nostrils – a combination of baby shampoo from her daughter's hair and the hint of open-fire smoke in the air along with that particular smell of early winter, that sharpness in the air as the first of the dark evenings settled in, still a novelty. At least she was home and Ruby was safe in her arms and once she could get inside she could sit down and talk to Will and he'd make everything fine again. Martha just wanted to lock the door of her house and never emerge.

She had driven home from the meeting with Dan in a daze, thoughts hurtling through her mind. Would this mean that she might have to move back nearer to London? Would it mean that Dan would have Ruby at weekends? That she'd only ever see her child on school nights and for half the school holidays? What would happen when Dan and Paula would take her on exotic holidays and expensive day trips? What if they turned her against Will entirely, when he had done so much for her?

Martha fumbled on her key ring for her house key, growing angrier by the second. Damn Dan! Everything up until now had been perfect – how *dare* he turn up like this and suddenly make Ruby into a child of a divorce? How dare he take the cosy bond that Martha and Ruby shared exclusively and break it? Make life be about choices, taking sides? Take up her time travelling between two houses when it could have been spent painting pictures, or baking, or going to the zoo? Martha paused on the top step with the key to the front door in her hand and took a deep breath, ordering herself to calm down in case she had a complete meltdown with Ruby still in her arms.

She had been surprised to see Will's Volvo in the driveway – normally he was never home before Martha, especially midweek. She was equally surprised to hear voices coming from the kitchen. She closed the front door behind her as quietly as she could and crossed the hallway, taking the first steps on the stairs as lightly as she could so that they wouldn't creak and wake Ruby.

Making sure that Ruby was settled, Martha made her way quietly to the bathroom. She knew she had to go downstairs and join Will and their guest, knowing that Will would expect it of her. She checked her appearance in the mirror in case the visitor was someone important for Will – someone from the university perhaps, or someone interested in publishing some of his work. Then again, it could be another bloody ghost geek, she thought. It wouldn't be the first time she'd come home to find Will poring over a laptop with someone from one of the city's amateur paranormal groups, trying to pin down the precise moment that a shadow seemed to twitch or a piece of dust floated past a camera.

She became aware of the smell of food as she went downstairs – a roast by the smell of things – which would indicate that whoever was downstairs was staying for dinner. A dinner which would take some time to cook, so it looked like she was in for a late one. A slight sense of panic gripped her. She needed Will to herself – to sort things out between them first and then explain about Dan. She didn't need him scoffing down a plate of chicken with someone who wanted to only discuss the merits of full-spectrum photography and then disappear up to his office to exchange ghost stories and analyse green, grainy digital video.

She frowned. She'd have to try to get Will on his own and tell him that something important needed to be discussed concerning Ruby. Ruby always came first to him. She knew he'd understand, even when she explained why she hadn't mentioned to him before that Dan was in town. He'd be able to help. Make Dan go away and then leave them in peace, leave them to get back to how things were before.

Martha was deep in these thoughts as she pushed open the kitchen door and saw Will first, leaning in his habitual position against the counter top, the kitchen windows black behind him. It was in these windows that she saw someone reflected who stopped her in her tracks. Martha did a double take, gasped and turned to her left to face the man sitting at the kitchen table. Momentarily her thoughts of Dan and feelings of panic washed away and she beamed with delight at Gabriel who was holding a glass of white wine in his bejewelled hands. Martha looked at Will, who smiled at her, and then looked back at Gabriel, who winked and raised his glass slightly in a silent toast. "Hello, my love," he said, grinning, and she grinned back as she went and leaned over him to give him a hug.

They were slightly tipsy by the time the meal of roast chicken was finally finished, hours later. In the meantime, Ruby had woken, been bathed hurriedly and put straight back to bed, exhausted. It gave the adults the chance to catch up.

"Seriously, Gabriel, you were the last person I expected to ever see sitting at the kitchen table again!" said Martha, reaching into the fridge for another bottle of wine.

"Remember, it's a school night!" grinned Will, but without his usual note of caution in his voice. He beamed at Martha as he held up his glass for a refill and they giggled as she slopped a little over the side in pouring. He even went so far as to hold his face up for a kiss, which she returned gladly, causing Gabriel to tut in disgust.

"Get a room!" he scoffed. "Top me up first though, my dear?"

Martha grinned back and gladly filled his glass before returning to her own. She felt light-headed with relief – firstly that Gabriel and Will were reunited, and secondly, Gabriel's presence there meant that she didn't have to think about Dan and the whole custody situation. It had become clear that she wasn't going to get Will on his own that night, and anyway she didn't want to, seeing him in such a good humour for the first time in months. There would be plenty of time tomorrow to talk through what was going to happen with Dan – he'd said he'd stay in Edinburgh for as long as it took, so let him. Let him camp out in a lonely hotel room at his own expense while waiting for an answer. As it stood, Martha realised that she held the cards and as she looked around the room at her partner, their estranged friend now returned, and the remains of an excellent meal, she decided that she was in no hurry to play them.

Martha plonked back down in her seat and picked up her glass. "To Gabriel and Will!" she said. "Reunited at last!"

Gabriel's response was to roll his eyes and stand up unsteadily from the table, pushing behind her and forcing her to scooch her chair in to the table so far that she could barely breathe.

"Outta my way!" he said. "A man's gotta do what a man's gotta do! Lav's upstairs, I take it? Never mind, I'll find it myself," and with that he was gone, listing slightly to his right as he did so.

Martha heard the bottom step squeak loudly under his foot and listened for a moment for any sounds from Ruby. She turned her head sharply, however, as she felt something a warm touch on her hand, and realised that Will had leaned across the table to cover it with his own.

"I have to thank you," said Will softly.

Martha cocked her head to one side. "Why?" she asked.

Will nodded his head toward the ceiling. "You just brought me back to my senses a bit. I'm so sorry I was annoyed with you – if you hadn't told me you'd seen Gabriel – it's difficult to say, but it sort of made him *real* again. I know that sounds like complete nonsense but I guess I had taken an out-of-sight-out-of-mind attitude to things. I've been so pig-headed. Without what you said to me – well – I wouldn't have gone and looked at the manuscript of my book. It all reminded me that – well, there's still research there that could change everything – how people think about the paranormal – maybe prove my point that it's an undiscovered science. He's vital to that – the best link I have and I've screwed it up by being stubborn. And on top of everything . . . I've missed the grumpy old sod. So I phoned him up and invited him over and we've talked . . ."

"And I've explained to him that I am not a total whore!" came a voice from the doorway as Gabriel rejoined them. "I can still maintain my integrity as a medium while actually earning a reasonable keep – is that not correct, William?"

Will nodded in response. "I can see now where you're coming from – doesn't mean I agree with it, but who am I to argue? And maybe you're right – maybe you being on TV could be a good thing – at any rate, you went onto that show with the best of intentions."

"Well, now, my dear," grinned Gabriel, taking a sip from his glass, "integrity's all well and good but being a tour guide wasn't going to buy me furs and diamonds, now was it?" He made an elaborate hand gesture in the air and sat sideways on his chair, crossing his legs theatrically.

Martha rolled her eyes – being tipsy made Gabriel automatically camper.

"If I'd only known what a total sham that show was going to be before I signed up for it though," Gabriel continued, resting his chin in his hand. "I mean there are so many of those shows where they take things seriously. What's that one – *Ghosts Wanted* – I mean, all they do is film the actual investigation on that one – none of these pieces to camera where someone says that, if only they'd known they were going to see something that would change their lives forever or that irrefutably proves that there's life after death, they would have made sure to have a camera with them at that precise moment . . ." Gabriel's words trailed off. "I've forgotten how I was going to end that sentence," he said matter of factly.

Martha laughed aloud while Will grinned, looking at Gabriel affectionately.

"What I mean to say is that, much as I love being a wee bit more comfortable, I can't wait for my contract to be up next month and get back to doing things proper. If I still can, that is."

Will leaned back from the table and folded his arms against his chest. "Is it true then, what Martha was saying?" he said, suddenly serious. "About Laurence being gone?"

Gabriel nodded. "Did she tell you about my . . . *visitor*? My nocturnal friend?" he asked.

Martha nodded. "I did, didn't I, Will?" she said, eager to prove that she had kept her promise to Gabriel.

Will asked Gabriel to elaborate and Gabriel began to tell the story of what was happening in his apartment, backed up by Martha as an eyewitness to the handwriting and the fingerprints. Emboldened by wine, he told the story almost in a cavalier fashion, showing none of the fear and emotion he had displayed in front of Martha in his flat. She was glad of that. It made his story seem far more rational and believable in front of Will who was looking at it through a scientist's eyes.

"Truth be told," said Gabriel, "I haven't the faintest notion what to do next. I mean, I speak to spirit – well, I normally speak to spirit, but I need my guide and for some reason he's up and left. I don't know if he's ever coming back either and that scares me more than this guy coming in at night does, I think. If I don't have Laurence, it makes me a *bus tour guide* and I can tell you, Mummy doesn't like that one little bit! Not at all!"

Martha snorted. "Gabriel, you're such a snob!" she interjected. "There's nothing wrong –"

She was cut short by Will who had remained silent through the whole thing. "There's one thing to do for starters," he said, serious and sober suddenly. "We need to conduct an investigation – equipment, recordings, an overnight stay – all the usual stuff – it's obviously the only way that we can try to get to the bottom of this."

"Fair enough," said Gabriel. "I was hoping you'd say that – I'm all for it. There's also the pressing issue of Dubhglas – did Martha tell you that I've been summonsed back to one of my childhood haunts? Except it sounds like it's not me who's doing any of the haunting these days."

Will shook his head. "No, she didn't . . . that is to say, I didn't . . ." He glanced across at Martha, a sheepish expression on his face.

She smiled and nodded her head, as much as to say all was forgiven.

Will cleared his throat. "Tell me again," he said to Gabriel and watched with interest as the medium slipped his hand into the top pocket of his shirt and withdrew the envelope that he had shown

Martha in his apartment. He handed it to Will who unfolded it and read with interest, raising his eyebrows as he got to the end. "That's a bit odd, isn't it?" he said as he placed the paper flat on the table.

Gabriel nodded. "I've told you about Gifford before. He's not a man given to hysterics. I just thought that this might be of interest to you. Plus, it adds another layer to things, I think." He took a swig from his glass. "I'm even more confused now because this might be connected with Laurence's disappearance. You both know that Dubhglas Castle is where Laurence died."

Martha and Will exchanged a look. This wasn't a subject with which Gabriel was comfortable.

"I can't help but wonder if whatever's going on there – enough to get Gifford, a man stonier than something you'd find on Easter Island, to write to me looking for help – is connected with Laurence's spirit going missing? I feel that I need to go there for some reason, but I don't know what that reason is. I need help. My schoolboy logic dictates that if I can somehow sort out what's happened with Laurence – see if he'll come back to me, or if I can find him somehow – then perhaps I can communicate with this man who's been following me." He fell silent for a moment and looked from Will to Martha and back again. "Whaddya think?" Then he added in a giddy, childish voice, "*Will you come to the party, Will?*"

Will and Martha didn't smile.

Will sat forward, reaching into his jeans pocket to pull out a small notebook with a tiny pencil stuck in the spiral binding. "First thing's first, we need to sort out investigating your flat, try to see if we can find out anything about your stalker. And then you need to tell me everything that you can about Dubhglas. And about how Laurence died."

It was after one when Martha slipped away from the table and headed for bed, leaving Will and Gabriel in deep discussion about the proposed investigation. Truth be told, she had tuned out of much of the conversation, focusing unavoidably on her own thoughts, thinking about Dan's face opposite her in the hotel and how she was going to deal him. She just had to talk to Will, she reasoned, but tonight hadn't been the night.

She fell asleep feeling hopeful for the first time in months, lulled by the hum of voices from the kitchen below and the wine and good food. It'll be all right, she thought to herself. Everything was going to be fine.

CHAPTER 16

1963

There was no denying that having young Laurence McKenzie around Dubhglas Castle changed the place for the better. There was something in him – some infectious joy, some lightness of heart – that made it brighter. He had arrived with his parents on a Friday night, devoured three helpings of roast pork and apple crumble, and had barely batted an eyelid when his parents left again the following morning. Claire had seen them climb into their car – the father, the Captain, folding his bulk into the driver's seat without a second glance – the mother, a tall woman with blonde hair in a neat perm, staring back at the facade of the castle sadly, longing to see her son peer back at her through one of the many windows . . . but he was already gone, tearing down to the kitchens to find Martin Pine and take him in search of a fishing rod.

Mrs Turnbull was right too. Having Laurence around turned Martin into a child himself. He'd arrive into the kitchen, breathless and scratched from pushing his way through thorny bushes near the lake or with the knees of his trousers torn from climbing rocks. He and Laurence would beg lemonade from Claire and then pelt off again in search of another tree to climb. There was always noise when Laurence was around. A favourite loud game involved whooping around the kitchen table wearing headdresses fashioned from Mr Turnbull's ties and chicken feathers, until Mrs Turnbull would usher them outside, her patience sorely tried.

And then there was the added work. The boy loved to swim and Claire seemed to be caught in an endless cycle of washing clothes that he had worn to jump into the lake, towels with which he had dried himself, or hanging out bed-sheets that he had lain on while damp. And there was a constant trail of wet footprints leading across the halls and the kitchen floor where he would enter, having run dripping all the way up from the lake for something or other. "I'll build you a swimming pool!" she had heard Mr Calvert laughingly promise him and more than once sincerely wished that he'd get on with it. It was bad enough dealing with the workmen's mess, but dealing repeatedly with the damp signs of Laurence's presence tended to get on her nerves a little.

When Mr Ball was around, there was always noise too, but nothing like the happy noise that accompanied Laurence as he skipped through each day with his childish innocence. With Mr Ball there was shouting – shouting at Martin, shouting at Mr Turnbull, shouting at the maids – even shouting at Mr Calvert, although the staff tried to turn a deaf ear to anything that they heard upstairs. Everywhere, there was Mr Ball's huge braying voice, with an accent even more difficult for Claire to understand than Martin's. When she heard that voice she was never so thankful that her place was in the kitchen because, as terrifying as he was to hear, he was twice as terrifying to the eye.

Claire didn't think she had ever seen a man so wide. There was something about the way that Mr Ball – 'Uncle Jack' he insisted on being called by everyone, staff included – carried his great bulk, that made him seem to fill spaces with his very being. He owned the castle, she knew. And Mr Calvert, then, was the child of Uncle Jack's widowed sister. "That's all you need to know," Mrs Turnbull had told Claire firmly. "Except that if Mr Ball says 'jump' you say 'how high?', do you understand? Or there are consequences . . ."

The housekeeper hadn't elaborated on what those consequences might be but Claire didn't care to risk finding out. His appearance alone terrified her. On the few occasions that she had actually seen him she had tried to cower in corners to avoid him, his great broad shoulders, thick neck and forearms and long legs taking up room everywhere he turned. He walked with his hands casually slung into his pockets, his neck buttons left open. It was his attempt at looking relaxed, Claire understood. Except he looked anything but. He looked like trouble to her.

And, of course, there was the scar. The red and purple disfigurement that ran up the left side of his face from his mouth almost to his ear. "'Is Glasgow 'alf-smile," Martin had called it, himself smiling ruefully as he did. Claire had no idea what he meant. Nor did she understand what Martin meant when he observed that "the fella wot did it never got the chance to even it off on account of how Uncle Jack 'ad 'im in a 'alf-Nelson quick as you can say Jack Robinson and snapped 'is neck for 'im." Martin seemed to know a lot about Uncle Jack. And Claire wasn't sure that she liked that side of him. But he rarely spoke or passed comment. Just made himself available to do Uncle Jack's bidding at any time, as they were instructed.

Claire understood from Mrs Turnbull that Uncle Jack was in some way responsible for Martin being at Dubhglas, and she was perceptive enough to understand that Martin seemed to owe him something. But other than that, there was nothing else to be learned about the great, hulking presence of the man who had come up from London, quite simply because no one would talk about him.

When Uncle Jack was around there was also, quite often, the sounds of things being broken – cups and glasses thrown around. Furniture being shifted in the library – Mr Ball's throne room, as Mrs Turnbull called it. And the relentless jingle of the bell around that cat's neck, the vicious feline that everyone tried to avoid – but it always seemed difficult to steer clear of Tiger. Before long Claire noted that Mrs Turnbull had tended wordlessly to almost everyone on the staff, including Martin, who needed help for bites and scratches administered by the sleek grey beast. The only time, she knew, that they were safe from attack, was when Uncle Jack indulged in his unusual habit of taking Tiger out for a 'constitutional' at any time of the day or night on a red leash which he wound proudly around his thick fist before parading the beast like a show-cat around the grounds.

As the summer stretched on, Claire gathered from snatches of overheard conversations that the staff found it unusual that he should stay at the castle so long. Hidden in the drills of the kitchen garden while she gathered potatoes for dinner, she overheard two of the maids discussing him. "He's disgusting," she'd heard Dots whisper vehemently. "I have to pick his clothes up off the ground – he just leaves them lying there, scattered all round the room. And more often as not he's broken something else up there. Yesterday it was his ashtray of all things and I had to clean up all his filthy cigar butts and scrub the carpet where it made a stain. And then I nearly knocked his blessed camera over. He'd kill me stone dead if I damaged that. Or the cat."

"Sssssh!" hissed Esther. "If he hears you, you're done for! What I want to know is why he is here so long this time."

Claire saw her glance back toward the house, terrified lest they be heard.

"He only ever comes for a week in the summer and then takes that filthy beast back with him to the pit where he came from."

With her lips sealed and her eyes and ears wide – her lifelong pattern – Claire gleaned that according to the staff, Uncle Jack had far outstayed his welcome.

His presence stirred an unease in the castle that she hadn't noticed before he'd arrived. A feeling of anxiety, a shade of darkness that Claire hadn't felt before. A darkness that she recognised from her past life, that she could never quite shake off, no matter how hard she tried.

CHAPTER 17

November 20th

"Missed a bit," remarked Gabriel, pointing a finger at something Martha couldn't quite see on his now pristine kitchen floor which she had just finished mopping.

Martha sighed and rolled her eyes as she tipped the bucket of grimy water down the sink and sluiced it out with fresh water from the cold tap.

"Not funny," she said drily – it was the fifth time Gabriel had cracked the joke since they had started the first clean-up his flat had seen in quite some time. There were certain areas which had to remain untouched, of course – the areas with evidence of spirit presence – but Gabriel's ghost visitor clearly didn't frequent the kitchen and Martha had been detailed to make it fit for purpose.

The medium giggled and wandered back toward the living room, completely idle, humming one of his favourite Smiths' tracks, occasionally bursting into a line from the song. Martha grinned as she finished cleaning the Belfast sink. It was nice to hear Gabriel back to his usual sarcastic and perky form, nice to be helping him out even if that meant doing everything for him, nice to be focusing on menial tasks to take her mind off everything that was happening.

It was an unseasonably mild day in November and where she should have been shivering with the windows open wide to air the rooms throughout the apartment, Martha was glad of the breeze to cool her down after the energetic mopping she had just given the stone tiles in the kitchen – the one room where Gabriel had steered clear away from a Georgian feel with modern shaker cupboards, a Gaggia coffee maker and a wide American-style fridge. Dan's words, "must be some money in ghost hunting", sprang to her mind as she took long steps over the wet tiles to return the bucket to the small utility cupboard off the kitchen.

The thought of Dan made the tightness in her chest return, the sick pain behind her ribs that she'd forgotten while she mopped and scrubbed. She still hadn't spoken to Will about everything that was going on – Dan's request for increased custody, the unpaid maintenance – even the fact that she'd met with him remained a secret, and Martha was becoming increasingly panicky as she realised that the longer it went on, the more deceitful it looked. And the angrier Will would most likely get about the whole thing. Not to mention the fact that she could only assume Dan was still hanging about Edinburgh, waiting for a response. He'd given her no indication of when he might be leaving – surely he'd have to go back to work at some point, she thought, and then realised that she was merely thinking that in the hope he'd go back to work and forget about the whole thing. Which just wasn't going to happen.

Then there was the investigation tonight, adding to the general niggling stress. Gabriel had begged her to come and she'd reluctantly agreed. She didn't want to rock the boat – she hadn't seen Will as excited about an investigation in months. This time, he seemed to have lost the panicky air that he sometimes had about him in recent months, giving a sense that it was imperative that he gain some conclusive evidence on each occasion, and if he didn't then something terrible was going to happen.

"*La la la la la laaaaaa!*" crooned Gabriel, re-entering the kitchen and coming close to Martha's face and waving his arms about in what he thought was an accurate impersonation of Morrissey. Martha couldn't help but giggle as he stepped away, humming tunelessly and doing his shimmying dance all around the wet floor.

"I've just cleaned there!" she pointed out, as he left a large footprint on a tile.

Gabriel didn't miss a beat and simply continued to dance,

changing the words of the tune to "*You missed a bit, you missed a bit, you missed a biiiiit!*"

Martha chuckled and turned to flick the kettle switch. "You're very perky all of a sudden," she observed.

Gabriel broke into laughter and drew the dance to a halt, leaning into a cupboard above her head for two Cath Kidston mugs and a tin of teabags. "Nothing wrong with a bit of perk every now and again," he replied.

"Even with tonight coming up?" asked Martha, leaning back against the worktop.

Gabriel opened a drawer for a teaspoon and bumped it shut with his hip. He shrugged his shoulders. "The sun is shining, my dear, and tonight maybe a piece of the puzzle will fall into place. I'm just pleased that I'm finally doing something to find out what's going on with the visitor and in a few hours' time I might have regained some of my sanity."

Martha found herself shuddering at Gabriel's use of the word 'visitor' and felt again the creeping dread of what was to come.

As if he read her mind, Gabriel, turned slightly toward her, keeping an eye on his task as he shovelled two large sugars into the floral-patterned mug. "Thanks for agreeing to come along by the way," he said.

Martha's eyes widened in mock surprise. "A *thank*-you from Gabriel McKenzie? Do I detect . . . *sincerity* in your tone?"

"Just don't tell anyone," he warned. "I've been showing way too much emotion lately. You're holding me in a vulnerable position. And no running to the tabloids either doing sympathy-and-tell stories – 'TV Psychic is Actually Human' and the like."

The kettle started to whistle and Gabriel reached into the fridge for a small jug of milk.

"Depends on the fee they offer me," shrugged Martha and smiled. "I could really do with the cash."

Gabriel turned to look at her and frowned. "Now hang on a minute here – you've just released a small puff of sincerity yourself, haven't you?"

He continued to study her face and Martha didn't know where to look.

"Are you having money troubles?" he asked.

Martha blushed and looked at her feet.

"You bloody are," said Gabriel, continuing to stare, having stopped all tea-making activities.

Martha shuffled slightly and then turned her back, opening and closing cupboard doors and peering inside. "Have you any biscuits?" she asked, in an attempt to change the subject.

"Of course," replied Gabriel, not moving. "There's a packet of turn-round-and-tell-me creams right over here!"

Martha stopped her over-earnest search and turned to face Gabriel. "Fine," she sighed. "It's not money troubles as such – I mean, people out there have real money troubles – people who can't feed their families, or are out of work long term and on benefits and –"

"Yeah, yeah, I get it, the peasants," replied Gabriel impatiently.

"*Gabriel!*" said Martha, shocked. "That's appalling – you can't speak about people like that."

"We're not talking about 'people', my little pauper," he replied, turning back to pour water into the two mugs as the kettle clicked off. "We're talking about *you*."

Martha rolled her eyes to heaven. "I'm far from a pauper," she said. "I just have some . . . some *concerns*, that's all."

"I thought you two were bloody loaded individually, never mind with your vast wealth combined?" said Gabriel. "And what about Desperate Dan? Doesn't he pay his way for Ruby?"

Martha sighed again. "Not at the moment, no," she said, feeling again the niggling ache in the pit of her stomach at the mention of her ex-husband's name. She suddenly couldn't hold it in any longer. In for a penny, she thought, as she blurted it out. "That's another thing I'm concerned about. He's here. In Edinburgh. I've met him."

Gabriel's eyes grew wide and he slopped some of the tea he was handing to Martha on the floor. "What?" he spluttered. "He's *here?* Old Brideshead himself? Is he still all blonde and dishy like you told me? Like your wedding snaps? All Ice Queen?"

Martha frowned in annoyance. "Gabriel, the floor!" she exclaimed, momentarily distracted.

"Screw the floor!" shouted Gabriel in response. "What on earth is Mr Hot-But-Sneaky doing in town?"

Martha managed to prise the cup of tea from Gabriel's grip and took a sip. "That's the stupidest name you've ever made up, Gabriel," she observed flatly, avoiding answering the question, reluctant now to continue the conversation and regretting starting it, regretting also having ever told Gabriel about her disastrous marriage over Bellinis once.

Gabriel was having none of it, however. "*Martha!*" he shouted, annoyed.

"Okay, okay," she said, and placed the cup on the worktop behind her before turning back and telling Gabriel everything – about the phone calls, the delivery of the thistles, the encounter in the alley and finally their meeting at the hotel where he had announced he wanted access to Ruby. Gabriel listened in amazement, taking occasional sips of tea.

"I haven't managed to talk to Will about it yet," finished Martha. "And while I'm at it he's another one of my concerns. Have you noticed he's a bit . . . well . . ."

"Bloody livid all the time?" finished Gabriel.

Martha couldn't help but laugh joylessly. "Oh dear," she said. "You've noticed. And the irony is that he's actually been in brilliant form – comparatively speaking – since you and he started talking again and he got all excited about tonight."

Gabriel blew air out between his lips. "*Pfff!* Comparative to what? A charging rhino with haemorrhoids? A peeved honey badger?"

"A what?" asked Martha. Why could Gabriel never take anything seriously?

"Oh, saw it on *QI*," said Gabriel. "Little thing. Bites your nuts off apparently." He suddenly re-focused. "But very angry. Like Will."

"Well, I can barely hold a conversation about what to have for dinner without him flying off the handle and stomping off these days," she observed. "How the hell am I going to tell him my ex is back in town, looking for access to Ruby? You know how he feels about her."

"I don't envy you," Gabriel replied matter of factly. "In fact, Will's humour is the reason why I've asked you along tonight – to be a sort of buffer in case he gets cross with me again. I don't think he's fully forgiven me for my terrible betrayal."

"Oh thanks very much," said Martha, sarcastically. "I've a feeling when I finally get around to telling him about Dan then I'll be the one needing a buffer. What time is it, by the way?"

Gabriel glanced at his watch. "Oh shit, time you were heading off. Angeline's expecting you at five and it's half past four now – by the time you get the car and if there's traffic –"

"I know, I know," said Martha. "I'll head off now to get her. You won't mention any of what I've said to Will, will you?" she asked, pleadingly. "Only I need to find the right time and get him in the right mood."

"Bloody right you do, lady," retorted Gabriel. "And the sooner the better. The fact that you've kept your powder dry for so long makes it seem like you're up to something. Now I know you're not, and you know you're not, but Will doesn't and – as you so rightly pointed out – we all know how he feels about Ruby. And Desperate Dan for that matter."

"I know you're right," Martha nodded.

"'*There may be trouble ahead!*'" Gabriel sang, wagging a finger at Martha, only half in jest.

She nodded and put her mug into the sink. "Okay," she said, determinedly. "Let me just close the windows and then I'll go get Angeline and we'll get tonight over with and then I'll do it. He'll know really soon, and that's final."

Gabriel nodded. "Sounds like a plan," he said. "Now, I'm going to run down to the shop and get an actual packet of biscuits for tonight. Can't contact the dead without Jaffa Cakes. Are you okay to let yourself out of here?"

Martha shuddered. In the last few moments she had managed to push the thought of contacting the dead out of her mind – replacing her concern about the investigation with her concern about her life in general. She nodded. "Go ahead," she said. "I'll be fine."

Gabriel was already halfway out the kitchen door and she heard the jingle of his keys and the slam of the heavy front door of the flat a moment later, leaving the apartment in silence. Martha sighed and leaned over the worktop to close the kitchen window. The sun was still shining but the afternoon had begun to turn cold.

She worked her way through the apartment, closing all the windows as she went, silence gradually filling the space as she shut out the noises from the street below. The living room was her last port of call. Martha wandered gingerly into the room. Something about it always made her feel uncomfortable, and her eyes were immediately drawn, as they always were, to the corner of the ceiling just to the left of the chimney breast. She couldn't understand why her attention was always focused there, but something about it made her uneasy, made her afraid almost *not* to look at it, just in case if she looked away something might suddenly be there when she looked back.

Martha closed her eyes and took a deep breath, telling herself not to be so stupid. She squared her shoulders and entered the room boldly, taking big strides to the first window and closing the sash window behind it. She then headed for the other window and found herself glancing nervously at everything on the desk as she passed it. There was an open notebook, but thankfully no sign of the message in ghostly handwriting that Gabriel had shown her before. She was comforted that it wasn't there – she'd thought about it more than once since leaving the flat the last time. The inhuman hand urging the reader to '*do it*', over and over again. She shuddered, and turned to plump a couple of the cushions on the couch as if to physically shake the thought from her mind. Again her eye was drawn to the ceiling to the left of the fireplace and she had to drag her gaze away, skimming the photograph of Laurence with his brick and his medal on the mantel on the way down.

All of a sudden the room felt very cold and Martha turned and scurried over to the second window, surprised to see that the blind was down. As she took the final step toward the window, she gasped in shock as a sudden gust of wind blew through the window and back again, sucking the blind against the window frame and causing it to rattle loudly. Martha screamed in fright and ran from the room and down the hallway, leaving the window wide open. She grabbed her handbag from the hall table and opened the catch on the door with trembling hands. It couldn't have been, she reasoned to herself. It was just your imagination – you're just nervous about tonight, she scolded herself as she ran down the stairway that wound down through the Georgian building.

She knew that the noise and sudden rush of wind had been enough to give her a substantial fright, but what had really scared her, had made her blood run cold and her whole body start with shock was what she had seen *in the blind*. What had made Martha run from the flat was the fact that when the blind was sucked back out by the window she was sure that, for a split second, as if watermarked into the blind's fabric itself, she had seen a face. A face with an open mouth, looking like a person trying to speak or shout or scream through the material of the blind. Martha reached the front door of the building and slammed it behind her, not pausing for a second as she rushed down George Street to get to her car, to get away. She felt sure, as she did so, that somehow she had just seen the face of Gabriel's intruder. The face of the visitor itself.

CHAPTER 18

As she drove toward Leith, Martha tried to imagine what the person she was being sent to pick up was actually like. It was helping her to focus her attention away from what she had just seen. What you *thought* you saw, she reasoned with herself, her heart still pounding slightly even as she drove further and further away from the flat to collect Gabriel's guest for the evening. Another medium. Brought in to communicate with Gabriel's ghost as he could not.

Gabriel said that he knew Angeline Broadhead from one of the spiritualist churches he attended occasionally. As she drove, Martha composed a mental picture of the medium as tall and witchlike – long hair, unkempt, possibly dyed red or purple, floaty clothes, lots of bangles and rings. It made Martha even more apprehensive about the night ahead – if this medium was into things like candles and invocations it would just add a whole unnecessary element to the evening and make it even more frightening – for Martha, that is. The others would probably love it, she reckoned.

Will had been sceptical about using another sensitive at first but on Gabriel's insistence he consented to have Angeline there, if only to perhaps spark something in Gabriel himself. Will was determined to remain sceptical of anything that Angeline might say and trust instead in his equipment. Martha glanced at the time on her car clock. Will should be arriving at Gabriel's flat around about now to set up for the evening – to wire the apartment with cameras and recording equipment, check normal levels of heat and sound so that he could detect any anomalies later. He was also conducting initial investigations to check levels of infrasound and electromagnetic frequencies. If they were found to be high, he'd explained once, it wouldn't be the first time that someone's scary experiences could be put down to being caused by the electrics. As Martha drove, she reasoned that it was actually most likely to be old wiring in the flat that made her feel spooked all the time, and her so-called vision at the window was just a by-product of a nervous imagination and stress. She started to feel slightly better as she turned into Elm Place, the pretty cul de sac where Angeline lived.

They drove in silence on the return trip, Angeline staring fixedly out of the front window. She reminded Martha of some kind of tenacious terrier, her attention fixed on a single point. She looked nothing like she had imagined her. She wore a headscarf for starters, and a tweed skirt and flat shoes, topped off with a green anorak. At first sight, in fact, Martha was struck by how much like the Queen she looked. Off for a spot of shooting at Balmoral, maybe. Followed by tea and shortcake. And some chatting with the dead.

Giving her the odd sideways glance, Martha made her way back through the rush-hour traffic into the city centre. She parked as close to Gabriel's flat as she could and killed the engine.

"Well," she said nervously, not knowing quite how to break the silence, "this is us, here at last."

She was rewarded with a warm, if slightly distracted, smile and a quiet "Thank you, dear" but that was as far as the communication went.

Gabriel let them in with a flourish of his arm and a hearty hello. Martha followed Angeline, who just padded silently straight past Gabriel and down the corridor, peering left and right into the rooms along the way as she went. Martha fell back and let her get ahead before turning to Gabriel.

"Where did you find *her*?" she hissed.

Gabriel glanced down the hall after Angeline and put a finger to his lips. "She's dynamite, isn't she?" he said admiringly. "A wee pocket-rocket – small medium at large!" Delighted with his own joke he followed Angeline down the hallway, leaving Martha to follow, bemused and slightly nervous.

As she entered the living room she brushed her face and made a *'pfff'* sound as she walked straight into a cobweb. She plucked frantically at her scrunched-up eyes and nose in an attempt to remove something that she couldn't see. Or feel with her fingertips for that matter.

On opening her eyes again, she was puzzled to see that Angeline had turned to stare at her intently. "Interesting," she said quietly. "Seems our visitor has been here already."

Puzzled, Martha finished flapping at her face, satisfied that the cobweb was gone, and opened her eyes. The room was mostly dark now, lit dimly with candles and a glow from the streetlights outside through the closed blinds. She looked away quickly, reminded of what she had seen, terrified in case she saw it again.

For a brief moment she wondered should she tell the others about her experience. She couldn't deny that it was something. A year ago, she might have convinced herself that it was nothing – just her imagination or that fabled trick of the light that everyone was so fond of referencing at times like this. But she knew that she couldn't do that. At the same time, however, she couldn't shake the habit of a lifetime – the feeling that if she didn't verbalise it, then it might never have happened. She remained silent.

The candle glow made the living room almost inviting – if it hadn't been for the upturned glass on the coffee table and the faint glow of the infrared cameras dotted around the room. A séance, Martha realised. They were all going to have to join hands and wait for who-knew-what to happen in the room around them. She felt terrified all of a sudden. Even the presence of Will standing beside the fireplace didn't calm her. He was more like an executioner awaiting the arrival of a prisoner than her boyfriend. He stood to the left of the fireplace, hands clasped behind his back, dressed in a pair of black jeans and a black turtleneck sweater, blending into the shadows. Martha's eyes flicked upwards, involuntarily, to the ceiling above him, drawn to the same spot as always. She looked back at the coffee table to find Angeline watching her intently.

The medium nodded. "That's right, dear," she said softly, looking at the spot herself, and then turned her attention to sitting down on one of Gabriel's expensive cream sofas, arranging her skirt under her in such a way that it didn't crease.

Martha stared at her, puzzled. What did she mean by that? Martha looked at Gabriel, who was gazing at her in a strange way. She looked down at her shoe suddenly, pretending to notice a spot of dirt to avoid his stare. She didn't want to have that conversation. He frowned and bent to Angeline to check if she were all right. Will was completely emotionless, staring at the group and holding aloft a piece of equipment that Martha recognised as a thermal imaging camera. He operated as if none of the other three were there and Martha realised that he was in work mode and wouldn't be joining in, just watching the proceedings with a detached eye. She also knew exactly what he could see on that camera. The outlines of three figures – herself, Gabriel and Angeline. They would be red and purple against the black of the room around. At least she hoped it was only three figures. She feared the moment that they might be joined by a fourth. Another heat signature visible only on the small hand-held screen and not to any of the living in the room.

Martha felt very alone as she took her place on the couch opposite to where Angeline was sitting, eyes closed, deep in thought, Gabriel by her side.

A hush of anticipation settled across the room and they sat in complete silence. Martha felt helpless as she looked across at the two mediums, hands folded on their laps as if in prayer, eyes tightly shut. Martha glanced at Will who was staring intently at the proceedings. She felt the silence begin to grow unbearable, longed to shout out to break it, to run from the room and home.

A long sigh echoed through the room. Martha realised that it was Angeline and felt her entire body go tense as a tiny, softly accented voice filled the room.

"Young man," Angeline began, eyes still closed, addressing someone who wasn't there – in body anyway, "I call upon you to make yourself known to me, to reveal yourself to us. We know you're here – you've already made a start – but I need you to speak to me and tell me exactly what you're doing."

A silence fell again, the same thick soundlessness that had begun the session. Martha was afraid to move and realised that she was holding her breath, for fear of making a noise.

"You have nothing to be frightened of," said Angeline. "We are here in respect – not to mock you or to hurt you. We simply want to communicate with you. I know you've been trying to talk to us so now's your chance. I'm listening."

Again, the silence, except for one of the candles on the mantelpiece guttering slightly. Martha shifted uncomfortably on the couch.

Suddenly, Angeline opened her eyes.

"My dear, can you open the door for us?" she said.

Martha thought it an odd thing to say, then noticed that Angeline was staring at her. "You mean me?" she said, pointing at herself nervously, hoping that Angeline would just continue talking to someone who wasn't there.

"Yes, please," said Angeline, nodding.

Martha's heart sank. Angeline continued to watch her expectantly, however, and something in her stare made Martha realise that she wouldn't take no for an answer. Reluctantly, she rose from the couch and padded over to the doorway, glancing at Will as she went for some sort of support but he was completely absorbed in checking that his digital video recorder was aimed at the door she was about to open. Martha's trainers squeaked softly as she crossed the room.

The door was forbidding in the candlelight – the handle cold to her touch as she gently placed her fingers around it. Martha froze before turning it, terrified that there might be something on the other side – something terrible like she had seen before. Something decaying and rotting and evil. She turned her head back to the couch and saw that Angeline had taken Gabriel's hand and was holding it tightly on her lap, her eyes once again closed, but an expression of anticipation across her face. Again, Martha felt completely alone. Against every last piece of will in her being, she turned the handle slowly, hearing it squeak slightly, and pulled the door toward her. It jammed for a moment on the saddle-board and she gently tugged to release it. It juddered, vibrating in her hand. She felt as though she was wired to the electricity mains – her whole body tense and expectant, finally understanding what people meant when they said their hair stood on end with fear. With a gentle creak the door swung toward her and she dared herself to lift her eyes and glance as she stepped backwards. It was almost a disappointment for her to see that there was nothing there. Nothing strange happened at all in fact – the candles on the mantel, the desk and the coffee table flickered with the breeze from the open door and the room was filled suddenly with cool air and, oddly, the smell of fresh Christmas trees – like opening the door to a living room on Christmas morning. Martha breathed it in. It was beautiful actually.

Relieved to find that the hallway before her was empty, she glanced back toward the couch and saw that Angeline and Gabriel were doing the same – taking deep breaths and savouring the festive smell. Must be one of Gabriel's neighbours, thought Martha, bringing home their tree early. Maybe Gabriel's building put one in the hall for the residents? It was quite posh after all . . .

She let go of the door handle, extended her fingers, realising just how tightly she had gripped the handle. She returned to her seat on the sofa. As she moved, so did Will, carrying an EMF meter and his camera and looking at both with interest. He passed her without acknowledgement, and she glanced after him as he walked to the doorway, lights flashing on the small piece of equipment.

The silence returned to the room again, as the candles grew still.

"Welcome," said Angeline slowly, and sat forward on the couch, bringing Gabriel with her by tugging his hand. She stretched her left hand across the table toward Martha and Gabriel opened one eye, saw what she was doing, and did the same with his right.

Martha realised that the hand-holding time had come and squirmed uncomfortably forward on her seat. This is supposedly where they combined their energies to make the spirit stronger, she thought. *Please don't let there be a spirit*, she thought, even though she knew there was. She could feel it. She gripped Gabriel's warm hand with her left hand and loosely took Angeline's cold one with her right.

"Now if we can all concentrate and focus," said Angeline softly, "we can help this poor man to tell us what's troubling him."

Martha shivered involuntarily. "Shouldn't we do some sort of . . . I dunno . . . protection spell or something?" she said timidly, her voice trailing off as Angeline's eyes shot open and the tiny woman fixed her with an angry stare.

"I am not a circus conjurer," she snapped abruptly, rolling the 'r's' as she spoke. "We are here to *help* someone who has passed on. The dead cannot hurt you, Martha, only the living."

Angeline closed her eyes again. Martha felt confused. The last time she had done this – with Gabriel – he had given her some protection and she knew from experience that the dead *could* do harm. Martha glanced at Gabriel for support but his eyes remained closed.

Suddenly, Angeline's head tilted to one side. Martha felt her energy drain from her and she grew hot as she realised that something was about to happen.

The air suddenly felt alive with electricity. Will swung the EMF monitor in the direction of the trio at the centre of the room and the candles guttered again. Martha heard a click that she recognised as a small recorder being switched on and she felt Will move behind her to lean over the coffee table and place it there.

There was no way of explaining it but it really felt as if there was another person in the room.

"*Mhmmm,*" nodded Angeline suddenly, looking as if she were in conversation with someone sitting beside her. "Can you tell me a little more about what you want us to know? I need some more."

Martha felt Gabriel's hand grip hers tighter as he too opened his eyes and looked at the tiny woman having her one-sided conversation. Martha tried to ignore a feeling of panic that rose in her. She was used to Gabriel being the strong one, knew that he should protect her – manage the situation like he had done before. Now it seemed, as she saw him grow alarmed, he was as vulnerable as she was. And that didn't give Martha any confidence at all.

She inhaled deeply as Angeline nodded again, took a deep breath and turned her attention to the table. "I have a man here who is a little anxious. He says his message is only for you, Gabriel, and he's been trying to reach you for a long, long time. He needs you to then pass the message on to others."

Gabriel gave a slight nervous cough. "Is this the man who has been following me around," he said, his voice cracking slightly as he said the words.

Angeline leaned over again and cocked her ear to her unseen conversation partner. She nodded. "He's been trying to get your attention, Gabriel," she confirmed.

Gabriel snorted. "Well, he's bloody well done that!" He glared at the unseen visitor. "Who are you?" he demanded suddenly, making Martha flinch at the volume of his voice in the quiet. "Why aren't you talking to me directly? What's with all the sneaking around?"

Angeline squeezed his hand. "Now you should calm down too, Gabriel. Our friend here says that he's new to all this and he's been doing his best because it's very important. He's been trying to get hold of you for a very long time – even from before he passed."

Gabriel sighed. Martha could see that he was frustrated. He was clearly not getting the information he wanted from whoever – whatever – was conversing with Angeline. Martha supposed that for someone like Gabriel, being unable to conduct his own communication must be like losing a vital sense – hearing, perhaps, or even taste. Suddenly, she found herself feeling sorry for him. Before she had always felt that it must be such a curse to talk to the dead.

"Does he know where Laurence is?" asked Gabriel softly.

Silence fell again, as Angeline turned her ear to listen for a few moments. Finally she shook her head. "He says that he only knew him when they were both living."

A look of confused dismay crossed Gabriel's face.

Angeline cleared her throat suddenly. "I have a name, Gabriel," she offered, concentrating deeply. "He says that you might know him. And that he didn't do it."

CHAPTER 19

Back at Calderwood, Gabriel practically snatched the whisky that Martha had poured for him from her hand, knocked it back in one go and handed the glass back immediately for a refill. Martha's eyes widened and she unscrewed the bottle.

"Thanks for letting me stay," said Gabriel, taking a more sedate sip from the second glass and rolling it around his mouth to savour the taste. He closed his eyes, more in relief than in pleasure. "Oh that's fine," replied Martha, finally tasting her own drink and grimacing slightly at the strength. She normally never touched spirits – of any sort, she thought to herself – but tonight was an exception on all fronts. She wasn't as shaken by the events in Gabriel's apartment as she thought she might be, but she was slightly spooked. She was glad that the baby-sitter had kept a fire burning in the living room and she had turned on all the lights in the house. It was already serving to make her – and, oddly, Gabriel it seemed – feel better.

Gabriel swirled the whisky in the crystal glass. "Ridiculous as it sounds, I'm really not sure I could have stayed in my flat by myself tonight after all that," he said and stared into the fire, almost regretfully.

Martha curled a leg underneath her as she sat down on the couch beside him. "I hope you'll be okay in the front room upstairs – it's full of Will's crap, but then again, so are all the others. I've

125

made the futon up for you. You know it ain't the Ritz . . ." Martha shrugged. She knew she was babbling but wasn't sure what else to say.

Gabriel had been visibly disturbed by Angeline's revelation, by being made aware of the identity of his ghostly stalker. The name had been vaguely familiar to Martha but she wasn't sure where she had heard it before. She wondered why Gabriel was so upset by it, but didn't want to ask for fear of upsetting him more. She had never seen him so unnerved.

"Will should be back shortly," she said, glancing at the clock on the mantelpiece, more to break the silence in the room with chit-chat than anything.

Will had opted to drive Angeline home, presumably to quiz her on the night's events, and Martha had been delighted to let him. She didn't want to spend a second longer with the strange woman than she had to.

Martha shuddered and took another sip from her glass, trying desperately to think of something to say to break the silence.

Gabriel sighed suddenly and Martha glanced at him.

"That was all . . . pretty . . . intense?" she volunteered.

Gabriel nodded his head in agreement. "It surely was," he said, exhaling deeply again. "I was *not* expecting that outcome, I can tell you." He shook his head, as if in disbelief.

"I mean, to find out you were right," said Martha. "About being haunted, that is . . ."

"Least of my worries now," observed Gabriel. "It's *who's* doing the haunting that's blown my mind." He directed his thoughts inward, and fell silent for a while. Then he suddenly turned to Martha. "And as for you, dark horse . . ." he said, taking a swig from his glass.

Martha looked at him, mystified. "What on earth do you mean?" she said, eyes wide.

"Well, you never told me before that you had any sort of a sixth sense for these things," said Gabriel, indignant.

"What sort of sixth sense?" asked Martha, genuinely bemused.

"Well, *my* sort of sixth sense!" barked Gabriel "I mean, what did you see in the corner when you looked up? You looked like you definitely saw something there! Have you been holding out on me?"

Martha herself was growing annoyed. "I just felt a bit funny, that's all. I didn't see *anything*." She wished he'd change the subject. She knew that what she had felt in that room was more than just discomfort but that wasn't a conversation she wanted to have with him now. To do so would mean acknowledging something that she didn't want to talk about, didn't want to face.

Gabriel rolled his eyes and persisted. "But you must have! Angeline whispered to me before we started that that's where his spirit is drawn."

"That's where whose spirit . . ." Her voice trailed off as she finally acknowledged what Gabriel was saying to her. "You mean your ghost."

Gabriel nodded at her, eyes wide as if she had just figured out something so basic that it was inconceivable that she wouldn't have known all along. They stared at each other like this for a while until Martha looked away and reached down for her glass. She couldn't hide from him the fact that she felt uncomfortably drawn to the spot every time she entered the room.

And then there had been the face in the blind . . . She shrugged away what Gabriel was trying to say to her.

"Hope Will's okay on the road," she said to change the subject.

The night had turned icy after the unseasonable warmth of the day. She had been surprised to find frost forming on the windscreen of her car and the sky bright with distant twinkling stars when they had finally emerged from the apartment, although the bracing fresh air had been such a relief. Angeline's identification of the so-called visitor had brought proceedings to an abrupt end. The room had suddenly gone flat and Angeline had shook her head, saying that the man was gone – didn't seem to have any energy left, much to Gabriel's disappointment.

Gabriel gave Martha a lingering look but didn't pursue their conversation any further. He swigged back the last of his drink and waved his glass at her to get him another refill.

Martha simply stuck out her tongue. "Get it yourself," she said haughtily and he grinned weakly before accepting defeat and levering himself from the couch to walk to the cabinet where the whisky bottle sat. Martha felt braver on seeing him smile and the mood lightened somewhat. "So," she said, "do you think that tonight helped, creepy and all as it was?"

Gabriel shook his head again but more in disbelief than denial. "Hard to say," he replied. "On one hand it solved one mystery – yes, I am being haunted – yes, someone has been trying to get in touch with me. On the other, though, it's just made things a million times worse – I've got more questions now than I have answers – great big bloody questions. I think I know now why Laurence has backed off, for example, but I've no idea how to get him back and no idea if somehow there's a connection between this ghost following me and my being asked to go to Dubhglas. I'm totally stumped in fact."

Gabriel rejoined Martha on the couch as she looked at him, waiting for him to elaborate on what he had just said. Gabriel continued to look into the fire, deep in thought. They sat like that for a while until he finally noticed her looking at him.

"You don't know what I'm talking about, do you?" he said.

Martha shook her head, aware suddenly that she was missing out on some vital information that was apparently common knowledge.

Gabriel sat forward in his seat and looked at her again, a half smile playing on his face. "You're really clueless, aren't you?" he said.

Again, Martha nodded.

"You don't know who the ghost is? Who Martin Pine is?"

"No, Gabriel, I don't know who Martin Pine is," she said impatiently. "Obviously tonight's events have meant a lot more to you than to me so if you want to explain, then feel free. If not, I'm just going to go to bed. With the lights on. All of the lights on and –"

She was interrupted by the sound of the key in the front door and Will entering quickly, stamping his feet against the cold and shutting the door gently behind him. He was with them in the room in a second, removing his coat as he strode in and throwing it on an armchair. Martha watched him as he looked expectantly at Gabriel, giving neither of them a greeting.

"Gabriel, I need your permission," he said, suddenly.

Gabriel turned a lazy eye to the figure standing over the couch. Martha felt the cold of the evening coming from Will and shivered slightly.

"Well, hello to you too, Will," he said sarcastically.

Martha could see his eyes beginning to glaze a little. He had eaten nothing all day while they had cleaned and now the whisky was taking its toll. Will strode around the couch and threw himself down in the armchair near Gabriel's seat.

Will's face bore a serious expression. "Okay, sorry. But don't you see, Gabriel, this could really be important? If we find out that Angeline's got it right, maybe it could reopen the case files or something, get him acquitted – imagine the publicity it'll generate? Another innocent man banged up for years and imagine if his case was reopened because of *paranormal evidence*? Imagine!"

"What are you talking about?" asked Martha, interrupting Will's stream of words which made absolutely no sense to her.

He ignored her. "We can do this step by step, get Angeline in touch with Pine again and then see if we can prove what he tells us? Video our sessions with an independent observer . . ."

Martha's eyes flicked to Gabriel who was shaking his head.

"Easy, William," he was saying. "We don't know if Pine's telling the truth – it goes against *everything* that was accepted in a court of law. And, besides which, he's already served a sentence . . . if he's innocent, then why didn't anyone raise an objection before now?"

Will was sitting forward in his chair with excitement. "Gabriel, there are hundreds of people out there who have been victims of miscarriages of justice. Just let me look further into this?"

"Please, will someone tell me what's going on?" Martha cried. "Gabriel – you were about to explain to me who Martin Pine was?"

"You don't know who Martin Pine is?" Will said in disbelief.

"*No*," growled Martha.

Gabriel looked over his shoulder at Will and sighed. "We clearly can't finish this conversation unless Lady Mushroom in the dark over there has everything explained to her," he slurred disparagingly. "Will you tell her, Will, or will I?"

Will responded by sitting even further forward in his chair and fixing his eyes on Martha, a trace of an excited smile playing on his lips. "This could be huge," he said. "Really important on so many levels. Martin Pine was convicted of murder. But if this is true, what he told Angeline, that he was innocent . . . if this is true then Martin Pine is innocent of killing a child."

Martha's attention suddenly returned to Gabriel as the penny dropped and she remembered where she had heard the name before. "Laurence," she said to him.

Gabriel nodded and drained his glass.

Martha looked back at Will. "Martin Pine is the man who killed Gabriel's brother, isn't he?"

Will nodded and sat back in his seat.

"And went to prison for it?"

Will smiled. "The very one," he said.

"That's what I meant when I said it explains where Laurence is gone," added Gabriel. "Pine murdered him, and now he's managed to scare him off in the afterlife as well. But why? And why is it all kicking off now?"

Will remained silent for a moment before going to the knapsack he had carried in with him and taking out his notepad. "I've got a theory," he said simply, thrusting the pad at Gabriel.

Martha couldn't help but recoil in horror as she recognised it, the scrawled, so-called spirit writing still shocking to her eye.

"I picked this up on my way out, for a closer look," said Will as Gabriel hesitantly accepted the pad. "Look at it – both of you – and see if you can see what I think I can."

Gabriel stared at the message for a moment before handing it to Martha. "Just tell me what you think," he said.

Martha reluctantly accepted the notebook and forced herself to look closely at it.

"The words," urged Will. "The ones we can make out say 'do it'. But just because they're the only ones we can make out doesn't mean they're the only ones there."

Martha looked up from the pad and shook her head. She handed it back to Will gladly.

"Look . . . there are all sorts of loops and squiggles on here," said Will, tracing his fingers around some of the markings on the page. "But you've seen spirit writing before, Gabriel, haven't you?"

The medium shrugged in the affirmative, still glassy-eyed and only half-listening.

"Sometimes the shapes that spirits make on a page don't necessarily relate to what they're trying to say, however – you've told me that before – that spirits find it difficult to summon up the energy to do this properly."

"True," replied Gabriel, becoming slightly more absorbed in what Will had to say.

Will looked from Gabriel to Martha.

"So what if the message that we're seeing here isn't complete?" he asked. "What if we can't make out the whole thing because he couldn't manage it? What if it's not a repeated instruction, but actually a number of attempts to say the one thing?"

Will held the pad up so that Martha and Gabriel could both see it clearly. They stared at it, and at him, bemused. It was Will's turn to give a sigh of impatience and tap the page with his forefinger.

"What if the message isn't actually telling you to 'do it', Gabriel? These lines and squiggles here – my theory is that these aren't decorative – they're an unsuccessful attempt at writing other words." Will paused and looked at them again. "Let's open our minds for a moment to the possibility that instead of telling you to *do* something, he's telling us that *he didn't* 'do it' . . . just as Angeline said . . ."

CHAPTER 20

1963

Jack Ball closed his left eye against the trail of smoke that snaked up from his cheroot. Monarch of all I survey, he thought to himself as he took it all in. His land as far as the eye could see – all his, well, in his name anyway – the lake glistening in the distance. A surge of power ran through him as he paused for a moment, taking the cigar out of his mouth and placing it in the crystal ashtray that was balanced on the windowsill. Who cared if it toppled off and broke? He'd just get himself another one. Another ten. And get himself the factory it was made in, if he was that way inclined. He reserved his caution for the camera sitting alongside the ashtray on the sill. Now that couldn't be replaced.

He was a tank of a man, broad and tall, with a boxer's physique. A heavyweight. He sniffed deeply and bent over, placing his hammer-like fists on the windowsill and leaning on them, to fully take in the scene before him.

It was a glorious summer's day, the breeze warm, the sky cloudless. A butterfly flitted past the open window. Jack Ball didn't see it, however. Didn't see the sparkle of the sun on the water, or the freshly mown lawn that led down to it, or the gorse on the distant hills or the roses blooming yellow, coral and red in the carefully tended beds beneath him.

Jack Ball saw none of these things because he was watching something else that interested him far more. With intent he gazed at a particular corner of the scene, staring at every movement, trying to catch every word that was thrown. Because among the apple trees that grew just below his bedroom window, Martin Pine was playing Cowboys and Indians, which irritated Jack Ball mildly. He was almost a man. Why was he being so stupid as to play kids' games?

Martin Pine was of little use to him these days, however. Jack plucked the stub of the cigar out of the ashtray with one thick hand and rolled it between thumb and forefinger contemplatively before bending down to look through the viewfinder of the camera. It wasn't Martin Pine that was of any interest at all to Jack Ball, in fact, on that summer's day. It was his playmate, his companion, that captured his attention. The Indian in the game, 'wah-wahing' with one hand over his mouth and the other holding an axe, a chicken feather tied around his forehead with a scarf, face daubed with what looked like lipstick.

Jack Ball took a deep drag of his cigar. He knew he could just go on down there for a photograph, ask him to smile for the dickie-bird and all that palaver. But that defeated the purpose. Took all the fun out of it, out of capturing the moment. "I can see you, but you can't see me," he whispered as he clicked twice, then straightened and stared. Stared at Laurence McKenzie dodging deftly between the trees, lost in the game, laughing aloud with joy as he played. Time for a stroll in the sunshine, he thought.

The bell that Tiger wore around his neck jingled as he made his way down the stairs, heralding Jack's lazy descent behind him. The day was warming up to be a scorcher, the cool halls and passages of the castle providing only a temporary respite from the heat outside. The fine weather made him feel languorous and lazy in his movements. He was never too fast on his feet if he didn't have to be. Mind you, in his line of work, sometimes he had to move at the speed of lightning. And he could if he needed to, but these days, as he neared his forties, he felt that he had earned himself the right to slow down a little. Enjoy the finer things in life – after all, he'd earned them. Like this place. His little Scottish bolthole. Who'd have ever thought he'd go to Scotland, eh? To his own castle. Putting Speccy in charge of this place was turning out to be a right little money-spinner. If Ricky Gordon could only see him now. Only you couldn't see much from the bottom of the Thames, could you?

Jack smiled lazily to himself and took his time as he made his way down into the empty hallway of Dubhglas Castle.

Jack opened the interior door, Tiger slipping out before him into the porch, the cat's grey tail giving a final swish as it disappeared through the open heavy outer doors. He should really get her lead, Jack thought to himself, but feeling the sun warm his thick forearms as he stepped out from the shadow of the castle he decided he couldn't be bothered. Tiger never went too far from Daddy, he knew. And if he decided to take a bit of a flit then there were plenty of servants here to go after her for him. Another perk of this Scottish-castle business, he thought to himself. Back home, he never dared let Tiger out of his sight in case she slipped out and didn't come back. Jack clenched his fists at the thought. Woe betide the soul who'd dare hurt his beauty, he thought. Tiger could stand up for herself, of course. But it wouldn't do to take the risk.

It didn't concern him that he couldn't see the cat now – he could still hear the little bell she wore on her red collar somewhere nearby. He wanted a diamond-studded one for her, he decided. There was nothing too good for Tiger.

The sun felt warm on his skin, his shirt sleeves rolled up, his collar open. He strolled, with slow, measured steps, swinging one foot in front of the other, around the side of the castle, taking deep breaths of the fresh Highland air. He felt proud of himself. He rounded the corner that took him out around to the back of the castle, through a small grove of apple trees and stopped for a moment, surveying the scene before him close up.

Tiger trotted through the freshly mown grass, tail held high, eager to investigate the game that the two boys were still playing, further down the lawn. Martin was pretending to fire a gun at Laurence, who defied the invisible bullets and continued to whoop and dance in circles. They were oblivious to their observer, absorbed completely in the action. Again a shudder of irritation ran through Jack as he watched Martin participate so actively in this. If he'd been seen playing kids' games when he was eighteen then someone would have taken a belt to him, and rightly so. What next, tea parties?

His irritation grew as he watched Laurence bend to rub a hand down Tiger's back and saw Martin pull his hand away.

"Don't go near that bloody cat – it'll give you a disease," he heard him hiss and Laurence stepped back quickly, but not quickly enough as Tiger took a swipe at his outstretched hand.

Jack heard Laurence exclaim in pain.

"Show it here," he heard Martin say and saw him take the proffered limb, examining it closely, waiting for thin trails of blood to show, but they didn't. He was still unaware of Jack watching him, his face black.

How dare he, thought Jack. Lad deserves a kicking for speaking about Tiger like that. Again, subconsciously, he balled his fists and took a single step in Martin's direction before calming himself. He'd make him pay later. Revenge was a dish best served cold, after all.

He watched the boys at play for a few moments more. So innocent, he thought to himself, watching Laurence's complete absorption into the scene that they had set for themselves. Jack stepped a little way back into the shadow of the apple trees, eager not to be seen just yet.

"You no kill Um Big Chief!" shouted Laurence, aiming an imaginary bow and arrow at Martin.

"You ain't nothin' but a thievin' Injun varmint," the older boy replied and again fired his invisible gun with its undiminishing supply of bullets.

Jack watched from the cover of the shadows as the game made its way back toward the trees where he stood.

He watched intently as Martin tried to dodge Laurence – a wiry, athletic boy if ever Jack had seen one – and failed, tripping up in the process and leaving himself wide open for the capture which duly followed. Laurence was smaller but strong, and he had the advantage of standing on two feet whereas Martin was sprawled on the ground, helpless with laughter in between his mock groans of pain. Giggling, Laurence hauled him to his feet.

"I take your scalp to my tribe now, white man!" he barked in a gruff voice and hauled him as best he could toward one of the apple trees.

Martin resisted, pulled away, but was weakened with laughter and Laurence set his jaw in a determined line and began again to pull the taller boy to his place of imprisonment. Martin giggled and pulled against his captor, using his superior strength to eventually free himself from Laurence's grip. Unbalanced, Laurence staggered backwards.

Expecting to land on his back, Laurence was shocked when he felt something soft break the fall. Jack's bulk helped him to keep some balance and he turned quickly as he righted himself, vaguely registering the look of fear that crossed Martin's face as he did so, the smile gone suddenly, his attempts to run away thwarted. On seeing who had blocked his fall, Laurence too felt a ripple of shock go through him, and he took a step back from the great hulk of a man who was shaded by the trees and looking at him so intently.

Laurence knew of Uncle Jack, and he had been here once or twice before when Laurence had stayed and he seemed to be always around this summer. The place felt different when he was here, somehow. Laurence didn't think he'd ever been this close to him. The smell of cigar smoke that came from his clothes momentarily overwhelmed the scents of summer – the mingled perfumes of the cut grass, the roses, the cleanliness of the air. Laurence's nose wrinkled slightly and he stepped backwards again. A moment's pause fell between the three, broken by Jack.

"Don't let 'im escape, lad," came a voice that was gruff but attempting to be playful. Jack nodded toward Martin. "'Ere, let me give you an 'and." And with that Jack joined in the game, lumbering after Martin with a roar while encouraging Laurence to join him, encouragement that made Laurence stare at first but within moments re-enter the spirit of the play wholeheartedly with that innocent thrill a child feels when an adult joins in as an equal.

Within moments, Uncle Jack had managed to seize Martin. So entranced with the imaginary Wild West was Laurence that he didn't notice that Martin's cry of pain was genuine as Jack grabbed him by the hair to stop him in his tracks, yanking back his head, *and then letting go as quickly, shifting the grip to his collar. Laurence caught up with them and, grabbing Martin's arm, he could do little but skip alongside the big man as he pushed their prisoner back to the apple trees to pin him against the bark. To complete the capture, Laurence fumbled with a rope that he had taken from Mr Turnbull's shed and fixed to his belt.*

In the lull of the action, only Martin saw the look that Jack gave him and felt the fear of retribution, although he couldn't think what for. In turn, Jack took the moment to fully look at the boy whose neck he could break with a single snap. He was finished with him, he realised. It had been all right when the fellah was a lad. A bit of fun, bit of distraction. But now – now he was going to be eighteen in a couple of weeks and that made him a man. And if Martin was a man, then that would make Jack a poof and that was one thing he wasn't. How dare this kid make Jack Ball, of all people, look like a nancy boy?

Martin winced as Jack's face filled with colour suddenly, growing red, then purple, all the time his dark eyes staring down at him. Jack looked away again suddenly and saw Laurence still fiddling with the rope which had caught itself on the buckle of his belt.

"'Ere. Give that 'ere, lad," he said, pulling the rope from Laurence's hands a little too roughly.

The child stared up at him, the rope taken from him and with it the joy of tying Martin up and beginning his dance around him, like a proper Indian that he'd seen at the pictures.

Jack moved quickly with the rope. "This is 'ow you tie up your enemy," he grunted as he wrapped it tightly and deftly around Martin's body and the tree behind him, passing it from hand to hand with a speed that belied his bulk, pulling it tighter after each circuit, ignoring Martin when he cried out in pain.

The knot that held him in place, pinning his arms to his sides, was firm, leaving Martin only able to twist his head from side to side and kick his legs out, completely helpless as he felt the hemp dig deeper into his skin the more he moved.

"Good and tight," Jack continued, his face growing redder by the minute, deep in concentration on the task at hand. Martin's eyes

filled with fear as they always did when they saw that familiar level of concentration and power.

Helplessly bound, he glanced at Laurence who looked on, confused. his game taken from him.

And now the axe.

Small as it was, it was a real one, taken without permission from Mr Turnbull's toolbox earlier that morning, along with the rope, for the purposes of the game. Martin's face turned back to Uncle Jack who was bright purple now, sweat glistening across his brow, his face distorted with the effort. Martin watched, as did Laurence, as without warning the giant of a man raised the axe in the air high above his head – as high as the first floor, thought Laurence as he stared, fear and disbelief creeping into his bones, eyes wide as Jack turned to look directly at him. Laurence winced as he studied the face properly – the pockmarks on the brow – and that scar – the one that ran jagged up his cheek, that made him look like he was smiling. Except he wasn't.

"Do you wanna scalp 'im, Big Chief?" boomed Uncle Jack and Laurence began to tremble, raising a small hand as he shook his head to indicate no, that he didn't want to scalp him after all. But to no avail. Jack continued to stare down at the small boy, pulling his arm back further to give more impetus to the blow that the boys were sure he was about to let fall.

"No, Uncle Jack . . ." Martin said . . . distant, irrelevant.

Jack stared at Laurence, at the small, perfect, rounded face before him, eyes wide with fear, breathlessly beautiful.

Very meekly, Laurence shook his head and repeated what Martin had said, whispering the words. "No, Uncle Jack."

The moment froze in time – the small child, terrified – the skinny teenager still now, too filled with fear to even struggle against the ropes in this game that had gone so horribly wrong – and the man, angry and dominant, the axe poised high, high in the air, ready to fall.

And it did.

There was a 'swoosh' sound as it sliced clean through the air, guided by the immense power of the arm which drove it. And then a terrible, dead thud as it embedded itself in its target with such huge force. The air filled with a child's scream followed by a low groan from the intended victim. And then, ridiculously, the jingle of a tiny bell as a grey cat wound its way around its master's legs.

The axe handle juddered for a moment as Jack let go of it. It would take a strong man to pull it out of the tree, just above Martin's head where it was now firmly stuck. There was a silence. A silence of relief, of suspended reality.

"You said you didn't want to scalp 'im," said Jack in a low voice. "So I didn't scalp 'im."

And Martin Pine watched in terror as the older man suddenly placed an arm around the boy's shoulders and pointed to the house. When he spoke, it was as if everything was normal, as if what he had just done had been as natural as picking daisies, or strolling around the gardens.

"I don't know about you, Big Chief, but a morning of not scalping my enemy gives me a terrible 'unger," grinned Jack. "'Ow about you? 'Ad any breakfast? I don't 'alf fancy some o' that lovely 'ome-made jam on me toast. Ooh, and a kipper or two, whaddya say?"

As he spoke, he began to move toward the house, pulling the child close to him, Tiger slaloming between his legs as he walked.

Martin still couldn't move, pinned to the tree not just by the rope but by fear, by the idea that if he stayed completely still then everything would be fine. His usual reflex.

"What about Martin?" he heard Laurence say.

"Oh, don't worry about the Sheriff," Jack replied, his voice growing distant as they drew near the house. "I'll send one of my men to release 'im in a while. Won't do 'im any 'arm to stew a little. Make 'im think twice before hunting down Um Big Chief again, eh?" And he giggled.

Had Martin been able to get his hands to his ears, he would have pressed them there to block that out. That cold, mirthless giggle. He knew it only too well. Along with the feeling of fear that pervaded his very being around Uncle Jack.

Martin rolled his eyes slowly upward, toward where the axe was wedged in the tree. Not even an inch from his head, he reckoned. He had felt it on impact, had been sure it was the end of him, sure *that Uncle Jack was going to scalp him for real. How had he avoided hitting him, wondered Martin, his thoughts straying back to the moment of impact. It wasn't something he was going to forget in a hurry. And he didn't. It stayed with him throughout the whole rest of his life, the fact that while swinging that axe with all of his human power, Jack Ball had never once looked at Martin Pine. In fact, hadn't once taken his eyes off the terrified face of Laurence McKenzie.*

CHAPTER 21

November 22nd

Sue, laden down with folders and newspapers, burst in the front door as soon as Martha opened it, still in her dressing gown. "Here, take these!" she urged, jumping from leg to leg and pushing the stash into Martha's hands. "I gotta pee! And put the kettle on – I'm *dying* for some breakfast. Well, a ciggie and a cuppa." She hobbled toward the stairs, clearly having driven much of the distance from London to Edinburgh through the night without a stop and feeling the ill effects.

Martha took the bundle of paperwork that was thrust into her arms and struggled to prevent the contents of one folder spilling all over the floor. "I thought you'd given up?" she called after her friend. "I thought that Simon said –"

"Simon said that he and his wife weren't together any more," Sue called back. "But then someone posted a 'congratulations on the new arrival' message on his Facebook page. And they didn't mean a puppy!"

Martha gasped. "Are you serious?" she called.

"Well, what's a girl to do?" Martha heard her call back down the stairs. The slight echo to her voice indicated that she had entered the bathroom. "Kettle!" she hollered and Martha heard the lock click.

Shaking her head, Martha stepped into the kitchen to fulfil her request.

Sue made no reference to her new single status as she sipped tea at Martha's kitchen table, listening first-hand to the account of the séance at Gabriel's apartment and the subsequent theory that Martin Pine might be innocent.

She pondered the details, an expression of disbelief on her face. "Wasn't he upset though?" she asked.

"Who?" responded Martha, pouring a second cup from the pot.

"Gabriel," replied Sue. "You know – the guy who killed his brother is put away for life – justice done and all that – and now all of a sudden, according to someone who sees dead people, the guy didn't do it at all so they have to start all over again? Didn't it dredge it all up for him?"

Martha shook her head. "He was a bit wobbly at first but you know Gabriel – he's been remarkably rational about the whole thing. What's shaken him most is the fact that he was right about being haunted. He didn't think it was possible for a medium to be haunted as such. And finding out that it's Pine has thrown him completely."

Sue's brow furrowed. "But it's his little brother, isn't he sad about it?"

Martha took a sip of tea. "Laurence was Gabriel's older brother," she corrected. "Gabriel never even knew he existed until his late twenties so it's a bit difficult to grieve for someone you didn't know, I guess. Plus, Laurence is Gabriel's spirit guide so he usually sees him all the time. To Gabriel he's not dead, but now he's missing and he wants to figure out how to get him back. He's so confused by the whole thing and wonders if we look further into this whole Pine being innocent thing then maybe it might get Laurence back." To Martha it made perfect sense.

Sue stared at her for a moment. "Do you really believe all this?" she asked sceptically.

"You know I do," Martha replied. "You know . . . what happened in Norfolk. And Gabriel helped me and I think he's really sincere. I know it sounds nuts."

Sue shook her head. "Freak," she mumbled.

"I'm not a freak," protested Martha, smiling.

Sue, in turn, grinned. "Nutter," she said.

Martha shoved her playfully and Sue laughed as her elbow slid off the table. "*Ow!*" she exclaimed and rubbed her funny-bone, still smiling. "Well, if you're a freak then I'm a freak's friend." She reached across for one of the files that sat on the table. "Because while you've been going all 'Is there anybody there?' on me, I have been knee-deep in archives and actual facts and I have rummaged out as much as I possibly can about Martin Pine and, apart from the fact that his name is the reverse of a small and rare mammal, there is really nothing complicated about this guy." Sue's face grew serious. "And from what I can find out, it was a pretty open and shut case – two watertight witnesses, no alibi, two bodies and a history of crime for Mr Pine. I'm really not sure how we're going to prove that he's innocent and that the voices from the other side are telling us the truth." Sue made a round 'oh' with her mouth and wiggled her fingers, giving a moan in a hollow and ominous voice. Her version of a ghost.

Martha sat forward in her chair. "Did you say *two* bodies?"

Sue started to organise the files and sheets of paper before her. "I most certainly did," she replied. "Where's it gone? Here. Okay – you ready?"

Martha nodded.

"Here goes. Martin Pine was convicted and sent to prison for the murder of Laurence McKenzie who we all know and love, and also – and this is the interesting one – the murder of a Jack 'Wrecking' Ball – a notorious gangland criminal."

Sue paused, took a swig of tea, and glanced over her glasses for a reaction from Martha who stared at her, open-mouthed.

"Jack 'Wrecking' Ball," Martha repeated and a smile tugged at the corner of her lips. "I know it's not funny, but 'Wrecking' Ball? What was he, a wrestler? *Jack 'Wrecking' Baaallll!*" Martha mimicked a ringside announcer and giggled.

Sue stared at her friend. "Martha. Can we take this seriously? Do you know how much stuff we have to get through? And you won't be making fun of this guy when I show you this file." She looked serious as she tapped another of the manila folders in the pile before her.

Martha suppressed the grin and took a mouthful from her mug. "Sorry," she said playfully, giving a last giggle before controlling herself.

"Okay. Let's start with what I've found out about Pine," began Sue, pulling a fresh sheet of handwritten notes dotted with the occasional shorthand squiggle from the pile before her.

"Right. Martin Archibald Pine, born in Hoxton in London's East End in 1945 to a widowed mum, Gracie Pine. His dad, Private Archibald Pine, died in a crash while Martin's mum was pregnant – they were both teenagers when they got married – Archie never saw active service. I'd surmise that theirs was a shotgun wedding judging by the dates, but Archie never saw his son and Gracie never remarried so Martin Pine remained an only child." Sue paused for breath.

"That's quite sad, isn't it?" Martha observed, peering at the page in front of her friend.

Sue shrugged. "Stuff happens," she said, simply, smoothing her long blonde hair behind her ears as she consulted some more notes.

"Our Martin seems to have been quite the scamp. He was expelled from school for constant truancy and left completely at fourteen which would have been in . . . 1959 or so. Now here's where it all gets a little more serious. Over the next couple of years, Martin was in and out of borstal – all for petty theft, shoplifting, progressing to breaking and entering and so on. Looks like our boy was probably headed for Pentonville until he got involved with a certain Firm which was hard at work in the East End at the time," Sue paused and looked at Martha to make sure she was following.

Martha looked back expectantly at Sue. "So he got a job then?" she said, scratching her head with her pen.

Sue lowered her head and looked at Martha over her glasses. "Not really," she said. "He became involved with a certain *Firm*."

Martha stared blankly at Sue, realising that Sue expected her to know something that she didn't. Martha felt a glimmer of annoyance. Why was everyone doing this these days?

Sue rolled her eyes and sighed. "The *Krays*, stupid!" she said, flicking through a number of printouts of newspaper pages that she took from a file before her and pushing them at Martha who gasped in surprise. "Reggie and Ronnie Kray and their associates.

It was London's East End in 1962, for heaven's sake – the Krays more or less owned the place and any criminals, petty or otherwise, were more than likely involved with them. Martin Pine was no exception but how exactly he met them, we don't know."

Martha waved her hand to get Sue to stop mid-stream. "How have you found all of this out in the last two days?" she asked, waving at the pile of paperwork.

Sue took a mouthful from the cup that Martha had handed her half an hour ago, and grimaced as her mouth filled with cold dregs. "*Eurrrgh,*" she said, "Oh we'd better make a hot cup – this won't do at all!" She stood, made her way to the kettle and filled it. "How I've found out has been an absolute stroke of luck," she said, popping the kettle back on its base and flicking the switch. "It just so happens that I worked with the editor of the *Hoxton Chronicle,* Maggie Ross, about six months back on a story and once I found out from the 1961 census that Pine was an Eastender, I was able to give her a buzz and she not only said she'd help, but she sent a poor intern in on a Saturday night to gather up as much as she could find on Martin Pine and Jack Ball and mail it all to me so I owe her a massive drink, therefore you owe me one in turn!"

Martha grinned. "There's bigger mugs in that cupboard just over your head," she said drily.

Sue grinned back and turned to take a teabag from the stone jar on the worktop. "Fair enough," she shrugged. "Anyway, the *Chronicle* has been in existence since the 1800's and Maggie computerised their whole records system when she took over as editor about three years ago and, as she has a large touch of OCD, you can find anything at the drop of a hat in there so our intern didn't have too difficult a job to do – just a very long one as both our boys were extremely busy throughout the late 50's and early 60's. At least Martin was, up until he got involved with the Krays, it seems. The last report we have of him in about 1962 lists him as an employee at the Gigi Club, Frith Street, in Soho which was one of the clubs that the Krays controlled. Around then he was fingered as a suspect in an assault on an elderly woman in her home, but somehow he managed to disappear completely until he turned up in court in 1964 for the murders of Laurence McKenzie and Jack Ball."

Sue blew on the fresh cup of tea as she sat back at the table.

Martha leaned back in her chair and sighed, milling the information around in her head. "It seems a bit unlikely though, doesn't it?" she said.

"What bit?" replied Sue.

"Well, it's a long way to go from being a shoplifter to a cold-blooded killer," said Martha, her brows furrowed.

Sue nodded in agreement. "True," she said. "But we're not finished with all this lot yet."

Martha regarded the reams of newspaper and scribbled-on foolscap pages before her. "Can we take a break?" she mock-whined in a childish voice.

Sue shook her head and grinned. "On to Jack Ball," she said, pulling open the file with a flourish. "Now this guy. He is a piece of work. He is your stereotypical gangster. He's so gangster that he makes Al Capone look like Cliff Richard. Take a look at this." She pulled a sheet of photocopied paper from the pile in front of her and passed it to Martha.

Martha took it in both hands and gasped slightly. "Wow!" she managed as she stared at the image on the sheet before her.

The photograph was copied onto an A4 sheet from a news article which she could see was dated 1960, and featured a close-up shot in profile of a man who, Martha felt instantly, exuded some sort of power. A fat hand was raised toward the camera in an unsuccessful attempt to hide his features but he'd completely missed his mark and the face was still clear, the head turned slightly toward the lens, the expression one of disgust. The man was big but solid, dark hair slicked back to one side. His eyes were narrowed into slits as he glared at the camera which added to the sense of danger that he generated. His lips were curled and there, clear as day, was a long scar which ran from the corner of his mouth upwards along his cheek. Martha had heard of this kind of maiming but didn't think she'd seen it up quite so close before.

"Does he have one to match on the other side?" she asked, all mirth drained from her voice as she ran a finger along the disfigurement, tracing its length on the paper.

"Not sure," replied Sue, suitably impressed at the response of her friend to the image before her. "That's the clearest photo of him I could find. That was on his release from prison in 1960. You can see the headline . . ."

"'*That's Enough, says Mr Ball*,'" read Martha aloud.

"Exactly. He announced to the press that day that he was getting out of a life of crime and going straight for once and for all. My guess is he was just moving towards a more corporate veneer to his crime with added undertones of extreme thuggery. And the odd murder. According to himself, he was hanging up his crime-doers cape and going straight on the family fish stall in Billingsgate."

Sue's face was grave as Martha's eyes met hers.

"It's weird to say but just to look at him," Martha observed, "just an old, photocopied picture of him . . . you can almost sense evil coming from him. Does that sound nonsensical?"

Sue shook her head. "For once I completely agree with you. For example, what sort of things does a person have to get tangled up in to get a scar like that? *Eeurrrgh*!"

They both stared at the picture for a moment before Martha gave an exaggerated shudder. "What exactly did he do?" she asked tentatively. "Or do I really want to know?"

"What didn't he do, more like," stated Sue, taking some more documents from the file in front of her. "Right. His back story is a little foggy up to a point. No one really knows what happened to him but at some point in his history his parents died and he was taken in by his much older sister, Anna Calvert, and her family. His parents were found dead at home in what was presumed to be a gas leak but to my mind . . ." Her voice trailed off and Martha's eyes grew wide as she understood the implication.

"You don't think . . . ?" she gasped and was answered with a shrug.

"Who knows? Anyway, this guy fell in with those lovely Kray twins and all of their associates quite early on in the game – no surprises there as to how he came across Martin Pine then. At first, Ball seemed to be a hired hand – or fist, rather."

Sue searched through another few pages and passed a sheet across to Martha. It was a list of criminal charges and convictions from the early 1950's.

"Literally as long as my arm," Martha observed, glancing through the sheet quickly.

"Too right," replied Sue. "The intern actually sat down and made this list out for us, bless her, because it was quicker than copying the reports. Look at the sort of stuff that he did – assault, GBH, battery, breaking and entering, criminal damage – he didn't use those paws for drinking out of china cups, I can tell you."

Martha nodded in agreement.

"It was in 1958 that he got sent down for murder for a guy called Richard Gordon whose body was found in the Thames," Sue continued. "His neck had been broken following a violent beating and he'd been chucked over a bridge somewhere. Anyhow, Ball was sent down – listen to this for a nice guy. *'As Mr Ball was led down to begin his life sentence for the murder of the unfortunate Mr Gordon, he was seen to gesture to the gallery with his fingers in a 'V for Victory' sign and was heard to say: 'Two years, worth every minute.' It is not known for sure what Mr Ball means by this but residents of East London can sleep safe in their beds tonight knowing that this man is finally behind bars.'*"

"But he was sentenced to life – what *did* he mean by two years? Oh! But he *did* get out in 1960 . . . how . . . oh . . ." It dawned on her what Sue was getting at.

"Yes. He *knew* he wouldn't serve life so he did his token couple of years for the sake of appearances and then won his appeal on 'a technicality'. Amazingly, a new witness turned up or something." She looked Martha right in the eye. "The Firm looked after the legalities," she said, and paused to let that sink in.

Martha pushed back her chair, stood up and stretched.

"So anyway, it's after this it all gets interesting," Sue went on.

Martha stopped in her tracks and leaned against the worktop by the sink. "'Cos it's been deadly dull up till now?"

Sue smiled and refocused. "So, after his release, and his declaration that he was going straight, he disappears off the criminal radar until 1963 when he turns up floating in a lake in Scotland. He was brought back to the East End for burial . . ."

Martha sat back down again. "Let me guess – horses with plumes, glass carriage, flowers spelling out 'Wrecker' or whatever his name was? Some dude with a cane leading a procession through the streets, Newgate Cemetary . . ."

Sue smiled again. "Now you're getting it! Although it wasn't Dickensian times, love! No Newgate, and the flowers spelled out . . . let me see . . . 'Uncle' . . . from his devoted nephew, Christopher Calvert, who inherited Mr Ball's Scottish residence, Dubhglas Castle, on his passing."

Martha took a moment to let the information sink in.

"So Ball *owned* the castle? And Gabriel's godfather is Ball's nephew? How the hell did he go from being in jail for murder to working on a fish stall to owning a bloody Scottish castle? And how did he end up dead then? And why? *Aaaargh*, the mind boggles!"

Martha made an exaggerated gesture of pulling her hair and Sue laughed.

"I know! I know!" she said. "I don't have all the answers – I have to show all this to Gabriel and find out what he knows – it's his bloody family history after all. I'm sure Ball didn't crack open his piggy bank to afford a castle but I haven't figured out yet where his cash came from. But I guess we've established how all the action came to be taking place up in Scotland – obviously Ball knew Pine from London and their criminal associations – my guess is that he maybe installed him at the castle because he was, I dunno, a trusted employee-slash-henchman maybe? And he brought his nephew up there to live with him because he was what they call *fahmily* possibly and somehow almost all of them ended up dead except for Pine whose ghost says he didn't do it. Case closed!"

Martha flung her head back and sighed, running her hands down her face. "So how did Martin Pine murder Mr Ball. And Laurence? And why?"

"Cut and dried, it seems, on paper," replied Sue. "There were two witnesses who testified – have a look at these . . ."

She handed Sue another photocopied sheet where two photographs were printed side by side. One of a thin, tall man with glasses and greased-back hair, wearing a suit and entering what looked like the Old Bailey. The second was of a young girl. The photographer had caught her just as she had taken a glimpse in his direction and had captured her with her full face upturned to the camera. She was young, slight and pretty, Martha noted, except for one flaw. Her left eye was turned inwards while her right was dead centre, where it should have been. For a moment Martha had to stare to see if she was looking directly at the camera or not.

"Christopher Calvert himself – Gabriel's godfather and Ball's nephew – and a Claire Drummond who worked at the castle at the time. Both arrived on the scene and found Martin Pine standing on a jetty at a lake on the castle grounds, a bloodied oar at his feet, showing all the signs of a struggle with two bodies found later when they floated to the surface – Ball had received a blow to the head and drowned, Laurence was throttled and then drowned. Bodies, murder weapon, guilty-looking young man . . ."

"But motive?"

"Yes. Motive. Not pleasant. Christopher Calvert himself testified that Martin Pine liked to visit Laurence's room at night-time, if you know what I mean? Spent a lot of time alone with the kid, Calvert said that he had 'concerns'. Evidence states that Ball caught Pine on a night-time boat trip alone with Laurence and tried to stop it, but Pine overpowered him somehow, bashed him on the head, finished him off, and then drowned the kid, presumably to ensure his silence, but he got caught in the act by Drummond and Calvert and was carted off to prison that same night."

Martha grimaced.

"Things just went from bad to worse for Pine," Sue went on. "He was brought back to London to be tried – that assault charge was still outstanding. And to make matters worse, all of this happened the day *after* his eighteenth birthday so he was tried as an adult and got two life sentences. All sounds a bit fishy to me."

"You mean 'sleeping-with-the-fishy'," quipped Martha.

Sue rolled her eyes.

"Yeah. That too. Now. I am going for a well-deserved fag break and you're going to make us some lunch. We deserve something nice. Because later on, when the boys get here, we're going to have to go through all of this again and see if Gabriel can throw any insider knowledge on the situation. And then I, the bearer of all this news, freshly single and operating solely on the energy generated by the love for my best friend and her nutty boyfriend, am going to get absolutely *steaming* drunk and cry on your shoulder about my love life. Is that okay?"

Martha took a deep breath, stretched and smiled. "Sounds like a plan, Sue. Thanks, by the way. For all this . . ."

She swept her hand across the table before her, indicating the hours of work that Sue had done. And for what? To support some bonkers theory of Will's based on information gleaned from a woman who claimed she was talking to the dead?

"*No problemo*," replied Sue, pulling her cigarettes from her handbag and fishing a lighter from her pocket. "Oh – and have a glance in that green folder there." She made toward the back door and struggled with the key.

"What delights await me there?" asked Martha, reaching toward the pile of documents.

Sue popped the cigarette between her teeth to free her hand to fight again with the lock. "Someone in there I think you should see," she replied, the words coming through the side of her mouth. "A certain Mr Pine."

For a split second, Martha withdrew her hand from where she was gently sliding the green folder from the pile before her. Martin Pine. The visitor. He was the one player that she hadn't laid eyes on yet and she wasn't sure if she wanted to. Presuming, of course, that she hadn't seen it already . . .

Gently she drew the file towards her and laid it on the table, glancing at the back door which was left wide open, the faint smell of cigarette smoke wafting in from outside. With a measured hand, Martha opened it and there he was, another photocopied image but clear as day. Thin, with a shock of tousled hair. Exactly as Gabriel had described his pursuer. Martha was suddenly taken aback. She wasn't sure what she had expected to see – what the face of a supposed double-murderer, a child molester, was supposed to look like – but she was sure that it didn't look like this. His hands cuffed, flanked by uniformed policemen who were leading him somewhere, Martin Pine, like Claire Drummond in the earlier picture, had looked full on at the camera and Martha was stunned to see that the face, his living face, with its wide eyes, full lips and frightened expression, was barely more than that of a child's itself.

Martha felt goose-bumps prickle all over her body that weren't caused by the open back door. She held the picture up toward the light to get a better look, disturbing, as she did so, another sheet of paper from the file which floated gently to the ground. She bent to retrieve it, noticing as she picked it up that it was yet another photocopy of a newspaper page.

It was a short piece. "Body of Local Recluse Found" read the headline. Martha pictured it tucked away at the bottom of the left-hand page in a local newspaper. She laid the photograph of Pine to one side to peer more closely at the typed information. It was from the *Hoxton Chronicle*, the paper that Sue had mentioned.

"Police have identified the body found yesterday at the Mulberry Gardens flat complex as Martin Pine, 65. They were alerted when a neighbour became concerned. Sharon Todd (35) first believed that something might be wrong when she experienced a strong odour through the walls of her own home. This coincided with her son, Jayden, witnessing flies crawling on the inside of a pane of glass in Mr Pine's door. When they were unable to gain access, Hoxton police station was notified and the residence was entered by force. It is believed that the body had been in situ for quite some time.

'The man who lived there barely came out,' Todd stated. 'You'd see him occasionally but no one would have noticed if he went off the radar for a while'.

It is believed that Pine moved to the flats in the late 1980's on his release from prison. He had no next of kin and the police are appealing for relatives to come forward although they confirmed that at this stage they feel such an occurrence is unlikely."

Martha felt sadness wash over her as she read. She glanced again at the picture – the man-child being manhandled up the steps of a courthouse. And then to this . . . dying alone in a flat complex, neighbours so distant that they only noticed something when the stench of his body pervaded their living space. And no one to claim him. No one to love him, to take his body and bury him, to say goodbye . . .

She shook herself then. Urged herself to get a grip. The man was supposed to be a paedophile, for heaven's sakes, she reminded herself. A killer . . .

But again she looked back at the picture of the boy. The look in his eyes. Angeline Broadhead's words ran through her mind again: *"He says he didn't do it."* What if she was right? What if he didn't and, having died alone, his spirit had come back prove his innocence?

Martha stared at the picture for another while, until one more thing caught her eye. The date on the piece. June. Roughly six months ago. The previous summer. The exact time that Gabriel had begun to experience strange things. *"Why now?"* Gabriel had asked. Was this why? Had Martin Pine's ghost left his body and instantly come in search of Laurence's McKenzie's brother, she wondered. Was he so desperate for help that his first act in spirit had been to go find a link back to the boy he murdered? Unable to rest until he proved himself innocent?

Martha smiled up at Sue as she re-entered the room, rubbing her arms and stamping her feet in the cold. Then she closed the file, keeping a hand on top of it, unable to let it go. Maybe it was true, she thought. Maybe Martin Pine really didn't do it.

CHAPTER 22

1963

Martin shoved his hand over Laurence's mouth to stifle the noise. The child was helpless with laughter – Martin realised he shouldn't have been clowning around, but he hadn't allowed for the fact that the kid was such a giggler. And it was infectious too. Within seconds, he had stuffed his own oversized jumper into his own mouth because he couldn't contain himself either. And the more they laughed, the more they wanted to laugh. Any second now and he'd wet himself and then there would really be what for. He couldn't expect Laurence to take the rap for that from Mrs T.

Martin shone his torch in the boy's face, causing a fresh explosion of muffled laughter, and he dissolved again at this, but soon managed to control himself. If anyone caught him – Mr Calvert, Mrs Turnbull – or worse – then he'd be on the next train back to London and he knew what waited for him there. He burned with shame at the thought of how he'd knocked that old lady over as he tried to get out of her flat, her clock stuffed into his coat. She'd been flat out on the ground when he looked back. He hadn't known whether she was living or dead – still didn't. And he didn't know why he'd broken in at all. It's not like he needed the cash. Maybe he'd just needed the thrill, but it had been a hollow one. He could be facing a murder charge if he had to go back home.

He always said that he didn't pray, but every night he did. That the old lady was alive, that he'd be forgiven and that he wouldn't have to face a life behind bars. He'd had a taste of borstal when he was younger and he knew that prison was much, much worse. He was a different person then. He knew better now. And he was so very, very sorry.

With one sweep of his arm, he pulled the eiderdown back from over their heads, effectively demolishing the tent they had made using two chairs to prop it up.

The boy's face fell. "Aww, Martin!" he began, but was silenced by a finger pressed to his lips and an aggressive "Sssssh!".

Martin couldn't be cross with the lad for long, but he had to think about himself.

"It's time for bed now, Lozza," he said and Laurence giggled quietly again.

"That's a silly name," he observed, obediently standing to attention, the leg of his red-striped pyjamas falling to his ankle from where he had pulled it up to his knee in order to absent-mindedly pick at a scab there while Martin told his nightly tale.

"Well, if you came from where I come from, you'd be called Lozza all the time," Martin informed him, waiting for Laurence to climb onto the iron-framed bed and turn around into a sitting position before pulling his covers back over him and turning to pick up the eiderdown with which they had made their bunker. "Or Larry. Which d'you prefer?"

Laurence raised his index finger to his chin and cocked his head to one side to show that he was thinking. "Lozza," he said finally, a little too loudly.

"Will you shut it?" whispered Martin with a smile. "You'll get me into all sorts of trouble – I shouldn't be here!"

"Sorry, Martin," whispered Laurence meekly. "But it's not like Godfather would read me a bedtime story. And you're brilliant 'cos you make them up yourself."

"You forget about them stories, do you hear?" replied Martin softly, tucking the boy in. "I probably shouldn't tell you them ones, about the ghosts an' all. They'll give you nightmares."

"Uncle Jack said he might tell me a bedtime story sometime," said Laurence as he watched the older boy smooth down the covers.

Martin froze. He felt something drop in the base of his stomach and a tremble in his legs, as though they were about to turn to jelly.

"No," he said, aloud, the word out there before he could stop it. He wanted to tuck Laurence in and lock the door. That couldn't happen. Not to Laurence. It was too late for Martin but not this kid. This lovely, vibrant, innocent kid. Martin hadn't had much of a chance to be a kid but Laurence – he had a whole life in front of him. A life that was clean somehow. He raised his hands and gripped Laurence fiercely by the shoulders. "You don't ever let Uncle Jack tell you a bedtime story, do you hear me?" he growled, squeezing the boy as he did so.

Laurence looked back at him, uncomprehending, his face beginning to fill with fear. "Martin, you're hurting me," he whispered.

Martin didn't hear. He stared directly in Laurence's eyes. This message was the most important one he could give the boy. How could he make him listen? His eyes bored deep into Laurence's, as if somehow by doing this he could burn the message into his brain.

"Never. Do you hear me?" he said. "You don't ever let Uncle Jack in here at night-time. Do you understand?"

He shook Laurence gently with each syllable to emphasise his point. He had to make his point, had to make him listen.

Laurence's face turned from confusion to anger. "Get off me, Martin!" he said aloud. "Get off!"

Martin slowly released his grip and Laurence propped himself up on his elbows. Martin took a step back, his heart pounding in his chest.

"I'm sorry Lozza," he said. "I didn't mean to hurt you but do you understand me? Did you hear what I said?"

Laurence scowled at him, raising one arm to rub his shoulder where he felt sure there would be a bruise. "Get out, Martin," he said crossly. "And my name's Laurence. Not Lozza."

With that he turned his back dramatically and yanked the covers over his head.

The older boy stood there for a moment longer, staring at the child's frame, his shape under the quilt. After a while he stepped toward him, laid a hand where his shoulder was and apologised again. "I'm sorry Loz–Laurence. I really didn't mean to hurt you. I just got carried away. You're my mate, right? 'Ow about some fishing tomorrow if the sun's out, wotcher think?"

There was no response – Martin hadn't expected one – and he turned and softly padded across the room toward the door. His hand was on the doorknob when he heard the small voice behind him. "Awoight, mate."

Martin smiled broadly. He was forgiven. Laurence wouldn't attempt a cockney accent if he was still cross with him. What a great kid. Grinning, he turned the handle, stepped gently outside onto the mezzanine and pulled the door silently shut behind him.

Had he been three steps closer to the stairs, he'd have tumbled down them, most likely breaking his neck in the process. As it was, he was far enough back so that when the silent shape slithered through his legs, causing him to fall over, he remained safe. He hit the floor with a thump and an involuntary 'Ow!', recovering quickly enough however to try to make out the shape in the dark of what had tripped him. The hiss that greeted him as he leaned toward the culprit made it abundantly clear that only one creature could have done that. Bloody Tiger. And without her warning bell on tonight.

Martin froze again at the hiss. Tiger wasn't allowed to roam the castle by herself at night. She slept in the bottom drawer of that stupid filing cabinet in Uncle Jack's room. On top of a pink satin quilt, of all things, emerging only to pounce on the odd mouse that scampered across the ancient floorboards. So Uncle Jack said. Uncle Jack . . .

From the corner of his eye, Martin saw the hulking black shape. It looked as though it was detaching itself from the wall beside Laurence's door. How long had he been there? Why was he there in the first place? What had been his intention? Martin felt panic fill his body, forcing him to his feet quickly, his breaths coming short.

"Well, well, well, as they say," came the low rumble in the darkness. "If it isn't Martin Pine, leaving the bedroom of a young boy on a summer's night. Tut tut, young Martin Pine."

Martin felt the voice get closer to him, felt an energy that was *familiar and repulsive, and took a step back towards the balustrade behind him as Jack Ball stepped toward him and into a shaft of light from a window high over the stairs. Shaded dark blue, Martin made out the familiar features. The small eyes, the scar. The face loomed at him in the darkness, something about it more threatening than usual.*

"I'm not sure my nephew is going to be happy to hear about this, Martin," growled Ball.

Martin stayed silent, waiting for a moment. To do what, he wasn't certain – bolt, punch, kick – give in, as usual. "The staff sneaking round to the top of the house in the middle of the night? Visiting young boys as they try to sleep? Telling 'em that they didn't mean to 'urt 'em . . ."

He'd heard. Heard what Martin had told Laurence. Heard the warning . . .

And now he was going to take those words and twist them. Make Martin sound like him.

"No," said Martin in a strangled whisper. "You know I didn't do anything!"

The response came in a placatory tone. "Come on, Martin, me old pal. Me old mucker. We go back a long way you an' me, don't we? All the way back to Gigi's. And Bow Street Station . . ."

He left the implication hang in the air.

"Good times, eh, Martin?"

He leaned a little closer.

"But it wouldn't be so good if you 'ad to go back now, would it? What with all that little-old-lady business. You were right lucky Uncle Jack was able to save your skinny little 'ide, wasn't you? And what a lovely place ol' Uncle Jack found for you to live, eh? If I were you, I'd be very grateful to Uncle Jack. Very grateful indeed. 'Cos if you're grateful enough, Uncle Jack might just let you stay on after he's finished with you. But only if you're a very good boy."

Martin's stomach lurched and he felt the gorge rising in his throat. He fought it back. He had to stay strong, alert. He looked at Laurence's door again, behind where Uncle Jack stood. There were two of them now, he suddenly understood. He had to protect the two of them.

"Now. You can start by running along. Go on – on you go – good lad. I'm just going to check if my nephew's godson is all right after his . . . nocturnal visitation from an older boy. And once I'm sure he is, I'll sleep very soundly. Very soundly indeed . . ."

And there it was. The giggle.

"What's going on? Who's there?"

Martin thought that his legs would buckle underneath him. He fought back tears of gratitude as he heard the voice come from the passage behind Jack and saw the hideous face that loomed over him withdraw from the shaft of light, frowning and then composing itself as he turned to face his nephew in the dark.

Christopher Calvert carried a small torch and the beam took in first Jack's face and then Martin's, pale and terrified.

"What on earth is going on?" asked Calvert again, pushing his glasses up his birdlike nose and squinting.

"It's all right, Speccy," Jack growled back.

"Ain't nothin' to worry about. Me and Tiger thought we 'eard a mouse, didn't we, Tiger?"

Martin froze again as he saw Jack turn his attention back to him, his face turned away from Calvert so that the younger man couldn't see the expression that gleamed in his eyes, the expression of sheer contempt as he spat out his words.

"But it was nothing. Nothing at all," he spat, his words directed straight at Martin. Then more softly, "Isn't that right, Tiger?"

There was the noise of a door opening then, and all three turned as Laurence's tousled head poked out of his bedroom door, squinting as Calvert shone the torch in his face. "What's going on?" he said, his voice husky with sleep. "I was just falling asleep and I heard all this noise."

"It's nothing, Laurence. Back to bed," snapped Calvert brusquely and ushered the boy back into his bedroom, accompanying him and closing the door behind them both.

Martin was almost sick with relief. Mr Calvert wouldn't hurt a fly, never mind his only godson. He worshipped that kid like a son. He'd never do anything to harm him.

He saw his moment then and fled for the stairs while Jack stared at the closed door of the boy's bedroom for a moment. He was fast, *he knew. He could be gone before Uncle Jack even turned, safe for one night at least. And Laurence too. He ran hastily down the steps, toward the hall below, feeling escape in his veins. Until he heard the deep whispered growl come from the darkness above him, echoing through the empty space of the hall.*

"Loose lips sink ships Martin," it said. "You remember that."

CHAPTER 23

November 28th

"It's no good, Maisie," said Martha at last. "I'm going to have to just go and get this prescription filled and go home."

Maisie Gordon threw her eyes to heaven. "Hallelujah!" she exclaimed, gratefully. "You've spent two days sounding like Darth Vader and as for your humour – my God!"

Martha managed a weak grin. She knew Maisie was right and that she should have gone to the doctor first thing Monday morning but she had stupidly carried on.

Martha ran her hands across her cheeks, as if that in some way would alleviate the constant nagging irritation from her sinuses that had troubled her since the weekend spent poring over the back-story of the Dubhglas murders with Sue. So much information, and none of them were any the wiser as to what Gabriel was experiencing.

She stood up from her desk and drew her handbag over her arm, ignoring yet again the juddering sensation from her phone which was on silent in the outside pocket. Dan again, she was sure. Over the last few days he had bombarded her with text messages and calls that she had ignored, a constant barrage of 'need to see you's'. and 'it's urgent's'. It didn't help that she had finally confided in Sue, told her friend of her concerns at his intentions, expecting support, yet Sue had been nothing but matter-of-fact in her response. She had been expecting this turn of events all along, she said. "Maybe having a baby is the new black in advertising," she'd shrugged. "If he's Mr Family Man he might land a particular client or something – you know what he's like." Martha knew Sue was right and it had made her even more inclined to ignore the texts. She knew it was stupid but a part of her wondered whether, if she continued to ignore them, he would just go away.

"I hate to leave you," said Martha to Maisie who wrinkled her nose.

"Trust me. I'd rather you left me," Maisie replied.

Martha could never tell if she was serious or not.

"Just go," said Maisie, with a grin, making a shooing gesture. "And don't come back till you're better. Please."

Martha grinned. "You're sure?"

Maisie simply pointed to the door in response. Martha blew her a kiss of gratitude and Maisie covered her mouth and nose to jokingly prevent infection. With that, Martha was gone, pulling on her coat as she walked down the stairs and out onto the street.

It was dark by the time she emerged from the pharmacy, antibiotics in hand, and decided to flag down a cab. The painful sensation in her face had grown stronger as the afternoon had progressed and she longed just to climb into bed and sleep.

She needed to be better for Friday, she knew. For their appointed date. The thought of visiting Gabriel's Highland castle made her feel physically ill, yet it was all arranged. Gabriel had insisted. All of them, Ruby included, were due to leave Friday morning, and then pick up Sue on the Saturday morning from the train at Dubhglas village. The trip hung over her like a cloud, she realised, as she settled herself into the back seat of the taxi. She remembered the wording of the letter Gabriel had received – *a delicate issue of a supernatural nature* – and now she was up to speed on everything that had happened there, those grisly events. Gabriel knew little more than what they had gleaned from the newspaper reports so he could cast no fresh light on anything. He'd been kept in the dark about it his whole life, with summers spent at the castle at the bidding of his parents, yet all detail about Laurence kept from him until he discovered the truth of his death by accident as an adult.

Suppressing a shudder, Martha rummaged in her handbag and withdrew her phone. At least deleting texts from Dan might take her mind off what was ahead in just a couple of days – heaven knew he'd sent enough of them over the last day or so. There hadn't been one since she had left the office – that one asking once again if she was free to talk anytime soon.

The air was thick with heavy frost as she got out of the taxi at the bottom of Calderwood's driveway and made her way up toward the house. The driveway was prone to ice, she knew, and it was safer to walk on the grass verge than drive up the slight incline. Besides which, she loved the feeling of breathing in a frosty evening – the scent of the actual cold itself, infused with chimney smoke and city smells. She felt an unanticipated thrill at the thought of Christmas also and her stomach did a childish lurch of excitement. Martha smiled, heartened again by the sight of Will's car parked outside the door. It was unusual for him to be home before her. And it meant that Ruby would be too, which made her feel even more excited.

Martha didn't bother searching in her handbag for her well-buried keys, instead choosing to ring the doorbell for Will to let her in, taking a final moment to savour the evening, the twinkle of distant stars in the sky and the first sheen of frost forming on the bonnet of the Volvo. The door opened suddenly and she was bathed in light and a delicious smell of cooking from indoors.

"Have you been outside at all?" she asked, glancing at the scene around her one last time before turning back to Will with a smile. A smile that disappeared as soon as she saw the stony expression on his face.

"Whatever's the matter?" she asked as he turned his back on her and walked toward the kitchen without so much as a greeting. Her heart sank. What was wrong with him now. Martha frowned and stepped into the silent hallway, pushing the door shut with her foot before shrugging off her coat and unwinding her scarf. She slung her belongings over the bannisters of the stairs and straightened her clothing, taking a deep breath before walking toward the kitchen. Heading into battle again, she thought to herself.

Again, there was an unexpected face at the kitchen table but on seeing who it was this time, Martha stopped dead in her tracks and instantly felt blood rush to her cheeks. There, in the same place where Gabriel had surprised her only a few nights ago, sat Dan. He was nursing a mug of something as he gave her a weak smile. On his knee, staring at his face, sat Ruby.

Martha reeled, tried to take in that he was here, opposite her, in her own kitchen.

"I tried texting you over and over," said Dan, in a tone that suggested he was trying to calm her down, even though she hadn't uttered a word.

She noticed that his eyes were red-rimmed and he had a sniffle. Everyone's bloody sick, she thought to herself. "Dan," she said abruptly.

He pushed a stray lock of hair away from his eyes. It immediately flopped back again. "Sorry to just land on you like this, but I needed to speak to you urgently. I thought you might be at home – I hope you don't mind?"

Martha gritted her teeth and held her breath. She could feel temper rising within her and didn't want it to come out, didn't want a scene in the kitchen, in front of Will. She was having trouble dealing with how surreal this felt. A part of her had banished Dan from her life and had begun to treat him mentally as if he didn't exist. Yet here he was, representing something that she had tried so hard to leave behind, sitting in front of her, intruding on her new life.

And then there was Ruby. Martha's chest heaved as she tried to control herself. Daughter and Father. Meeting each other for the first time. And without her here. Without her presence to protect Ruby from him. Martha suddenly felt weak and vulnerable, violated somehow. As if it was somehow inevitable that her fears should come true. That Dan would just take Ruby away from her forever. She sank onto the nearest kitchen chair, aware suddenly that her head was pounding, her swollen sinuses throbbing and her legs had turned to jelly.

"I couldn't get hold of you but I need to speak to you urgently about a certain matter," he said. "I reckoned that maybe your phone was broken or lost or something so I just came here – I didn't know what else to do."

Dan spoke quickly and earnestly – keen, Martha thought, to reassure.

"Will was kind enough to let me in," he added, a smile breaking out on his face as he glanced in Will's direction.

Will was standing at the cooker, stirring something he had been busy with since Martha had walked into the kitchen. He turned his head to give Dan a weak grin and throw a sidelong glance at Martha, before turning back to his cooking.

It suddenly hit her that of course Will was still completely in the dark about Dan's appearance in Edinburgh. She still hadn't managed to tell him about their contact – had hoped to keep it a secret until Dan was gone. Shit, thought Martha. She had a lot of explaining to do.

Ruby interrupted the scene by sliding off Dan's knee, giving him a flirtatious toddler's grin as she did. He watched her leave the room, his expression blank, but Martha was sure she could see a vague look of wonder in his eyes. It made her feel sick. Martha felt a rush of desperate protective love as she watched her daughter.

"I've been explaining to Will why I had to see you, actually," continued Dan.

"It seems that our Ruby . . ." he began, pausing after he said it, seeming to realise that he may have overstepped his mark.

"Well, it seems that Ruby has come into some property. In the south – Cornwall. My Aunt Ellen – you remember her, don't you Martha?"

Martha glimpsed Will stiffen at the allusion to the shared memory. As it happened, she didn't remember an Aunt Ellen, but Dan could be very secretive about certain things. His extended family being one of them.

"Well, Aunt Ellen died a few weeks ago – she was ancient, you know. Ninety-something. Natural causes – don't worry!" Dan laughed at his own joke.

"But she owned quite a bit of land. A big estate near Padstow – it's a tourist haven now, of course, but for some reason she decided to leave a chunk of it to Ruby – I'd been corresponding with her, you see, in the last few years, and she knew about Ruby and what a mess I'd made . . . Well, that's all for another day. Anyway, her will was read last Friday and it seems that Ruby is to get a portion of the land – which could be worth a fortune by the way."

Martha continued to stare at Dan. Land? For Ruby?

"Thing is," Dan shifted slightly in his seat, "we've got to sign some documents or other. It's not legal until both of her – parents have signed on her behalf, it would appear."

Martha closed her eyes and opened them again. This was really the last thing she wanted to listen to right now. She wanted to go to bed and have a rest and wake up tomorrow with everything sorted out. Surely it could wait? Portions of Cornish land weren't going to go anywhere after all, were they?

"And that's the next thing," said Dan. "We've got to do it really soon or else there's some clause which hands the land on to someone else. We have to do it Friday, in fact. That's why I've been trying to get in touch with you over the past few days."

Martha reddened as she felt Will turn to look at her again.

"I've taken the liberty of booking us an appointment with a solicitor here in Edinburgh for early afternoon on Friday – I really hope you don't mind?" continued Dan.

Martha was jolted back to reality. "Friday?" she repeated. "This Friday? Why? What could be so vital about these documents that we have to sign them Friday?"

Dan shrugged. "It's the clause in the will – they need to be done by the end of the month. Old Ellen was a funny old bird. I suppose she just wants to make sure that everything's done and dusted as soon as. If you'd replied to my texts at the weekend . . ."

Dan's voice trailed off and Martha looked at Will who was looking straight back at her now, eyebrows raised.

"Oh God, we're going to Dubhglas on Friday . . ." she remembered.

"That's a pity," Dan said. "But it's Ruby I'm thinking of – property is still worth something, even in these times – and the location is absolute prime land for development . . ." Dan glanced up at Will and back at Martha. "The thing is, it could maybe pay for private school or university or something. And I'd feel in some way that it might make up for my – not – being there for her for the past two years."

There was a loud clatter as Will almost upended the saucepan he was stirring. Martha felt uncomfortable.

"How long will it take to sign these forms?" she sighed.

Dan smiled. "No time at all, I think," he said. "I've booked us an appointment at 2 p.m. – they should have all the documents up from Padstow by then. All we do is sign on the dotted line and then that's it – we just get on with our day."

He looked expectantly across the table at Martha who sighed again.

"Fine," she said. "That okay with you, Will? You and Gabriel can go ahead and I can drive up with Ruby on Friday afternoon? So I'll be there to pick Sue up from the train as planned on Saturday morning at Dubhglas station."

Will shrugged and continued to stir the sauce. "You're Ruby's parents," he said simply, without turning round.

An uncomfortable silence descended on the room.

It was Dan who eventually broke it. "Sue Brice, eh? Still friends after all these years? Wow! Old Sue was always a tough nut to crack." He smiled, looked again at them both as if expecting them to join in and found himself looking at Will's back and Martha's stony expression. "Right then. That's settled. I'll call you tomorrow with all the details." He stood from the table and pushed his chair in quietly, glancing again at Will for a moment, and then scanning the room until he spotted his coat slung over another chair. He reached for it, adding, "You look absolutely done in, Martha, if you don't mind me saying."

Martha stood also. "You don't look so amazing yourself," she responded and indicated that Dan should walk through to the hall.

"Oh this," said Dan, sniffing and pointing at his face. "Just a cold," he said dismissively. "Scottish winters and all that. Not used to them." He moved to the door where he paused. "Thanks so much for taking me in," he piped in Will's direction, to no response.

"I'll show you out, Dan," Martha said, a slight tone of warning to her voice. She didn't want Dan to stay a moment longer to make it any worse.

Ruby was busy playing shop with some cans of beans and a

baby doll in the living room as they passed and Martha made a point of going straight to the front door, opening it and standing aside to indicate that Dan should leave. "She's got a lot on in there," she said, with a half-hearted smile, hoping that Dan would understand that a father-and-daughter farewell wouldn't be appropriate under the circumstances. If nothing else, she didn't think she could bear to watch them together again. A gush of frosty air filled the hallway.

Dan fiddled with the buttons on his trendy duffel jacket and glanced to where his daughter was playing, but took the hint and made no effort at a goodbye. He fished a scarf from one of the front pockets and flung it around his neck. He always had that knack, remembered Martha. Of just throwing something on and looking marvellous.

She shook herself back to the present moment and shuffled her feet. "Thanks for . . . the information," she said politely.

He nodded, and pulled a pair of gloves from the other pocket. "No trouble," he responded, stepping over the threshold and out onto the gravel.

Martha stepped out behind him and crossed her arms against the biting cold.

She couldn't help but notice how beautiful the garden looked. She hadn't spotted the full moon earlier but it completed the perfect winter scene for her. The whole garden was illuminated with a clean white glow which made it look festive and mysterious at the same time. Frost twinkled lightly on the ornamental iron lamppost that she had added to the garden when they moved in.

Dan looked at it also and smiled. "Narnia?" he asked.

Martha stared at him and nodded. He'd remembered. *The Lion, the Witch and the Wardrobe* was one of her favourite books – an inspiration for her own books – and she had always said that she wanted a lamppost in her garden when she 'grew up'. She blushed slightly as she remembered pestering Dan to get one for the house in London when they married. He had always refused – and rightly, she knew. The gardens in their street were tiny and her magical lamppost would have looked contrived and tacky.

Here in the large and private garden at Calderwood, however, it was perfect. And in the moonlight, with frost twinkling on the newly bare branches of the trees, it looked magical to Martha. She felt very tired all of a sudden and she sighed loudly, closing her eyes for a moment. She realised that she was in no rush to go inside, to face explaining everything to Will. This was a mess of her own making. If only she hadn't ignored the texts and just dealt with Dan . . .

She opened her eyes again to find him smiling at her, his face handsome in the moonlight.

"Go inside," he said softly, "or you'll freeze."

Martha smiled back briefly before stopping herself. "Bye, Dan," she said quietly and turned to go back in. She heard him take a deep breath of the winter air.

"Oh and Martha," he added, pausing as she turned back to face him, one hand on the door frame. Dan looked around him at the garden and waved his hand around. "It's a beautiful home you've got here," he said. "Narnia's just right for it."

Martha said nothing. It felt odd, but she was somehow touched that he had remembered the lamppost, not to mention that he had been kind about it – he hadn't always been. She nodded, almost imperceptibly, and went inside, pulling the door closed behind her.

With a deep breath, and her arms still crossed, she walked across the hall and back into the kitchen where Will was washing the saucepan that he had been stirring so vigorously. Martha paused for a moment and gazed at him. The muscles moving under his blue shirt as he scrubbed, his hair just skimming the collar. A wave of love ran through her, followed by a wave of regret.

"I'm so sorry, Will," she said softly.

Will stopped what he was doing and looked over his shoulder at her, pausing as if to contemplate whether or not to say anything. Martha was relieved to see him turn fully, leaning back against the counter top as he did so. He reached for a tea towel to dry his hands and looked at her for a while, studied her tired face, her hair which hung limp over her ears.

"He's right," he said, nodding in the direction of the front door. "You do look done in."

Martha responded by shrugging and returning to her seat at the kitchen table. Her whole body ached. She ran her fingers through her hair and squeezed her eyes shut for a moment. "I am, a bit," she replied. "It's been a really long day. And I don't feel well."

"I got a fright," said Will, soft but stern. "I come home early to cook us a meal – to try to spend an evening together. I've taken what you said on board, you know." He paused for a moment. "And then the doorbell rings and there's this stranger outside asking if this is Martha Armstrong's residence. I was taken aback at first but then it hit me that that something had to have happened to you . . . and, for a second, I thought you were in hospital or . . . worse . . . and that Dan was a policeman or someone come to tell me. And then he used my name and finally I recognised him. From your wedding photos – the ones I forced you to show me."

"I'm *so* sorry, Will. For not telling you he was here in Edinburgh and that I'd seen him . . . and . . ." She felt a wobble in her voice and stopped to try to rein the tears in.

Will threw the tea towel on the counter top behind him and crossed the room quickly. "Martha, it's okay! Jesus, I'm not angry with you. I was just so *worried*. I just got a fright – I was so delighted to see you when you got home but the whole thing was so *weird*. Your ex sitting like that at the kitchen table – after everything you've told me about your marriage. He was only here for a few minutes before you got home – thankfully!" Will's expression was sincere as he sat down opposite Martha at the table and reached out for her hands.

"It's just that you're angry – quite often lately," sobbed Martha, a combination of relief and exhaustion making the tears hard to stop. "And we haven't been spending time together and then this happens – I mean, Dan here in our kitchen . . ."

Will squeezed her hands tighter. "I know, I know," he said, his voice reassuring. "I know that I haven't been easy to live with but the last week or so . . . I want to change that. Get back to how we should be – how we used to be, for heaven's sakes! Since I fell out with Gabriel I just . . . lost the run of myself. I got completely absorbed in work because, I dunno, I had to prove to him I could do it without him or something. Does that sound really stupid?"

Will mirrored the teary smile that Martha offered him. She

shook her head and sniffed. "No," she laughed. "Just very . . . like a stereotypical *man*."

Will squeezed her hands again. then reached out and ran a hand down the length of her cheek. "Dan said he'd been in town for a while, that you'd met him?" he probed.

Martha nodded. "I'm so sorry. I wanted to tell you – I was going to on the night that Gabriel came round so I couldn't then – and after that it just never seemed like the right time. And I was scared that you'd blow a fuse and then – you know what I'm like – I put things off sometimes, pretend they're not happening . . ."

Will laughed. "Boy, do I know that one!" he said and Martha made a sheepish face.

"He hasn't been paying his maintenance money either," she said. "I should have told you that too but I thought he'd cough up – he's never been unreliable before so I didn't want to . . ."

"Didn't want to face up to it," interrupted Will, his voice more serious now. He brushed Martha's hair behind her ear. "Why didn't you mention that to me? That has to have worried you?"

Martha shrugged. "I suppose I didn't want another quarrel," she said quietly. "I should have told you but you've been so . . . preoccupied . . ." Her voice trailed off. As honest as they were being, she didn't want to make any sort of an accusation that could turn into a row.

Will bowed his head and withdrew his hand from her hair to rub it across his face. "I know I have. Look, I can't say I'm happy about Dan rocking up here like that, but I have to acknowledge that my recent behaviour has been to blame for . . . why you didn't tell me anything."

"I never intended for him to come here. I just . . . hoped he'd go away. I don't want him having anything to do with us . . . but the horrible truth is that he's got rights . . ."

"And for some reason he wants to use them?" added Will.

Martha nodded.

Will thought for a moment. "Then what we have to do is keep our noses absolutely clean around him," he said decisively.

Her face grew dark. "Can't we just tell him to sod off?" she said in a low voice.

Will leaned back in his chair. "I'd bloody love to," he smiled. "But for now we need to play along. See what he wants, and don't give him any cause to – I dunno, get worked up about things."

"You mean go to the courts? For access or something?"

Will looked at her with kindness in his eyes, sensing the growing panic that she felt. "I genuinely don't know," he said. "I don't really understand how all of that stuff works but all I do know is that I don't want him upsetting our little apple-cart, our little family." He nodded in the direction of the living room, from where they could hear a loud and tuneless rendition of 'Twinkle Twinkle Little Star'. "On the upside, this property thing is interesting. Do you think it's genuine?"

Martha's eyes widened. "Christ, who knows with Dan? I suppose I have to give him the benefit of the doubt if there's the slightest chance it's going to benefit Ruby – maybe he genuinely *is* making amends. God, Will, why does it all have to be so complicated?"

Martha's thoughts turned inwards as she moved on to the logistics of the upcoming Friday in her head. "Friday's going to be a nightmare now – I've told the childminder she can have the day off, and the chances are that I won't get out of that meeting till three . . ."

"Look," said Will, in a businesslike fashion, "why don't you skip all the stress and wait till Saturday to come up to Dubhglas?"

He stood from the table and Martha watched as he crossed back to the cooker and peered inside. It struck her suddenly that she could smell roast beef and she realised she was starving. "Did you make Yorkshires to go with that?" she demanded suddenly.

Will laughed. "You and your Yorkshires," he giggled. "Look, logically, it makes a lot more sense to just pick Sue up from the airport here in Edinburgh on Saturday morning, no? She gets in early enough – and then the three of you travel together, in daylight. Think about it – that appointment could take longer than expected and, if it gets frosty on Friday evening, then I really wouldn't be happy about you and Rubes travelling in the dark on your own – this place sounds pretty remote and I'd rather have you on the road accompanied by someone with a sense of direction."

Martha looked around for something to throw and found a

table mat to hand which she launched at Will across the kitchen. He laughed again as he deftly dodged the missile.

"I have a perfectly good sense of direction," she retorted, smiling as she watched him crumple his nose in disagreement. She mirrored the gesture. "You're right," she giggled. "I don't." They laughed together for a moment, until Martha stood and crossed the kitchen into Will's open embrace. She sighed at the familiar smell of him, the comfort that came from him. He was right, she thought. They shouldn't do anything to upset this apple-cart, as he called it. This life that they were building for themselves.

"You know it makes sense." Will's voice was muffled where her left ear was pressed against his chest. "And besides which, it gives me and Gabriel the chance to have a little snoop around on the Friday night without freaking you out and then maybe we might just enjoy this party on Saturday? We're due a good knees-up, you know."

Martha nodded vehemently. It had been a long time since they'd gone out together. She thought to herself that she'd prefer an intimate restaurant somewhere – not a castle in the back of beyond, milling with locals, and whatever 'significant activity' Gabriel's butler friend had referred to. But it was something. And it meant that for a couple of days she could be away from Edinburgh. From the now-constant presence of Dan.

"I know you'd rather not stay in the castle," said Will, out of the blue.

Martha drew her head back and looked up at him. "Have you stolen Gabriel's powers?" she asked. "Is that where they're gone?"

Will was smiling as he looked fondly down at her face. "It's just that I thought we all need a bit of a break – I thought this might be nice until we have time to get away properly, in the New Year, maybe. And Gabriel says it's a really amazing place."

Martha rested her head back against his chest. "Amazingly bleak and haunted, more like," she offered.

Will chuckled and she felt his lips touch against her hair. "A bit," he agreed, and squeezed her to him. "It'll be fine," he said softly, and Martha knew that he didn't just mean the weekend in a draughty old castle.

She smiled broadly as her daughter came pelting into the room as fast as her legs could carry her, clutching a doll whose hair had been sucked into a permanently upright position.

"Dolly!" she offered and Martha swept her up into her arms, making their hug into a family one. She pressed a firm kiss on Ruby's cheek and felt Will's arms encircle the two of them. He was right, she knew. It was going to be fine.

CHAPTER 24

1963

Claire's first summer at Dubhglas Castle stretched into a haze of long, warm days but she was too busy to notice. She spent every hour that she could with Mrs Turnbull in the kitchens, learning how to cook every dish that was served at the castle, from Mr Calvert's favourite roast lamb, to sherry trifle for Laurence. For the most part she adored rolling her sleeves up and taking on each task as though it were the most important of her life. Whatever job she was given she embraced fully – from selecting vegetables or herbs from the kitchen garden, to crumbing bread for stuffing, to painstakingly shelling peas.

The one fly in the ointment, however, was the constant presence of Uncle Jack. The man terrified her. Large, powerful, unpredictable – she'd lived her whole life under the shadow of men like that. The more she saw of him, the more she feared him.

It also didn't help that Martin, in some odd attempt to alleviate the shadow that Jack Ball cast over the castle, had developed a habit of playing practical jokes on her, sneaking into the kitchen behind her back and hiding things that he seemed to know instinctively that she needed. "Whatever do you mean that I hid it?" he'd respond, wide-eyed with feigned innocence as she demanded futilely to know the whereabouts of the cheese grater, or

175

the pudding bowl, or the potato masher or the vegetable knife. The jokes made her flustered and stressed. She couldn't bear to be teased or taunted in any way. It reminded her of being back at school, always the butt of the joke. He always seemed to be at his worst just when Uncle Jack was in one of his black moods, or when Mrs Turnbull was on her day off.

Laurence had a particular fondness for sponge cakes and Claire had recently been assigned the duty of making them as a treat, on Mr Calvert's instructions no less. It was imperative that she get them right, she knew. So important.

Which was why it made her so frustrated that she couldn't find the whisk one Sunday when Mr Calvert had taken Laurence out for the day and Martin was bored and petulant in the kitchen. He'd been hanging around since lunchtime, watching Claire, and his very presence distracted and irritated her. Every now and again he'd stand up and begin to mooch around in his boredom, lifting pan-lids here, pulling things from drawers and examining them, all the while humming a tuneless dirge. Claire longed for Mrs Turnbull to come back and give him her habitual smack and order him away to do something useful.

"Martin," she sighed eventually, "what have you done with the whisk?"

He didn't look up, but continued to spin the bottle of vanilla essence around and around on the kitchen table. Claire waited for a response, received none, and bit her lip as best she could.

"Martin," she tried again, sweetly. Catching more flies with honey, Mrs Turnbull called it.

"Martin, have you got the whisk hidden on me?"

She tried her best to add a playful tone to her voice but she couldn't quite manage it.

Again, he spun the bottle around and around. It thrummed in circle after circle, shooting suddenly across the table as well as rotating. It was all Claire could do to slam her hand on it before it rolled right off the table.

That did it. Mrs Turnbull's vanilla essence was something that she had been warned to use sparingly. And here was Martin, sitting at her table, hiding her things, humming his stupid tune, about to break it and waste the lot.

"Martin!"

Claire had meant to shout at Martin, to snap at him and speak in the tone that Mrs Turnbull used when she meant action. Instead she burst into tears right there at the kitchen table, managing only to wail his name as the crying completely stole her speech. Martin looked up at her with a start.

She didn't know where the tears had come from, or why they wouldn't stop but by the time they finally began to dry up, she felt as though she had been crying for hours. She felt helpless. She should never cry. Never. That showed weakness and made the beatings worse, made the hand over her mouth clamp firmer. Then why was she crying now, over a stupid whisk?

Martin stared at her, mouth open, across the kitchen table. Every few moments he would try to find a word but to no avail. He'd never seen anything like this before. And he was clueless as to what to do. His old ma never cried, and if the girls on the road cried when he pulled their pigtails, well, that was all part of the game, wasn't it? Only meant you liked them, after all.

He stared at her as the sobbing became more sporadic and the tears began to dry. Eventually Claire's face looked a little more like itself and she lifted a floury white hand to wipe an eye. A speck of flour caught on one of her eyelashes and it was that which spurred Martin into action.

"Hanky!" he blurted. He scrabbled in his pockets, retrieving a piece of red cotton that had seen better days. He hesitated in handing it to her, noticing as he held it out how dirty it was, but he found himself too far into the action to stop.

As it happened, Claire didn't even look at the rag but just accepted it being pressed into her palm. She wiped her eyes, the tiny piece of flour catching in the cloth, and blew her nose loudly.

"It's on the top shelf in the pantry," murmured Martin quietly.

Claire opened first one eye and then the other, a puzzled look across her red and puffy features.

"What is?" she managed to ask

"The whisk," came the reply. "I was going to get it for you, I promise. I didn't mean to make you cry."

At once, Claire felt ridiculous. She hung her head, resisted the urge to pull her hair down over her eye as had been her habit for as long as she could remember. She smiled apologetically at Martin, who regarded her now with a face filled with confusion and uncertainty. Claire found her heart grow soft and shrugged in helpless laughter as he continued to stare at her.

"Thanks," she managed, before laughing again.

Martin joined her, giggling softly at – at what, he wondered? What were they laughing at? He didn't care. He just joined in, happy and relieved to see her lift her head so that a shaft of light from the high windows caught her features suddenly. Her eyes glistened from the tears and her nose was red, but her smile was so beautiful.

"You must think I'm terribly stupid," she said softly, sniffing, unable to catch his eye. "My father always told me I was stupid so I expect I must be and this just goes to show . . ."

"I don't think you're stupid, Drum," said Martin suddenly, his laughter ceasing abruptly. Again, he looked at her, puzzled.

"I don't think you're stupid at all. Did your old man really call you stupid?"

Claire continued to stare at the window. She was silent for a few moments, her mind acting against her will, forcing her to think of something that she didn't want to. She frowned and Martin was sure that the tears would start again but she stopped herself in time. She looked down at the mixing bowl before her, took a deep breath, and waved her floury hand in the direction of her face.

"I must be," she said quietly. "I mean, my eye . . ."

"What about your flippin' eye?" demanded Martin, a slight tone of annoyance creeping into his voice.

Claire inhaled deeply at his tone, as if trying to suppress a fresh bout of tears. She looked up again at the window. "It means I'm a bit soft, I suppose . . ." she whispered, her words trailing off as she tried to keep the emotion in.

What Martin did next would stay in her memory forever. The awkward youth stood up from where he had been sitting at the table and walked around to face her where she stood in her dusty apron, flour up to her wrists. He still had a look of confusion on his face, but it softened slightly into something more defined as he stopped before her, reached his hand up slowly, and unexpectedly brushed his thumb across the eyelid of her left eye.

Claire had flinched, instinct reminding her that no one raised a hand without pain following. Not this time, however. Martin was gentle as a feather. She felt her eyes close under his fingers. There was no sensation of hurt. no gouging, like her brother had done once in a fit of rage, trying to push the eye back into her head. "Yi'd be better off wi' a hole in yer hid than tha' thing," she remembered him say, his voice thick with whisky. She shuddered at the memory, and regretted it because it made Martin pull his hand away. He took a step back, embarrassed.

"Sorry," he said in a voice that was uncharacteristically low for him. "Dunno what I was thinking. I didn't mean to hurt you, I mean, does it hurt when you touch it?"

Claire stared at him, suddenly conscious of the short distance between them, their breathing shallow in the silence of the kitchen. The shaft of light from the window shone down between them now and she saw dust motes sparkle in the light across Martin's chest.

"No," she whispered. "It just reminded me . . ."

"Only when I look at your eyes," continued Martin, finding it difficult to look directly into them, "I just see now that they're a really nice colour. Green and that. I mean, at first I used to notice the one that looks the wrong way . . . I mean, there's nothing wrong with it, but you know what I mean . . ."

Claire smiled as she watched Martin struggle with the words.

"And you're not stupid!" he said fiercely.

Claire flinched again, this time at the sincerity that she saw in the eyes that looked back at her.

"You're learning all that stuff from Mrs T all the time," he said, "like baking them cakes and stuff, and you know all about the things in the garden – the herbs and all that. I've been here a year and I don't know the difference between 'em and a blade of grass!"

Claire smiled again, but melancholy tugged at the corners of her mouth. She wasn't used to people speaking to her like this. She wasn't sure it had ever happened.

Martin took a deep breath and continued. "And I think you're flipping marvellous actually. And you must know I like you 'cos I *hang round here all the time when I can and you make lovely lemonade and things are great since you came and I'm really glad you never went to Glasgow and that you stayed 'cos I think I'd really miss you if you left."*

Claire frowned. His face was gone completely red, even to the tips of his ears.

"And they're nice here and all, don't get me wrong. I mean I love Mrs T to bits but . . . well, she's Mrs T, innit, and there'd be Mr T to reckon with and I don't even fancy her . . ."

Claire found it harder to understand his accent as he spoke faster and faster, his eyes darting from his hands up to her face and away again, as if ashamed or nervous to look at her.

"What are you on about, Martin?" she asked softly. *"Please slow down, I can't understand you."*

"Can I kiss you?" he asked suddenly. Blurting the words out. Immediately he regretted it and his hands flew to his mouth as if to try to stuff them back in.

"I'm so sorry, Drum, I shouldn't have asked you that. That was cheeky."

Claire gasped, feeling her stomach leap at his words, as if an electric current went through her body. She felt a sudden dart of nerves hit her and her legs and hands trembled. She stared at Martin, trying to take in what he had just asked, while he burbled in his odd accent, bright red with embarrassment. She looked at his face, into his now-troubled eyes, at his full lips, his slightly sallow skin, the small brown mole on the line of his jaw that she had never noticed before.

"Not now, Martin," she said suddenly.

Martin stopped talking, bringing his gaze up to meet hers shyly.

"I'd . . . rather you didn't just now," she continued. *"But maybe . . ."* she let the words trail away. She wasn't sure what she meant, wasn't sure what she wanted Martin to think she meant. She needed to think.

It was only a matter of a week or two before the kiss finally came at the back door in the late afternoon sunshine with the sweet smell of grass in the air and dusk beginning to fall. It was the first of many kisses, snatched here and there, fleeting exchanges on the stairs or in the kitchen garden. Giggling, shy, joyous kisses when they found a second to be alone together. And as the summer stretched on, seeming endless, the shadow of Uncle Jack didn't seem so dark, and the threat of Claire being found by her family diminished. Because in the days and weeks running up to Martin Pine's eighteenth birthday, he realised, as did Claire Drummond, that he was in love. For what would be the first and only time in his life.

CHAPTER 25

November 30th

"Bloody stupid bastard!" said Will, slamming the palm of his hand lightly against the steering wheel of the Volvo. "Stupid arrogant shit, coming up here and thinking he can just swan in and take over!"

Beside him, Gabriel covered his ears. "*William*!" he barked. "Language, *please*. You're offending even *me*. And it's offence enough that we're driving to the party in this heap of *tin* when you have a perfectly decent car sitting back in Edinburgh!"

Will ignored him and continued to focus on the road ahead. They were on the last lap of their journey to the castle and Gabriel was directing proceedings with the occasional twitch of a finger in the appropriate direction. Will was finding it hard to focus on the narrow, unknown road and the subtle gestures.

"Will you just *tell* me where to go," he sighed, frustrated. "You're not at a bloody auction!"

Gabriel eyed him sideways. "I mean, my godfather is a very wealthy man, and what's he going to think of me turning up in *this*!" He swept an arm around him, looking disdainfully over his shoulder at the back seat which was covered with discarded jackets, empty water bottles, chocolate wrappers and bits of paper and pens. Further behind, the hatchback boot was filled with Will's equipment, packed carefully into neat cases. The whole car had a faint smell of coffee and Gabriel's eye was drawn to the source, an empty cardboard cup that rolled in and out from underneath the driver's seat.

"You know the equipment doesn't fit in the Lexus," growled Will suddenly.

Gabriel jumped a little. He hadn't expected a response yet – normally it took at least ten minutes' more badgering to provoke an answer to his complaints.

"So let's run through all this again," said Will. "Just so I'm clear before we get there – Christopher Calvert is your godfather, but he was also Laurence's, am I right?"

Gabriel sighed. "I really wish you'd listen for the first time when you're told stuff," he said petulantly and took a deep breath to begin again. "My understanding is that my mum used to work for Christopher and made him Laurence's godfather. When Laurence died, Christopher was distraught – he loved him to bits apparently – so, when I was manufactured – hastily, to replace him – they gave the stewardship of me to Calvert as well. Sort of like getting a new puppy when the old one goes to a farm in the countryside."

"Gabriel!" Will exclaimed. "That was uncalled for!"

Gabriel swung his head sharply toward the driver's seat. "So was the several hours of moaning about Desperate Dan that I've had to listen to all the way up here! But did I say a word? No, not I!"

"All right," conceded Will, interrupting him sharply. "I know I've been banging on about it. Sorry."

"Accepted!" barked Gabriel. "Now take the next left."

Will did as he was instructed before picking up the conversation again. "And you don't know anything more than that?"

Gabriel cast an eye out the passenger window to take in the scenery through which they drove – bleak and beautiful in the mid-morning sunshine. He shrugged. "Truth be told, I've found out more about this place from Sue's clippings over the past few days than I knew in my whole life. Jack Ball, for instance, is someone I know nothing about. No one ever spoke to me about any of this stuff – not even Laurence. By the time I started coming here for my annual summer penance, it was as if time beforehand had been obliterated. Next right."

Will turned sharply, sighing again at the lateness of the instruction. Once around the corner, he glanced at Gabriel, his brow furrowed.

"Wasn't that a bit odd?" he asked. "No one talked about any of it, ever? And you're at least, what, fifty now?" He smirked and Gabriel sniffed loudly, fixing his attention out of the window.

"I'll choose to ignore that comment," he replied drily. "Now feast your eyes on this . . ."

He pointed out the windscreen just as they took another bend in the road and Will gasped, as through the bare trees on his left he caught his first glimpse of the castle about which he had heard so much. He could see it in the distance, smaller than he'd expected, but complicated – turrets and towers, ancient dark stone set amongst trees. For an instant he'd catch it, a fairytale structure one minute, then disappearing into the trees again before emerging to show itself off from another angle – a stately gothic home.

Will tried to keep an eye on the road but kept finding himself distracted by the castle looming like a dark shadow on his right-hand side. Gabriel barked more instructions, and Will did as he was told. It wasn't long before they turned in through two high gateposts, once magnificent, but now missing a brick here and there and struggling a little with a growth of ivy.

"Here we are," observed Gabriel.

Will lowered his speed, taking in the long driveway spread out before them, twisting and curling out of sight under the overhanging bare branches of oaks twisted together over time. The castle had all but vanished from view once they had taken the turn, hidden behind tall rhododendron bushes.

Gabriel waved at the screen of bushes. "All the better to overwhelm you with when you do actually get there," he informed Will.

"This is a proper stately home job, Gabriel!" remarked Will.

"Why the surprise?" replied Gabriel. "I told you – it's the real deal. Built in the 1860's for some minor royal or other, architecture loosely modelled on Glamis Castle. We'll get Martha to talk to Godfather tomorrow – he knows all about it and she has the stamina for all that historical stuff." He waved his hands dismissively as they drove under a low bridge, still with no sign of the main building in sight.

Will rolled his eyes. "It would do you well to brush up a bit on your history," he observed. "What with all the talking to people from the past that you do."

"Not any more," came the rapid-fire response. "I am currently not a medium, my dear boy. I am simply, shall we say, a *mediocre*. You can park in there,"

Will turned the wheel sharply left, steering through a gap in the high wall on their left and found himself in a courtyard, edged with ramshackle, disused sheds on three sides. There were a couple of other cars already parked there – a Mercedes and a BMW.

Gabriel tutted. "They'll all know I've arrived in *this*," he muttered, almost under his breath.

Will gasped. "Well, maybe if you bothered to drive every now and again you might see fit to spend some of your hard-earned cash on something that *doesn't* embarrass you!"

Will killed the engine and pulled the keys from the ignition, stepping from the car onto the rough ground underneath and gasping slightly as a blast of freezing cold air hit him full in the face. Despite the brightness of the winter sun, it was bitterly cold. A few degrees lower than Edinburgh and heaven knew it had been cold enough there when they'd left. Will slammed the driver's door shut and opened the back, reaching in for his coat which was slung across the seat.

Wordlessly, Gabriel stepped from the car himself and immediately set off, trudging away over the gravel surface of the makeshift car park, toward a gap in the wall opposite. Will watched him over the roof as he went.

"Here, aren't you going to carry something or am I your Sherpa now as well?" he barked. Gabriel barely turned and made yet another of his dismissive hand gestures. "Someone will come and get all that for us!" he shouted over his shoulder and marched on without a second glance.

Will couldn't help but smile. Being friends with Gabriel was sometimes like being a servant to a particularly petulant royal, but he was nothing if not entertaining. Will slung his overcoat on hastily and slammed the car door shut before taking off after his friend at a jog.

Dubhglas Castle didn't so much welcome Gabriel through its double doors, as seem to consume him. At one moment he was striding ahead of Will along a gravel pathway which cut through a well-tended lawn leading toward the house, the next he skipped up the castle steps and disappeared. A pair of thick, fortress-like external doors were pulled open and secured to the front of the building with hooks, revealing a small entrance porch at the top of the steps and then a pair of flimsier doors within – white-painted wood frames with glass panels. Gabriel's disappearance into the mouth of the castle gave Will a moment to stop and take it in full on. It was tall but compact – a mini-castle, more or less, with a fairytale round tower winding its way up to a pointed roof to the right-hand side of the main body of the structure – a functional square of a building which was flanked on the other side by a square tower topped with turrets. The overall effect was of something cobbled together out of different buildings from varying eras that didn't quite fit. Will turned and scanned the landscape. There was nothing for miles – just the heather and bare trees beyond the castle grounds. He stared at the bleak beauty for a while, lost in how desolate yet extraordinarily beautiful it all was.

Feeling the cold seep in through his feet, he shoved his hands firmly into his pockets and with a final glance upwards at the ancient stones of the building's façade, Will, too strode the remainder of the way to the entrance, climbed the steps and turned the old-fashioned brass knob of the internal door. On entering the hallway, the faint hint of must and old cooking hit him. There was no sign of Gabriel.

Will scanned his surroundings – it was impressive for a country home, but not the great hall of a castle that he had been expecting. To his left, a carved wooden staircase wound its way upwards to a mezzanine area on the first floor. Dark oil paintings hung on the wall directly in front of him – Highland landscapes, hunting scenes, along with an obligatory stag's head, all underneath the canopy of the mezzanine. Before him but slightly to the left and through an archway, the hall extended down a dark passageway at the end of which stood two large, solid doors, modern and not quite in keeping with the others around the hall. He reckoned that the two on his left led to rooms inside the square tower while the one on his right, almost underneath the stairs, led through to the thin, round tower. The floor was tiled in traditional black-and-white tiles – clean, but chipped and cracked here and there – the flowers on the heavy, antique table which stood as a centrepiece before him were faded plastic. The décor, the smell – Will felt he'd like to throw open a window, give the place a lick of fresh paint and some brighter wall hangings. It was like the home of any other elderly person who lived alone, he reckoned. Musty and in need of a little care but then again, not only was the owner old, the structure was, too.

Will glanced around for Gabriel and frowned that there was still no sign. He stepped a little to his left to better see down the straight passageway toward the back of the castle, peering into the gloom. He couldn't make out much but didn't have to stare for long because a muffled flushing noise nearby indicated a presence and Gabriel emerged, wringing his hands, from a door on the right-hand side of the passage.

"Oh, I needed that!" he observed, and wiped his hands on his coat before shivering. "Is it just me or is it absolutely bloody freezing in here?"

He joined Will in the hall and they stood, peering back down the corridor and up the stairs.

"*Shop!*" Gabriel called loudly, and pulled his scarf up to his nose to show exactly how cold he was.

They turned sharply as the first door into the square tower opened, the first to the left of the main entrance, and saw a man emerge. He was of medium height, medium build and with a full head of brown hair, tinged with grey over the ears.

"Mr McKenzie!" he said in greeting, his voice distinct and clear, his Scottish accent faint.

He strode across the hall toward where they were standing.

"Gifford! The very man!" Gabriel exclaimed joyfully and they shook hands firmly. "This is Will Peterson." Gabriel stood back to allow Will and Gifford to shake hands.

The exchange complete, the three of them stood in an awkward circle, unsure who should be the first to speak.

"Did you enjoy your drive up here?" Gifford asked.

"It was lovely –" began Will, only to be interrupted by Gabriel.

"I wouldn't have called our mode of transport 'enjoyable'!" he sneered, taking a sidelong glance at Will. "But the countryside is just as stirring as ever. Is my godfather round?"

Gifford shook his head. "He's not, Mr McKenzie. In fact he's away for the night – he said he had some business to attend to in Edinburgh, ironically, at head office. None of the guests come for the Christmas party the night before any more, so he took the opportunity to go to the meeting – truth be told, I think he overlooked the fact that you were arriving today."

Gabriel frowned. "His head office? But surely he's retired at this stage?"

Gifford nodded. "For the most part," he replied, his 'r's' soft. "But I believe that the board of Violet's Frozen Fish was making some sort of presentation to him at their annual dinner to mark the occasion as he was head of the company for so long and he felt he had to go along. He finds it terribly difficult to sit still for long, if you don't mind me saying."

Gabriel grinned. "I can well imagine, Gifford," he replied.

"Do you have baggage with you?" the butler asked, changing the subject.

Gabriel nodded toward the door. "Quite a bit," he said. "We've brought some added extras in response to your invitation . . . we hoped to be able to take a proper – eh – scientific look at things? Once we've had the chance to chat with you, of course." He thought he saw Gifford blush slightly and avert his eyes.

"Very good," Gifford replied. "I'll send Callum down in the golf buggy later – would that be an idea?"

"That would be a great idea," said Gabriel reassuringly.

Will watched the exchange between the two men. "Would it also be a good idea to have a little chat with you now, Mr Gifford?" he asked, a hint of eagerness to his voice. If Gabriel's godfather wasn't around, and no guests were staying overnight, then they had a perfect opportunity.

Gifford reddened again. "I suppose that's why I asked you to come," he said, with a tone of resignation to his voice. "I just need to finish some arrangements with the caterers – they need their instruction by lunchtime or else who knows what we'll be eating tomorrow night. It's all a bit too much for Mrs Hibbert these days so we hire in professionals. Would you mind awfully waiting for me in the library while I telephone them?" He indicated the room from which he had just come. "I'll just make the call from my office downstairs and then we can get down to business. No time like the present."

Gabriel responded by giving the man a warm clap on his shoulder. "Is there Talisker in the library by any chance?" he asked mischievously and was rewarded with another of the man's enigmatic smiles.

"Isn't there always at Christmas?" Gifford said softly, and then with the tiniest of nods in Will's direction, he excused himself and disappeared through a door underneath the turn in the stairs, leaving Will and Gabriel to enter the library.

Once inside, Gabriel headed straight toward a shelf which was laden with bottles and glasses. While he was busy, Will took the opportunity to try to text Martha but tutted when he glanced at his phone and saw the complete dearth of coverage bars. He'd have to try again later.

Gabriel, finally clutching the much-longed-for glass of amber liquid, plonked himself on an upholstered armchair and gulped the first sip, smacking his lips theatrically as he did so. Will had refused the offer of a glass but as he returned the phone to his pocket and sank into the chair opposite, he wondered if he might retract his refusal and have something to calm his nerves. He couldn't tell why but, as he took in his surroundings, the room itself made him edgy. He wasn't sure if it was the wood-panelled ceiling, the dark tiles each individually decorated in the centre with a small fish, the great gothic window which looked out over the front of the castle but seemed to let in no light or the high shelves of heavy books which lined all four walls. The end of the room furthest from him was virtually in complete darkness – he could just make out the looming shape of another stag's head keeping a watchful eye on the volumes. The furniture was scattered about – more of these high-backed, gilt-framed chairs, occasional tables, more plastic flowers, some of them in Victorian-style domes which always gave him the creeps. Just behind him was a piano, covered with a black cloth, bearing yet another glass case in which a stuffed weasel was frozen in motion as he crossed a log, a small field mouse dead at his feet, the tongue of the tiny creature lolling to one side while the weasel beamed in victory. It felt like a Victorian funeral parlour, Will thought to himself and continued to look nervously around.

"Sure I can't tempt you with a Talisker?" Gabriel cajoled him. "'The king o' drinks', Robert Louis Stevenson called Scotch whisky." He sipped noisily from the glass and regarded Will imperiously.

Will coughed and shook his head, shuffling his feet uncomfortably as he continued to scan his surroundings.

"It's horrible in here, isn't it?" said Gabriel after a while.

Will didn't need to pretend, and didn't want to. He knew that Gabriel had picked up on how the room made him feel. He didn't need his psychic gift for that. He replied by nodding, turning his head to nervously study the weasel again, and then looking back at Gabriel who stared back wordlessly for a few moments – until he leaned forward suddenly in his seat, grabbing his throat while simultaneously making a guttural hiss from the back of his throat.

Will jumped, emitting an involuntary grunt of shock. Gabriel began to giggle, leaning back in the chair, satisfied that his impersonation of having one's throat ripped out by a weasel had done its job.

"Jesus, Gabriel!" sighed Will once he had calmed down a little.

That served only to reduce the medium to helpless mirth and Will watched as a tear ran down his cheek.

"I'm so . . . sorry!" Gabriel gulped. "But you're normally so *brave*! So *unflappable!*"

Will couldn't help but join in. "I know," he spluttered, "but this room gives me the total creeps – it's like the set of a Hammer horror for Christ's sake!"

Gabriel groaned and wiped the last of his laughter-tears from the corner of his eyes. He pointed to a photograph, framed on a small side-table to Will's left. "You haven't seen an up-to-date shot of the old man yet, have you?" he asked, sniffing.

Will leaned forward and peered in the gloom at the picture. It showed a proud, thin elderly gentleman, glasses perched on his nose, wispy hair askew, proudly holding a huge fish and surrounded by smiling schoolchildren.

"He'll need a pretty big potato to make the chips!" Will observed with a smile. He had seen the pictures in Sue's collection of the young Christopher Calvert on the steps of the Old Bailey, almost fifty years before. He was now in his eighties, Will calculated. He had changed little – a slight stoop with age of course, but his smile was broad and his eyes bright.

Gabriel gave a small snort. "I think that's probably the local school's fishing contest. Loves his fish, does Godfather. At work and at play . . ." He leaned in for a closer look himself. "He's a real animal-loving, kid-encouraging, philanthropist type – wait till you see the drawing room – there's a sort of shrine to everything that he does for Dubhglas village. The church fete, the village games, the annual mince-pie and mulled-wine reception that he'll do next weekend – he takes his role as Laird very seriously, and he's very popular. The original Local Hero, my godfather."

"He made his fortune in the fishing industry?"

Gabriel nodded. "The Violet's Frozen Fish range. Fish fingers, fish toes, fish spleens – if it had gills then it's frozen in a bag by my godfather's company – which was apparently named after my mother I'll have you know . . ."

Will gave a start as the door opened and Gifford came in, approaching on silent feet, in soft shoes, and sat down in a chair on Gabriel's right-hand side, perching on the edge of the seat.

"I do apologise for that delay," he said calmly. "I hope you don't think I'm being too familiar, joining you for a conversation like this?"

Gabriel waved his hand dismissively. "That's what we're here for," he said, and took another swig from his whisky. "Care to join me in one of these, seeing as Will refuses?"

Gifford looked shocked. He stammered a little as he tried to refuse politely. "I'm – I couldn't – not while I'm on duty, thanks, Mr McKenzie," he managed and pulled his feet closer to each other until he sat in what Will thought must be the tensest position he had ever seen, his back ramrod straight, shoulders back, knees together. The man's demeanour made him appear as though he had travelled through time from a bygone age of servitude.

There was something else, though, Will noted. Something he saw in his eyes. His whole tense body screamed of someone who was very nervous indeed. His instinct was to be kind to the man.

"How can we help you, Mr Gifford?" he asked, and leaned toward him.

Gifford glanced uncomfortably first at Will and then at Gabriel.

"Will's a student of parapsychology," Gabriel said reassuringly. "He knows about these things. And if you're – frightened – or unnerved by anything, then it's Will's job to put you straight."

Gifford looked at him, and then back at Will. It was clear that the man didn't know where to start.

Still in his upright position, he cleared his throat and searched for words. "I'm not really sure how to begin," he said.

Will leaned further toward him, eager to hear what he had to say. He was rewarded by Gifford jumping up with a shocked expression on his face.

"Tea!" he barked. "I never even thought to offer you tea!" He looked aghast, as though he had himself committed murder. It took a few moments for Will and Gabriel to get him to sit back down, to reassure him that tea wasn't required. To appease him, Will requested the whisky which he had earlier refused. Gifford was more at ease serving others, it was clear.

When they eventually settled him, he took a deep breath, raised his eyes heavenward and began slowly. "I wouldn't normally so much as acknowledge this sort of thing," he started, "but as I said in my note to you, Mr McKenzie, we're not too sure where to turn for help. Because it's not just me. If it was, I probably wouldn't have approached you." He hesitated for a moment, keen to show that he meant to trouble no one. "It's the staff, you see. They're . . . well . . . uncomfortable with something in the castle. And when they're unsettled, so am I. We're really not too sure what's going on, but we know that we don't like it." He paused for a moment to look again at their faces, make sure that they were listening. His discomfort was palpable, but then again, so was the fear that they could feel coming from him.

"Go on," Will said, encouragingly.

"Over the past few months . . . about six months or so, in fact," Gifford continued hesitantly, "we've been able to feel something about the place . . . something that shouldn't be here. Do you understand?"

Will and Gabriel made reassuring noises.

"Absolutely," said Will, making eye contact with Gifford who responded by turning slightly toward him.

"At first I thought it was the maids being silly," continued Gifford. "We have two who work part-time – they alternate mornings and afternoons each week. It works quite well. And then if we're entertaining at night – if Mr Calvert has, say, some of his committees up here, or a guest or two – then there's a couple of the girls who we hire casually. They're in college so they work evenings and weekends to earn some pocket money."

"What is it that made you think they were being silly?" asked Will, gently steering Gifford back on course.

He cleared his throat again. "Well, they started saying silly things – refusing to go into some of the rooms because they said they could hear noises . . . breathing, if you must know. They said that there were unpleasant smells about the place too. Tobacco smoke for one, when no one in this house touches the stuff. I thought it was their imaginations, all feeding off each other – a mass-hysteria thing. But then Mr Johnson, the gardener, said that he'd been getting a drink in the old kitchen downstairs – I can show you around later, Mr Peterson – we've a brand-new kitchen down there but the old one is still in use as a sort of canteen for the staff. Not that there are much of us any more, of course. Anyhow, where was I?"

Gifford looked blankly at Will, trying to retrace his steps.

"Mr Johnson?" prompted Will, reaching into his inside pocket to take out the small notebook and pen that he kept there. It had come to the point in the story when he needed to start taking notes.

"Oh yes. Mr Johnson. Well, he smelt the smoke too. And he was the first to see something. It was a mist, he said. In front of the old cooker down there. He turned his back to fetch a teabag and when he turned back to get the kettle it was there in front of him."

"Did this mist take a form? A person, or an animal?" asked Will, matter of factly, scribbling as he did.

Gifford shook his head. "Not that Mr Johnson saw," he replied. "He dropped the teabag and ran outside as fast as he could. Said he felt stupid afterwards but I could tell it really shook him."

"When did this happen?" interrupted Gabriel, now leaning forward too on his seat.

"Around August time," replied Gifford.

Gabriel smiled. "I mean, what time of the day was it?"

Gifford smiled slightly. "Terribly sorry, Mr McKenzie," he said, allowing a short laugh to escape his lips. "It was dusk. Mr Johnson was doing the lawns – he comes in for one full day a week to do them and stays as long as it takes. He had finished mowing and was just taking a break before cleaning down the mower. He always takes a cup of tea out with him to the shed – and that's when it happened."

Will looked up from his notebook. "That must have been unnerving," he said. "Anything else?"

Gifford's eyes widened and he leaned closer to Will. "That was just the start of it. Since then it's got more frequent – in here, for example. Whichever of the maids was on the first shift used to come in and clean first thing in the morning. But soon it got to the point where they'd wait till their shift crossed over at lunchtime so that they wouldn't have to be in here alone, and so that it would take them half the time. Stuff . . . moves, you see. It ends the day where it should be, and then turns up somewhere odd the morning after. Or it might be in its right place, but upside down."

"Classic poltergeist activity," noted Will. "Who's here at night-time, Gifford?"

"Only Mr Calvert," came the reply. "The maids go home, I live in the village, Mrs Hibbert lives in her little house out the back, across the courtyard. Mr Calvert wouldn't do such a thing and besides which he doesn't believe in this sort of thing. He doesn't seem to have experienced or noticed anything out of the ordinary in fact."

"Or if he has, he's not saying?" offered Gabriel. "He's getting old after all – he's at the prime age for doing things like leaving his glasses in the fridge or his teeth in the car or whatever."

Gifford was having none of it. "He might be advanced in years, Mr McKenzie, but his wits are entirely about him!" he snapped.

Will noted this. "What else?" he asked.

Gifford turned again to face him, calmed himself a little and thought about where to rejoin his story.

"We started to have more concern when one of the night girls was helping serve dinner around the start of October," he continued, his voice low. "She came in here to get something – to check the fire maybe, or for Mr Calvert's nightcap. And then she came screaming down to the kitchens – I've never seen anyone so terrified."

"What happened to her?"

"A glass, Mr Peterson. A glass like the one you're holding in your hand right now. Someone . . . something . . . threw it at her and it just about missed her head, by inches, and smashed on the hearth. There's a chip gone out of the hearth, in fact – there, look – but there was no one in here at the time. I saw the broken glass with my own eyes however."

Will wrote furiously for a moment and then looked back at Gifford who was clearly becoming more and more unsettled at his own account of events. The butler shuddered slightly as a cold breeze ran through him, someone walking over his grave.

"And what else then?" Will prompted again.

"After that it was almost constant. The girls said that they felt as though they were being watched, or followed upstairs. Then those mists started to appear upstairs as well – mainly on the mezzanine. They saw shadows where there should have been none. Callum, the odd-job boy – he only works weekends because he's still at school – he had to leave early one day because he said he felt something around his legs – something warm, like a small animal. And that's the other thing, we've all heard a little bell jingle around the house but there aren't any pets here – or goats or anything like that. And there's still the breathing noises behind you when you least expect them, and then when you turn there's no one there. And we've all had things thrown at us in here."

Will glanced nervously around him, as if he expected to be hit with a missile any second.

"No one's ever been hit, but the breakage rate is very high." He paused. "There's just an odd feeling about the place too. I'm a sensible man, Mr Peterson, but I can't deny that something's changed round here. It's colder too, somehow – like room temperature has dropped a few degrees, despite the time of year. I've worked all over the world – in restaurants, castles, stately homes – I used to stride through Dubhglas Castle without a care, but since all this started, I find myself jumping at the slightest thing, looking behind me, seeing shapes out of the corner of my eyes, racing to get my coat on in the evenings to leave and I am not a man who shirks his duties."

Gifford's expression had grown deathly serious, his eyes wide.

"So you've had personal experiences, Mr Gifford?" urged Will.

His response was an emphatic nod. "We all have, Mr Peterson," he stated. "And then *these* started appearing on us one by one – we don't feel ourselves getting them, but then they're there, and we don't know where they've come from. Callum got the first – the poor boy feels terribly threatened, I have to say. I found this earlier today . . ." He pulled up his sleeve and held his left arm out into what little fading light there was, turning the underside toward Will first, and then towards Gabriel.

Will pulled his phone out of his pocket and immediately photographed what he saw on the soft flesh of Gifford's arm. Four long scratches, stretching almost to his elbow, red as though they were fresh.

"Does that hurt?" asked Will, concern growing in his voice. He had seen this before in photographic evidence but never in the flesh, literally.

Gifford shook his head and pulled down his sleeve hurriedly, as if he was ashamed. "We might feel a slight sting but that's all. No one knows where they come from, no one finds them until after they've appeared – on the ankles, the base of the back, the wrists, the arms like me."

Will looked at Gabriel, his face grave. "That looks demonic to me. Gabriel – what do you think?"

He was surprised to see that Gabriel's expression was unconvinced.

"Have you shown these to anyone outside the castle, Gifford?" Gabriel asked.

"Only to my father," replied the butler. "He's mostly bedridden – he's the reason I came back to Dubhglas, actually. He lived in the village all of his life, the local greengrocer – he delivered fruit and vegetables to the castle – he's known it well. When he got too sick to live alone I packed my bags and came back. I showed him the first of the scratches when they appeared and he said the strangest thing. 'That'll be a tiger,' he said, and he told me to get some cream on it before it went septic. I tried to get him to explain what he meant but he said 'Better not to talk about these things' and would say no more. He rambles, however, muddles the past with the present and so on . . ."

There was silence for a moment as Gifford looked from Gabriel to Will and back again.

"There's one more thing that you should probably know, Mr McKenzie. Something else that I've seen . . ." He paused nervously.

Gabriel stiffened again in his seat.

"Only it's something . . ." continued Gifford quietly, "something that none of the other staff have seen. And I haven't told any of them about it. But he was there, in the hallway. I saw him by the front door. Dripping wet, one shoe missing from his foot."

Gifford looked again at Gabriel, seeing if he understood.

Gabriel didn't for a moment, a chill suddenly piercing his heart that was far colder than this grim room smelling of age and peat fires when he did.

"It was your brother," said Gifford softly again, looking Gabriel right in the eye. "Out there, in the hallway. I saw a boy, a dripping wet boy with one shoe. I never saw him alive but somehow, I just . . . knew who it was. I saw your brother, Mr McKenzie. I saw Laurence."

CHAPTER 26

November 30th

Standing in the hallway, Martha eyed her reflection in the mirror over the hall table. She didn't look too bad, she thought, taking in the expensive full-length coat she wore over a knitted black dress. Her make-up was carefully applied over her pretty features and the copper highlights in her short bobbed hair caught the light and shone.

Smoothing down the coat, she tutted as she felt the tickle of a stray thread from her sleeve. She contemplated tugging at it but resisted the urge. With quick steps, she hurried into the living room and across to the pottery bowl on the mantel where she kept a small nail scissors, snipped the thread, and shook it from her finger into the open grate.

She looked up as she heard the car outside crunch over the gravel and gave herself a final once-over before the taxi-driver beeped his horn. She hurried out of the front door, locking it carefully behind her. Dan had texted her the address of the solicitors which was somewhere near Canonmills. It was near enough, she knew, but in an area with which she was unfamiliar. And it was stressful enough meeting Dan without the added hassle of finding the place, and she was notoriously unlucky with parking, so a cab it was.

Will's advice to play it safe rang in her ears as she stepped into the cab and called up the text message that Dan had sent with the address, showing it to the driver who knew immediately where he was going. Martha sat back in the cab and relaxed, taking in the fresh winter's day as she made the short trip.

She couldn't help but stare around her at the beauty of the grey, stone crescent of buildings as she stepped out of the car. She was in plenty of time, she knew, and was contemplating strolling a little further along the road to see what lay around the next corner when she spotted Dan, waving at her as he walked hurriedly out the front gate of one of the houses.

"Hallo!" he shouted in his friendliest way and Martha raised her hand in quiet acknowledgement. He was out of breath as he reached her on the pavement.

"Hi," he offered in his smoothest voice.

Martha recognised the voice. Herself and Sue had a name for all of his tones and personae. This one was called '*Reserved for lady clients*'. In a way it was vaguely flattering that he was using it on her. Toward the end of their marriage he had barely been able to bring himself to grunt a 'hello'.

"Hi," she managed back. "Have you been in already?" She nodded toward the building through whose gate which Dan had emerged.

"Yes, I have . . . wow, you look absolutely fantastic . . . if you don't mind me saying so . . ." Dan's voice trailed off as he looked appreciatively at his ex-wife.

And again, thought Martha. This time the Hugh-Grant charm-offensive manoeuvre. He's really pulling out all the stops.

"Thank you," she said brusquely. "So, shall we go in?"

Dan gestured with his hand to show he was gathering his thoughts. "Em . . . actually . . . are you okay for time? It's just that it seems we've got a wait on our hands." He stretched his lips in an 'isn't this awkward?' way and Martha sighed.

"Do you know how long?" she asked. "Only I absolutely have to pick up Ruby at five today. There's absolutely no one else that can do it – Will's gone to Dubhglas ahead of me – and I've mucked the childminder around enough already – she was supposed to have the day off today."

"No probs at all," stated Dan flatly, making a point of crossing his hands in a gesture that emphatically said 'No way!' "I've been chatting to the receptionist and she says that the most we'll be waiting is half an hour, forty-five minutes tops. Mr Neil – that's our guy – has got a couple in with him apparently . . ." He curled his nose up and nodded back at the building. "*Divorce,*" he whispered loudly.

Martha couldn't help but smile at the irony of it. "Lucky we were never like that then, eh?" she replied, surprising herself with the ease with which she referred to those horrible days. They hadn't communicated directly, of course. She did it all through her solicitor. Clean, quick and painless. Well, less painful than everything that had led to the divorce in the first instance.

Dan took his cue and smiled back at her, rolling his eyes exaggeratedly. "Something like that," he said and a moment's silence followed. "The receptionist said that there's a little greasy spoon round here somewhere where we could get some coffee . . . if you like?"

He pointed down the street behind Martha and she nodded, glancing at her watch and then falling into step beside him. It was a movement at once familiar and surreal to her – walking along beside a man she had sworn to love forever, as she had done so many times over the years they'd been together. She felt odd, as though she were outside her own body. She, of course, hadn't broken the promise to love him forever. She stole a glance sidelong and upward to take in his face and was struck again by just how familiar those features were. Still, she thought, it wasn't that hard to fall out of love with someone who has taken you for a complete and utter fool.

She stayed silent while they entered the cafe and took a seat in a booth near the window where she looked out at the quiet street while Dan went to the counter.

She caught a whiff of his familiar aftershave – Dolce and Gabbana Light Blue – as he deposited a mug each on the table. Once sitting, he rummaged in the pocket of his duffel coat and deposited sachets of sugar and stirrers on the table. Martha took one and shook it into her drink, stirring it carefully and looking back out the window as she took a sip. She felt edgy as she struggled to think of something to say, and then wondered why she should bother saying anything at all. Yet Dan was being so *nice*. She wasn't comfortable. She just wanted to get this over and done with. And more than that, she burned to figure out his agenda.

"Mr Neil should have some photographs to show us," began Dan, catching Martha mid-thought. She didn't understand what he meant for a second and looked at him blankly. "Photographs of what?" she said and then it dawned on her. "Oh, you mean of this land in Cornwall?"

Dan nodded. "Beautiful part of the world, Padstow. Have you been?"

Martha nodded. "Will's parents live in Cornwall. Near Mevagissey actually. I've been a few times."

Dan smiled. "Must be serious then. Meeting the in-laws."

Martha scowled at him, forcing him to change tack.

"Will's a really nice guy actually," he observed lightly. "So good of him to let me in like that the other night – a complete stranger at the door."

"What's the catch to this property?" Martha said suddenly, desperate to change the subject.

"Is it zoned for a big car park, or is there a new road going to run through it or something? Is it swamp? On the side of a hill? There must be a catch."

Dan shook his head and took another sip of his coffee. "No catch that I know of," he shrugged. "Little Ruby's going to strike it lucky when she turns eighteen, I'd imagine."

There was a pause for a few moments and they drank their coffee in silence. After a while, Dan made to speak, hesitated, and then tried again. He looked as if he was having difficult forming the words.

"Martha . . . what's she like?" he said. "Ruby? I'd love to know what she's like . . . I don't know a thing . . ."

Because you walked out on her to go live with your mistress, thought Martha sternly as she stared at him, surprised by the question and even more surprised by the genuine look of interest in his eyes. "I cocked up so much," he said quietly. "I don't deserve to know, but can you bear to tell me anything about her at all?"

It wasn't so much the humility he expressed as the sincerity with which he asked the question that made Martha start, slowly, to describe her precious little girl. "She's beautiful," she began hesitantly. "Well, you've seen that for yourself. She's good – really good, and very very clever – above average for her age . . ."

A broad smile spread over Dan's features, one that verged on pride. He looks like he actually means that, thought Martha, pausing for a moment to take another sip of her coffee.

"What does she like?" he asked eagerly. "Does she have a favourite toy, or a game or something?"

"Em, there's Hugo, her bear," began Martha and, as she continued, driven by the desire to somehow show him what he'd missed out on, she was encouraged by his responses. He smiled, he laughed, he made all the right noises. By the time that they realised they should get back to the solicitor's office she had begun to believe that he actually cared about what he was hearing. And what was more, she had begun to enjoy telling him.

Dan was right in his assumption that Mr Neil would have photographs. And that it was a beautiful part of the world – he knew it well as it happened and he was keen to chat at length with Martha, sharing knowledge of the area. In the end it was close to four o'clock when they emerged into the dark of the evening, another hard frost already beginning to sparkle on the ground and the sky filling with stars above the regal buildings around them. As they passed through reception on their way out, they noted an angry-looking couple in their mid-fifties seated on opposite sides of the waiting area, both drinking water from paper cups, the man accompanied by a bored-looking woman with make-up that had seen better hours and her red jacket crumpled above her black pencil skirt, a pile of papers and files perched on her lap. Dan and Martha heard the receptionist's side of the short exchange that took place as she answered an internal call.

As Dan held the front door open for Martha, they heard her say, "Mr Neil will see you again now." Dan caught Martha's eyes and widened his own, jokingly placing his hands to his neck and pretending to throttle himself.

Martha giggled quietly and dared to glance behind. "Mr Neil

must have felt the need of a break before embarking on their case again – they look like they're about to *murder* each other," she whispered.

Dan smiled in return. "There's a lot to be said for how we did it," he said and then winced as though wishing he could take it back. His cheeks burned red in the light from the doorway and Martha grinned again as they made their way down the path back out onto the street.

She stopped to rummage in her handbag as she felt it vibrate slightly and pulled out her phone which blinked on and off to indicate an incoming call.

"How goes the day?" Martha heard Sue say brightly on the other end of the line. She glanced at Dan, pointing to the phone to indicate that she needed to take it.

He nodded graciously and hung back to let her walk on a little way to speak in private.

"Whereabouts are you?" Martha asked, guessing that some sort of moving vehicle was the answer but with Sue, that could be anything from a limo to a tank.

"Surprise, surprise! Just about arriving at your house actually," came the reply. "My interviewee this afternoon cancelled in time for me to reschedule my flight up so I threw my spotted hanky over my shoulder and thought I'd go see my old mate, Martha. What about you, still with Brideshead?"

Martha glanced back and took another few steps further from Dan. "Affirmative," she said in a low voice. "We were delayed thanks to the War of the Roses – tell you later."

"How's it going?" quizzed Sue in an equally low voice.

"*Compliqué*," replied Martha. "Lots to fill you in on. All being on our best behaviour."

"Which character are we wearing?" asked Sue.

Martha could hear the smile in her voice. "*Four Weddings*," she replied, smiling herself.

"Really?" Sue's tone was shocked. "Better than *Sleeping with the Enemy*, I guess."

"Lots," laughed Martha aloud.

"Anyway, I've picked up some duty-free Limoncello for a

change, because I know that you want an early night. Anything else I can pick up on the way?"

Martha glanced at her watch again. "Rubes actually. Would you mind? I'm not sure how long it's going to take me to get a cab and I'm sure there will be traffic. You pass by the childminder's door on the way. She'll be able to lend you a car seat. You do remember her house?"

"Do I *ever* forget where I've been before?" Sue replied, indignant.

"You don't mind, do you?"

"Not at all. Myself and Ruby Doo could do with a little bonding time," Sue reassured her. "I've learned some new Polish swear words this week that I think might be of interest to her."

Martha ignored her. "And you know where the spare key is?"

"Sure do. Leave it with Auntie Sue. I'll have a curry menu and a nice glass of the finest yellow drink known to mankind waiting for you. It's one of your five a day, you know, lemons . . ."

Martha laughed. "I think I'll pass," she grinned. "Look, I'll see you in a bit – thanks a mill."

"*Salute*," came the faint response as Sue ended the call in her usual fashion, by growing bored and removing the phone from her ear before she said farewell.

Martha returned her own phone to her bag with a grin and turned to see where Dan had got to. He was standing only a few feet behind her.

"I didn't mean to eavesdrop," he said, "but I couldn't help but hear the last bit . . . am I right in thinking that there's someone else to pick Ruby up now?"

Martha nodded and eyed him suspiciously.

"Oh good. That's a nice surprise . . . I mean, you don't think that you'd be able to take a little more time out and, I dunno, grab a bite maybe?"

Martha looked alarmed, looked again at her watch, opened her mouth to decline the invitation but was interrupted.

"Only there's another couple of other things that I need to discuss with you and this might be a good time to do it. All that unpaid maintenance business – I'm really and truly sorry about that so I'd like to take the opportunity to buy you a meal and talk. What do you say?"

Martha hesitated. She felt unsettled. Just wanted to get home – to get away from him and his niceness. To get away from how easy she had found it to talk to him earlier, pouring her heart out about Ruby. Then again, Will had said to play the game by Dan's rules. Keep him close so he couldn't make any sudden moves. And now he had more to discuss with her, including the unpaid money? What now? Had he won the lottery? Bought out the company?

"Look, let me just text Sue and see if she's okay for a couple of hours without me," she said tentatively.

"Great!" replied Dan, enthusiastically. "We'll walk toward town, shall we? See what comes up along the way."

He held out his arm to indicate the direction that they should take and Martha fell into step, taking yet another look at his expression and feeling surprise that she could see nothing there but sincerity. She began to text as she walked. A couple of hours, max, she decided. They had a long drive ahead tomorrow so then home to bed.

Dinner with Dan. Something that she hadn't done in years. A plate of something, see what he had to say and get the maintenance discussion over with. Where was the harm in that?

CHAPTER 27

Dan and Martha stumbled upon the tapas bar almost by accident. It was called Gaudi's and its enticing red-painted woodwork and the soft glow of lamps from the window lured them in off the freezing street. A few dishes, Martha thought, and then home to Sue and Ruby. She was feeling tired and the cold was hard to kick.

"These Scottish winters are *harsh*," observed Dan emphatically, handing over his coat to a waiter. Martha nodded in agreement and reluctantly handed hers over too, opting to keep her scarf on for a while until she warmed up.

The waiter then led them to a table at the rear of the restaurant.

Dan slid along a banquette against the wall, under a shelf bearing a large ceramic dragon, and laced his hands together, blowing into the gap between his thumbs and forefingers to warm them.

Martha sat down on the leather straight-backed armchair which had been pulled out for her and shunted it in toward the table slightly, then took a moment to look around at her surroundings.

The restaurant was cosy and just a little mysterious, lit by small table lamps throughout, which glowed warm from under red and pink shades. Small fairy lights had been strung along the picture rail – a nod to the season that approached without a full commitment to all things festive. The walls were painted in warm colours and the artwork paid tribute to the architect after whom the restaurant was named – ceramic pieces, pen-and-ink sketches of his famous buildings. An inviting smell floated through the swinging kitchen doors.

Martha settled herself, accepted the menu that the waiter handed her and began to study it, raising her head to glance at Dan when she realised he hadn't yet even opened his own. She saw that he was turned awkwardly in the seat, lying partially across it, looking above him to take in their ceramic companion on the shelf above. He turned and smiled, pointing at the mosaic dragon, faithfully recreated from the original with its blue, yellow and ochre tiles.

"Remember this guy?" he said. "Parc Guell?"

Martha smiled. "I don't remember him as much as I remember how ill I was the day we went to see him," she replied and resumed studying the menu. She wasn't expecting the hearty guffaw that Dan gave in response.

"What was it you ate again?" he laughed.

She smiled, continuing to stare at the menu. "Prawns," she replied.

"Prawns! That's right." Dan laughed again and took another look at the ornament before finally opening his menu, chuckling. "Have you been back? Barcelona?"

Martha glanced at him to see what he was getting at, but he was running his finger down the list of tapas plates as he spoke.

"I have actually," she said. "We – eh – Will has, well, *had* a place there so we've been a couple of times."

"Nice," responded Dan. "Remember the first time though, eh? That Mayday weekend when you ate the prawns . . ."

"Okay, Dan, I get it, I ate the prawns," growled Martha but with a lightness to her tone. She found that couldn't stop herself smiling, however much against her will it was to remember times like that with Dan. It hadn't all been bad, she conceded to herself. At the beginning, when they were just starting out . . .

The thought came as a revelation to her. For the two years since she had discovered his deception she hadn't been able to think of him without bile rising in her throat, without thinking that if she ever saw him again that she'd kill him with her bare hands. And yet here she was, at a table in Edinburgh, having spent the last few hours together, and it was all strangely civilised and mature. It didn't feel *normal* by any means, but it wasn't so odd as to make her feel that she wanted to get up and run.

They were momentarily interrupted by the waiter who stood silently by the table awaiting their order.

"Oh, um, I'll have the –" began Martha.

Dan cut across her. Again.

"Let's have the cheese and meat selection," he began, running his finger again down the menu until he found the items he'd earmarked. "And a big old plate of *patatas fritas* . . . and some olives . . . you like olives still, don't you, Mar?"

He stopped himself suddenly, looking straight at her.

She thought she detected him blush yet again.

"Christ, I'm doing it again – I'm really sorry. What would you like?" he said apologetically.

Martha shook her head and sighed. "Not at all. That's fine actually. All of that will be great." It was exactly what she had chosen herself from the menu. That was something that used to often happen to them, she remembered – that they'd order exactly the same dishes.

Dan slammed his menu closed. "That'll be all, thanks," he said, handing the leather-bound folder back to the waiter. "Oh, and a bottle of house Cava as well, please."

"Not for me!" exclaimed Martha. "I have to get back – and I have a long drive in the morning."

The waiter hesitated.

Dan looked sheepish and stuck out his lower lip. "Just the one glass, eh?" he pleaded. "To celebrate what we've just signed. For Ruby?"

The waiter glared at her and Martha felt uncomfortable under the scrutiny of the two men. Reluctantly she nodded. "Just the one then," she said quietly and Dan beamed at the waiter who lifted her menu from the table where she'd laid it and without a word made his way back to the kitchen.

There was a silence between Martha and Dan for a few moments.

"You must know Barcelona quite well, then?" Dan asked.

Martha shrugged and looked around her. It was true, this wasn't as difficult as she thought it might be but she still found it tough to look her ex-husband in the eye.

"Not really," she said. "We tended really to stick to the gothic quarter, the port, the beach – the apartment was in the heart of the old town."

"Oh wow, not near that church, was it?" Dan clicked his fingers as he tried to remember. "What was the name of it?"

"Santa Maria del Mar," replied Martha quietly.

Dan jumped on the response. "Oh my word, what an amazing place that was – do you remember sitting in the square outside just as evening fell? Drinking rosé and just watching the world go by?"

Martha hated to admit it but she did remember. Vividly. She looked at the picture in her head, her younger self, in a white linen skirt and a dark-green cotton top. Her hair was darker then and longer, and she'd worn her shades, face turned upward toward the sun, with the promise of her whole life ahead of her. It was their engagement-celebration weekend Dan was referring to, she realised. She remembered the diamond solitaire ring, bought three weeks previously in Antwerp, sparkling on her finger. It was shoved in the very back of her underwear drawer now. They were genuinely in love then, she thought. A whole life ahead of them. It was hard, for a moment, to feel as harshly toward Dan as she normally did.

Dan, leaning across the table, roused her from her memory.

"I have a confession. I've sort of brought you here under false pretences," he said in a low voice, picking up the salt cellar and shaking it from side to side, watching the grains shift as he spoke.

Martha sat up, at once tense again. "What do you mean?"

"Oh God, nothing sinister," he replied reassuringly. "I only mean that I knew this place was here and I thought you'd really like it – we loved Barcelona so much. I've eaten here a couple of times actually since I've been in Edinburgh."

Martha was at once curious. "How long exactly have you been here?" she asked. "And don't you have to go back to work some time?"

"Work," repeated Dan, an odd smile crossing his face. He paused as the waiter arrived and undertook the ceremony of opening the Cava, allowing Dan to taste, pouring Martha's glass and then topping Dan's up before leaving the bottle in an ice bucket on the side of the table.

"To new beginnings!" toasted Dan.

Martha followed suit by clinking her glass against his, but she remained silent. She wasn't quite sure that she wanted to celebrate new beginnings with Dan just yet, if ever. They sipped from their glasses and Dan smacked his lips appreciatively before continuing.

"Where was I, oh yes – work. Yes. Well, that's what I wanted to talk to you about. There's a big new beginning taking place on that front actually, in that I've left A&M and I'm setting up on my own. That's how I have all this time to spend here in Edinburgh. Change is as good as a rest and all that."

Martha's eyes widened at the news. She couldn't quite believe what she was hearing. Dan had always worked at A&M, had fought his way up from being an assistant to being one of the best account directors that the advertising agency employed. He was ruthless and always hungry for new business. He was their golden boy, their biggest asset. She had been sure that he would have been in line for a directorship at some stage, maybe even MD? Yet here he was, going solo?

"Is it a good time to do that?" she asked tentatively. "With the recession?"

"I've got a few core clients who have agreed to come with me," he replied, taking a sip from his glass. "Tom Anderson won't be happy about it but that's how business works. It's enough for me to be getting on with it until I can build my client base."

"I thought you loved it there?"

Dan took another slug. "Oh I did. But there just came a time about six months ago that I thought . . . I just decided that I wanted something different. To claim my own space, you know? Not be Dan Smith from A&M any more but be Dan Smith from Dan Smith Advertising. Maybe that sounds silly?"

Martha shook her head. "Not at all," she replied. "When I had my book published I felt exactly the same way."

"God, yes, I'd forgotten about your book," replied Dan, draining his glass and reaching for the bottle, topping both glasses up, even though Martha had barely taken a sip. "Congratulations. You achieved your dream, didn't you?"

Martha nodded again and drank automatically from the glass.

She didn't know why it upset her, why she felt emotional to hear him say that. When they were married he hadn't paid any attention to her dream. It didn't rate on his scale of achievement. And yet here he was . . . first Narnia and now this. Maybe he had known her a little better than she thought, she realised. Maybe her memories of him – her feelings about him – were coloured slightly with two years of accumulated bitterness. Could it be that Dan Smith wasn't actually such an awful guy? She'd only gone and married him once, for heaven's sake! Could her judgement have been *so* wrong?

"And Paula and I have split up," he added suddenly.

Martha choked sharply on the fizzy liquid and fought back a full-on coughing fit. She reddened. That was the news she had waited those full two years to hear, what she'd hoped he wanted to tell her in The Scotsman. And now here it was. Her eyes widened as she took it in. She had thought, with the passage of time, with settling down with Will, that the news wouldn't have such a huge impact on her. But it did, she realised. The longing to hear those words was so ingrained in her that on hearing them, her subconscious jumped to attention. *There*, it said. *There you go. It's over. She doesn't want him. Or he doesn't want her. You can have him back.*

She flinched at her own thoughts. She didn't want him back. He was the last person that she wanted back in her life. She took a large swig from her glass to focus herself on something.

"I'm sorry to hear that," she managed and was greeted with another of Dan's grins. This time she looked at it, full on. That hundred-watt smile, she remembered. The foppish look, the single lock of hair that hung down his forehead like a matinee idol. Her heart gave a little start, out of habit she decided, some long-forgotten bodily function, some muscle-memory triggered in her body without her permission.

"You don't mean that," he said, smiling softly and stood. "Just nipping to wash my hands." He slid out from behind the table, leaving Martha to greet the waiter who was just arriving with their food.

Martha took the opportunity to check her phone, to text Sue to let her know that she had monumental gossip, changing the words to 'big news' before she sent it. It seemed almost disrespectful to label this as tittle-tattle when somehow it felt bigger, more important than that. Sue texted back almost immediately to let her know that she was fine to hold the fort, and that Ruby was smoking crack cocaine. Martha smiled. A smile that turned sour as she checked through her other messages and saw that there was nothing from Will. She'd asked him to let her know when they arrived in Dubhglas and they must have been there for hours now, however much they might have been delayed on the road. Couldn't he just text her and let her know that they'd arrived safely?

She was disturbed by Dan's return to the table and returned the phone politely to her handbag. They began to eat in silence.

By the time that Martha pushed her plate away, feeling ready to burst at the seams, she had fully warmed up and was feeling exceptionally relaxed. The Cava was sweet and the meats and cheeses had been particularly good.

"That's the trouble with tapas," she observed as Dan spooned himself another plate-load of *patatas fritas*. "I always think that they're never going to fill me and then I completely overindulge. I'm stuffed." She rubbed a hand across her stomach and Dan raised his glass again in a toast. Martha sipped at her drink, toying with an olive on her plate, rolling it around with a knife.

"What would you say to some copywriting work?" Dan said suddenly.

Martha stopped what she was doing and looked at him full on. "You mean advertising copy?" she asked.

Dan nodded and reached for a piece of bread with which to swipe the sauce from his plate.

"You're an award-winner, and now a successful children's author – just the calibre of person I need. You're the best at your game. It would be a real help to have you on board."

Martha trailed her finger through the condensation on her glass. "I don't know, Dan," she said. "I hated the advertising game." She'd never dared admit that to him before, she realised. He loved it, so therefore she had to love it too. But he was right. Whatever about how much she liked or disliked the industry, she was bloody good at coming up with the goods.

"I totally respect that," said Dan.

Martha knew she should have felt shocked at that but right now she felt too mellow, too relaxed to let it get to her. Dan respecting her. Whaddya know, she said to herself. Didn't see that one coming.

"So we'd do it on your terms – you could work part-time, freelance – whatever suits you. Obviously you're going to be here and my office would be in London. Unless, of course, you thought it might be a good idea for me to set up here in Edinburgh?" He offered the statement teasingly almost, popping the last of the bread in his mouth and pushing his own plate away, leaning back against the banquette for more comfort.

Martha widened her eyes again. She was relaxed in her own seat, feeling terribly comfortable and the way that the bubbles shot to the surface of her glass and exploded there looked too beautiful for her to look away. She noticed Dan's gesture for the waiter to bring a second bottle but couldn't bestir herself to object.

"I've no ties to London any more," he continued. "In fact, I've now got more ties up here than down there."

This time Martha looked, out of habit. To assess his expression, see the sneer that she felt sure must be there. It wasn't. He was looking at her almost from under his eyelashes, sussing her out, genuinely awaiting her response. She straightened in her chair.

"Ruby," he explained. "And you."

The statement fell between them on the table. *You don't have me*, she knew she should say, but she didn't. She let it hang. There was a certain merit to the idea after all. If he was going to be more of a dad to Ruby, for example, then his being based here would mean that there wouldn't be that horrible separation of sending her to London to see him if it came to that . . . with the added fear that she might like it there . . .

And Martha had to admit to herself that there was a part of her that was enjoying this. It was a revelation – revisiting the past, being reminded that their years together hadn't been a total waste. She'd been so angry after they'd separated. Over time, she knew that the anger was mostly aimed at herself, for allowing herself to love him so much, to give herself up for him. And now, hearing that he had some shred of respect for her dreams and concerns? Finding that it could be easy again. It could work, she found herself thinking.

"Trial run," she heard herself say. "I call the shots. I write, and write only. I don't deal with the clients. I sit in an ivory tower, or – better still – my *house* – and produce the goods and you pay me and that's that, okay? I am *untouchable*!" She giggled.

Dan laughed too. "You've got it," he replied. "That's great to hear, Martha. Thank you. Such a relief that I've got the best on my side again."

The statement was loaded. They looked straight at each other as Dan topped their glasses and handed Martha's hers.

"A toast," he said. "To the newest – to the *second* member of Team Smith. Gawd bless 'er and all who sail in 'er!"

Again, Martha didn't repeat the words but she clinked her glass enthusiastically and smiled sincerely across the table.

"You don't think Will would mind, do you?" asked Dan, sinking back into his seat and crossing his legs, making himself more comfortable.

Martha shook her head. "Don't see why he would," she replied. She was aware of a very slight slur in her voice all of a sudden and made a mental note to order a strong coffee. "It's all money, isn't it? Which reminds me, where's Ruby's maintenance money gone? Is that your start-up capital? Are you taking food from your daughter's mouth to rent a glitzy office? Did you use it to buy one of those 'zecutive toys, you know the ones with the dangly balls?"

They both burst out laughing. At least he's tipsy too, thought Martha, proud of herself for having brought up the subject in such a diplomatic way.

"It's a fair cop!" laughed Dan, holding his hands up. "I'm really sorry about that – no, I mean it! I'm going to get the whole lot to you when I free up some assets. It's a bit complicated, and I'm awfully embarrassed about it. Things haven't been – easy of late."

His face grew sombre and Martha felt sorry for him. No matter what sort of a bitch Paula was, it wasn't easy breaking up a long-term relationship. Of all people she knew that. He wouldn't be the first to get up and run away somewhere. She shuddered for a moment as her thoughts strayed to when she ran herself.

"I get that," she said, veering back onto the conversational track. "Look, sort it when you can, okay? When Dan Smith Advertising goes absolutely global . . . hey, couldn't you come up with a better name than that, actually?"

Dan smiled again. "I kind of hoped that you'd do that for me," he replied.

Martha waved a hand in the air. "On my to-do list," she said flippantly and took a large gulp from her water glass. She was feeling awfully hot.

There was a long silence between them, a silence that Martha noticed after a while had gone on too long. There were implications to it now. It had a *significance* of some sort.

Dan broke it. "Are you happy, Martha?" he asked out of the blue, looking straight at her.

She felt her initial discomfort return and she looked away – down at the remains of their meal, at the crumpled napkin on his plate.

"Because I'm not," he continued and leaned over the table towards her.

She didn't flinch as his hand covered hers where it rested on the table. It was just a gesture, she thought, glancing momentarily at where his wedding ring used to be.

"I cocked things up so royally," he said, almost in a whisper.

She forced herself to meet his gaze.

"I had you, and a lovely home and a beautiful baby and I threw it all away. I'm so *sorry*. And the horrible thing is that if I had it all again I'd probably do the same – screw it up in some fool way and then I'd lose you both forever. I'm not good enough for you, Martha. Never was, never will be. But at least let us build *something* together, eh? Give me a second chance . . . with Ruby, with the company . . ."

His voice trailed away but Martha continued to hold his gaze for a few seconds too long. She whipped her hand away suddenly. "I think we'd better go," she managed, the words slurring together slightly.

He withdrew his own hand from the table quickly and coughed. "You're right," he said. "Let me get the bill."

He paid in cash, quickly, and it only took a few awkward

minutes for Martha to find herself standing outside again in the bitter cold, her breath coming in clouds, tinged yellow under the streetlights. They stood, facing each other. A little too close, thought Martha, but then again she didn't want to step backwards because she wasn't sure of her balance. And a cab would surely come any second. To take her away, let her think all of this through. All these old emotions that were surfacing. Dan seemed so sincere, so *different*.

"I'm sorry if I embarrassed you," she heard him say softly. He took yet another step toward her. "But I'm not sorry for what I said. I'm going to come straight out with this, Martha, and say that against my better judgement, against knowing what's good for both of us, I'm throwing my hat back into the ring. Do you understand me? I'm going to fight for you. Because seeing you here, seeing how you are, how comfortable in your own skin, how beautiful . . . I realise just what an idiot I've been, what a bloody fool."

Martha stayed still as she felt his hand skim her cheek. The same gesture that Will had made across the table in their home a few nights previously. Will. Still no communication from him. All the way up in Dubhglas and he couldn't be bothered letting her know he was okay. Up there chasing ghosts, like he always did . . .

Dan was kissing her before she knew it. It felt so strange, yet so familiar at the same time. His lips were full and warm against the chill of the evening and she was conscious of his breath, his scent – all of those things that she had once loved, once taken for granted, old and new simultaneously. She had longed for this moment, she knew. She'd never admit to anyone, not even Sue, but this, for so long, had been her dream. There was something perfect about it – so *right* – in the crisp, clean frost of the evening on the quiet street. Just the two of them. Like before. *New beginnings, right?* Instinctively, Martha felt her hands reach up and slide across Dan's shoulder-blades, across the breadth of his back, and in response she felt his hand clasp around her neck, just below her ear, the gentlest of touches. And suddenly she couldn't stop herself as she kissed him back.

CHAPTER 28

Will and Gabriel had almost to physically restrain Gifford from serving them a formal meal in the dining room that evening. He was full of apologies for the fact that the housekeeper was unavoidably away and had prepared their food in advance. The house was unusually quiet, he'd explained, as apart from Callum there was never a need for staff these days if Mr Calvert wasn't on the premises.

Will was keen to get started and he finally persuaded the butler to serve them their evening meal in the staff canteen in order to have a proper look around the room where the gardener had seen the mysterious mists. Once the meal was finished, he then insisted that Gifford finish for the evening, making sure that any other staff were gone as well. There was much work to be done.

It was pitch dark when they found themselves at the beginning of the investigation, in the same two chairs in the library as earlier, when the white-faced Gifford had told them of the sighting that he believed to be Laurence. Since then, Gabriel had been more or less silent. He had helped to unpack the equipment and set it up, but without a trace of his usual banter. Will knew something was wrong when Gabriel dropped a small camera on his foot and didn't even whine.

They sat in the silent darkness of the library, the all-consuming blackness of the house at night cloaking them. Gifford had shown them around the castle – they had both been glad to leave the stuffy, grim atmosphere of the library earlier. But now, sitting there again, Will felt it close in around him and took deep breaths to steady himself.

Gifford had taken them to what he called the 'hot spots' and Will had taken note, later setting cameras to record, linked to the bank of computers that he had placed on a trestle table in the hall. Motion-sensors were set on the stairs and toward the rear of the library, trigger-objects had been left on the kitchen table downstairs where Will had also reverted to old-fashioned methods, shaking flour along the kitchen floor to try to catch footprints. It was archaic, he knew, but it had worked for him once before and he thought that if there were anywhere that a floury footprint might happen, the old, barely used room would be it.

Upstairs, on the mezzanine, yet another camera was trained on the door of a bedroom near the top of the stairs where Gifford said that the strange mists were seen most frequently. Will had his own theory about mists but he hadn't wanted Gifford for a second to believe that he doubted a single thing that he had said. Too frequently, these mists were caused by grubby spectacles, or cigarette smoke, or steam from a bathroom door left open after a shower. There was much else of what Gifford had said, however, that he couldn't instantly debunk. Like the scratches, for instance. All that would take a little more work.

Will shifted in his chair and glanced behind him for the reassuring red dot that indicated the DV camera attached to the wall near the window was working and, assured that it was, he glanced at the second camera he'd set up, trained on the fireplace. He ran his thumb along the small voice recorder which he held loosely and then looked for Gabriel, just about visible in the glow from the small screen of the thermal imager which he held. Gabriel sat completely still, staring at the apparatus. Will was filled with concern for his friend.

"Why don't you take the voice recorder and give me the thermal?" he whispered. It somehow felt wrong to speak out loud in the thick silence of the building. For a second he was aware that, even though he had thought the castle small, there were still many rooms around and above and below him that were empty. Or at the very least should have been.

Gabriel didn't respond. Will only knew that he had agreed to the swop when he felt the thermal imager thrust in his face. They fumbled in the dark for a few moments and, once the exchange had taken place, Will sat back a little in the chair and allowed the silence to settle around them again.

Gabriel sighed loudly and Will grinned in the dark.

"You all right?" he asked, softly.

Silence again, followed by the creak of Gabriel settling in his chair.

"I'm not sure," came the whispered reply. "I mean, Laurence? Here? *Haunting* the place?" Gabriel's voice rose a little above a whisper as a tone of desperation entered his voice.

The thought inspired Will to scan the room with the imager to detect any figures, any change in heat signatures, any indication of an apparently empty seat being occupied by something unseen. He saw nothing out of the ordinary, but he knew that didn't mean it would stay that way.

Gabriel was silent for a moment before continuing. "Has he retired from being a spirit guide and gone into the haunting business? He could have bloody *told* me first!"

He ended the sentence on a high note and Will suppressed a laugh, trying to stay focused on the task at hand. He knew he should be shushing Gabriel so that they might catch an unseen voice on the recorder or hear even the slightest movement in the room but he knew that would be like trying to get water to flow backwards. Best to allow him to let off steam, he decided.

Gabriel's tone grew serious again. "Actually I find it a bit upsetting to think of him like that. Presenting as he was when he drowned . . ."

"We don't know for sure it was Laurence," said Will. "We don't even know for sure that Gifford actually saw anything. There are any number of reasons for hallucination –"

"Hallucination my eyeballs!" hissed Gabriel. "Did you see the man's face? That was no hallucination. He saw it all right. And as for the smells and the noises and the mists – what the hell do you reckon is going on?"

"Steady, Gabriel," warned Will. "We have to remain sceptical about everything. For example, some wires might have shorted about the place, causing a smell of burning and some smoke . . ."

Gabriel snorted.

Will could tell by the sound that his logical explanations were being rejected. They needed a break, he thought. The darkness was beginning to get to them. A coffee and they'd be fresh to move on to another location perhaps . . .

Will jumped as Gabriel's voice suddenly boomed out in the darkness: "If there's someone here – anyone – Laurence? – if you're here, then I'd like you to show yourself to me. Do you hear?"

Will tutted. "Gabriel, there's no point in trying to provoke a reaction. The mood you're in, you're just going to talk over anything we might catch."

Gabriel laughed. "Going by Gifford's tale, the main things we'll be catching are objects hurtling through the air –" He stopped speaking suddenly and the two men held their breath.

"What?" whispered Will, his senses alive. He scanned the room quickly again. There was nothing. No sound, no images. He sensed Gabriel relax.

"Sorry," he said. "I thought I heard something. I'm not used to being a normal bystander in one of these things. Usually, I have my brother here giving me directions but seeing as he's decided to start *wearing a sheet and clanking chains*!" He raised the volume of his voice toward the end of the sentence.

"Easy," whispered Will.

There was silence for a few more moments, broken eventually by Gabriel again. "Martha's not going to like this one bit, I can tell you," he stated with a sniff.

Will uncrossed and crossed his legs where they were growing stiff in his chair.

"It'll be different tomorrow night," he suggested. "Black tie party, lots of people around. Probably some electricity in use . . ."

Gabriel snorted. "You go ahead and think on that, mister," he laughed. "Martha's not fooled by lights, cameras and action. She's what you might call intuitive. Probably more intuitive than I am at the minute in fact. I'm keeping an eye on her."

"I tried calling her earlier but there's no bloody coverage in this place. Looking forward to her getting here, actually," said Will, sounding strangely embarrassed.

No sooner were the words out than Gabriel jumped on them.

"Looking forward to getting her away from Desperate Dan, more like!" he barked.

Will blinked as Gabriel suddenly flicked on the small torch he carried with him. Gabriel's face was illuminated suddenly, looking at once frightening and indignant as Will's eyes adjusted. "Turn the light off," he ordered, weakly. Gabriel still had some steam to let off, it seemed. Will sighed, glanced at his watch in the faint glow of the torch and settled a little, waiting for the onslaught.

"Oh Will," Gabriel scoffed, "why don't you just put a big coloured spot on her and Ruby's backs and then Desperate Dan will know they're your property and leave you alone?"

Will rolled his eyes. "Helpful," he said.

"Look, if Martha's to be believed – and I think somehow she is – she doesn't want him round any more than you do. She *was* married to him so I think she knows best what his marks out of ten for being a total bastard are, am I right?

"I don't know," Will said. "She has a history with this guy and now he's started showing an interest in Ruby – and that's all Martha ever wanted – for the three of them to be a proper family and now here he is offering that on a plate. And he's one of those bloody handsome types as well."

"Oh William, is he an absolute *dish?*" said Gabriel sarcastically. "'Cos –"

"All right, all right – I get it!" hissed Will. "Can we get on with the investigation? We have a lot of ground to cover. It's still not nice having Dan round, okay? And things between me and Martha . . . need a little polishing."

"I know," said Gabriel, jumping in quickly. "I've stayed with you guys at the Bickerage, remember?"

Will glanced at the medium. "The *what?*" he asked.

Gabriel carried on regardless. "It's a bit *Wuthering Heights* round at yours in fact – lots of storming off and brooding and silences and whatnot."

"Well, I've been busy," blustered Will.

Gabriel nodded. "I know, Will. Busy will keep you warm at night when Martha's snuggled up with Dapper Dan, the Handsome Man. Why not be in a chilly castle somewhere while Daddy Dan, the Fathering Man, is being all fathersome a hundred miles away from you . . . Am I painting a picture?"

"I *get* it," snarled Will. "And before you paint anything else, Van Gogh, have a look at this."

Will rummaged in the pocket of his coat, worn to stay as warm as he could. He had asked Gifford to ensure that the central heating was off, to prevent any unnatural heat signatures interfering with their results. He found what he was looking for and thrust it toward Gabriel who shone the torch firstly directly in his face, and then lowered it.

"What am I fumbling for in the dark here . . . *ooooh*!" Gabriel gasped as he opened the small red-leather box marked with the antique shop's address and logo, and held his torch over it to fully inspect the diamond ring within, nestled in the red velvet.

The central oval diamond was surrounded by half-moon sapphires, themselves surrounded by a ring of tiny brilliant cut diamonds, all set on a gleaming platinum band.

Will looked fondly at the piece of jewellery as it gave a light sparkle in the torchlight. "Edwardian. Do you think Martha will like it?" he asked nervously. "Only I've been chatting with Sue behind her back . . .".

Gabriel's eyes and torch shot up from the ring to Will's face, his expression aghast.

". . . and went for completely the opposite of what she suggested," Will continued. "Sue went on the net and found this site where the rings are titanium, set with unpolished pebbles – they're meant to symbolise that our love is a rock, apparently."

Gabriel grimaced. "So this is it, then? The big proposal?"

Will nodded and Gabriel fell silent, taking the ring from the box and placing it on his little finger where it went no further than the top of the nail.

"What?" said Will suddenly. "It's all right, isn't it? The ring, I mean?"

Gabriel raised his eyebrows. "Of course it is, from a diamond and sapphire point of view . . ."

"But . . . ?" replied Will, growing panicky.

"You're sure it's not a kneejerk to the reappearance of The Amazing Dan? Are we a little insecure, darling?" He reached over to try to rub Will's cheek with his huge hand.

Will smacked it away. "I hardly managed to get that picked, sized and delivered in two days, now did I?" he snapped. "No, I've been planning this for a while but I wasn't sure when was the right time. When all this cropped up, I thought it might be nice to propose in the Highlands." He was glad of the darkness to hide the fact that he was blushing.

Gabriel shone the torch on his own face, as if putting himself in a spotlight. "Take your time, Will," he said in a deep, warning voice. "Do this right – make it something she'll remember because you're doing it from the heart – not because you're reacting to her ex-husband turning up on the scene. Do you understand?"

Will smiled. "Are you saying you think it's good then?" he asked.

Gabriel folded his arms and grunted. "I shall want to wear something smart for the wedding," he said, snapping the torch off as suddenly as he'd snapped it on. "None of this hired top hat and tails nonsense. Proper tailoring. Designer. Now do we need a change of scene maybe?"

Will smiled and stood up. "I think so. You've completely ruined the atmosphere in here anyway." He stretched, and heard Gabriel rise also. "Let's go out to the hallway maybe and do a little EVP work? A lot seems to have happened out there –" Will stopped suddenly, remembering too late that the hallway was where Gifford had said he'd seen Laurence's ghost. "Are you all right with that?"

He felt Gabriel thrust the ring box back at him in the dark and took it carefully, shoving it deep into his pocket again. Gabriel's torch was reactivated, this time used to light their way from the room. They moved slowly as they negotiated their way around the furniture.

"How do you think all of this is actually connected?" Gabriel suddenly asked.

Will stopped, confused.

Gabriel stopped too, and turned to him. "Only I was hoping beyond hope that all of this would help me to figure out what's going on in my flat in Edinburgh. But now I'm more confused than ever. It seems like out of the three major players in what happened back in '63 only two of them are on set and of those two one's on location. So is Laurence haunting here to get at Pine or something? Only Pine's off in Edinburgh on his jollies, leaving me love letters. And where does that Ball character fit into things?"

He stopped short suddenly. Both men turned their heads toward the door of the library and began to move at the same time. They'd both heard it. Cutting faintly through the silence outside – they'd almost missed it by talking but the two of them had definitely heard it. There it went again. The jingle of a small bell.

Gabriel reached the door first, flinging it open and stepping heavily out on to the tiled floor of the dark hallway.

Will was right behind him. "*Turn off your torch!*" he hissed as he made it out into the hall behind him, the atmosphere different out there, less cloying and stuffy than the library but still smelling musty and now damp. And freezing, freezing cold.

The two men stepped hurriedly out to the centre of the hallway and listened again, standing beside the polished round table with its artificial flowers, scanning the room in opposite directions.

Will's breath quickened with excitement and the familiar frisson of fear he experienced when something like this happened. He held the heat detector in his hand at arm's length and began to slowly scan the space.

"*Turn on the recorder,*" he hissed at Gabriel.

"*Done,*" came the response.

The months of estrangement hadn't rendered their familiar patterns rusty. It was almost instinctive now, every move practised over time.

There was nothing for a few moments. Just their breath in the darkness. Will ran the thermal imager around the space, starting from the library door, around to the front door and past the windows which registered completely black with cold, and then across the wall which flickered between green and blue. Up the stairs then. Nothing.

When he finally saw the red image on the screen he felt a bolt of shock hit him like electricity. The heat source that finally registered on the screen was that of a man. Will's eyes shot from the screen up along the mezzanine and to the wall just beside the first door at the top of the stairs. Of course he could see nothing for a second, his vision requiring adjustment.

"Who's there?" he shouted upwards. Then he muttered to Gabriel, "Up there – the first door – there's a man standing there." It had to be Gifford, come back to see what was going on, or Calvert – maybe he'd come back earlier than expected and had got in when they were in the library – or Callum – he'd been very curious about their equipment indeed when he'd helped to load and unload it on its trip from the car park in the golf buggy.

He glanced down again at the screen and was stunned to see the shape still there, still distinctly human. Another bolt of fear suddenly shot through him and he felt himself go involuntarily warm against the severe cold of the space. At that moment, Gabriel, too, made out the black shape leaning against the wall of the upstairs area with his naked eye. His heart, too, gave a jolt. He wasn't used to this. To being frightened of what he could see. He could communicate with these souls, he thought to himself, frustrated. He should be able to make out his features, feel his thoughts or some of his emotions – but all he could perceive was a shadow. The unmistakeable shadow of a large man, leaning against the wall. And it wasn't moving, wasn't going anywhere. It looked, for all the world, like it was watching *them*.

For a moment, there was a standoff – Will, glued to the small screen in his hand, trying to see would the figure turn out to be something else . . . a suit of armour perhaps . . . but there wasn't one up there. He'd been up and down while they set up – there was definitely no armour, no wax figure on the mezzanine. Nor would they register as a heat source, he berated himself.

Gabriel, meanwhile, was unable to tear his eyes away from the figure. This . . . this shape . . . it seemed blacker than the blackness itself. Completely immobile. Steady as a rock. *Challenging them.*

When it moved – when it seemed to peel itself off the wall where it leaned, both men felt as though they had been hit by lightning. Will's head shot up toward the vision as the figure turned on the screen before him. He wanted desperately to see it for real. Gabriel took a step backwards, startled by the sudden movement. He had just been growing used to the idea of a still figure – but then it *moved*. And so did they.

Will ran first, his legs operating independently of his mind. He made for the stairs, fumbled briefly for the bottom step, tripped and brought his foot down heavily with a bang on the first wooden tread. The noise seemed to mobilise Gabriel suddenly and he bolted after him, the two of them beginning an unsteady yet rapid ascent with Will one step ahead. He tried to focus on the figure but kept having to look at the stairs to try to make out the shape of the next step, to stay alert for the first turn. He then realised that Gabriel was now further behind him, stopped dead in his tracks.

"Will . . ." he said.

Will realised from his tone that Gabriel wanted him to look again at where their quarry stood.

And stood it did. The shape was perfectly still, poised at the opening of the passageway which led off the mezzanine down to four or five small guest rooms, where Gabriel and Will themselves were to sleep.

Will drew himself to a sudden halt and stared in its direction. It was unflinching. *Fearless*, he thought to himself. And there was something about the figure's stance to suggest a challenge, as if it wanted them to follow. After a few moments they did, Will suddenly gripped with a fierce rush of adrenalin as he took the rest of the stairs two by two, the surge of energy through his system making him sure-footed.

And still it stood there, waiting, waiting . . . until Will reached the top step and then with a speed that exceeded anything natural it disappeared in a blur around the corner and down the passage. Will made it just in time to see it vanish. To see it melt through the wall into one of the rooms along the passage. In the darkness, Will felt sure it was Gabriel's.

Gabriel was behind him in an instant. "Where did it go?" he gasped, his breath coming short.

"There," Will panted in response, pointing down the corridor. "Torch," he commanded, and Gabriel complied.

They peered down the passage where they had seen the shape disappear. The walls were painted the same green as downstairs, the doors made of sanded and varnished wood, the floor the same, but with a single strip of green-patterned carpet running down its centre. But there was no shape, no figure, no person to be seen. Vanished, impossibly, through a wall into a room.

Gabriel stared down the passage. He felt a slump hit him as it flashed across his mind again what he'd seen. The shape moving. Like a person, observing them. Taking it all in. *An intelligent haunt*, he thought to himself. He knew Will would sit down and start to go through his endless 'what ifs' to try to disprove it. But Gabriel knew what he had seen. That great, hulking, dark shape poised above them as they looked right back at it. He glanced behind him suddenly at the camera which had been affixed to the top of the bannisters. He'd put it there himself earlier – they could prove it, he could see it again, see if what he thought was true . . .

But as he shone the torch on the balustrade his heart sank again. Not only was there no red light, but the camera was lopsided, hanging to one side, barely held in place by the gaffer tape he had wound so assiduously around the wood and the camera to make sure that it stayed in place. And worst of all, it was facing completely the wrong way. They must have knocked it off in their ascent, he thought to himself, although he couldn't recollect either of them registering the bump or hearing the probable ripping noise of the tape as it dislodged itself.

Then again, maybe we didn't do it, he realised. Maybe someone else had. Something else. Someone who didn't want to get caught, but still wanted his presence felt. A big presence. A strong presence.

Gabriel inhaled deeply as Will turned to look at him and both of them wordlessly acknowledged what they had seen. They'd have to go after it, of course. Just take a breather for a moment and then go in pursuit of it down the icy pitch-black passages of Dubhglas Castle in the dead of night.

CHAPTER 29

Will woke with a start. His mind reeled at a thousand thoughts a second – he didn't remember going to sleep, didn't even know where he was for a moment. He knew that the sleep had been deep but he had no idea how long he had been out for.

After a few moments his mind began to slow down, to pace itself slightly. He recognised at first the faint smell of damp in the room, the hint of mildew, and then registered the cold. That all-consuming chill. He exhaled – knew that if he could see it there would be a cloud. Slowly, he sat up. The bedroom he had been allocated in Dubhglas Castle, he remembered.

He'd hated it on sight – aesthetically it was grim enough but it also had that feeling about it – something unwelcoming about the walls themselves, as if the room wanted to be left alone for once and for all.

Will wondered what time it was and pushed himself upright, reaching out to the bedside table where he had left his watch when he had climbed onto the bed to just gather his thoughts for a moment. Gabriel had nodded off on him first, he recalled.

Afte the sighting, they had followed the shape into Gabriel's room, and set themselves up there to keep a vigil, propped themselves up against the pillows on his bed to see if anything else might happen. Will had kept scanning the room with the handheld camera as they waited in the silence until he heard Gabriel's heavy, regular breathing and felt the slight thud on the covers where the thermal imaging camera had dropped from his hand. He should have woken him straight away, Will knew, should have kept going but he'd retreated to his own room which was next door instead for fresh batteries and a moment to gather his thoughts. He hadn't intended to sleep – they had other rooms to visit, EVP sessions to conduct – tonight was their only chance to be completely alone in the castle.

Except they weren't, were they? And for the first time ever, Will had to acknowledge that he just couldn't face it. Couldn't face leaving the room again, as creepy as it was. Couldn't face setting foot out there into the warren of freezing passageways, the maze of corridors leading to room after room scattered higgledy-piggledy throughout the gothic structure. He was normally fearless. He had no issue with dark corners or basements or churches or great halls or tunnels – or anywhere that spirits might lurk. His taste for the paranormal, for trying to prove his theory that yes, there was some sort of existence after death, to chase down his prey, as it were, had served only to embolden him over the years. But this place . . . with its freezing pistachio-coloured walls and air of gloom . . . This had crept into him. Had entered his subconscious, had made him feel the urge, since the second he'd walked in the front door, to constantly glance behind him. For once, Will Peterson had to admit that he was too scared to carry on with the investigation.

His watch showed 5 a.m. He glanced at his mobile on the bedside table beside it, still devoid of coverage bars and he groaned as he realised he had completely forgotten to try to text Martha again, completely distracted as he was with setting up the equipment and the investigation itself. Not that she'd be best pleased anyway if he texted her at that time of the morning, but he felt a pang, missing her, wanting to hear the familiar comfort of her voice. Instead, he decided to get an hour's sleep – he had to be up again shortly regardless – he could call her from Gifford's office later, perhaps, although he'd see her in a few hours in any case. In the meantime, the equipment had to be dismantled and packed away. Get it done before dawn, before the staff returned.

Will glanced around the room. He had left the main ceiling light switched on, along with three sets of dim wall lights and had also pulled back the curtains and opened the shutters when he'd entered earlier. He couldn't bear them closed – he felt claustrophobic with them shut. *Buried*, he thought grimly, and then banished the thought.

He studied the windows for a moment, the clear panes, the glass warped in their old wooden frames which looked as though they would crumble and surrender under the lightest touch. His gaze strayed around the rest of the room – the rusted metal filing cabinet that stood to one side of the window, the oriental screen beside it, the hideous portrait of a nun that hung over the fireplace. It felt like sleeping in an old furniture storeroom, he thought, his eyes darting again and again around him. He fought against the anxiety that gnawed at him. He acknowledged that piece by piece there was nothing sinister about any of the odd furnishings individually but, even without the chilling events he had witnessed that night, their effect as a whole, when combined with the smell of damp, the dreary décor and poor lighting, did nothing to create an atmosphere that he might want to sleep in, to surrender himself in.

Neither did the sudden sound. The hollow, echoing boom like a kettle drum. *Or like someone kicking a filing cabinet,* he figured later. He was upright in an instant, scanning the room again, still able to see everything around him. For a moment. The boom was followed by a 'pop' above him – and then a second – and he found himself gradually plunged into darkness as the light-bulbs in the wall lights, with their dim glass shades, blew – all three of them, one after the other, followed by the main light in the centre of the ceiling.

Will looked around him quickly, breathing deeply, to quell the panic rising in his chest. His eyes adjusted and he began to make out shapes in the dim light afforded to him by the windows. It was barely anything, but he was glad of it. He had no torch – he'd left it with Gabriel. He made a face of frustration as he felt the fabric of his pocket yield beneath his hand where the flashlight should have been.

The noise rang in his ears as he scanned the room again, picking out the shapes, re-establishing what was familiar. His heart raced as he focused on the picture over the fire, the shape of a large wooden chair to the left of the hearth, the small armoire to the right . . . and just out of the corner of his eye, the scuttling movement of something – something large – sliding in behind it, into a gap that was too small for a person of even average proportions. Will gasped and jumped to his feet, trying to catch sight of the object but, as with all things when they are looked at directly in the dark, it grew darker and less distinct. And that was when he heard the first sound. The breath.

Then there was another sound, an exhalation. This time from the corner of the room immediately to his left, from behind the ensuite bathroom door that he had left open. There was someone there, in the room with him, behind the door. And there was no one else in the castle. Other than the shape they had seen . . .

He tried to block out the earlier shadow, tried to stay in the moment. Tried to apply his tried and trusted logical thinking. Someone *must* have entered when he'd dozed, he reasoned. Will forced himself to think logically and then took a step toward where he had heard the breath, pushing rationality to take over.

It was as his hand reached out to touch the door, to pull it toward him and reveal what lay behind, that he again saw movement out of the corner of his eye at the opposite end of the room. Will swung around. He could see nothing there now, but what he had seen was a person – he was sure – standing up from the wooden armchair suddenly. Will stared at the chair. His heart pumped. There was nothing to be seen now down that end of the room, directly or indirectly. *What the hell had he just witnessed? Were there two people there?*

He was distracted again by yet another noise, this time from behind him, from the other side of the bed. This time he was sure he had heard a voice, a man's voice. Will couldn't make out directly what had been said, but he knew there was substance to the sound, that it was more than a breath. But there was *still* nothing there that could be seen with the naked eye.

Will knew that he should be excited by this, that it was what he dreamed of as a paranormal investigator, but he couldn't feel anything other than a growing sensation of dread in the base of his stomach, an electric current of fear charging through his veins as he looked this way and that, following the noises and the shadows. What was going on?

Another movement. A shuffling noise. This time again back at the armoire. He swung his head to the left enough to just catch something again in the corner of his eye, but he wasn't fast enough. And then another voice, from the bathroom this time. Will swivelled his head as quickly as he could to catch up with each new occurrence, but it was all so fast. He gasped as the room went still and he looked from side to side, frozen. He was barely aware of his body other than the dead dull fear in the base of his stomach. Was that it, he wondered, or was there more?

And when more came, Will felt completely overwhelmed. It started with a footstep on the floor tiles of the bathroom, but as fast as he could turn his attention there, another movement, more shuffling, came from the fireplace end of the room. This time it seemed like there was definitely more than just one person *or thing* moving. The movement seemed to grow, always outside of Will's exact line of sight, always just below or worse still just above where he was looking. And it seemed to increase in seconds. In a matter of moments Will realised that while he couldn't pinpoint one exact spot of movement that it was almost like the whole end of the room was filled with movement, like the darkness was seething.

And there were more voices. Male voices, all of them. It started as a shuffling noise and grew in seconds to a whisper, getting louder and louder. Will could make out individual words, he was sure. "*You!*" he heard again, like a bark. More whispering and shuffling. Will's chest rose and fell rapidly and his head twisted suddenly back toward the bathroom as the sounds began in earnest on that side of him also. He felt the panic rise further and further within him, his investigator's logic gone, and the flight instinct took hold. What should he do? He had to get out of there, but the movement, the shifting of the darkness, was taking place again before him, over toward the door of the room where he longed to go, to get out of there. All the time the noise grew louder, the sense of presence stronger. He had to react, had to *do* something – what could he do? Will's brain was overloaded, his thoughts a jumble of terror and panic.

"*Stop!*" he shouted suddenly.

Allowing himself to speak, to hear himself say the word seemed to settle him somehow. And for a half second, the movement did stop. It was enough time for something to click in Will's brain. He had no idea what was happening, had no idea how to stop it. Will's hand immediately dropped to the pocket of his trousers and he fumbled around for his mobile, tearing his eyes away for a second from the unseen mayhem that was growing closer by the second around him, his fingers skimming the keypad until he found the torch app. He needed desperately to see what was going on. It was pure instinct, however, that made his finger rapidly jab at the next icon on the screen. His camera setting. In a second he held the device upright and jabbed it with his finger. The room was suddenly and brilliantly lit by the flash. And then again, and again. Will swivelled the camera around the room, taking photo after photo, the flash constantly illuminating segments of the room, leaving a white residue on his eyes, blinding him to everything except the apparatus in his hand.

And as he took the pictures, the noises grew quieter and the movement receded, as if the bright light of the flash was somehow fighting back, sending these inhuman shapes and sounds back into the corners of the room from where they had come.

In a matter of moments, Will stopped, lowering the phone from his face, and peering into the silence, squinting against the flash image which burned into his eyes which was also gradually dissipating. Eventually he could see as clearly around him as the darkness would allow, could see that all was still.

Suddenly the door burst open with a crash and Gabriel all but fell in, as if he had been pushing with all his might.

"What the fuck's going on?" he demanded, breathless.

Will could barely think about him being there. His mind was racing at a mile a minute and he stood there, frozen, tense.

"Are you all right?" barked Gabriel, still standing in the doorway, gripping the handle.

Will felt his heartbeat begin to slow a little as the silence gained a grip once again on the room. He realised he could move his feet again and took a step that enabled him to reach over to the bedside table and turn on the lamp there which immediately flooded that side of the bed with a warm light. Inspired by this, Will looked at the wall above and spotted there a black switch which he flicked upwards, turning on, with repeated flickering, the welcome fluorescent glow of the bathroom strip light.

He sank down on the side of the bed and took in the panorama of the now-lit room, watched by Gabriel who still stood frozen at the door.

It was all quiet. All still and most importantly, bright. There was no intrusive or unwelcome movement, no mysterious voices. All the furniture stood where it should. The room was clear. Will felt his heart gradually return to a more normal pace. What had just happened, he wondered. Had he imagined it? Had he had some sort of out-of-body experience? A seizure? He inhaled deeply and shook his head to clear it. Slowly, he felt the pounding in his heart recede and his breath to return to normal. It was as if he had been literally stunned.

It took a while before he thought to look at the phone. The photographs. He lifted the device, activating the touch screen to call up his photo album, eager for some proof of what he had just experienced. He found himself disappointed when, as he flicked the screen back, shot after shot revealed a room that was fuzzy but empty. The flash had illuminated the fireplace, the armoire, the bed, the door – all of these things, time and time again, blurry with the movement of the camera but just as they should be otherwise. Gabriel, still silent and worried, stepped closer, approached the bed where Will stood. Will felt a tension from him, the same as his own. He looked up, directly at him, saw his white face, his tired eyes. Still, Will couldn't speak.

He looked back at the phone. What he had just experienced wasn't normal, he reasoned. He was sure it wasn't a figment of his imagination – there had most certainly been something – or things – in the room with him. Maybe, just maybe, he might have captured something on his phone, some light anomaly perhaps? Will flicked through the images faster and faster, knowing that it was unlikely that he had captured anything. Until he reached the one of the bathroom door, the last one that he had fired off, he calculated. For a moment he was completely transfixed by what looked back at him from the screen. Because there, blurred and somewhat indistinct, but unmistakeable, was the form of a man. Broad shoulders, a torso, legs visible to the knee. And his face was clear – two eyes, a nose, and a mouth fixed in an expression of rage. The right arm was raised high above the shape of the head, the hand clenched in a fist. Will inhaled deeply as he try to take in what he was seeing. It was a man, a furious man standing before him. Staring at the face Will couldn't deny the creeping feeling that he was in the presence of pure evil.

"Look . . ." he managed, and thrust the phone at Gabriel, feeling the tense electricity between them. There was so much to take in – he felt fully charged, overcharged even.

Gabriel took the phone and gasped as he saw – and recognised – the shape in front of him. He met Will's eyes and nodded. It was all he could manage. So much information, so much significance.

"That's not all," Gabriel managed, pointing back out the open door.

Both of the men were managing to speak but neither could fully take in what they were saying and hearing. Sound, for them, was like it is before a faint comes on. Distant, yet something desperately sought for, a return to something, something to cling on to.

Will's head spun but he tried his hardest to focus on his friend with his wide-eyed stare.

"It's not all, Will – *he's* not all. Pine's come." Gabriel glanced at the wall that separated his room and Will's, distantly wishing that his body could somehow stop juddering and start feeling like his own again. "*Pine,*" he said again, for emphasis. "I woke up when I heard a noise in my room. A scratching noise, like someone writing. I was coming in to tell you when I heard all the noise from your room – he left me another message while I was asleep. On a notepad in my room. Pine's *here.* As well as Laurence according to Gifford. And now this guy . . ." He handed the phone back to Will.

Will lowered his head again to look at what he had captured on screen, his whole body on fire. "He wanted me to see this, didn't he?" he said breathlessly. "I mean, it's not impossible to catch paranormal stuff on ordinary cameras – it happens all the time – but this? Something this clear? And just when I wanted it to happen most?"

Gabriel nodded in agreement as Will looked up directly at him. "They're all on set now," Gabriel said. "And something's going to happen. Something more. Because they're *all here*. All of them, Jack Ball included."

CHAPTER 30

Gabriel and Will sat in silence in the kitchen – the new, gleaming kitchen with its strip lighting and modern equipment – having removed all traces of their investigation from the old one. A part of Will kicked himself – why hadn't he persevered? Why hadn't he carried on with the investigation when there was so much energy in the house? How could he have thought it was gone dead when so much had happened? Why was he hiding out in the kitchen with a cup of tea and Gabriel for protection? Because he was scared, that's why. He'd *never* been this scared before – unnerved, uncertain, but never truly scared. Then again he hadn't had an experience like that before. He had to admit that alone, in that room with the darting shapes and hideous whispering he had never felt so close to evil in his entire life. He pulled again at his sleeve and looked in disbelief at what he had found there. Four scratches, like claws, embedded in his arm. He hadn't felt it happen but it was identical to what they had seen on Gifford's arm.

Gabriel's forehead was ridged with concentration. Glancing at him, Will guessed that his fear was somewhat less – after all, he hadn't seen anything he wasn't already familiar with – but he was completely confused and overwhelmed. They both jumped at the sound of a door being unlocked and opened somewhere in a passage nearby and watched as the kitchen door swung open and an elderly woman Will hadn't seen before appeared. She, in turn, gave a start at seeing them but then recognised Gabriel.

"Good morning, Gabriel," she said. "Welcome to Dubhglas."

"Morning, Mrs Hibbert," he managed.

She nodded at him, taking off her coat and bustling through to the door to the adjoining original kitchen of the castle, before coming back in and heading for the kettle.

"I'm so sorry I wasn't here yesterday to greet you when you arrived but I had some appointments that I couldn't miss," she said in a soft voice. "Can I make you gentlemen a cup of tea?"

Will raised his empty cup as Gabriel politely refused and they excused themselves, aware that the normal day at Dubhglas was about to begin and they still had to tidy up the miles of cable and equipment that they had set up so carefully the previous night. It felt like a million years ago, thought Will as they emerged from the kitchen. He checked his watch. It was six thirty. Later than he'd intended making a start, but they still probably had a bit of time before the normal household routine kicked in, and before Christopher Calvert returned.

Gabriel had been insistent that his godfather shouldn't see what they had been doing. "He doesn't believe in ghosts," he'd explained. "He told me once I had fey ways and I replied by asking wasn't she in *King Kong* and earned a clip around the ear for my troubles!"

They had laughed as they worked but there was no laughter now as they made their way up the back stairs that led to the main hallway. It was still dark outside of course. Will felt anxious as they surfaced through the door under the turn in the stairs and into the main hallway to be greeted by pitch blackness. He was relieved when Gabriel found a switch and they were suddenly bathed in a dim light. Their spirits lifted a little more as they worked, focusing on winding up the cable, packing away the laptops, ensuring that each camera was removed from where it had spent the night, leaving no marks on wood or paintwork. It took over an hour to get everything done but Will was satisfied by the job. Everything was packed away as it should be, he was certain. And he knew where everything was when he needed it. When he began the task of searching through the footage for evidence.

Normally this would fill him with excitement. He'd fidget anxiously, longing to settle down in a room, alone, with a coffee and his equipment, searching, searching for evidence of the paranormal. As a dark, damp dawn crept slowly over Dubhglas, however, he could think of nothing that he wanted to do less. When he thought about it, he was unsure which he dreaded most – finding something on the tapes that would remind him of the terror of the night before, or shutting the door behind him again in that bedroom.

It was his fear of the room that led him to seek out the housekeeper again to obtain the keys to the golf buggy that Callum had used the day before to ferry the equipment to the castle, and undertake the return journey in the bleak morning, soaked through in a sodden fog. He didn't care, however. His equipment was valuable to him and he didn't want to store it in that room. Not if what Gifford had said was true about the destructive nature of this so-called spirit. He didn't want anyone – or anything – tampering with the evidence.

He saw Gifford when he made his final journey back from the car park. He was standing beside Gabriel on the mezzanine overlooking the front door as Will re-entered. He was pleased to see that Gabriel was studying the place where they had seen the shadow seem to step from the wall and watch them.

"We need to analyse all the evidence, of course," Will heard him say as he climbed the stairs. He hoped that Gabriel was being discreet about what they had both experienced. They needed something more concrete before they went and terrified an already frightened man.

"Oh hello, Mr Peterson – you should have let me take your equipment back to the car." Gifford held out his hand to Will apologetically.

Will shook it briefly and then handed the keys of the golf buggy to the butler. "Not at all, Mr Gifford," he said. "But, can you tell me again about the mists you see here? Where exactly do you see them?"

Gifford pointed a finger at the first bedroom door, exactly where they had seen the figure the previous night.

"Here, as I told you," said Gifford. "Directly outside this door here."

Will and Gabriel glanced at each other.

"Would you like some breakfast?" asked Gifford, suddenly. "I'm afraid I'm not looking after you gentlemen very well!"

Will made to refuse politely but then thought better of it. Gabriel took the words from his mouth. "I'm absolutely famished, Gifford," he said. "But I think we might need just a little fresh air first – what do you think, Will?"

Will nodded. He'd had some already as he drove the golf cart back and forth. He didn't fancy another soaking in the pervasive Highland mist of the morning, but knew by Gabriel's tone that he wished to speak to him in private.

"We'll take a turn down to the loch, I think," said Gabriel. "And then do you think Mrs Hibbert might do some of her scrambled eggs for us?"

Gifford relaxed. This was familiar territory for him. Not spectres and mists and strange noises. "Would that be with smoked salmon or something more substantial?" he asked eagerly.

"Oh, I think a full Scottish on the side might be in order?" smiled Gabriel and Gifford relaxed even more, eager to get to work. To do something normal. "A walk to the lake will add to my appetite just that bit more."

It certainly added to Gifford's delight. He took off with an efficient, silent step down the passage while Gabriel took Will's arm and led him down the stairs.

To Will, the weather had improved slightly as they walked around the house to the back lawns, passed through what had once been a copse of trees, now white-painted stumps, and onto the grass which was saturated. The morning mist hung there, gloomy, soaking everything in all-encompassing greyness.

Gabriel tutted loudly as he glanced down at his shoes and saw that they were sodden in a couple of steps. He pulled his coat tighter around him and looked up, closing his eyes against the mizzle and sniffing loudly. "What a *dreich*," he commented emphatically.

They walked on down the lawn in silence for a few moments, each man lost in his own thoughts.

Will dug his hands into his pockets and turned fully to look behind him at the building, to take it all in. He studied it silently, peering at every window, at each turret, as if he didn't wish to miss anything that he might see. Satisfied that there was nothing to be noticed – this time – he turned back and took in what was now before him.

Dark grey, barely visible amongst all the other greys of the morning, on the far side of a thick copse of trees at the bottom of the sloping, carefully tended lawns, the lake was just visible.

He was distracted suddenly by Gabriel breaking into a gentle jog and looked at him in surprise as he aimed a perfect kick at a tall mushroom that he had spied slightly to his left.

"Gooooal!" mouthed Gabriel quietly and joylessly as he watched it break and scatter over the grass. The action hadn't been as satisfying as he thought it might be.

"A lot happened last night," offered Will. "I think we might have seen Jack Ball's ghost, what do you reckon?"

He was surprised to hear Gabriel's response. "Wasn't the one I wanted to see," he replied bluntly.

"What do you mean? What else did you want to see . . . oh . . ." Will stopped as he realised that of all the phantoms that they had encountered the night before, none of them was the one that Gabriel had wanted to witness. None of them had been Laurence. "I'm sorry, mate. Does that upset you?"

Gabriel paused for a moment and took a calming breath. "I'm just so confused. So hurt that he's manifested to Gifford who is a complete stranger to him. And it distresses me to think that he's presenting in this form – as he looked when he died. The wet clothes, the missing shoe – that's exactly how those paper cuttings described it. I've never seen him like that." Gabriel moved on slowly. "That's how he must be when he's here, I suppose. I never thought that he actually *be* anywhere other than with me but maybe this is where he is when he's not . . ."

Will glanced sideways at his friend, unsure what to say, and they carried on in silence, finding soon that they had reached the trees at the bottom of the lawn. Gabriel fell in behind Will as they negotiated the narrow path in single file.

"I may as well hang up my hat," said Gabriel eventually.

Will turned his head, but only enough to hear him more clearly. He was afraid that he would go head over heels on the network of damp tree roots and slippy leaves and moss that lined the floor of the thicket. "Why's that?" he called behind him, concentrating hard.

But Gabriel didn't answer. They were silent as they crossed the last few dangerous feet of ground and then emerged from the shadow of the trees onto a small beach against which Dubhglas Lake lapped serenely.

Will halted and stared. The water itself was the same grey as the sky. He gazed out over to the horizon, barely visible. The mist was thick on the other side of the lake but he imagined it would mirror exactly the side on which they stood. Now, there was nothing there, just the dark, grey void of fog and water, and the eerie silence that surrounded them, broken only by the lapping of the water on the black shore and the occasional sound of a bird, even though Will could see nothing on the gentle slate-coloured waves that bobbed into the distance.

"I just wish I could *communicate*," Gabriel sighed, helplessly.

Will turned to look back up the hill beyond the trees to where the castle stood. He stood on a small rock and could make out a window here, the fairytale turret – a full view impossible with the trees. He was still aware however – always aware – of it dominating the landscape.

"Normally this house is teeming with spirits," continued Gabriel. "I've been coming here all of my life and I don't think I've ever seen the same one twice. And none of them are nasty or anything. The odd poltergeist but they're more likely to rearrange the ornaments and the place is so big no one even bloody notices that. It is the *worst* house in the world if you're dead and looking for attention. No one – no one living, that is, has ever been afraid to be here and that's important. You heard what Gifford said – it never bothered him until the past few months."

"But this time?" probed Will, glancing at Gabriel who was shaking his head.

"I don't know for sure but, even without my gift, something about it feels so . . . empty," he replied. "Like they've all gone . . . on holidays or something."

"Except for Martin Pine," continued Will. "And Laurence, and the mysterious Uncle Jack."

Gabriel shrugged an 'I suppose so'. "I don't know why – and this sounds totally rubbish, I know, but humour me . . ."

"Don't I always?"

"It's as if they've all stood back or something. That they're all watching to see what happens, like waiting for the curtains to draw back on a play."

"A three-hander," offered Will. "Starring Martin Pine and his alleged victims?"

Gabriel turned to face the house. "Exactly. I just wish I knew the plot."

"You and me both," said Will emphatically. "There *is* something horrible going on in this old place – and that's a lot coming from me." He stepped down from the small rock he had used as a podium to get a better view of the castle, and glanced at his watch. "Had we better think about breakfast?" he suggested. "Things might be better after this full Scottish you've promised me."

"We'd better, I suppose. The old man'll be back soon enough. Here – we'll go up this way. There's an easier path through the kitchen gardens." Gabriel indicated that they move to their right and the two men began to stride purposefully along the beach. The sounds of the lake carried in through the reeds on the shoreline.

They had turned off the beach and begun to climb a path when they heard a distant shout coming from the direction of the house. They couldn't see its source but then heard it again.

"Hi! Gabriel!" it came, a man's voice, clearer as it came closer.

Gabriel's face softened slightly. "The old man. He's here." His pace quickened a little. "Godfather!" he called back.

Will looked at him sidelong. It seemed such an odd, archaic way to refer to him but then again so much about this place fitted in with that description. He was pleased to see the sincere smile that spread across Gabriel's face as the figure of his godfather became visible from behind some privet hedges ahead. He really was very fond of him, thought Will.

Christopher Calvert looked like a bird – a stork, perhaps, Will thought, as his thin figure darted down through the mist, arms wide. He and Gabriel embraced warmly.

"Christopher, great to see you!" said Gabriel. "You're looking marvellous as always!"

The older man responded by pulling apart from his godson and patting his stomach. "And you're enjoying the good life, it seems," he with a grin. "Pursuing your acting career as well – good man!" Gabriel looked at Will out of the corner of his eye and then back to Calvert.

"Gifford saw you on the telly and pointed you out. Good to see you're not doing that awful bus-conducting any more. That show you're in is something terrible though. You should try to get a part in something worthwhile – I like that *Desperate Housewives* myself. The redhead – *woof*! This your guest?"

Gabriel stepped aside to allow Will and his godfather to greet each other. "This is William Peterson, my friend and colleague – of sorts."

"Pleased to meet you, Mr Calvert," Will said as they shook hands. "Your home is . . . eh . . . beautiful."

Gabriel coughed loudly and the old man indicated that they should walk together back toward the castle.

"So sorry you were left all on your ownio last night in this old place," he said. "The timing was terrible but the board of the old company were having a dinner last night and wanted to make a fuss with a presentation type of thing. Which isn't *my* type of thing, as you know . . . you know me, the behind-the-scenes man. Anyway, I went. Thought it was time to do it. Time to start drawing lines under things and all that." The old man took a breath from his rapid-fire explanation and then continued. "So, that's the job taken care of. Goodbye, thanks very much, here's the door and all that. Just this place now." He looked up at the castle and stopped suddenly, his breathing a little laboured from the walk. He put his hands on his hips, pulling in his green waxed jacket as he did and showing how thin he actually was. He gazed up at the building, drinking it in, completely silent.

"Anyhow," he said suddenly, clapping his hands together and rubbing them briskly, "best get on. Have you had breakfast yet? There were nice smells coming from the kitchens as I passed."

"Your housekeeper is making us a cooked breakfast," said Will. "Will you join us?"

The old man raised his hands in refusal and took off again at his brisk pace, the others following. "No time, I'm afraid," he said over his shoulder. "I've a lot to be getting on with before tonight – the Christmas-tree people aren't here yet and there's a lot to be done." He pointed a bony finger at a back doorway. "Best be off. Like I say, tonight won't be as big as the other years. Your old ma and pa are on their way, Gabriel, and then your other friends coming from Edinburgh, and a couple of my old staff and the usual contingent from the village. We'll make it jolly though, eh? Might be the last year I do it so let's make the most of it. See you both anon." He sped up, veering to his right and up to a long set of French windows at the rear of the castle, through which Will could make out a function room. He watched him go, darting inside without a second glance, his mind already on to his next task.

"So that's your famous godfather?"

Gabriel nodded. "Getting a bit doddery by the sounds of things."

Will snorted. "Just sounded a bit preoccupied to me. And I think someone's been a bit liberal with the truth about their career path? Acting?"

Gabriel smiled. "Curiouser and curiouser," he said playfully.

Will looked up at the castle before him. The mist had lifted a little and there was a brighter tinge to the sky. He suddenly caught a whiff of bacon coming from the back door. "*Ooh*, smell that!" he said enthusiastically as his stomach betrayed him with a growl. "Let's have some bangers and then decide what's next, eh?"

Gabriel didn't respond and Will wasn't surprised. His own cheeriness was completely forced, of course. He had to acknowledge that he didn't want for a single second to go back in there. Neither of them did. To face whatever was going on – whatever was yet to happen.

A fresh concern suddenly crossed his mind. Martha. And Ruby. This was no place for them now, now that they knew what presences were already here, not now that there was an expectation of more. A fresh urgency gripped Will. He had to contact Martha somehow. Tell her to abandon the plan to come along. What had he been thinking, arranging for them all to come here? Thinking that they could somehow have a relaxing countryside getaway? He felt foolish suddenly and a wave of regret washed over him as he felt the bulge of the ring box in his pocket but he was quick to banish it. Another time, and certainly another place, he decided.

"Let's go in, Gabriel," he said, his tone serious.

Breakfast would have to wait, of course. He had to try to get hold of Martha.

CHAPTER 31

"What the *fuck* have you done?" hissed Sue as Martha shuffled into the kitchen at Calderwood. Eight o'clock already, the time read. Martha had intended to be up and out by half past. But her head felt so foggy, her stomach sick. She had been surprised when she had woken up on her own pillow, truth be told. Worryingly, she had no recollection of getting there, of even getting back to the house.

Sue stood, arms folded, the steam from an untouched cup of tea wafting gently upwards on the counter top beside her. Martha could hear the happy sounds of the children's channel coming from the living room and knew that Ruby, at least, was content.

She sank down on the kitchen chair nearest the door and pointed at the cup of tea. "Can I have one of those?" she asked faintly, resting her aching head in her hands and squeezing her eyes closed. She was exhausted, she knew. And a part of her felt still slightly drunk.

Suddenly, she remembered. She caught her breath and held it as she tested the memory, then allowed it to replay fully in her mind. That conversation with Dan . . . kissing him outside the restaurant.

Sue proceeded to do as she was bidden – to fetch the longed-for cup of tea but to also make as much noise as possible as she did so. It didn't matter, regardless. At the memory of what had happened, Martha suddenly tasted the food, the wine, *the kisses* over again and her stomach lurched. She almost knocked the chair over as she bolted for the downstairs bathroom. She barely managed to pull the door shut behind her so that Ruby wouldn't come to investigate as she was violently ill.

Strangely, it made her feel better. When she could stand, still trembling from the ferocity of the attack, she didn't return to the kitchen but instead made her way upstairs and stood under the shower for a good fifteen minutes, washing the night away from her. Letting the hot water cleanse her, giving her time to think. She dressed in a pair of jeans and a sweater, and threw the few remaining items that she needed for the weekend into her travel bag, relieved beyond reason that she'd had the foresight to pack cases for herself and Ruby the previous morning. With some make-up applied and her hair dried, she felt well enough to make her way back down the stairs and greet her daughter, who had barely noticed that she hadn't seen her mum that morning. She had Auntie Sue who gave her jam on toast and the occasional breakfast Hob Nob, and the delights of cartoons.

Quietly, Martha carried her case outside the front door where she saw Sue loading her own travel bag into the boot of her Audi.

"I'll drive!" Sue barked, slamming the trunk shut. "Give me your keys."

It was a command, not a request, and Martha was relieved that she wouldn't have to get behind the wheel. She still felt so woozy, so hung-over. How had she managed to get that way? She was sure she'd only had a few glasses of the Cava – Dan had worked his way through it fairly comprehensively from what she could recall, but she'd done her best to behave once she'd realised that it was going to her head. Yet here she was, unsure she'd get through a breath-check should that arise.

She managed the simple task of fitting her case into the boot, sweating profusely as she did so, and made her way back inside and into the kitchen where Sue was dressing Ruby. Martha took a bottle of water from the fridge and sipped some to cool herself down. Her cheeks burned suddenly as another memory of the previous night, of those embraces on the street outside the restaurant, played back in her mind. She banished the thought. Still, Sue said nothing.

There were no further words between them until they were well on the road.

"I haven't blown your cover by the way," said Sue sarcastically, out of the blue. "Will doesn't know that you didn't get back till God knows what time last night."

Will, thought Martha. She'd been blocking the thought of him from her mind. With a trembling hand, she pulled her phone from handbag and checked it, finding it completely dead, the battery empty. She wasn't sure when that had happened – maybe late the previous night, maybe that's why he hadn't been in touch? Maybe he'd been trying all along, and she'd got so cross about it . . .

"Thank you," said Martha quietly, her lip wobbling.

Sue negotiated a roundabout. "But I can't guarantee it's going to stay that way, Martha." She glanced in the rear-view mirror. Her soother lolling from her mouth and Hugo clutched to her chest as usual, Ruby had nodded off the instant the car had started to move. Sue turned her attention back to the road. "I don't know what the hell happened last night," she said bluntly.

Martha squirmed uncomfortably in her seat. This wasn't one of Sue's comedy telling-offs. This was the real deal. Her friend was livid with her. And she had a reason to be too.

"The last I knew, you were having some late lunch with Dan after signing those papers. *I* agreed to mind your daughter for a few hours. I heard you struggling with the front-door key past midnight. What on earth were you doing with Dan all that time?"

"I think I've made a terrible mess, Sue," wailed Martha, finally dissolving in tears.

Sue sighed and drove on in silence while Martha wept it out.

"I suppose we've time for a cup of tea – neither of us have eaten," Sue said after a while, her tone softer, as she indicated a left turn into a service station and pulled up outside.

Martha had never believed in the hot, sweet tea theory for a shock but, as she sipped her way through the cardboard cup while leaning on the bonnet of her car, she had to confess that it seemed to be doing the trick. The terrible headache and nausea seemed to be lifting slightly. It had also helped to finally spill the story to Sue who had listened patiently throughout, quietly drinking her own coffee and picking at the Danish pastry she had selected.

"I kissed him, Sue. I cannot believe I kissed him. I don't even think I had that much to drink – he must have kept topping up my glass when I wasn't looking."

"I doubt he held your nose and poured it down your throat," sniffed Sue. "Had you finished taking your antibiotics?"

Martha groaned. That was it. She had mixed her medication with the wine. That explained why she had felt so . . . relaxed . . . so quickly. Why she had let her guard down so easily? With Dan of all people! Her cheeks burned again as some of their conversation came flooding back to her. More than the kiss, that was the biggest betrayal of all. Agreeing to work with him again, talking about having him back in her life, planning his move to Edinburgh to have him nearer . . . for more than a moment *wanting* that to happen . . . She hadn't told Sue that part, she couldn't. Couldn't bear to verbalise the betrayal. It was bad enough that Sue thought their interaction was purely physical. If she knew that on some level that Martha had contemplated giving herself emotionally too . . . Martha couldn't bear to think of it any longer.

"Martha, I really don't know what you were thinking," Sue said, and fished for her cigarettes in her pocket. She glanced in through the car window as she did and saw that Ruby was still out for the count. She flicked her lighter and inhaled deeply.

The smell of fresh smoke assaulted Martha's nostrils and her stomach lurched afresh but she thought better about saying anything. Now was not the time.

"Either do I, Sue," she replied with a sigh.

Sue inhaled sharply again and blew a long plume of smoke out into the crisp air.

"I suppose we have to look at the positives," she said loudly.

"And what might those be?" replied Martha, the question a statement of desperation.

Sue examined the cigarette in her hand. "You're not dead," she offered, managing a slight grin. "You did make it home in the long run."

Martha smiled weakly and sniffed. "Not dead yet," she managed.

There was silence for a few moments between them.

"What am I going to do, Sue?" said Martha meekly. "I've cocked this up so badly . . . when Will finds out he's going to hate me . . ."

"You're going to say *nothing*!" barked Sue suddenly, making Martha jump with the intensity of the statement. Sue cast the butt of her cigarette on the tarmac and ground it in with the ball of her foot.

"What do you mean . . . ?" began Martha.

"*Nothing*," repeated Sue vehemently, looking Martha straight in the face with a rare intensity. "Did you mean what happened to happen?" she demanded. "Did you go out to eat with the intention of kissing Dan?"

"No."

"Did you mean it when it did happen?"

"Christ, no, you know that!"

"Do you mean it to happen again? Do you intend having a relationship with him?"

"How can you ask that?"

"Then shut up about it. You get hold of Dan when you get back to Edinburgh and you tell him there's been a massive mistake and that he's to get out of Dodge and that you're happy with Will et cetera. Tell him that you were off your face because of your antibiotics – tell him anything but just face up to what you did and make it right. You can't undo it."

"You mean lie to Will?"

"No – just don't tell him the truth – that's different," replied Sue, rummaging in her coat pocket for the car keys. "It's not going to do him any good to hear about it and as you have no intention of getting your marriage back on track I suggest we all shut up about it and take that wonderful British approach – the 'never-speak-of-it-again' one."

"But this is a massive betrayal," said Martha, stepping around the car and waiting at the passenger door for Sue to unlock it. She couldn't quite believe what she was hearing. Sue was prickly but honest as the day was long. Martha wouldn't have dreamed for one second that her friend would have advocated keeping silent about this, deceiving someone like Will.

"Absolutely right," nodded Sue, casting her coat into the back seat and sliding behind the wheel. "And you've got to live with it forever and ever but Will doesn't. He loves you and he loves Ruby and he doesn't need to be hurt. The fact that you're a cheating liar is something you can carry round like a millstone forever and ever and that'll be a lesson to you to never do it again."

"Wow, thanks for the kind words," replied Martha as she slid into the passenger seat and pulled the belt around her.

"Martha, you are my oldest friend and I love you dearly," said Sue, turning directly to face her. "But sometimes you do stupid shit and you have to stop doing stupid shit and stop forever. I know this involves being dishonest but it's the best I can come up with under the circumstances. If you tell Will that you kissed Dan – and feel free to do that – it might make you feel better but you'll break up a happy family – and for what? Something that you barely even remember doing with someone that you despise? Maybe I'm not Claire Rayner but this is the best I can think of to keep things the way they are. You'll just have to find a way to deal with the guilt – it's not like you slept with him, is it? Oh God, please tell me you didn't sleep with him?"

Martha shook her head. She had a recollection, however vague, of being in a taxi. And if Sue had heard her come in at midnight then she couldn't have. Did that mean, however, that she wouldn't have? She flushed. It didn't feel right not to tell Will but she couldn't think of anything that would feel right. Maybe Sue's way was the only way to minimise the hurt?

"What if Will finds out?" she asked quietly. "What if I lie to him now and then he finds out later? Won't that make it worse?"

Sue grunted slightly as she reversed the car out of the spot they had parked in, concentrating as she peered over her shoulder. She put the car into first.

"I don't know," she replied firmly. "I don't have all the answers. Like I told you, this is the best I can come up with. You can take my advice or leave it."

Martha nodded and they proceeded in silence out onto the road. Sue was right, she told herself and took a deep breath.

The midsection of the journey was undertaken in silence, just the low hum of Radio 4 in the background. When Ruby awoke, demanding drinks and a banana, it was a blessed relief. It was another distraction for Martha to sing songs with her the remainder of the way, clapping hands and making silly faces through the gap between the top of the seat and the headrest.

The countryside eventually grew bleaker around them, a mist suddenly enveloping the car as they wound along narrow roads. Sue flicked on the windscreen wipers, switching between 'intermittent' and 'fast' as the mist grew thick, then abated, then grew thicker again. She exchanged Radio 4 for some music from her MP3 player as they drove on and Puccini filled the car, adding to the atmosphere created by the increasingly misty landscape, odd white shapes looming at them from the verges, terrifying at first, nothing but weather-beaten trees and hedgerows on closer inspection. Even Ruby grew still and silent as she looked out the window. There was only so much 'Wheels on the Bus' that even a toddler could take, Martha reckoned.

"Channelling Inspector Morse here somewhere?" she chanced, nodding towards the source of the music – an attempt to play with her friend who was focused on peering through the haze created by the mist.

A smile played on Sue's lips but she concentrated and forced it away. "Quiet!" she barked. "This is the best bit."

A soaring voice filled the air from the car speakers as Martha peered again at the bleak landscape, alien in the fog.

"Where the hell are we?" Martha asked and followed Sue's finger to the screen of the Sat Nav.

Sue tapped their location, a blue arrow on a completely white background. "Here," she replied. Martha laughed. "Didn't realise my car was so prepared for off road!"

Sue slowed the car down a little slower. "It's not. And I think we're a bit lost and the Highlands is not somewhere I want to be a bit lost in, particularly as the Great Fog sets in and . . . oh! Maybe we're not lost after all."

The glimpse of stone through trees caught both of their attentions at the same time.

"Bloody hell," whispered Martha, taking in the vision that peered from the trees at them.

"This is it all right," said Sue in a more assured voice and sat more upright in her seat, accelerating into a higher gear as the road seemed to improve a little before them. "This sounds just like Gabriel described it. Spooky, haunted Scottish Castle."

Martha groaned. "Do you think there's even the slightest possibility it isn't?"

Sue shrugged. "You're the big believer – what do you think?"

Martha knew what she thought and glanced nervously out the window as they drew closer, turning up the main driveway and catching sight, through the mist, of the chimneys, the turrets, the towers. Sue braked suddenly as she spotted a crude, hand-painted sign reading 'Car Park' and she turned slowly into the gravelled courtyard edged with disused farm buildings.

Martha recognised Will's Volvo, parked amongst considerably more modern and expensive vehicles. She giggled. "Gabriel must be so ashamed," she observed.

Sue smirked as she pulled in beside a gleaming Mercedes. She killed the engine, and with it the music which had just started to swell again. "Right then," she stated. "We're agreed. No mentioning of the war and good times to be had by all?"

They turned to face each other and Martha nodded reluctantly. She didn't want to lie to Will and she still felt terrible about the night before but she couldn't think of anything else to do.

"Good," Sue stated, pulling the keys from the ignition and stepping out of the car.

Martha stepped outside too, hit immediately by the blast of freezing damp air that filled her nostrils. She inhaled sharply and exhaled again, the mist refreshing after the heat of the air-conditioning. Sue suffered from smoker's circulation and required her travel temperature to be just a little higher than Martha would have liked.

Martha took in her surroundings as she prised Ruby from her seat. The toddler, too, glanced around her almost nervously. her bright eyes darting about her as she took it all in. She would normally attempt escape the instant she was released from the constraints of her car seat, wriggle from Martha's arms, excited by the stimulation of new surroundings. Today, however, she snuggled into her mother's chest, looking upward at the grey sky and squinting as she felt the dampness hit her face.

They trudged across the gravel with a quiet focus and then, as Will and Gabriel had done the previous day, made their way onto the path through the lawns, and across the short distance to the castle steps. Martha glanced around her as they walked, as quickly as they could, toward their destination. The lawns were well-tended, she noted. And the gravel surrounding the perimeter of the building was dotted with pruned rosebushes. It must be spectacular in the summer, she thought to herself, and turned for a moment to look behind her. The view took her breath away. To their rear, the sky had turned from the misty dull grey that had surrounded them throughout their trip, to a menacing black. A storm cloud, still in the distance, but approaching. Casting its shadow on the already grim horizon. The view was a landscape of grey and black, as if all the colour had been sucked out of the countryside. She turned back toward the castle, felt how it somehow seemed to wait for her to enter. So unwelcoming. Ruby saw it too and Martha watched her daughter's face for a moment, the bright little eyes filled with apprehension as they drew closer. It must be enormous to her, thought Martha, and hugged her tighter. The toddler looked at her mother, trusting her, and then back again at the castle as they reached the entrance with its heavy wooden doors opened back against the walls.

They entered the porch and Martha jumped suddenly as she reached out for the brass doorknob of the inner doors and an unexpected figure loomed at her through the panels of glass. Fear swelled in her as the handle of the door was wrenched from her hand and the door swung open, the air from inside filled with a medley of odours – must, damp, pine needles – *like in Gabriel's flat* – and a familiar scent that she couldn't place for a moment.

"Hello, gorgeous!" she heard a voice, and felt instant relief at seeing Will before her.

He had obviously seen them coming across the lawn. She couldn't stop the flash of irritation that ran through her as he pulled Ruby from her arms and stood aside to let them in.

"Hi, Sue –" he began, but Martha interrupted him.

"Why didn't you text me when you got here?" she demanded, regretting the words the instant they came out of her mouth.

Will's response was to laugh nervously, which made her even more irritated. "Have you checked your coverage bars? What's your excuse?" He replied and turned his attention to Ruby who was excitedly pulling his hair. "I've been trying to ring from the landline all morning but there was no answer."

"My battery's gone," she replied simply, avoiding eye contact with him. Of course, he'd had no coverage. Now that she could see the place, it all made perfect sense. She watched him kiss Ruby's little fingers which were now tugging at his lips and felt her heart swell a little.

Martha closed her eyes for a moment and leaned over to briefly rest her head against his chest which prompted him to take her into a one-armed embrace. Maybe it would all be okay, she thought to herself, before turning to look at him and raising her face for a kiss.

She heard a familiar vomiting sound as Gabriel came up behind Will.

He laughed as he greeted Sue with a brusque "Brice," as he was fond of doing.

"McKenzie," she replied and a conversation began between them, snappy banter back and forth as was their habit.

Martha watched her friends bicker and felt Will's arm close more firmly around her as he guided her further into the hallway. She began to take in her surroundings for the first time and felt a small sense of dread creep into her as she surveyed the dark hall, the stag's head watching everything. And up the stairs . . . she found her gaze drawn up toward a wooden balustrade protecting a mezzanine area above her, off which ran a passageway. There was another stag's head up there, she noted, high on the wall, smaller than the other. But nothing else that would draw her attention. Just some doors, presumably leading to bedrooms. Still, she couldn't help but stare . . . *what did she think she'd see up there?*

"Missed you," she heard Will say softly, and he gave her a squeeze, his voice filled with concern. She pulled her gaze back to him. "Me too," she replied and meant it, so sincerely.

"How did signing those documents go?" he asked, and her stomach gave a dart of nerves.

"Oh, it was all right," she began. "There was a bit of a mix-up with the . . ."

She was interrupted by another voice coming from the doorway of the house.

"Make way! Make Way! Be upstanding for the arrival of the Christmas Men!"

Martha glanced at the doorway to see the figure of a thin old man in a burgundy pullover and a pair of beige slacks opening the glass doors through which Martha had just entered and placing small wooden wedges underneath them.

A red van had pulled up outside, disgorging two men in jeans and sweaters who opened the back doors of the van and began to remove items. Christopher Calvert waited on the top step for them and stood back as the first climbed the steps and entered, carrying a stack of cardboard boxes which he placed carefully on the floor in front of an enormous Christmas tree, already half-decorated with red, green and golden baubles. The second man followed with a long fir garland slung over his shoulder, like a snake charmer carrying a python. The smell of fresh pine filled the air.

The small group watched the proceedings intently. Martha pointed Ruby in the direction of the Christmas tree as the first man exited and then returned, this time with a box marked '*Lights*'.

"Look, Ruby!" urged Martha, feeling a frisson of childlike excitement run through her at the festive sight. She couldn't resist Christmas. Maybe this weekend could be fun after all. Once some twinkling lights were brightening the place, and they warmed up from the soaking outside, they might actually start to enjoy themselves. An image of Dan's face lowering itself to hers suddenly flashed across her mind and she blocked it, feeling herself flush again. A mistake, she told herself. A mistake that was over.

"That's Christopher Calvert," said Will in a low voice, with a nod in the direction of the elderly man who was barking instruction at the 'Christmas Men' as he had called them. "Gabriel's godfather. I've been watching him in action all morning – he's the most energetic human being I've ever seen. Like an eighty-year-old Usain Bolt – but out of his mind on espressos and Red Bull."

Martha giggled. "Not sure I like the sound of that!"

The men were bringing in more garlands and a giant wreath. Martha watched the chaotic scene unfold, the old man with one hand on Gabriel's arm, the other pointing upward at one of the portraits, Sue gazing in the direction he indicated, her expression rapt, Ruby jiggling up and down with excitement, the noise growing and growing.

And then the breath on her ear.

Martha slapped a hand to where she had felt it tickle her and turned, suddenly, to see who could be standing so close. But there was no one. The noises seemed to quieten for a moment as she looked from right to left, taking in the murky passage that lay behind her off the hallway. Surely no one would have sneaked up behind her, blown in her ear and run off again? And it wasn't so much a blow as a breath . . . like someone leaning over her shoulder, watching the scene unfold, just like she was doing.

Her thoughts were interrupted by Will squeezing her shoulder protectively. She allowed herself to be absorbed back into the moment. To listen to Sue laugh charmingly as the old man flitted between telling some tale or other which also made Gabriel beam, and giving instruction to the two decorators who were growing increasingly soaked as they traipsed in and out with more and more paraphernalia.

The hubbub increased as from behind the pair of doors at the end of the passage which led toward the back of the building, the sounds of hammering began, punctuated by the occasional wheeze of what sounded like an accordion.

"That's the ballroom down there, where our festivities will be taking place tonight," she heard the old man tell Gabriel and Sue. "I'm not allowing a soul in there till it's done though. These local fellows come up every year from the village and decorate the place for me – I'd be happy with just a few garlands, but the ladies seem to love things that twinkle and, well, it's a great time of year and I like to start it early . . . oh, Hibbert – can we have some tea in the drawing room for our new arrivals, please? I expect you'll need a little warming up after the trip. This way folks, just through here"

Martha watched as Sue allowed the old man to take her arm and steer her through the archway and down the passage, disappearing through the first door on the left. Gabriel followed and Will set a wriggling Ruby down on the floor to toddle her way in at her own insistence. Martha stood back to allow them leave ahead of her, the buzz of conversation transferring through the door to the drawing room. As she stood there, the woman who Calvert had addressed as Hibbert caught her eye and looked at her directly. Martha stared back. There was something distinctly familiar about her, but Martha couldn't place her. The woman took a step closer to where she stood.

"It's Martha, isn't it?" she said kindly and Martha smiled in return.

"It is," she replied, glancing to one side of the woman to keep tabs on Ruby who was taking a few tentative exploratory steps toward the great Christmas tree which towered above her. "Don't touch that, love!"

The toddler stopped, looked back at her mother, and then back at the tree.

Mrs Hibbert glanced in her direction and smiled warmly. "That'll be Miss Ruby then," she said, joy in her voice. "Long, long time since there was a little one up here." She returned her gaze to Martha.

"I'm sorry to waylay you like this – but I wondered if you actually might like to come with me to my cottage and I can show you where you'll be sleeping? I'll get one of the maids to do the tea for the others."

Martha glanced again at Ruby, and then back at Hibbert, confused for a moment. "Won't we be staying in the castle?" she asked.

Mrs Hibbert shifted slightly from one foot to the other. "Mr Peterson had a word with me earlier – with Ruby being so small, we felt that . . . well, my cottage is a stone's throw away outside and it's very cosy. We thought you might be more comfortable out there as –"

"*Ruby!*" Martha screamed as the huge tree began to topple forward.

There was a shout as one of the Christmas Men lunged for the tree, thrusting a hand forward and pushing the fir just as it was about to crash down on the little girl, altering its course so that it crashed onto the boxes he'd carried in rather than on the child.

The great pine landed, bounced slightly and then settled, a little less than a foot away from where Ruby stood, still watching it with wide eyes.

Martha groaned with relief as she saw her daughter was safe, and scooped her up, pulling her close, holding her as the panic rose again around her.

"The damn thing was secured to the wall!" the decorator shouted.

"What's going on?" came the reedy tones of Christopher Calvert from the door of the drawing room, rushing out to see what had happened.

Will emerged behind him, rushing to Martha's side, demanding to know if they were all right. She nodded, breathless with shock, her hand rubbing Ruby's hair and cheek as she tried to soothe her.

"I don't know how that could have happened," the shaken decorator said to the other one who had just burst into the hall. "It was *tied* to the bloody wall! I secured it myself to that hook!"

"Well you should have done it tighter then!" growled the second man, bending to pick up a piece of rope which was lying on the floor underneath where the hook protruded from the wall. In an instant, Will had joined him, taking the rope from his hand and examining it thoroughly before turning his attention to where it should have been secured.

Martha turned and saw the face of the housekeeper was pale with shock.

Mrs Hibbert reached out and took a firm grip of Martha's arm. "It might be a good idea to come and get a cup of tea yourself, love," she said softly. "We'll go out through the front and around to my cottage. The castle isn't a good place for children."

Meekly, Martha hugged a bewildered Ruby to her and with a glance upwards at the mezzanine, she followed Mrs Hibbert away from the confusion and the noise, the questions and recriminations, and the now-still bulk of the fallen Christmas tree

CHAPTER 32

1963

Martin managed to smile at all those who stood around the kitchen table, loudly singing 'Happy Birthday'. Everyone was there for him – the ghillies, the maids, Mr and Mrs Turnbull, Drum carrying a cake lit with eighteen candles and iced with the message 'Happy Birthday Martin" in blue. "Claire made it all herself," he heard Mrs Turnbull say proudly over the chorus of 'For He's A Jolly Good Fellow' that had followed on, without missing a beat, from the birthday song.

Martin looked at Claire's beaming, proud face, and it made him feel better. He was exhausted of course. Exhausted with worry, although there was certainly a lot less to keep him up at nights these past few weeks than there had been previously. He'd had no nocturnal visitor for some time now. The relief when he woke in the morning without having seen Uncle Jack's sneering face appear around the door of his bedroom was huge. But that, in itself, brought its own concerns. If Uncle Jack wasn't paying his visits to Martin, then did it mean that he was going elsewhere? Hence the reason for Martin's exhaustion. He had taken to sneaking down to the entrance hall at night to keep an eye on Laurence's bedroom door. So that if the familiar shape loomed out of the darkness again then Martin could somehow raise the alarm. He'd pay for it *somehow, he knew, but he didn't care – couldn't care. He had to protect Laurence. Had to make sure that Uncle Jack didn't hurt another child. Then last night he had thought he'd heard voices from Laurence's room – but he hadn't, thankfully. But it frightened him more than ever. He'd woken that morning early, stiff-necked and freezing, having slept slumped against Laurence's door. Now, as he tried to smile through his birthday celebration, he could still feel the nagging discomfort in his back but it was worth it if it meant that Laurence had had an undisturbed night.*

Martin scanned the group again as their tuneless singing reached a crescendo. He smiled again as he saw them all. His family now, he realised. Now that he couldn't go back to London. Esther and Dots were doing a little dance, bumping their hips against each other as they sang. Mr T was glancing at his watch, eager to ensure that not too much time was spent eating cake when there was a house to be run. And there was Laurence, his little mouth open widest of all, belting out the song. But to look at him made Martin feel physically sick because behind him, a great paw placed on the child's shoulder, singing along with the rest of them but staring only at Martin with his cold eyes, was Uncle Jack.

Martin was no fool. He knew that the company Uncle Jack was supposed to own – Violet's Frozen Fish – was another way to launder money for the Krays. Out of the way like this, with Jack Ball, reformed character, at the helm, it could carry on undisturbed and unnoticed, a quiet money-spinning machine. He knew, too, that Jack Ball couldn't have run the company – that he was too violent, too preoccupied with other things – too thick – to know even the difference between a salmon and a herring. Martin knew that Christopher Calvert – Uncle Jack's nephew – had been brought up to Scotland and installed at Dubhglas for that very purpose. The skinny, bespectacled young man was a business genius and the company thrived under his diligent guidance, with the heavy hand of Uncle Jack behind him all the way, should it be needed.

And Martin knew that buying an old, rundown castle in the Scottish highlands with the profits was, to the gangster fraternity, an excellent spot for a bolthole, a hideaway, a safe house for thugs and criminals of all kinds who needed to be kept off the scene for a while. That's how Uncle Jack had justified bringing him there in the first place. He reminded him constantly of how the old lady he'd encountered during that robbery could well be dead, and that he was safer up here and out of the way. But Martin knew that he had been given a job and left there so that he was available for Uncle Jack's use any time that he chose.

Martin knew that Jack could only tolerate Dubhglas for so long, that he disliked the drab weather, the isolation. But Mr Calvert loved it, and loved the village, and had embraced the restoration of the castle, had made sure to employ locals in doing the work. He was a good man, Martin knew. A good man caught up in bad deeds. If he only knew about Uncle Jack, would he do something to help? Could he stop him? Erased some of those memories that haunted Martin. The scars. Or was he bound by the ties of family? Sometimes, on hearing Jack roar at Christopher, call him offensive names, belittle him in front of the staff, Martin felt sure that he couldn't be.

He shuddered at the thought of how filthy he felt after the great beast entered his room in the dark and knelt beside the bed. Always the same smell of dirty tobacco smoke off his clothes and his breath. Always the scar, looming over Martin's face as he woke.

As Martin watched the group encourage him to blow out his candles, he knew what he wanted most for his eighteenth birthday. The peace to sleep all night through. That's all he wanted.

He took a breath and gathered his thoughts and all his willpower into giving one of his beaming smiles back. He did love these people. The Turnbulls were like parents to him. And Claire – lovely, gentle, broken Drum. He'd seen the look in her eyes too from the very beginning. She was as damaged as him, he knew, although they had never spoken of it. That was why he had orchestrated to keep her here, probably why he had sought her out that day in the teashop. Because she was like him, she made him feel safe, like he had an ally, someone other than Laurence to carry on for. She made him feel brave.

He bent down and blew the candles out in one go, standing up again and beaming his fake smile as everyone cheered and Mrs Turnbull handed him the kitchen knife to make the first incision.

He held it in his hand, looking again at Laurence who was standing there, fists clenched, barely able to contain his excitement. Martin couldn't help but laugh. The kid had the sweetest tooth he'd ever come across. Cake meant more to him than the crown jewels.

Martin held the knife poised over the centre of the cake while Dots leaned in and removed all of the candles. Something made him look up, to look straight at Uncle Jack. The temptation was huge, Martin knew. He could just reach over the table and instead of plunging this knife into the sponge, he could plunge it into Jack Ball's black heart. The vision was so strong it frightened Martin. He could imagine the fat, scarred face register first surprise, and then pain, and finally fear as he realised what Martin had done. The blood already seeping out around the handle of the blade – dark red, filthy and stained. Then it would bubble from Jack's mouth and he'd stagger backwards before falling to the ground. Stone dead, and then he'd be gone. Forever. It would be over. Martin would be safe and Laurence would be safe. And so would all the other boys and young men that he knew must be out there, their lives tarnished by the hand of that evil thug. Martin couldn't bear to think about them too much. There might have been only one, he knew, but more likely there were hundreds. Who all felt the same as him.

It would be the perfect solution, he knew, to kill him there and then. To make sure that everyone saw it happen, make sure that they, too, knew it was finally over.

Instead, he averted his gaze, smiled at Dots as she removed the last candle with a flourish and sank the knife into the soft, creamy centre of the cake to yet another cheer from the assembled group. And Uncle Jack watched him, applauding with the staff as Mrs Turnbull leaned in and pulled the cake along the table toward her, making a swift head count before she began to deftly cut slices for everyone.

The cake cut, everyone's attention began to stray from the birthday boy. Claire was dispatched to get plates and paper napkins, Dots to get forks. Mr Turnbull himself made his way over to pick up the tray of lemonade and glasses that Mrs Turnbull had put to one side. Martin watched as Uncle Jack removed his hand from Laurence's shoulder and suddenly extended it across the table.

Towards him. He looked around to see if anyone else saw and then, unable to think of anything else to do, reached out to weakly accept the grip that the so-called master of the house extended to him. Jack smiled. In as much as he could. "Happy Birthday, Martin," he said in a low voice. "Just had to drop down to wish you Many Happy Returns."

Martin nodded, trying to extricate his hand, but Jack's grip tightened. Martin met his eyes, his mind flashing back to the first time that he'd seen him at the Gigi club. "You'll do," Uncle Jack had said then. Martin didn't know what he meant, but didn't have to wait long to find out.

Jack's stare seemed to burn through to Martin. "Eighteen. You're a man now, young Martin," he said menacingly. "All grown up."

And with that he released the grip. Martin's hand smarted from where his fingers had been crushed. And as Uncle Jack withdrew his hand, it fell again on to Laurence's shoulder, the space between fingers and thumb moulding itself around Laurence's neck. A touch of possession.

In an instant, Martin realised what had just happened. That by becoming a man, he was no longer needed. Released from his duties. No longer Uncle Jack's boy. But that meant it was definite. There was a vacancy created with Martin's coming of age. And his stomach flipped again as he looked at the innocent face of the boy who would fill it, if Uncle Jack had his way. Martin was a man now, the handshake meant. But that didn't mean that Uncle Jack didn't need a boy. Uncle Jack always needed a boy.

Martin grew suddenly aware of the loud voices of the staff around him, excited at this break from the daily routine and at the prospect of cake. Like a robot, he accepted the slice passed to him by Mrs Turnbull. smiled as Mr McAllister, the gardener, ruffled his hair. He felt as though he was outside himself as he forked a piece of the cake into his mouth. It was delicious – of course it was. Claire had made it. With love.

But suddenly it felt like poison in his system. He placed the plate on the table and fled, slipping past the others who stood, happily chatting with their forkfuls of sponge disappearing by the second. He couldn't keep it in, any longer, he knew.

Martin made it to the back door and a little beyond but no further before the piece of cake, along with the remaining contents of his stomach erupted from his stomach. He retched violently, his body purging everything he'd eaten that day. And as Martin Pine vomited violently into a drain outside the back door, he began to cry at what had happened to him. At how his life had turned out. At the thoughts, the recollections of everything Jack Ball had done to him. And what he knew he was going to do to little, innocent Laurence if Martin let him.

His insides cleared, Martin stood. He spat into the drain to clear his mouth out, and ran a fist over his eyes. No one would see him cry. Always ducking and diving, that's me, he thought to himself as he gathered himself together to return inside. He didn't know how he'd explain to Claire that it wasn't her cake that had made him ill. He could blame that on the excitement, maybe. Or a filched piece of pork pie.

He would protect Laurence, he vowed. From now on he'd do everything that he could to make sure the child remained unharmed. He'd sleep outside his door every night if needs be. But another child would not be hurt. Not if Martin Pine could help it.

CHAPTER 33

Safely ensconced in Mrs Hibbert's cosy cottage while the others caught a few hours' rest and Sue made some work calls at the castle, Martha kept half an eye on the window as daylight eventually gave up at almost four o'clock. It was as if the day just didn't have anything left and allowed itself to be overpowered by night, which brought with it a strong breeze and finally proper, freezing rain.

"What a shame," Mrs Hibbert remarked as she made her way around the small house, closing curtains as she went and lighting lamps. "I hope it doesn't put people off Mr Calvert's party. It's a small enough guest list this year as it is. Heaven be with the days when there would be hundreds of people milling around the place for the whole weekend – a shooting party then on the Sunday to clear everyone's head."

She sighed and turned back to Martha who was seated on a small sofa beside the solid fuel cooker in the kitchen, Ruby on her knee. The little girl had completely forgotten her encounter with the Christmas tree earlier. There had been plenty of diversion throughout the afternoon, of course. Will and Sue had joined them for lunch and playtime in the cottage while Gabriel spent the early part of the afternoon with his godfather as he buzzed through the castle preparing for the night's festivities. Mrs Hibbert, too, had scarcely sat down for a moment, running back and forth from her cottage to the castle kitchens, keeping an eye on the professional caterers which had been hired for the occasion.

Ruby had played for hours with the housekeeper's kitchen utensils – unfamiliar pots and pans which were all excellent musical instruments to a toddler. Martha was delighted that she had settled in so quickly, even though she couldn't manage to shake the memory of the falling tree from her mind. Another inch or two and it was down on Ruby's head. With such enormous force behind it. She shuddered to think what might have happened and picked Ruby up to hold her close for a moment.

Martha wondered if it might just have been too much to bring her along with them. She hated leaving her with anyone overnight – since Norfolk, she was even nervous leaving her for a couple of hours. And now Sue wasn't even going to watch her as had been arranged – Mrs Hibbert had offered to do it to allow Sue join in the festivities, to make up the numbers. She'd insisted so vehemently that Martha had felt obliged to agree. She'd have to get dressed up in her finery and make her way through the rain back into the castle, leaving her little girl with this complete stranger. More upheaval in her little life. Her mind strayed again to Dan – the kiss – all the things she had said at dinner only the previous night. Sue was right. She needed to get to him as soon as she got back to Edinburgh. Explain to him – face to face, of course. She didn't want to do it over the phone, not that she had a choice while at Dubhglas with the non-existent coverage – the house phone was too public.

The place seemed even more desolate and bleak as night set in. As if the rest of the world didn't just grow dark, but set the castle and its grounds adrift from the rest of civilisation. Some people loved this sort of thing, Martha thought. But not her. She craved lights, company, heat and comfort. And while all of that was available to her in Mrs Hibbert's home, there was still that threat just beyond the back door that opened on to a courtyard where log piles leaned against the back wall of the castle and herbs grew in pots scattered throughout. The threat that was just a few steps across the cobbles, always looking over the shoulder of the cottage. The threat of the castle which gave her the creeps. She wondered how Will and

Gabriel's investigation had gone the night before and then stopped herself. If they had found anything, she didn't want to know about it. There was time enough for them to tell her when they got back home.

Martha tried to block the negative thoughts and focused instead on Mrs Hibbert's kindness. The woman couldn't do enough for them. At first, Martha had been disappointed to see her sleeping quarters – a small room decorated in fawn and pink, with a single bed and beside it a low camp bed for Ruby. "She won't hurt herself if she falls from that," Mrs Hibbert had said reassuringly. "And we'll line the floor with pillows for her so that if she takes a wee tumble then it'll be a soft landing." And with that she had firmly drawn a pair of thick curtains, concealing a set of sliding doors which led from the bedroom out onto a small patio and then further into the orchard and the kitchen garden which ran parallel to the main castle lawns. "The lawns lead all the way down to the loch," the housekeeper had told Martha, pointing in the direction of where the water lay. Martha shuddered at the thought. That lake which was the cause of so much mystery. Not to the current residents of Dubhglas, perhaps. To them – should they even know about the murder – the case was cut and dried. A long-forgotten double murder by the odd-job man with a taste for young boys. But was that really the case? Martha gazed at the closed curtains, the vision of the darkening sky beyond them burned upon her brain.

As the evening wore on, the thought of staying in the cosy room with its beds for just herself and Ruby – Will, Gabriel and Sue were all billeted in the castle itself – appealed more and more as the house was buffeted by the worsening weather. The calm inside as Mrs Hibbert made tea and bustled about her chores while Martha and Ruby unpacked in their sleeping quarters, was occasionally shattered by a screaming gust of wind and the sound of rain being lashed across the long glass panes behind the curtains. An odd place for such a door, in the guest bedroom, but Mrs Hibbert explained that a previous resident, long ago – another housekeeper – had been ill for a long time and they had installed the doors so that she had a bright view of the garden and could be wheeled onto the patio on warm days. The cottage looked very old from the outside, she'd explained, but it had been modernised some time in the early 1990's. It was a little dated now, Martha thought – the pink, floral bed coverings and matching curtains with hand-sewn pelmets, the oatmeal carpet on the bathroom floor with its aubergine suite, the wallpaper decorated with cherry blossom flowers. But, like Mrs Hibbert, it was warm and certainly a lot less forbidding than the castle. As night approached, Martha found herself grateful to Will for making the decision to put her in here. "The castle's not a place for children," she remembered Hibbert saying just after the tree had fallen. Nor for her.

A plate of Violet's Fish Fingers and some thick homemade chips later and Ruby had fallen under the thrall of Mrs Hibbert who clucked away to her in her soft accent throughout the meal. Martha drained yet another cup of tea and glanced at her watch, realising that the time had come for her to prepare for the evening. She moved off the couch where she sat beside her daughter who had allowed the housekeeper to bounce her on her knee while crooning nursery rhymes in a low voice. Ruby stared, watching the woman's face intently, her eyelids growing heavy before she'd force them back open again and continue to watch her new friend. Martha smiled. This was something that Ruby didn't have, she realised. A grandmother. A proper granny to sing her these old songs and teach her how to bake, or sit for hours with her doing jigsaw puzzles. Her eyes widened as she saw Ruby finally succumb, and nestle into Mrs Hibbert's arms, relaxing against her chest, her soother lolling from her lips as she bounced her gently and continued to sing.

"You might as well take a chance on leaving now, my dear," said Mrs Hibbert softly, between the lines of a tune that Martha didn't recognise. "Why don't you get dressed in my room? It's the door next to yours – and you can be on your way. I'll take my chances with this wee one. If she'll go to sleep for me, then there's less of a shock if she wakes up and sees me with her."

It made sense, Martha knew. And she really had to get moving. She hesitated for a moment before pushing herself upwards from the cosy, threadbare sofa, and tiptoeing out of the room. She picked out the clothes she needed and then stepped under the shower for a quick wash before shutting herself into Mrs Hibbert's room to prepare herself.

When she emerged, Ruby was asleep in her bed and Mrs Hibbert was trying to figure out the workings of the baby monitor. Martha smiled, gently took it from her and pressed the 'on' switch.

"I'll most likely hear her from here anyway," Mrs Hibbert remarked, placing the monitor on the small, tiled fireplace as if it were cut crystal. "Don't you look nice though!"

Martha smiled and gave a little twirl, feeling the swing of the full-length, velvet, Empire-line gown in midnight blue which she had found in a vintage dress shop in Edinburgh. The bodice was decorated with tiny pearls, and the thick shoulder straps were trimmed with silver edging. She had teamed it with kitten heels in the same shade of blue and had pulled her hair back to one side with a diamante-encrusted fan-shaped comb. Mrs Hibbert stood back to admire Martha fully and, for a brief second, Martha was sure again that she recognised her from somewhere, that she had seen her before.

"Thanks so much, Mrs Hibbert," she said and meant it. "Not just for the compliment but for everything – for looking after us, especially when you were so busy today– it's really been lovely." Another gust of wind roared outside and the pelting rain against the house caused the monitor to crackle. Martha jumped. The damn thing always made her unnecessarily uneasy these days, especially in strange surroundings. "The afternoon with you has really been the calm before the storm – literally," she added.

The old lady waved her away. "It's a pleasure, dearie," she said. "Now get ye on up to the big house. Your friends are waiting and the wee thing – she's beautiful – is sound asleep in her little cot bed. No harm done. There's nothing to worry about."

Martha nodded, feeling that pang that she always had on leaving Ruby. Always. Without fail.

Mrs Hibbert saw the moment's hesitation. "She's perfectly safe, Martha," she said. "That's why she's out here with me. So she's safe."

Martha looked the housekeeper in the eye then, the words finally striking a chord with her. Did that mean that she would be unsafe in the castle then? The note from the butler to Gabriel said that the staff were all nervous. Why wouldn't that include Mrs

Hibbert, as sensible as she seemed? What had she seen up there? And why wouldn't a child be safe?

Hibbert broke the stare before Martha could open her mouth to speak, and bustled out of the door into the hallway, returning with what Martha realised was a black oilskin cloak and hat and a pair of wellington boots.

The old lady was smiling. "Now don't laugh at me, but I reckon this lot will complete your ensemble this evening."

Martha laughed as she allowed herself to be draped in the waterproof gear. Mrs Hibbert really had thought of everything.

"It's a short walk to the back door of the castle," she said wisely, "but it can be a wet one – I've many years experience of winters up here but I've never made the trip in gear so fine as what you're wearing so let's keep it fine, eh? There you go!" She pulled the sou'wester down heavily on Martha's ears and held her arm for balance as she slipped out of her shoes and replaced them with the boots which were a size or two too large. "Leave the lot inside the back door when you get there, and if it's still blowing a gale when you're coming back out – which I wager it will – then they're ready for you and you won't get soaked."

"Thanks again," said Martha as she allowed herself to be ushered down the small back hall.

She stood for a second or two at the open door, the hall suddenly filled with the sounds of the rain beating against the walls and down on the cobbles of the yard. The movement of the door triggered a sensor light and she saw in the distance the back door of the castle which she knew was her destination – Hibbert assured her that the plain brown door was unlocked and would lead her straight into a hallway where she should take the stone stairs up to the main body of the house. Martha smiled and thanked her again before tugging the hat down on her head and suddenly plunging herself out into the wet night, head down as she hurried toward the castle, all the time glad of the fact that Mrs Hibbert was watching from her cottage, observing her passage.

Reaching the door, with a great heave she pushed it open and made her way inside to the darkness and cold of Dubhglas Castle.

CHAPTER 34

Gabriel was the first person that Martha recognised on stepping through the doorway under the stairs into the main hallway which by now was busy with people in evening dress, milling around with drinks in their hands.

The Christmas tree which she had last seen lying across the boxes, was now upright and firmly secured, in pride of place in the hallway across from the front door where it greeted guests. It seemed friendlier now, festive, twinkling with lights, as was the garland wound around the stairway and the festive friezes atop each of the doors which led off the hallway. A couple of waiters circulated offering hors d'oeuvres – plates of crostini, mini-burgers and quiches. Martha's stomach gave a pang as she saw them. She had only picked at her meals all day, still too shaken by Ruby's near-miss with the tree to enjoy lunch. The air in the hallway was no longer musty, but now thick with the scent of pine from the Christmas tree, and of cinnamon and cloves coming from a great tureen on a trestle across the drawing-room door where a waiter ladelled out cups of mulled wine.

"Don't you look positively *splendid*," observed Gabriel as she reached him.

Martha gave a slight curtsey before taking in his appearance, then stared at him in disbelief. "You're wearing a kilt," she observed, stunned. "And those socks . . . Gabriel . . ."

Gabriel glanced down at his legs and reached an arm down to tug the end of the kilt, as if to make himself decent. "And your point is?" he queried drily.

"Your knees . . ." Martha continued, nibbling on her food and continuing to stare, a mocking expression on her face as she did so.

"I am a Scotsman, young lady," pronounced Gabriel in response, brushing his hand imperiously along the green and blue squares, "and this is my family tartan I'll have you know. Well, it's a tartan at least. Of that much I am absolutely sure. All is well in the housekeeper's outpost?" He flagged down a waiter and plucked two champagne flutes from his tray, handing one to Martha.

She accepted and nodded, looking around her then for Will. "Vicious night, isn't it?" she remarked, only to be greeted with his customary shrug followed by his attention being drawn across the room to a waving woman standing by the Christmas tree standing beside a man who was essentially an older version of Gabriel.

"That's my folks over there, actually," he observed. "Come and say hello, why don't you? Only for heaven's sakes don't mention ghosts, my brother, the Navy, the Territorial Army or Ally McCoist to my father. In that order."

Martha hid a grin as Gabriel took her arm and led her across the hallway toward the smiling couple.

An hour later and they were going in to dinner in the long banqueting hall to the rear of the castle. Will came to escort Martha and Sue in – Sue stunning in a backless, red halter-neck with matching lipstick and her blonde hair tight in a chignon. "You know me! I always keep something fancy in my overnight bag," she shrugged when Martha complimented her, as though it were the most natural thing in the world. And for Sue, it was. She was nothing if not always prepared.

Will was looking stunning himself in his dark-blue tux, his tie slightly loose at the neck from repeated tugging. Martha reached a hand out to straighten it and basked in his smile. Forget about last night, she urged herself. You didn't mean any of it. Look forward. This is what's important now.

It wasn't hard to be distracted from any such thoughts. Tall, festive flower arrangements stood at equal distances along the table which was covered with white linen and laid with red-glass goblets and tartan napkins held in shape with holly-topped napkin rings. Two more Christmas trees, smaller than the one in the hallway, flanked the fireplace behind Christopher Calvert who sat at the head of the table. Two more stood at the opposite end of the room where a small stage was prepared with a number of chairs, instruments atop them or at their legs. Martha noted the accordion with some dread. Outside, the rain lashed across the panes of glass which overlooked the lawns. It made inside seem cosier, the thick drops trailing down the windows catching the reflection from the candles and the tree lights and making the window sparkle.

And the food, when it arrived, was fantastic. A salmon and prawn starter served with crème fraiche on homemade potato cakes was followed by a creamy leek soup. The main course of simple beef and trimmings was delicious and Martha felt her seams begin to strain as she devoured the last mouthful of Yorkshire pudding and set her cutlery on her plate.

"You always do that, don't you?" grinned Will beside her.

"What?" She smiled hesitantly back, wondering what he was thinking.

"You save your favourite thing on the plate for last – like Yorkshire puds. I don't know anyone who loves them as much as you do."

Just then Gabriel appeared behind them, dinner jacket off and tie loosened. He hunkered down between Martha's and Will's chairs.

"*Whooh*! That was a good bit of scran, no?"

Martha was puzzled by the term. "Seriously, Gabriel, have you started to speak in tongues since we got here? And your accent is getting stronger too!"

"It's being around my dad," he giggled. "Military slang." He made a dismissive wave of his hand and continued to scan the room. His face was red from a combination of sitting near the fireplace and the wine he was clearly enjoying. "Those caterers are quite the job. You should hire them for your – emmm – parties. In the future. Any parties you might be having –"

"You having a good time up top there?" barked Will suddenly, changing the subject and nodding toward Gabriel's place setting.

Gabriel made his lips into an 'eee' of silent apology. "Och, you know, old folks' jokes – 'remember the times' – all that old yawn," he huffed as he glanced up the table to where his godfather, a sprig of heather pinned to his lapel, was engaged in conversation with Gabriel's parents who were seated on either side of him.

"You're having a great time, admit it!" smiled Martha.

"Do you think you might get to ask him about Pine?" said Will suddenly.

Gabriel's expression changed to one of uncertainty. "Not sure if it's the time," he said, raising his eyebrows. "It's not my parents' special subject." He stood up sharply, his knees cracking as he did so. "Oh, I've eaten too much," he groaned, and rubbed his stomach. Then, looking at Sue who was seated beside Martha but engrossed in conversation with the man to her right, he muttered, "I'd best have a word with Brice. Mr Duffy there next to her could be a really good catch for her actually. Local salmon smoker so he is." Gabriel raised his eyebrows and moved on to Sue and the salmon smoker.

Will slung an arm across the back of Martha's chair and surveyed the room.

"Did you get all that business done with Dan?" he asked suddenly.

Martha reached out and took a small swig from her wineglass, feeling herself go red as she did so. Thank heaven the room was so warm.

"The forms are signed anyway," she said. "I saw some photos as well. It looks lovely – we might take a trip there when we're with your folks next time and see –"

"Martha, when we've finished with dinner, I wonder could I talk to you about something?" Will interrupted.

Her heart froze in her chest. He knew. He must know that something had happened with Dan. What else could it be?

"It's not bad or anything," he continued, his own cheeks going a little pink.

He must have seen my face, she thought. Calm down, for heaven's sake! Don't give yourself away with a stupid guilty expression.

"At least I hope you won't think so . . ."

"Of course," she managed quietly, forcing a smile, feeling the shock of his request subside. It was probably something to do with his work, she reasoned. A six-month secondment to a haunted friary in Wales or something . . .

A shadow passed over her face for a moment, interrupted by the familiar clang of spoon on glass as speeches were announced. Christopher Calvert had risen to his feet and was demanding silence. He began to speak in a low tone that she could barely hear. It appeared that he was thanking his staff, the caterers – the usual thing, it seemed. Martha allowed her thoughts to drift off and she absent-mindedly pushed her spoon around the empty dish of panna cotta with rhubarb compote. It was so difficult to focus on the speeches in that heat. Her reverie was interrupted by applause as the speech ended.

Sue touched her arm to get her attention, announcing a little too loudly. "This is Mr Duffy, Martha! He smokes *salmon*, can you believe that?"

Martha extended her hand to greet the man and registered that while his face was distinguished, his greying hair still thick on his head, his eyes a steely blue, when he smiled his mouth was entirely devoid of front teeth, top or bottom. She could see Sue grimacing in a 'get me out of here' way and she spent the next few minutes engaged in a conversation with Mr Duffy conducted across Sue, trying to ignore the faint smell of fish and peat which was beginning to creep her way as she leant forward.

Her escape came when a team of staff entered the room and started to clear away teas and coffees. The initial whine of the accordion was the signal for toothless Mr Duffy to finally spot a fresh target and he excused himself and disappeared across the room, leaving Sue to vanish quickly to check if the weather was yet clement enough do some smoking of her own.

"Oh Christ, I hate ceilidh music!" Martha exclaimed, turning her nose up as a guitar and a fiddle joined the accordion and a joyful tune rang out across the room.

"You're not alone in that," came a woman's voice from behind her.

Martha turned sharply to see Gabriel's mother standing there.

She smiled and indicated that she should sit in the seat vacated by Sue.

The older woman was smartly dressed in a slate-grey silk shift, a shawl alive with exotic peacocks in blues and greens was draped over one shoulder to enliven the look. She was tall, her hair cut short and grey in colour. Violet McKenzie's skin was clear and her blue eyes bright. She really was an attractive woman, thought Martha as it struck her that she must be in her late seventies or even early eighties.

"That son of mine babbles on about you all the time, you know," smiled Violet, seeking Gabriel out in the crowd.

His cheeks red, he had headed to the dance floor and was attempting some sort of jig in his kilt. Martha did an exaggerated double take and it was Violet's turn to smile.

"It's good to see him enjoying himself up here for a change," she remarked, taking a sip from the glass of red she had brought with her. "He always hated it as a child. Hid in his room with earphones on, Christopher used to tell me. Had no interest in fishing or shooting or any of the outdoor stuff."

It was a simple observation but loaded, perhaps unwittingly, with comparison. Martha looked at Violet's face, as she in turn watched her son again, and realised that she was looking into the face of a woman who had lost a child. Whose firstborn had been taken from her. Alive when she left him for his summer holidays, then gone, without her being there with him when he died. Martha felt an incredible sadness sweep over her. How could she still come here, she wondered? Still function, cope, smile, *live* even? How did she get through every day?

"How's your little girl doing? Ruby, isn't it?" Violet asked politely and with real interest.

Martha averted her gaze a little too quickly and nodded. "She's great," she replied. "Sound asleep with Mrs Hibbert out in the cottage."

"I hope I can meet her tomorrow?" asked Violet. "I never thought Gabriel would speak with affection about anything that can't debate the finer points of religion with him, but he gets a real kick out of Ruby."

Martha smiled again. She knew that, but Gabriel would never have admitted it in a million years. Martha wondered exactly what sort of things he discussed with his mother when they chatted alone? He was close to her, she knew. Closer than he let on. Closer because of his father's hard line, his military discipline and methods. But in his own way Gabriel adored him too.

"This room is beautiful, isn't it?" said Martha politely.

Violet gave the room a cursory glance and responded with a shrug, the same as Gabriel's. "I've never liked this room," she observed. "Christopher built it on about fifteen years ago – he had some notion about turning the place into a wedding venue and this was as far as he got. The castle's completely unsuitable as is, of course. It needs a complete overhaul but try telling him that. He's always had his own ideas about this place, has Christopher. Stubborn old thing."

"You've known him a long time?" prompted Martha, covering her glass with her hand as a waiter bent toward her to refill.

He stepped back and then bent to Violet who held her glass up to him. She took a generous sip.

"All my life," came the response. "We were neighbours as children, went to the same school but not at the same time. I'm a wee bit younger – didn't stop me stealing his pencil-case and throwing it into a tree on the way home though!" She smiled at the memory and then tutted, shaking her head. "What a horrible cow I was," she giggled. "I suppose that's the way first love goes, though, doesn't it?" she added.

How candid, thought Martha. The source of yet another of Gabriel's traits.

"He was your first love then?" she asked.

"Absolutely." Violet nodded. "If you asked me then, or asked anyone on our road, you'd have thought that I was definitely going to be Mrs Calvert, suburban accountant's wife, seeing him off at the door each morning with a peck on the cheek."

"And what happened?" asked Martha.

The shrug came again. "This place, I suppose." Violet looked at her surroundings and Martha thought she could detect a hint of contempt in the glance. "Jack . . ."

The name hung on the air.

"Jack Ball?" Martha said hesitantly.

Violet looked at her in surprise. "You've heard of him then?" she asked.

"Just a little bit. He used to own this place, didn't he?"

Violet spluttered a little. "In name only, Martha. In name only."

"How do you mean?" prompted Martha, curious to hear about him, thirsty to hear tales of Jack Ball from someone who had known him first hand. Of course Violet would have – he had lived with the Calverts, her neighbours, for years.

"It wasn't Jack's money bought this place, but it made perfect sense to keep him up here. Like tying up the guard dog, I suppose," said Violet, her eyes glazing with the memory.

Martha straightened a little in the chair.

"Of course he never actually stayed put up here for too long. There was too much damage to be done down in London but after he served his time in prison he did things differently, kept his nose clean. He wasn't so thick that he didn't know he'd been given a great opportunity with this place by his . . . well, we'll call them bosses . . ."

Martha knew that she was referring to the Krays. Violet McKenzie had known the Krays. Bloody hell.

"He was the name behind the so-called 'business' that they'd throttled out of the Calvert family fish stall. He could have lugged mullet around indefinitely at Billingsgate but when the opportunity came to make it a bit more, he grabbed it with both hands. Literally by the throat. But his limited intelligence, shall we say, gave him only the insight that he needed someone to do his thinking for him, so who better than his sister's swotty lad? Clever old Christopher. *My* Christopher."

Martha looked on in surprise as Violet's gaze travelled across the room to the thin old man holding court still at the top table.

"I was Christopher's secretary for a while when I left school – during the transition from fish stall to factory."

A thought crossed Martha's mind. "Violet's Frozen Foods – Gabriel mentioned it was named after you, am I right?"

This was met with a dazzling smile. Violet shook her head. "What a lovely thought, but I'm afraid not! It was Jack who thought of the name. He was buttering up the real bosses of course – coincidentally Violet was the name of the main woman in their lives – their dear old mother. Jack thought if he ingratiated himself with them that he could be a big player. He wasn't fully content with the business they more or less handed him on a plate – he wanted to be like them. Strutting around London forcing people to hide from him. And Christopher could never stand up to Jack. He was a terrible bully, of course. A cuckoo in the nest – a big brawny child thrown in with his cousins who were all little sparrows. The difference made him mean. Especially to poor Christopher. He called him 'Speccy' because of his glasses, 'Birdy' because he was skinny, 'Swots' because he was brainy – wore him down so much that when he suddenly started to build him up again, telling him how he needed him to run his business, that he should forget about the skinny secretary next door – me – and take a real opportunity, Christopher was so grateful for the attention that he packed his bags and left for Dubhglas and never came back. It was the one thing that made me happy about the whole sorry mess. That Christopher inherited this place and that he loved it so much. He turned the business around, somehow managed to make it all legitimate. As for the castle, though – he's made a complete pig's ear of it, of course, but it makes him happy – one of his few pleasures in life save for the work he does in the village. And the boys, of course."

Martha glanced at Violet's wineglass, noticed it was half empty and realised that was another reason for her honesty.

"I met Phillip then, when Christopher had left to come up here, and we fell in love and had our son – it was complete coincidence that I moved to Scotland as well but Phillip was stationed up here. It was nice to be close to Christopher again. It meant I got to keep a bit of an eye on him, keep him as a friend. Jack isolated him up here completely. I felt I couldn't not ask him to be involved with . . . my sons. It was a connection for him, you see, a connection to other people. People who weren't Jack with that stinking cigar in his mouth and his camera round his neck and that filthy cat, Tiger."

Will swung his head abruptly to look at Violet. "*Tiger*?" he said, his voice intense.

Violet nodded. "He used to bring the animal everywhere with

him. It slept in his room, had the run of the place – it verged on feral, of course. A vicious thing. A rat got it in the end, I seem to remember. After Jack . . . died . . . there was no one to take care of it so it ran wild around the castle – wild enough to attack anyone who came near it, but too mollycoddled to be able to stand up for itself. No one was sorry to see it gone."

An expression of concern flickered across Will's face as Violet continued.

"I couldn't bear being around Jack, of course. Never could. So I used to leave the boys here for their holidays. Phillip approved of that, of course. Cut the apron strings, make men out of them. But look what happened . . ."

Martha felt uncomfortable. "So Christopher never married?"

Violet shook her head. "Never. He'd go on after one or two whiskys that I was his one and only. But I think his real love is Dubhglas. The village and the castle. He's made a real life for himself here. Probably better than I could have offered him – waiting by the door with his dinner made, ready to darn his socks. This way he got to carve out a real place for himself, do some good. And escape."

An uncomfortable silence fell across the trio, Violet's attention straying back to the dance floor to seek out her remaining son.

Will coughed politely. "Excuse me – I was actually just wondering if I might steal Martha away for a few moments?" he asked.

"But of course," said Violet.

Martha had turned to him in surprise. Surely he wasn't going to ask her to dance or something awful?

He saw her concern. "Don't worry, no dancing where there are accordions," he said, as if it were something he'd learned by rote. "I just want to show you something . . . nothing of . . ." he glanced at Violet who was staring intently at the dancing crowd, "a *supernatural* kind either. Look, just come with me for ten minutes and then I'll have you back here. I'll even staple you to your seat so you can't get up should an urge to break into dance strike you."

"All right then," Martha agreed, with some regret. She was fascinated by what Gabriel's mother was telling her. "If you don't mind, Mrs McKenzie?"

Violet was already distracted. "What's that? Oh, not at all, Martha. I'll see you later perhaps – but, if I don't, make sure that I get to give that wee girl a cuddle tomorrow, won't you? And enjoy the rest of your night!"

With a smile, Martha allowed herself to be steered away from the table by Will. Together, they walked out of the main doors of the function room and back along the passage that connected it to the entrance hallway of the castle, the sounds of the function room fading behind them.

CHAPTER 35

Summer 1963

"Can you look after that for me, Drum?" asked Laurence in a rush, retracing his steps from the lawn to the stone bench where she sat against the wall of the kitchen courtyard, dumping something cold and hard into her outstretched hand, and running again without a glance back toward the lake.

Claire looked at what he handed her and saw there his most prized possession – his swimming medal that he'd won at his local pool for lifesaving and which he wore proudly every day, like a war hero. Why had he taken it off now and given it to her?

She shook her head in puzzlement and sat back to wait for Martin, enjoying the last rays of the evening sunshine. Her eyes closed as she leant her head back, feeling the sun on her face, the heat sinking into her bones, the bench warm beneath her. She probably shouldn't be on the side of the wall overlooking the lawns, but it was such a beautiful evening she couldn't bear to sit indoors, nor in the shady courtyard between the castle and the Turnbulls' cottage.

The boy had started to call her Drum, she'd noticed. It was Martin's name for her. "Little Drum," he teased her affectionately. "Always banging on about something in that big loud voice of yours. Never shut up, you. Can't hear myself think with all that talking you do. Gives me a blummin' headache," he used to say, and the more she laughed, the more elaborate the effect of her alleged incessant talking had on Martin. "Rabbit-rabbit all day long. Nagging me about this and that. Can't get a word in edgeways . . ."

He was slightly late, she knew, but she didn't mind as it afforded her the chance to sit there and take in the last of the summer heat. Laurence's parents were coming in the morning to take him home for a new term at school. And then in the coming weeks, the evenings would start to close in and a chill would make the air sharp.

She glanced down again at the medal in her hand and blushed when she remembered how shy she had been around the boy when Martin had first invited her to spend time with them. "Is he some sort of lord, or royalty or something?" she had whispered to Martin when she was sure he couldn't hear. Mr Calvert treated him like he was a young king, she had noted, and so she did the same.

Martin had spluttered with laughter at the question. "God, no!" he had managed to exclaim eventually. "Kid's dad is in the army! They live in a bloody Semi D!"

She stretched in the sunlight and yawned, feeling warm and content, like she was on some sort of blissful island.

"Wotcher, puss," came a voice behind her and she pulled her arms down sharply from the stretch instinctively lest Martin launch an attack on her exposed armpits with tickles. "What's that you got in your hand?"

"Oh, it's just Laurence's medal," she said as he sat down beside her on the step, bumping his hip against hers to get her to move over. She wrapped the red, white and blue ribbon on which it hung around the bronze disc and stuffed it into her cardigan pocket. "He asked me to mind it for him and then went tearing down toward the lake. Does that boy never get tired at all?"

Martin glanced at his watch. It was going on for half past eight. "Evenings are starting to draw in," he observed. "Little tyke should be in his bed."

"It'll be quiet tomorrow when he's gone," observed Claire.

Martin nodded in agreement. "Yes, we'll miss the little fellah when he goes back, but home's the best place for him."

"But you'll have no one to play with any more," grinned Claire.

Martin looked at her for a moment, his expression deadly serious, before suddenly throwing an arm about her and ruffling her hair. Claire squealed.

"You're getting cheeky in your old age, ain't ya?" he laughed, his teeth gritted in mock ferociousness.

Claire laughed until he released her from the tight grip but kept his arm around her waist. She didn't move it. It made her feel safe.

They chatted for a long time, and then sat in silence for a while, watching the evening taking on that particular shade of summer blue. Claire rested her head shyly on Martin's shoulder and he pulled her closer to him as the sky darkened even further. Claire's attention was drawn to the first star of the evening twinkling overhead. She contemplated pointing it out to Martin but instead remained silent in his embrace.

"'Ere, check out that moon," he remarked suddenly, raising a finger to point at the great glow that was now just visible over the trees down at the lake.

Claire gasped. It looked close enough to touch, the craters and lakes clearly visible in the milky orb. She stared at it for a long time, overwhelmed, trying to imprint the picture on her mind as she often did with things that were beautiful – taking an internal photograph and saving it for later. It was a lifetime's habit for her to drink in things of beauty as if they were a dying man's draught, lest they be taken from her.

"That's beautiful, isn't it?" she said and the silence fell between them again as they took in the view. It wasn't long, however, before Martin turned his attention back to Claire and she raised her face for a kiss in which she lost herself. To them, it felt like moments, but the moon had travelled much higher in the sky by the time that they finally broke apart and Martin glanced at his watch.

"Blimey!" he exclaimed. "It's almost ten o'clock already! How did that happen?"

"Goodness!" said Claire, but she didn't budge, despite the fact that she knew she really should go to bed herself. She hated when her time with Martin came to an end and found herself trying to devise ways to make it last just those few moments more.

"I should go and check that Little Lozza is tucked up safely in his bed," he said, sitting up a little.

Claire snuggled further into his neck again, tried to make him stay. Five more minutes. "He's probably still down at the lake," she murmured.

"In the dark? On his own? He couldn't be. We just didn't notice him coming back up to the house – must have gone round to the front door."

"He's not on his own," she replied sleepily. "I saw Mr Ball going down there just before he did. I guess they're fishing or something . . ."

Claire's head was jolted upright as Martin sat up fully. "You mean Laurence is down there with Uncle Jack?" he demanded. "On his own with Uncle Jack?"

Claire nodded, looking at Martin in astonishment. She was tossed to one side as he jumped to his feet and stood, staring firstly at her and then looking down the lawn toward the lake.

"Whatever's the matter, Martin?"

"He's on his own with Uncle Jack," Martin muttered, almost under his breath. It wasn't directed at her. Without warning he broke into a run, calling over his shoulder back at her. "Get Mr Calvert! Mr Turnbull – anyone!"

"Martin!" Claire called after him, standing herself, brushing her skirt down. "What's happening? Why do you –"

"Just get someone!" Martin yelled as he pelted down the lawn in panic.

Claire watched him, bewildered, for another few seconds. She didn't know why he wanted her to do it, but she turned in the settling darkness and made her way back inside to fulfil his request.

CHAPTER 36

Martha held Will's hand loosely as they drew further away from the noise and warmth of the function room. It was cooler along the passage and Martha regretted not bringing a wrap. She cocked her head to one side to more clearly hear a noise that sounded to her at first like distant drummers but then realised that it was the rain, lashing against the castle, growing louder at every second. As they emerged into the main hall the sound seemed to fill the space as it battered the roof above and Martha looked upward as if it might cave in any second. A gust of wind screamed all of a sudden and she shivered violently. There was a whine to it that sounded almost human.

"Where are we going?" she asked Will quietly. Afraid to speak in case someone could hear her. She had never had a stronger feeling of being out of bounds, somewhere that she shouldn't be.

He halted and glanced nervously around. "I'm, eh, not sure actually. There's something . . . oh, shit . . ." He fumbled in his pocket – the left first and then the right, then dropping Martha's hand to search both at the same time. "I've forgotten it," he mumbled. "Wait there. I've left something upstairs Stay right here, okay? I'll only be a second. Don't move." Behind them noise from the function room grew loud for a moment and then faded again. Will and Martha both jumped as a voice came from the darkness behind them.

"Where are you two off to?" came Sue's voice. "I couldn't stay in there a second longer – everyone smells of peat. Or maybe that's still the toothless guy and I can't shake the stink."

She joined them and Will sighed, annoyed. "I've . . . eh, just left something upstairs," he said, looking directly at Sue.

Martha glanced from one to the other. The knowing look on Will's face, the sudden flicker of recognition on Sue's.

"*Oh shit!*" Sue exclaimed suddenly. "Em, that's where I'm going too. Upstairs. Bursting for the loo actually. Won't be a second"

In an instant Will and Sue had fled for the stairs, watched by a puzzled and hurt Martha. What was going on? Was Will sharing some sort of evidence with Sue, something that he'd found the night before that he didn't want to show to her? She pouted as they took off up the stairs together at speed. She made to follow them and then stopped herself. It was clear that they didn't want her with them – Will had told her not to come, after all. She glared after them, feeling left out and alone.

The feeling only lasted a moment, however, as a torrent of raindrops distracted her, beating solidly on the roof above. She shuddered. The hallway was dim now, the only illumination a single bulb under a dark glass globe that hung down from the high ceiling and the faint light provided by the Christmas lights on the garlands and the trees. Martha heard Will and Sue's footsteps clatter distantly upstairs and then fall completely silent.

She felt very alone in the space and looked around her, taking in the height of the ceiling, the stone floor, the heavy occasional furnishings dotted around the edges of the hallway, the doors downstairs, and up. Her eyes travelled to the doors that led off the mezzanine upstairs. Where did they all lead, she wondered, and all at once felt dwarfed by the possibilities.

"That was smooth," remarked Sue sarcastically as they stood outside the door of Will's room, waiting for him to open it. The lighting in the passage outside the rooms was so dim, like everywhere else in this damn castle, he thought to himself, that it was virtually impossible to see the lock to insert the rusty key that Gifford had given him.

"You weren't exactly the Queen of Cool yourself," he replied, distracted. Finally the door budged and he pushed it open, bracing himself in case there was something inside that he didn't want to see. A gush of wind screamed down the chimney, as they entered and he jumped. His hand flapped around the wall until he found the light switch and he was thankful that someone had replaced the blown light bulbs during the day, for what good they did.

"That's one more thing that this place needs – sixty-watt bulbs," he grumbled.

"Screw the bulbs," hissed Sue. "*Show me!*" Her excitement was palpable and infectious.

Will gave a quick glance around and saw the ring box where he had left it, on the bedside table. He reached across the bed, handed it to Sue and pointed at the bathroom door. "Just going to attend to some business," he observed, ignoring Sue's look of disgust which soon disappeared as he locked the door and she opened the box. Her face fell a little as she held the ring up to the weak light, turning it this way and that, watching it glisten and then, satisfied, she replaced it in the box, closed the lid and took in the room around her.

"Amazing interior decorator in this place, huh?" she called toward the bathroom, walking to the centre of the floor at the end of the bed and taking it all in with an expression of distaste. Her attention was drawn to the incongruous metal filing cabinet and she moved toward it, reaching out an arm to tug at the top drawer. There was no budge. No sound either of Will emerging from the bathroom. Sue grasped the key which appeared to be rusted into the lock on the top right-hand side. She tried turning it to the right first. Nothing. Then the left. She jiggled it – it was against her nature to see a key in a lock and leave it unturned.

Sue heard the toilet flush at the same time as another sweep of wind and rain drove against the window. Her attention was momentarily distracted by how loud it was, the gust of wind making a long whine trail down the chimney. For a second she glanced away from the key in her hand. And that was when it turned.

Her eyes shot back to her hand. *But that was impossible!* It was completely rusted shut. No one had opened this in years. But there, like it had been freshly oiled, it had twisted open. Like someone else had done it for her . . .

Downstairs in the hall Martha stood shivering in her sleeveless gown. What *were* Will and Sue up to? This was ridiculous. What was he thinking of, dragging her out of the function room for no good reason and then leaving her here in the cold dank hall?

A sudden noise drew her attention sharply toward a door behind and she swung around to look at it, sure that there was someone there. She couldn't see anybody, but something drew her toward it. "Hello?" she asked, hearing the word echo around the freezing hallway and taking a tentative step in the direction of where she had heard the noise.

Gently pushing open the door, she peered inside and instantly shrank back for a moment. Lit faintly by wall lights and with a soft glow from a dying fire, the room that must be the library, if she remembered Will's account of the castle correctly, was as intimidating as he had described. Curious, she gingerly took a step further in and felt silence close around her. There was nothing to be heard – not a trace of ceilidh music in the distance, not a footstep from upstairs. There was even a momentary lull in the storm.

Will emerged from the bathroom, drying his hands on a towel. "Bloody towels are like sandpaper! What's the matter?" He stopped in his tracks, catching sight of Sue's face, shocked in the dim light.

She pointed to the cabinet with her free hand, the other still grasping the key as if it couldn't let go. "I seem to have opened this somehow," she said cagily. Slowly, she pulled the top drawer open toward her.

Will threw the hard, threadbare towel on the bed and joined her.

They peered in, both recoiling from the cloud of must and stale air which billowed out. The drawer was deep, and dark. Sue reached her hand in and felt around inside. Will heard her palm brush against some sort of paper as she did so and he watched as she withdrew her hand, a number of photographs held in it. She turned toward the light with them as she checked the images, leaving Will to peer into the drawer again to see if she had missed any. She had. There was one stuck under the metal edge of the drawer. He was about to retrieve it when Sue spoke, a little breathlessly, and turned to show him what she held in her hand.

"This is Gabriel's brother, isn't it?" she asked, fanning out the six or so photographs in her hand and pointing to one of them.

Will peered at them, patting his pocket for his phone and the torch app which he had decided against using the previous night. He fumbled with it, and then held the small but powerful beam of light toward the images to get a better look.

"Sure is," he agreed.

The black-and-white pictures were shot from an open window out onto grass. Clear as day, two of them focused on one subject only. Laurence McKenzie at play on the lawn of Dubhglas Castle, deep in a game, unaware that he was being photographed

"They were taken out that window," observed Will, nodding his head in the direction of the curtains which were tonight closed.

"But the rest . . ." Sue pointed at the remainder and gathered them back into her hand, "weren't."

She flicked through them one by one so that Will could see under the scrutiny of his phone-torch again. They were of boys. Four different boys, aged roughly between the ages of eight and sixteen. Like the photos of Laurence, they had been taken without the subject knowing. One on a street, against the backdrop of a market. two in a park, the last out a window also, the boy playing hopscotch on the street below completely unaware that his image was being captured.

Sue looked at Will, an expression of discomfort on her face. "They're not exactly what you'd call offensive by today's standards," she said quietly. "But I find these images really unsettling, don't you?"

Will nodded, staring at the shots again and then looking away from them quickly, as though he shouldn't have looked at all. He took the prints from Sue's hand and wordlessly dropped them back into the drawer. He was about to shut it when he spotted the photo that had been left behind. He plucked at it to retrieve it and held it up to the light, doing a double take as he caught a glimpse of the subject. Again it was taken without the boy's knowledge, this one a little older than the others but thin of frame and slightly girlish of feature. Will held the torch up again and studied it more closely, recognising from Sue's files the image of a young Martin Pine. It was taken at what looked like a theatre, or a nightclub – Pine was sitting beside a showgirl in full costume and headgear who was showing daring amounts of flesh. The young man looked obviously uncomfortable at the proximity of the woman. And at first glance it seemed as though the woman was the subject matter of the picture. But taken in context with the other photos, Will felt sure that wasn't the case. He pocketed the shot and then shut the drawer gently.

"We'd better get back to Martha," said Will, clearing his throat. The wind gave another piercing whistle down the chimney and he stirred a little. "She's downstairs by herself – she'll be terrified," he said, reminded again that it wasn't safe for her – for Sue either, for that matter. After everything that had happened – those scratches on his arm, the tree falling so close to Ruby, Gabriel's sense that something was going to happen . . .

Entering the room, Martha had felt as though she were entering a different space and time somehow. She had stood there, taking it all in: the walls lined with book-laden shelves, hardbacks, paperbacks, leather-bound tomes – the clutter of chairs, occasional tables, display cabinets scattered here and there, the baby grand piano. In the gloom she had walked about the room cautiously, peering at the titles of the books on the shelves, studying the odd ornaments crowding every surface – she shuddered as she encountered a stuffed weasel baring its vicious teeth.

It was all so forbidding. As the whole castle was, in fact. Or was she just projecting her awareness of its nasty history on it? Poor little Laurence . . . Martin Pine . . . Jack Ball . . .

She had shaken off those grim thoughts. She couldn't allow herself to think of things like that alone in a cold, dim room. It was unnerving enough as it was, without allowing her thoughts to stray. Deep breaths, she had thought. Deep breaths. Time to leave. Will would be back any second now.

She moved towards the door. Then stopped suddenly and swung around. She thought . . . no, she was sure she had heard a noise come from the direction of the piano – like a breath, a sigh or a very light cough perhaps. She stood totally still, breath held for a moment, to see if she could hear it again, but there was nothing. Don't be ridiculous, she chastised herself, forcing her ear to see if she could pick up distant sounds from the party but to no avail.

She turned to go, then stopped and held her breath again, listening. She was sure she had heard the sound again.

Unnerved, she turned and glanced around the room quickly. The first time she could have easily just been hearing things – it happened all the time. There was a lot of extraneous noise that could be misinterpreted – the wind, the rain. But a second? An identical noise? An identical breath? A wave of goose-bumps ran down her bare arms as she became sure, all of a sudden, that there was someone in the room with her. Yet as far as she could see, there was no one else there. She was completely and utterly alone. Martha felt a familiar dread begin swell in her gut.

She exhaled quietly, terrified lest even the smallest breath or rustle of her clothing would cover another sound, and strained her ears to hear anything else that might be there. She was suddenly aware – overwhelmed – by the possibilities that lay in all the dark spaces – the alcoves either side of the fireplace. the spaces behind chairs, the ceiling, *under* the piano itself.

Martha felt herself start to panic and tried to control it. The noise had been like a breath, she thought, but it could have been anything – peat shifting in the fire perhaps? A mouse scratching? There is no one here, she urged herself. Be logical about things. And just *leave*.

But she couldn't leave. Frozen with fear, she found herself rooted to the spot, incapable of moving a step, afraid to turn her back on whatever might be there . . .

She suddenly turned her head, feeling in an instant like there was someone behind her. Nothing. The space behind her toward the window and the door was empty. No one had joined her in the vast and dim room.

No one had to, an inner voice said. *They were here already*.

Again, Martha took a deep breath and shook the voice away.

Then suddenly, again, just when her attention was focused elsewhere, there was a small, vague noise, a movement. There was no mistaking it. Martha stared in the direction of the bookshelves to the left of the fireplace. It had been something definite that time, she was sure. But it was the one area of the room that was relatively uncluttered. She could clearly see the shelves – about three feet of clear floor space in front of them, with no chairs, or small tables, or geegaws of any sort.

Martha found herself drawn to the space, unable to take her eyes away from it, as if staring at it for long enough might reveal to her what exactly had made the noise she had *almost* heard.

It was then that she noticed it. The book. She could just about make out that the cover was a burgundy colour, embossed with gold lettering, on the second shelf from the bottom, about a foot away from the floor. Where all the other books were firmly in line with each other, pressed right in to the back of the shelf, this one jutted out right to the edge. She found herself drawn toward it for some reason and took the steps from where she stood, surveying the room, to where the book sat, out of place and, she felt, somehow calling for attention, as if the other books were trying to squeeze it out – or it was trying to squeeze itself out. She watched, transfixed, as it did just that. The book edged itself out from the shelf and plopped the short distance to the floor. The other books relaxed into the space it had occupied and Martha stared in disbelief. The book had just *removed* itself from the shelves. *Classic poltergeist,* she heard Will say in the back of her mind. A spirit had done this. Someone was there, with her . . .

Enough, she thought, and turned sharply, ready to make for the door. She had barely taken a step when, out of nowhere, something hard hit her square on the eyebrow, just adjacent to her temple. The room flared white and Martha grunted, her hand shooting to the side of her head where the object had made its impact. She was dimly aware of the thud as she saw the book bounce off her skull and hit the floor. For a second she could think of nothing else, had to stop to allow the searing pain to fade. The impact dazzled her, confused her completely. There was a warm sensation under her fingers. It took her a few moments to realise that it was blood.

Will had already opened the bedroom door when he realised that Sue hadn't budged from her position at the filing cabinet. As he'd looked at her questioningly, she'd placed her hand on the second drawer down, her huge green eyes focused on Will's face.

He'd hesitated, thinking of Martha alone downstairs, then reluctantly closed the door again.

Sue had given the drawer a tug, her eyes still fixed on his face. It slid open and they'd looked down together, peering in nervously, afraid of what they might find. There was nothing.

Nor was there anything in the third drawer.

Then Sue's hand had made its way down to the bottom drawer and she'd tugged gently to open it but it had failed to yield. She'd pulled it again and it moved a little, but not enough to force it open.

Will had taken a turn then but was unable to get it open. He shone his phone-torch in and examined the edges closely, leaning right down to get a closer look.

"Have you got a nail-file?" he asked. "One of those metal jobs?"

Sue snorted. "Not *on* me right now, goshdarnit," she sneered. "I think I left it in 1965 along with my lace hanky and a fresh ribbon for my hair. A metal nail-file, Peterson? Seriously!"

Will looked at her and frowned. "Over there," he urged her, pointing to the back of the door where his jacket hung. "The pocket of my jacket – there's a penknife in there actually. Could you get it for me?"

Sue did as she was told, squatting back down to peer at what Will was doing once she'd handed him the implement. "A nail-file you ask for? When you've got the whole Swiss army in your pocket? Think, Will, think!" She tapped the side of Will's head for emphasis and giggled as he chipped away at whatever was holding the drawer shut. Both the discovery they had made and the relief of what they *hadn't* discovered had made her slightly giddy.

"This is well and truly jammed," he said.

Sue sat back on her hunkers and continued to prattle. "Where did you get the big sparkly ring, by the way? I did you a deal with those guys who make the really unusual pebble rings. Although I have to admit that Martha *will* probably prefer the shiny one. When are you going to do it? A moonlit walk by the lake in this weather isn't really on . . . oh!"

The drawer had shot open.

"What is *that*?" said Sue.

They leaned in further to see the drawer's contents more closely.

"What's all this stuff?" Sue asked, reaching a long, red nail in to poke at the pile of filthy pink, shiny fabric, for all the world like a quilt of some sort.

Silently, Will forced himself to reach in and withdraw something black that he could just about see among the folds of stinking fabric. He pulled the long strap all the way out from its soft hiding place and held it aloft, watching the camera swing from side to side. Something caught his eye suddenly and he lifted the apparatus closer to his face, holding it up to the light. It had faded a little over time but the monogrammed initials were still clear enough.

"I'm not sure what else is in there," he said, concentrating hard, "but I think we may just have found out who our photographer might be."

He dangled the camera toward Sue so that she could get a better look. It took a moment for her to realise what she was looking at, but when she did, recognising the initials as a J and B intertwined, she gave a gasp and bit her lip, looking at Will with wide eyes.

CHAPTER 37

Martha staggered through the library door back into the hallway. Her mind was a complete jumble, her heart pounding, her body electric with fear. She was only vaguely aware of being surrounded by the noise of rain beating like applause on the building. Instead, she was deafened by the jagged rasps of her own breath and the clatter of her feet on the hall tiles. What the hell had just happened? Her head throbbed where the book had hit her. And what about the blood, now seeping through her fingers from her temple? She stopped moving, her mind a blank, and turned to stare back at the library door, terrified lest whatever was in there should lurch out and that she should see it.

She staggered a few feet further toward the centre of the hall, a feeble attempt at making herself safe, creating a distance between herself and what had happened. She felt her palm, wet and sticky with blood, and the realisation dawned on her that she could be badly injured. She glanced up the stairs . . . where had Will and Sue gone? What was taking them so long? Anger mingled with the terror.

She had to be with people, she suddenly realised. Had to get some help. Still clutching her head, she started back toward the dining room, back to the party. A sudden moment of clarity hit her, however. She couldn't go back in there. A party, in full swing, and in walks a woman bleeding from the head, injured by an object thrown at her by something unseen? Martha trembled. No one would believe her for starters, they'd think she was crazy – and it would cause such a scene. Questions – people would ask questions that she couldn't answer. *Where the bloody hell was Will?*

She thought about calling for him, but was worried that it might attract more attention to herself in the silence of the hall. She could go upstairs after him, but she didn't know where he was. She hadn't so much as set foot on the first step since she got here, and she didn't want to have to go searching in the dark when she hadn't a clue where she was going. Not here, not now. Her chest tightened with another wave of panic and she looked yet again at the library door. She had to get away from there, reason out what had happened to her. She'd have to go back to the cottage. That was it. Mrs Hibbert . . . Gabriel said that the staff knew that something odd was going on. Perhaps *she* wouldn't think Martha was crazy . . .

She felt a fresh throb of pain from her head. Be practical, she thought. She had to get her wound seen to. The practicality of the thought spurred her onwards and she turned sharply and began walking at first, breaking into a run as the terror of what could yet come behind her gripped her.

Martha pelted back the way she had come when she had first entered the castle earlier in the evening, through the door under the turn in the stairs, into the dark passageway beyond. She paused for a second, feeling a little braver as the door to the hall closed behind her, a barrier between herself and what had just happened. Then fresh anxiety rippled through her as she was confronted with the darkness. She reached her free hand to the wall and felt for a light-switch but could find none. Stay calm, she told herself, her breath still coming in short gasps, keeping her hand pressed to the cold stone for security. Her eyes adjusted a little to the darkness and she looked down, teetering for a second on the edge of the top step of the steep flight of old stone stairs which spiralled down before her, which she had climbed to initially enter the castle. She took a deep breath and tried to ignore her racing heart as she began her shaky descent, her legs trembling, her knees threatening all the way to betray her.

It seemed like an age before she felt the different floor surface of the flag-stoned passage under her feet. There was a hint of light now, and sounds of people and clattering pots and pans. The kitchens, of course. A wave of hope washed over Martha. She contemplated for a moment seeking help from the kitchen staff – they'd have first-aid kits, training . . .

She banished it. Again, she couldn't face it. The scenario was too unbelievable. She was best braving the elements and just getting back to the cottage, getting out of the castle altogether. She reached out in the dark and found the wall opposite her, then turned left and felt her way along the wall.

It was growing brighter ahead of her, a passage off to the right throwing some light out into the passageway and she was able to remove her hand from the wall where it had guided her, finally able to see where she was going. She winced as her head gave a throb, and carried on, trying to move more quickly now, comforted by the faint bustle she could hear from the kitchens, a clatter of pans and glassware, conversation. She walked on, getting closer to the sounds. It was dark again down here, but she didn't care. She could feel the hint of colder air and knew that she was near the back door. Her steps quickened with relief. She wouldn't bother with the raingear – she knew she'd get soaked but she didn't have the time or the patience to fumble with it. She didn't care about her party dress, she wasn't going back up there anyway.

She glanced back, as though she might see something, the thought flashing across her mind that whatever it was that had injured her in the library could still be coming, could be *anywhere*.

She didn't see the dark shape before her step from a door on her right – wasn't aware that there was anyone – *anything* – in the small passage with her until she touched against it, the fingers of her free hand brushing against something too late for her to withdraw. Martha walked directly into a human form, her mind flashing white with fear, turning blank as she squeezed her eyes shut and finally screamed.

CHAPTER 38

The red handprint on Mrs Hibbert's pale pink sleeve where Martha had tried to fight her off was vivid. The blouse was ruined, Martha knew, and she burned with a sudden and fierce embarrassment, made more intense by her bubbling emotions, the residue of the terror she had experienced upstairs.

"I'm so sorry, Mrs Hibbert," she managed.

It struck her that she should make some attempt to let Will and Sue know where she had gone, but she felt so drained all of a sudden, sitting there in some sort of old kitchen, the woman fussing around her, peering at the cut on her forehead. It felt so warm in here, so comforting. She'd just stay here a while, have someone else look after her for a bit . . .

"That's fine," replied Mrs Hibbert in a soothing tone. "I must have given you a terrible fright stepping out in front of you like that. Your wee girl is fine by the way, I've left Laura with her – she's one of the weekend girls and she's very good. I'd only popped in here for a moment myself to find something Mr Gifford needed."

Martha blushed again. Ruby. It hadn't even occurred to her to be concerned that the woman in whose care she'd left her daughter was here in front of her. She felt exhausted and overwhelmed.

"That's such a nasty cut," fussed Mrs Hibbert as she crossed the room to the old Belfast sink under the high window and ran water into a bowl. She rummaged then in a cupboard until she found a first-aid box. Crossing back to the table, she removed a thick roll of cotton wool and dipped a segment in the water. She dabbed gingerly at the wound at first, tutting as she peered closely at it.

The room was lit by a single fluorescent strip that hung directly over their heads. Martha sat in a wooden chair at the head of a long formica-topped table with her back to the doorway. The chair faced toward an unused solid-fuel stove, old-fashioned but highly polished.

"You shouldn't have tried to come down in the dark, my dear," said Mrs Hibbert and Martha realised the old lady thought she had hit her head against the rough brickwork of the wall in the dark. "But of course you didn't know where the light-switches were . . . I should have told you . . ."

Mrs Hibbert looked up suddenly as someone entered. Martha couldn't turn her head but she heard the squeak of a door and the kitchen sounds that had guided her down the dark passages outside grow loud for a moment. A man's voice spoke.

"Everything all right here, Mrs Hibbert?"

"Everything's fine, Mr Gifford," the old woman replied, holding Martha's head still as she spoke. "We've just had a wee accident here but nothing to worry about."

"If you're sure then? I'll be off so. Thanks for finding that serving dish for me by the way. Sorry to drag you out on a night like this."

"Not at all." The old woman resumed dabbing at the cut, wetting a clean piece of cotton wool and swirling it over Martha's cheek. "Safe home and I'll see you tomorrow. We've ten for lunch."

"Ten. That's good then. Goodnight, Claire."

And with that, the squeak as the door closed again and the man was gone.

Mrs Hibbert concentrated on cleaning the cut.

"Is it all right?" asked Martha tentatively. "There was so much blood . . ."

"Nothing to worry about at all," repeated Mrs Hibbert. "I thought at first you might need a stitch but you don't. The cut's a little bleeder all right but I've cleaned most of it away. I'll put some disinfectant on it and pop a plaster on it. That should do you."

Martha was grateful. "Thank you so much," she said sincerely. "I really wouldn't fancy a trip to hospital on a night like this."

The housekeeper continued to busy herself with the first aid. "Och, I could sew you up myself in no time," she said, applying the disinfectant while Martha winced. "I've been in this job so long I've seen my share of slipped carving knives. It saved a lot of time and effort for me to learn how to do a few stitches." She smiled warmly and looked full on at Martha.

It was then that she saw it. The faint trace of the eye turned inwards, not as evident as when she'd first looked at this face, in the grainy photograph. Martha gasped.

"You're Claire Drummond, aren't you?" she blurted, without thinking.

The old woman stopped what she was doing. "How . . . how do you know that?"

Martha wished she had said nothing. "Your picture . . . I saw your picture . . . we were looking at the files about . . . what happened here. About Laurence . . ."

Concern spread across Mrs Hibbert's features and she stared at Martha. "How did you get that cut?" she then asked sharply. "It wasn't an accident, was it?"

It was Martha's turn to feel uncomfortable but she didn't have anything left in her to make something up. "I was in the library . . ."

Mrs Hibbert gave a start. She stood up straight, the expression on her face turning to pure worry. She turned her back on Martha to rummage in a drawer.

"There was a book . . ." began Martha, allowing the sentence to trail off, unsure if the older woman was listening to her at all.

Mrs Hibbert turned, brandishing a plaster, and came back to Martha, all the while avoiding eye contact.

She made to pull the package apart to retrieve the bandage inside but, as Martha's eyes travelled down to watch, she saw that her fingers were trembling violently and she gave up.

"I knew it. Knew that it was only a matter of time before someone got hurt in the castle," she said, looking away from Martha.

She was talking almost to herself and Martha leaned closer to hear what she would say next.

"I asked Mr Gifford if there was any way at all to cancel this party," the housekeeper said a little louder, her voice trembling, "but he said Mr Calvert was having none of it. He doesn't know he's here, of course. Or if he does, he chooses to ignore it . . ."

"Who doesn't know *who's* here?" probed Martha, a feeling of uncertainty creeping through her. Did the old woman understand what she'd said or rather what she *hadn't* said about how she'd obtained the wound? Martha at once became fearful of continuing the conversation, of facing what Mrs Hibbert might say next.

The housekeeper looked Martha straight in the eye finally, before she spoke.

"If you saw me in those files then I'm sure you'll have seen him too," she whispered, her voice quaking.

"Who?" asked Martha again, unsure whether or not she wanted to hear what she knew would come next.

It seemed to take an age for Mrs Hibbert to finally speak. "Uncle Jack," she whispered, so low this time that had Martha not faced her directly, had not read her lips, she wouldn't have known what the old woman had said.

Martha felt herself turn to ice.

"Jack Ball," said Mrs Hibbert by way of clarification. She looked around her, taking in whole room, as if checking that they were alone. "He's come back for someone. Come back for Martin."

Martha sat there in silence herself. She felt herself reel a little. She wasn't sure what to do, what to say next. "You mean Martin Pine?" Her voice shook as she spoke the words.

A tear rolled down Claire Hibbert's face and she stifled a fearful sob. She nodded and Martha sat back in her chair to take it in.

"It's all my fault," sobbed Claire, looking around the room frantically. "I made a promise to Martin and I haven't kept it yet – I promised I'd tell someone, that I'd give her the letter he wrote before he . . . There was an injustice done here. So long ago that you'd think it wouldn't matter but it does. If I'd just done what I promised him, then he wouldn't have to be here, do you understand? And if *he* wasn't here, then Jack Ball wouldn't be here and none of this would be happening!"

Martha leaned across and grasped at one of her hands which rested on her lap. "Calm down, Claire," she said softly. "I'm sure it's not your fault."

"But it is," gasped Claire. "We were in love, me and Martin . . . I should have said something . . . I *knew* he couldn't harm anyone. He didn't do it . . ."

"Wait, Claire, slow down," Martha said insistently, and then more quietly, "When you say he didn't do it, when you say that an injustice has been done, what do you mean? Are you saying what I think?" Martha paused, gripping the wrinkled hand, searching the woman's face. Could it all be true then? Could there be substance to it? She could only whisper the words. "Was Martin Pine innocent of those murders?"

Martha felt the warm old hand grasp hers back. Claire Hibbert looked down at where their fingers were joined, sniffed, took a breath, and looked up again. She nodded.

"That's right," she managed. "You *do* know about this, don't you? All of you? It's why you're here? Why Gabriel and his friend were here in the kitchen so early this morning?"

Martha blinked. This woman had actually been here when it had all happened. When Laurence and Jack Ball were murdered. If she said – if she somehow *knew* that Martin Pine was innocent, then all of this was true – the messages in Gabriel's flat, Will's theory about what they meant, Angeline Broadhead's chilling words . . .

Martha's head throbbed as she tried to take it all in. Up until now, it hadn't seemed real somehow, despite the newspaper cuttings and the constant conversations, despite actually going to the bother of coming to the castle. But suddenly, as she touched the woman's skin, she felt a strange connection to it all, felt the story suddenly come to life. It grew vivid in an instant, the characters not just pictures in Sue's file, but *real* people – here was one of them before her. And Martin Pine really could be innocent. A picture of his face, that photograph from the files, flashed suddenly in front of her eyes, so real that Martha felt she could reach out and touch it.

She watched as Claire Hibbert gently released her hand from

where it was intertwined with her own and, with weary movement, pushed herself upright. She walked slowly and with effort across to the worktop beside the stove where an electric kettle stood.

"I'll make us some tea, shall I?" she asked, and Martha shivered as a loud gust of wind screamed past the castle, flinging rain like a handful of pebbles against the window.

CHAPTER 39

The day was glorious as the woman stepped from the black cab and eyed the buildings nervously. She wished that she hadn't bothered with her heavy raincoat now. She took it off and draped it over her arm. The sky was cloudless, sharp blue as far as the eye could see. Which wasn't very far, she noted, as the five tower blocks soared high above her, casting shadows over the courtyard. This place was no different to thousands of other tower blocks across the world – children playing in the shade of the courtyard below, washing hanging on the walkways between the flats, women watching their offspring and sharing gossip with their neighbours, unemployed men staring with suspicion at the newcomer from doorways, cigarettes dangling from lower lips.

The boy – an old man now – lived on the fifth floor and the woman, too terrified to take the stinking lift, was bathed in perspiration by the time she reached his door. She hesitated for a moment to collect herself, smoothed back the grey hairs that had strayed onto her forehead during the climb and ran her hand under each eye to wipe away the light sheen of sweat on her cheeks. She took a breath and, after another second of hesitation, knocked lightly.

Everything about Martin Pine had turned grey in the years since she had seen him – his curly hair which remained thick, the faint traces of a beard appearing on his chin – even his skin was grey. He opened the door nervously and peered outside with his grey, sad eyes, registering no emotion when he saw who was outside. The visit wasn't a surprise after all.

The woman – Claire Hibbert, formerly Drummond – entered slowly, stepping carefully over the threshold and peering down the hallway before her. She couldn't help but wrinkle her nose a little. The smell wasn't of cooking or human waste or anything so unpleasant, but the air was thick with the musty smell of a human body and cigarette smoke. She had found Martin's smell reassuring once, but now it assaulted her and then enveloped her as she stepped timidly inside and he closed the door with its cracked frosted pane of glass behind her.

Nothing was said at first. Pine, remembering himself, twitched his arm in the direction of a door at the end of the hallway to indicate that Claire should go through. With a small nod of acknowledgement she did, taking four steps and pushing the door at its end, with its thick layers of yellowed gloss paint and scratched metal handle. She was hit at once by a wall of light – the beaming sunshine of the day filling the picture window that looked out over the square created by the grouping of the apartment towers. Claire blinked a little, registered that the smell was stronger here, and that there was little or no ventilation except for a small top window which was open an inch.

She stopped in the doorway and surveyed the room before her – everything was yellowed from smoke – the once-white walls, the stippled ceiling, the skirting. The net curtains which had been pulled to one side along a grubby curtain-wire were grey with age and dirt and she noted that the windowsill was dotted with occasional dead flies. The plain brown carpet tiles had seen better days as had the furniture – a once-beige suite with flattened cushions, a matching armchair facing a small portable TV. She could just about make out the shape of a quizmaster and two contestants on the screen through a thick snow. There was a coffee table bearing only an ashtray filled with butts, emitting a thin wisp of stale smoke into the air where a cigarette had just been extinguished.

As she looked around, Martin Pine pressed the 'off' switch on the TV. In an instant the room was thankfully silent, a relief from the deafening fizz of the white noise.

Through the silence, Martin made an attempt at speech, but blushed as no word came out – just a guttural noise, a mixture of a cough and a grunt. He cleared his throat, embarrassed, and tried again. Claire wondered when had been the last time he had spoken to another person?

"Welcome," he managed nervously on his second attempt, and as she heard his voice, the emotion finally hit her.

There he was. The boy who had kissed her at the kitchen door, held her close by the lakeshore that lifetime ago. The fresh-faced, cheeky lad who had shared his cake and his coffee that sweltering day when she had first run to Dubhglas. And this was what he was now, what he had come to, this grey old man for whom words refused to form. So alone.

The wave of feeling was tinged with nerves. She looked at her feet, folded her hands together as if in prayer and paused to control herself before replying.

"Hello, Martin," she said. There was so much more to say, but where to start?

"You got my letter then," he said, indicating that she should sit down in the armchair.

She managed a short smile, smoothed the skirt beneath her, and perched on the edge of the chair, to avoid the indignity of sinking into it. She took a moment to arrange herself – to place her handbag on the ground beside her, and carefully smooth the raincoat over the arm of the chair where it covered a multitude of small burn marks. Pine took her lead and sat himself on the edge of the furthest cushion on the couch, closest to the window.

Claire glanced up to find him looking at her, taking her in.

For a second, in the sunlight, there was a trace of the boy she had once known, and then he was gone – in his place, a worried and sad old man, thin-lipped and hard. And desperately uncomfortable.

She tried a warmer smile. "It's good to see you, Martin," she said. She had thought she'd forgotten her feelings from back then but here they were, despite their grim surroundings, despite the

309

hardness of the features that looked back at her. This was proving much more difficult than she thought.

"It's very good of you to come," he managed.

She shook her head in denial. "I was due some days off." She paused. "I'm going home this evening on the five o'clock train."

Silence fell in the room.

"By home, do you still mean . . . the place?" he asked.

"Dubhglas?"

"The castle," replied Martin.

Claire nodded. "I live in Mrs Turnbull's cottage now," she said. "Myself and my husband . . ." She paused, she didn't know exactly why but it felt wrong somehow to mention Jim. "Well, we moved in there when Mrs Turnbull had to go into a home. The poor dear couldn't look after herself – she was confined to a wheelchair . . ."

A look of dismay flashed across Martin's face and he lowered his head to hide his face. Claire paused, realising she had upset him. There was silence for a moment.

"And is your husband with you in London," he asked, raising his head, his eyes unmistakeably moist.

Claire shook her head again. "No. He passed away last year," she said matter of factly.

There was another silence.

"Sorry to hear that," mumbled Martin. "And sorry to hear about Mrs T as well."

Claire suppressed her own sadness, the sadness that welled in her sometimes when she thought about the past, thought about Mrs Turnbull, her once-capable saviour reduced to a withered, confused old woman who couldn't tell where she was from one moment to the next, whose body eventually ceased to function. Her sadness when someone was kind enough to express sympathy at Jim's loss. Their marriage hadn't been stormy or passionate, their tale not a great love story, but she missed his company sorely, even though she kept herself busy with the few hours she still did at the castle and with her reading. She wondered what to say next.

"You look well," said Martin suddenly, starting a fresh topic.

Claire looked at him to see him indicating his own face but meaning hers. "Your eye . . . it's different . . ."

Claire smiled despite herself and nodded. "It is," she said, raising her hand to it. Trust Martin to be still so upfront about things. "I had an operation some years ago."

Martin smiled back at her. "Nice," he said, and in his voice she again heard the young East End boy. For an instant it felt like she were reliving a film in her memory where the characters lived in a hazy place filled with warm yellow sunshine rather than the glare of today. It certainly didn't feel for a second like it was her own life she was remembering.

"Drum, I haven't got much time left," he said suddenly.

Claire reeled a little, felt as though she had been slapped. "You're unwell," she managed.

Martin nodded weakly. "Cancer," he said. He pointed at his cigarettes and lighter on the table before him. "Not much else to do in prison but smoke." He attempted a grin but failed. "The doctors say that I might have six months, tops. I'll probably have to go into hospital soon. That's why I wanted to see you. There are things I need to do before I . . . go. Things that need to be set straight . . ."

Claire found that she was holding her breath in. Holding her whole body in, if she were honest with herself. Martin. Her Martin. Dying. Talking in terms of months – sitting before her like this. Dying. All that part of her life, gone now. Those happy, happy days before that night by the loch . . .

Martin's face suddenly grew dark and he sat even further forward in the seat.

"I didn't do nothing to Laurence," he said. The words hung in the air for a moment as he fixed Claire with a stare. He spoke slowly, his words careful and measured. "And I didn't do nothing to bloody Jack Ball. Do you understand? I have to tell someone. What I said in court all those years ago – when I pleaded not guilty – I was telling the truth."

She'd been right all along. She'd always known it. Known that Martin couldn't have harmed the boy. But she'd never told another soul. Had just gone along with everything, too afraid to defend him . . .

"I never touched him in any way – do you understand? He was my mate. I never had mates when I was small – always had to be a grown up, always ducking and diving, and that's how my life's been

311

since. Laurence McKenzie might have been a kid but he was the best bloody friend I ever had."

Spittle glistened on Martin's lower lip as he grew silent again, his eyes filled now with rage and hurt, his chest rising and falling more rapidly with the exertion, his tired, rotting lungs unable to keep up. It was a while before he calmed his breathing enough to begin again.

"Uncle Jack used to . . . to hurt me . . . to do things to me . . . Do you understand?"

It took a moment for it to sink it, but when it did, Claire bit her lip hard in a futile attempt to stop herself crying at the shocking realisation of what he was telling her. He'd been abused. Just like she had . . .

The tears made her vision blurry and when she couldn't help but blink, one rolled down her cheek rapidly, followed by another.

Martin Pine looked away from her, as if watching her tears might be catching. He steadied himself to continue. "That's why I told you to go and get help that night at the lake, do you remember? I knew that Uncle Jack was done with me and was ready to move on to greener pastures." He looked directly at Claire. "I couldn't let Laurence be alone with him. When I knew that they were both down at the lake that night, I had to stop it. But you know what a bully Ball was. I couldn't have done it alone. And besides which, I needed someone else to see . . . to know. That's why I told you to go get help. To get someone who could have stopped him."

Claire watched him, her eyes wide, as he continued to speak, his breathing becoming more laboured as he went on.

"When I got down to the lake that night, it was dark of course but I could see clearly – there was a moon – a great, round harvest moon, do you remember that and all? You have no idea how vivid it all is still in my head. I've played it over a million times, Drum."

Claire nodded for him to continue.

"And there they were, just coming alongside the little jetty – you remember the one? With the ladder to climb in and out of the rowing boat? I was so scared, Drum – how could I have let that happen? Let Laurence be out there on his own with that evil piece

of work for so long? I couldn't help myself – I ran as fast as I could onto that jetty, shouting the odds, yelling for little Laurence to get out of that boat, yelling at Ball to keep his hands off him.

Ball tried to brave it out at first, you see. Started throwing faces at Laurence, cocking 'is thumb at me as much as to say 'who's this nutter then?' and trying to laugh it off only poor Laurence didn't seem to think it was so funny. His face was white as a sheet, Drum. To this day it haunts me that I don't know actually what happened out on that lake, to that poor little lamb.

But I wasn't going nowhere, I tell you. I could tell Jack was getting madder – his 'orrible face was like thunder and he started bellowing at me like a bull – he lurched to his feet and started shaking one of the oars at me while the boat rocked, telling me to get the hell back to the house and keep my nose out, but wild horses wouldn't have dragged me away from that boat. The boat was close enough now for me to help Laurence out of the boat and up the ladder. I reached out to him, I did. Except it was Ball grabbed my arm and pulled me right close to his face so that I thought I was going to fall in, or that he'd pull my arm clean out of its socket. I could feel his spit on my face as he told me to shut up and get out of his sight before he did me some real harm. His voice came from his boots when he was angry, and he was angrier than I'd ever seen him in my life. Angrier than I thought a man was capable of being."

Martin fell silent for a moment, partly to collect his thoughts, partly to regain his breath. Claire watched him retreat into himself, his face darken, watched him go back in time to that night, standing on the jetty.

"I can still hear Laurence screaming," he whispered softly, a tremble to his voice. "Screaming 'Stop, Uncle Jack!' and 'Let me off!' and yelling at him to sit down, that they were going to capsize. His little voice, Drum, screams that you'd think would wake the dead. He was terrified – the sound of it made me want to cover my ears – and still Ball was roaring at me and the boat was rocking from side to side. Then suddenly he let me go and hauled his bloody great fat body up the ladder – I was sure it would come away from the jetty – and he came at me, his eyes on fire, still with the oar in his hand. It was all I could do not to get hit by it once he started

swinging it from side to side like some bloody great pendulum on a grandfather clock. I could hear it making a 'whish' through the air, swinging past my ears as it went one way, past my legs as it came back, a swing with every step. He'd lost it Drum. I don't know what it was that night that finally drove him over the edge. There was no reason there, no sense. He was just like a crazy animal and he wasn't going to be happy until he'd hurt me.

And I couldn't run, Drum – do you understand? There was nothing to stop me turning tail and making a run for it back up the lawns but I couldn't. I couldn't turn my back on Laurence – something just wouldn't allow me to do that and all the while he was coming at me with this hatred in his eyes and then I lost my balance and stumbled and fell and I was sure I was a goner, a sitting duck. And then suddenly he stopped."

Martin raised his eyebrows as if somehow he was still surprised, as if the moment was completely unexpected, even though he had clearly lived through it, again and again, for years.

"Just stopped in his tracks. And his eyes sort of glazed over for a moment and everything went still. And I could see Laurence behind him – with the other oar in his two hands. The little soldier had only gone and climbed onto the jetty and brought the oar down on Jack's head. And for a moment we all froze solid. All we could do was stare at Jack, with his eyes gone all funny and his body starting to sag. There was a little trickle of blood just running down his face, a dark streak that ran down over his scar. He lifted up a finger then, real slow. And he wiped some of it onto his hand and looked at it. Like he'd never seen his own fingers before.

And then he let out a roar, Drum. A roar like a wounded animal. That just seemed to fill the whole night. I was sure that everyone in the whole world could hear that sound at that moment. And then Ball turned away from me. And did the last thing in the world that I wanted him to do. He turned on Laurence.

The little fellah wasn't quick enough to get away either. Even though Ball was stunned by the blow from the oar, it wasn't enough to floor him. I don't think a gunshot would have been enough to floor him – he was fuelled by a rage that I'll never forget. Pure bloody rage.

He got his fingers round Laurence's throat before I could stand up and even when I did I couldn't get at him properly to prise them off. They were like a vice, Drum. Like a crocodile or something when he gets hold of his prey and he won't let go. That poor kid never stood a chance."

He paused for a moment, overwhelmed. Claire saw tears form in his eyes as the tragic scene played out yet again in his memory.

"In the struggle we went into the water. All three of us. That's what happened. Still I tried to prize those big fat fingers from around Laurence's neck but it just couldn't be done. Even under the water I tried but we just kept going down and down. Ball couldn't swim, see? And even if he could I don't know if he'd have had the mind to. He acted like a great heavy anchor, just dragging us down and down further and the water got muddier and darker with all the silt and the mud that was getting dredged up with us all thrashing around."

Martin focused again on Claire, his damp eyes pleading for understanding.

"I only left Laurence for a few seconds, Drum. Just went back to the surface to get some air – just a few seconds – but it was enough. When I went back under, I couldn't see a thing. And it wouldn't have mattered if I did anyhow. There was nothing on this earth and probably the next that could have saved that child once Jack Ball decided he had it in for him.

"It's haunted me all these years, Drum . . . if there was anything I could've done to stop it all happening, I would've. But if I hadn't gone down there to the lake then who knows what Ball would have done to the boy? Or . . . would Laurence still be alive? Maybe it was my fault after all . . . maybe I did the wrong thing?"

He grew silent again and his eyes glazed over as he concentrated on the memory.

"I'm so sorry," said Claire through her tears. "I shouldn't have doubted you . . . I shouldn't have testified . . ."

"Him being dead and gone – that's something I don't regret for a minute. Sometimes, when I was inside, I'd actually wish I'd done it, wished I'd managed to finish him off somehow. Ball was a vile, spiteful bully, and he hurt me and Laurence too, I reckon. Just the once but that's enough, isn't it?"

"*He was no loss,*" *agreed Claire. She remembered suddenly Martin's face that night when she had told him where Laurence was gone, the pure shock, the fear that she'd seen in his eyes. She should have recognised it then. The same look of fear and panic that she'd always felt when she heard footsteps approach her room at night. A lifetime ago now.*

Claire was pensive for a moment, filled with regret. "*I never spoke up, Martin,*" *she said.* "*I never told anyone what you were really like – how kind you were – I could have, maybe, said something to your solicitor . . . explained that you weren't like that . . .*"

Martin laughed bitterly. "*My brief wasn't there to get me off. I was fitted up. Once the case was sent back to London, my fate was sealed. Please don't beat yourself up about all this, Drum. There was nothing you could have done. The odds were against me, all them years back. No matter what I did or said, there was no way I was ever getting out of that prison. There were forces at work – powerful forces who wanted me to pay for what they thought I did to Ball. The case was put together that I was the one who hit him with the oar and he fell in the water. The sickening part – the part that keeps me awake at night is that they twisted it to make it look like he was trying to protect Laurence from me. That I was some sort of dangerous predator who went on to hold the boy under the water by the neck until he drowned. As if I could, Drum. Whatever else Ball was, he had his uses to the powers that be. I knew that once I went down, I wasn't getting out and there was no point in even thinking about it. For a long time I cried – I raged about it all. About how unfair it all was – why me and all that. And then time went on and I just got used to it. That was how things were to be from now on. And I grew to accept it and with a little help from Him Above, I realised that there was no point in being angry. But when I knew . . . when I heard my days was numbered, then I knew it was time to act. Time to tell someone. It's his mother, you see? I can't stop thinking about her, and about what she must think of me. And I need her to know some peace, do you understand? I need her to know that he called for her. He called out for her as he stood in that boat, terrified of what Ball was going to do next. He was a brave little fellah – the bravest. If he'd grown up he coulda ruled the world.*"

Claire nodded. "She still comes to the castle at Christmas, you know. Mr Calvert hosts a party every December. She always comes, with that sad look in her eyes. And her husband comes, and their other son . . ."

Claire was surprised to see a smile cross Martin's face.

"She had another boy?" he asked.

Claire nodded in response, puzzled.

"What's he like – the other one?" Martin asked eagerly.

Claire thought for a moment. "He's a nice boy. Different from Laurence though. He's grown up now, of course, but when he was young – when he came for the summer, like Laurence used to, he used to hide in his room and read books, and listen to something called The Smiths . . ."

Martin grinned, eagerness showing in his face to know more.

"He hated going out shooting – he's the complete opposite to Laurence, actually, in that way," Claire went on. "The first time he shot a deer, Jim – my husband – found him crying behind a tree, although he swore there was just something in his eye. He was a funny wee thing – sharp as a knife. Looked exactly like him too, like Laurence. If you saw him now then you'd be able to see what Laurence would have looked like if he had grown up . . ."

Martin smiled wistfully. "I'd like that," he said quietly. "Wish I'd met that lad. What's his name?"

"Gabriel," said Claire with a smile. "There's a rumour – of all things – that he can talk to the dead. Mr Calvert would dock me pay if he heard me say that to anyone. But maybe it's true – there's sometimes a funny look in his eyes."

"You mean . . . he's like one of them mediums, is he?"

"Something of that sort, yes."

"Maybe he can talk to his brother then, eh?" Martin said with a smile. "I like that idea."

"I don't think I do," said Claire. "He doesn't come visit now so much any more of course. He joined the army like his dad, but he left – I'm not sure what he does now for a living."

Martin stared into space. "Funny to think that a whole lifetime has passed since," he mused. "That a kid's been born and grown to be a man all the while my life stood still. But I never forgot you, *though, Drum. Or Laurence. And I never forgot that damn castle either. It was home to me. I'd go back now . . . if I could."*

Claire blinked away fresh tears, taking him in fully – as skinny as ever, although she didn't know if that were still his shape or the ravages of disease. She breathed in, felt herself choke and a sob rose from deep within her.

"What are you going to do now?" she asked, her voice a whisper. His future – what little of it there appeared to be, was unimaginable to her. She knew that she'd get the train back to Dubhglas – she'd just leave here and he'd go back to his fuzzy television set and beyond that . . . hospital, ventilators, treatments . . . She looked at him sadly.

"It's been too long, Drum," he replied. "But I've been thinking and, like I say, I just want someone to know the truth. Can you tell her for me? Laurence's mother? Tell her I never hurt her boy?"

Claire stared at him, the look loaded with sympathy and desperate sorrow. She nodded a yes. It was the least she could do. She saw her tears mirrored in Martin's eyes then.

"Claire – that summer, when you came to Dubhglas, that was the happiest I'd been since I was a kid. Sure, I'd thought I was the big man about town when I lived in London, but I was just a troublemaker. Getting out of London – going to that castle and meeting the Turnbulls and then you was the start of a real life for me, despite everything that Jack Ball did."

"Martin, we were very young . . ." began Claire.

Martin shook his head, cutting her short. "I know that. We was a pair of kids, for heaven's sake. But it gave me a taste of what life could be like if I stayed on the straight and narrow. Without what you and I had, I'd have had nothing at all, do you understand? It was the only taste of life I'd ever had, and I savoured it every day for all the time since. Now I just want to get my house in order. I just want folk to know that I didn't do it, Claire. I really and truly didn't do it. Will you tell them?"

An image flashed across Claire's mind of Laurence's mother, of Violet McKenzie, and the light in her eyes that had been extinguished after her boy had drowned. Claire felt very small all of a sudden. It was as if a camera pulled up, up into the sky and focused back on her, growing fainter and fainter in that chair, till she was little more than a dot. She felt insignificant, but there were all these other lives, all these other people touched by what had happened. And now she had a responsibility to set it straight, to help. Suddenly the camera in her mind rushed back towards her closer and closer and closer until she was somehow inside herself again.

"I'll do that, Martin," she said.

The shadows of evening were long when she stepped back out of the archway of the Mulberry Estate. What a sweet name, she thought, for such a horrid place. The air was rich with the smell of a hot summer's evening. More and more people had emerged onto their balconies, some clutching cans of beer. The children were growing irritable as they played in the courtyard and she was glad to leave the place and hail another cab. She was nervous in London, exhausted by the day's events. By at last truly knowing what had happened. She longed to return to her place of safety, her little house in Dubhglas.

"Goodbye, Martin," she whispered as she glanced up toward the top of the tower block where he had returned to solitude, where his life was ending. Claire touched her bag which contained the letter he had given her – his testament, the truth – and knew in her heart that it was the last time she would ever see his face.

CHAPTER 40

December 1st

"I could only testify to what I saw," mused Claire Hibbert, nursing the half-drunk cup of tea. It had seemed to restore her somewhat, made her braver.

Martha, too, was calmer, more rational. Her head still stung a little but she focused hard on the woman's story, trying to memorise every last detail.

"And what I saw was Martin standing there – the oar stained with Jack Ball's blood at his feet. Martin was just standing there, soaking wet, looking into the lake. I stopped running – I just didn't know what to do – and then I realised Mr Calvert was behind me, shouting at me to go and get Mr Turnbull to telephone for an ambulance and for the police – I ran back to the house as fast as my legs could carry me and then I just waited with all the rest of the staff as the police came and the ambulance – all those flashing lights outside. We all wanted to see what was happening but Mr Turnbull sent a message that we were to stay indoors. A policeman came to talk to me, of course. And I told him what I saw but nothing more. What I told that policeman was what I repeated on the witness stand."

"That you'd seen Martin with the murder weapon at his feet and that he was wet?" asked Martha.

"That's all I saw," repeated Claire with a sigh. "In court, they said such awful things – that Martin had been . . . interfering . . . with Laurence . . . that his interest in him was what they called 'sinister' and 'perverse', and that Jack Ball had been trying to protect the child from him . . . that Martin had killed Jack and then dragged Laurence into the water and held him under by the throat . . . but it was the other way round . . . it was Laurence who hit Jack Ball with the oar on the temple . . . and it was Jack who strangled the boy while Martin tried to save him." She looked directly at Martha. "I saw Martin, you see, when he got out of prison . . . just the once last May . . . soon before he died . . . and he told me what really happened."

Claire shifted in her chair and for a split second glanced behind Martha, her eye catching something at the other end of the room before she looked back.

"Laurence was such a feisty little thing – no one knows what went on between himself and Uncle Jack in the boat, but Laurence might well have proved more than Jack could handle . . . And in the end he showed his mettle and fought back to defend his friend Martin. For all the good it did . . ."

As she told the tale, Claire's voice grew stronger, more powerful somehow. As if it were a weight lifted off her entire being to tell another person.

Martha caught her glance yet again behind where she sat.

"There are so many 'if only's', though," she continued. If only Martin hadn't gone down to the lake in the first place, if only Laurence had heeded his warning not to be alone with Jack Ball, if only Martin could have somehow got Ball to release his grip . . ."

"How ironic that a boy who loved to swim so much should die like that," observed Martha.

"When it got to court they wouldn't let Martin testify. He was never allowed to defend himself on the witness stand. And that lawyer that they got from London – it was like he *wanted* to lose. Like he didn't really care about Martin. Like Martin said, there were forces working against him. Martin was sure he'd been what he called 'fitted up'. I should have done something – said something about his character . . . about how he used to go to Laurence's room only to tell ghost stories at night . . . about how they were friends . . ."

Martha leaned forward. "There was nothing more you could have done, Claire," she said reassuringly. "You were young and afraid – they were clever people. And they wanted it sewn up neatly."

"That's what Martin said," responded Claire, looking again past Martha and down toward the back of the room.

Something in the look made Martha take notice. Her heart began to beat quickly as she turned slightly to look in the same direction. Then she stopped herself. Something in her made her think that she didn't want to look after all as a thought struck her out of the blue.

"Claire . . ." she said, "when you said Jack was back for Martin . . . what did you mean by that exactly?"

Claire's stare didn't budge from what she saw at the end of the room. That was answer enough for Martha. A chill ran the length of her spine. She stared intently at Claire's face where a hint of a smile played.

"I never go back to the lake much now," Claire said. "But I loved it down there. Loved how we'd hold hands and chat about our plans, or sit on the big rock down on the shore and skim stones. I often went back there over the years, even after I married Jim. Martin's Place, I've always called it. I always think of him when I'm there . . ." Her eyes were still fixed on the back of the room.

"I knew he was sick . . . when I saw him last May he knew he didn't have long. He had less than even he thought, as it turned out. And shortly afterwards, things started going missing around the kitchen – pudding bowls, soup ladles – and after a while I'd find them in the most unusual of places. He used to do that to tease me when we were young . . ."

The chill spread around the whole of Martha's body and she felt the hairs on her arms begin to prickle as they stood on end.

"It was when I found the whisk in the pantry that I knew," Claire said quietly and smiled again, her eyes still focused beyond Martha. "He did that once before . . ."

Martha felt her heart begin to race, felt a weakness run through her.

"He's here, Claire, isn't he?" she whispered, the question asked against her will.

The nod was barely perceptible.

Martha forced herself to turn in the chair, to peer into the gloom of the space behind her, terrified at the prospect of what she might see. There was nothing there of course. At first. But then Martha noticed, for a second, what looked like a mist in the corner. It was barely visible, but when she looked away, and looked back again, she was sure it was there. Her heart gave a great leap and she swung back to look again at Claire, her eyes filled with panic.

"It's gone now," Claire said, still staring at the space. Her gaze returned to Martha's face. "After that, all the other strange things started happening around here – the smells, Tiger – all the staff were disturbed and then Donald Gifford said he'd sort it and that he'd contacted someone to see if they could help. It's Gabriel, of course . . . though Donald didn't say so."

Martha leaped in her seat as there was a sudden crash. Then the kitchen door burst open.

Claire jumped to her feet. "Laura!" she exclaimed, shocked. The figure of a young girl, her hair damp, stood in the kitchen doorway. The sound of the storm grew louder from behind her, where she had left the back door open.

Martha looked back toward Claire. Wasn't that the girl she said she'd left with Ruby? Martha suddenly grew numb.

"The child, Mrs Hibbert . . ." panted Laura.

"What about her?" gasped Martha, leaping to her feet.

"The door – she opened the sliding door somehow!" cried Laura. She was soaking wet, her hair limp on her shoulders.

"*Is she okay?*" Martha cried, taking a step toward the girl with the petrified eyes. *Please, God, no – don't let her say what I think she's going to say . . .*

"The door's open, somehow," Laura panted. "Mrs Hibbert, she's gone!"

It was as if Martha had no control of her own body as she started running, past the girl, out into the passageway and toward the back door. She crossed the courtyard and rushed in through the open door of the cottage. When she burst into the bedroom where last she had seen her child asleep, however, her heart broke through the barrier at the sight of the empty bed, the ruffled covers, the dent in the mattress in the shape of Ruby's little body, Hugo her bear.

A matter of minutes and Ruby had been asleep here . . . safe . . . and now the room was freezing cold, the curtains blowing wildly as the storm found its way in. The wind, of course, Martha thought. Somehow the wind had managed to open the lock or break the door or blow something through it – but how? It couldn't have pulled apart those heavy curtains, nor broken the glass without leaving a trace somewhere in the room. The door was open but there was no damage – no shards of glass on the floor. There was a small crash as she stood there, as the bedside table lamp blew over in a strong gust of wind. All the while the rain beat its persistent tattoo on the windows.

Claire appeared at the door and behind her the terrified Laura.

"How did this happen?" yelled Martha, feeling a rage build up inside her.

"I don't know – the door is always locked – there's a small bolt. Always," panted Claire. "What happened, Laura? Tell me *exactly* what happened."

The girl was shaking as she spoke. "I went into the toilet – I'd only just checked her and she was sound asleep. I didn't hear anything with the flush of the toilet . . . but then when I came out I felt the cold in the hallway, and I heard how loud the storm sounded. I wondered if maybe a window had somehow opened, or if a branch or something might have broken some glass . . . I never thought for a second . . . I followed the noise of the wind into this room . . . I couldn't believe it . . . she was just gone . . . I rushed out and searched for her outside but there was no sign of her . . ."

"Someone at the party must have taken her," tried Martha. Her head was working overtime – where could she be gone? *Someone* had to have opened the door. She crossed the room, walking around the beds and stepped over the threshold out onto the patio where she was instantly buffeted with a gust of wind and pelted with ice-cold rain. She didn't feel it. She was paralysed by the panic that grew within her by the second.

She went back into the room and demanded of the girl, "Did you hear *anything?*"

"Nothing, I swear. But the sound of the storm was so loud I wouldn't have. For a second I thought I heard a wee bell, like if someone had tassels on their clothes or something but then nothing."

Martha caught Claire Hibbert's eye and every ounce of colour drained from her face. Her body started to tremble uncontrollably. "Get Gabriel!" she hissed at Claire, before she turned and ran out into the night, into the storm, with no idea where she was going.

She heard Claire's voice call her back but she couldn't stay, couldn't stand still. It was as if she was pulled out into the night. If he had Ruby . . . if what the girl had said was true . . .

Martha ran as quickly as she could across the patio at the back of the cottage, dodging fallen flowerpots, and then on, under a trellis shaped like an arch, bare and white against the darkness, like an arc of stripped bones. As she did, the sensor light on the cottage blinked off and she was plunged into complete darkness.

The dress was sodden now, clung to her body, soaked through in the matter of moments. It felt a ton weight, the wet velvet slowing her down as she ran. Her hair, too, was stuck to her head, to the sides of her face. The drops of rain were like hard pellets of ice hitting her skin. She had to keep running, had to find Ruby . . . but where?

In an instant she knew. Knew that reason was too much to hope for. Knew that it wasn't a living soul that had made their way into that room and taken her daughter, or guided her, or forced her. Knew that there was one place that Jack Ball would take a child. The lake.

Martha ran even faster. She felt the ground grow soft beneath her feet, stumbled time and again as the kitten heels wedged themselves in the soft earth, feeling rage and frustration grow every time she had to pause to pull them out again. For a moment, she contemplated removing them, running barefoot, but her mind was clear enough to reject this as a poor notion. She pelted on, without a clue where she was going – except she knew that the lake was this way.

She had been running across open ground – soon, however, the space narrowed to a pathway lined on both sides with dark foliage. Martha almost froze with terror as she suddenly felt damp leaves stroke her arms as she ran. For a second, she was full sure that they weren't leaves – that they were arms, reaching out to her in the dark. The mental image made her run faster, to escape them, to escape her own thoughts.

Suddenly, through the storm, she was sure that she heard a child's voice. She stopped dead, her heart pounding against her ribcage with fear and the strenuous exertion. But the wind screamed, leaving only the crying of the gale. With a groan, she picked up the sodden skirts as best she could, and began to run again.

When eventually she felt the ground grow soft underneath her feet, when the bushes ahead of her parted and when she stepped onto the black shore of the lake, a gust of wind hit her, so strong that it almost knocked her off her feet. Martha stopped, her breath coming in great gulps, her chest burning. She was here, here at the lake. Where she was sure Ruby would be. She could see little. The night was black, the sky free from light pollution but filled with layer after layer of cloud spilling torrents of water from the sky. Martha was aware of the water ahead of her, the sound of the downpour hitting it with thick, relentless drops. The ground felt muddy underneath her. She felt her footing go in the soft earth and staggered as she tried to balance herself, all the time her eyes searching frantically, forcing them to grow more accustomed to the darkness, to see if there was any sign of her precious child.

And then she saw the shape move out of the corner of her eye. It frightened her. Despite the fact that she sought a living thing – oh God, please let her be alive, she thought – she was still surprised to see movement. She lost sight of it for a second while the wind blew more rain against her, but there – there it was again. A small pale shape moving out toward . . . no, *into* . . . the lake.

"Ruby!" screamed Martha, racing as fast as she could to reach her baby before the waves could. She could hear the lake in turmoil, seething and rushing. As she grew closer, the small pale shape – Ruby in her pale pink sleepsuit – became more distinct, as did the lake. And somehow, *somehow,* it seemed that Ruby was floating above the water. Walking, as if on it, but yet above it. If she were *in* the lake, then surely it would only take seconds for her to disappear. And as she grew closer, Martha realised that Ruby wasn't floating above the surface, but walking along a small, dark jetty which Martha hadn't made out before, the blackness of the structure indistinguishable against the high water that lashed at its supports. The jetty. Where it had all happened before.

Martha grew closer again and watched as Ruby stopped a few feet from the end of the jetty. A fierce gust of wind suddenly attacked from their right, from across the lake. It shoved Martha sideways, helpless against its strength. She screamed. If the gust could move her on the low shore, then surely that was it – Ruby would be lifted like a leaf out there on the water's edge, and tossed into the water.

Yet she wasn't. The child stood there, stock still, facing out into the water, as if she wondered why she could go no further.

Martha wanted to scream but instead hauled the dress up again and scrambled up the steps onto the wooden pier, felt the old and rotten wood creak dangerously under her feet. It was too dangerous to walk on, she surmised. With both eyes still firmly fixed on her child, Martha dropped to her knees and began to crawl along the feeble wooden structure. Her weight, made heavier by the bulk of the sodden velvet dress, might prove just too much for the wood beneath her. She couldn't risk shouting at Ruby either, frightening her, knocking her off whatever balance she had achieved that had so far kept her from being cast into the seething water. Martha's heart raced at a mile a minute. She longed to scream, to lunge for the child but her little girl was so calm as she stood there, even though the wind came in persistent gusts now, buffeting them both, threatening every second to blow one or both of them into the swirling waters. Martha couldn't allow herself to think about that. Because that would be it. If Ruby slipped from the pier, if she fell in there, then she would never be seen again. She must reach her. She couldn't lose her, it just wasn't possible, yet here it was, so close . . .

Martha crawled on, slowly testing the beams with her hands, leaning her weight on them, before following with her knees. She had to suppress the urge to call out to Ruby. What if the little girl turned and lost her balance? Or got a fright and stepped forward?

She was almost there now . . . only feet away. Still Ruby never moved, never swayed. A terrible thought struck Martha. What if the spirit had done something to her already? What could he do? Her body seemed fine, but what if he was inside her head? Forcing thoughts into her little mind? Things that she would never forget? How on earth had he got her down here? How had he made a tiny child come all this way by herself?

"Ruby," she whispered gently, unable to hold back from uttering her daughter's name any longer. She manoeuvred herself gently around the side of the child, crawling past her, so that she was able to position herself directly to her front, between her and the edge of the jetty. That achieved, Martha knelt there, barely able to keep her eyes open against the rain which now lashed fully across her face, water dripping in streaming rivulets down her cheeks, her chin, her bare neck and chest and her exposed arms. It was like being showered with freezing pins. But at least she was *there* now. Between Ruby and the water. All she had to do was take her in her arms and they'd be safe, the two of them.

They were close enough that Martha could see her little features, could make out the small shape of her pale little face in the dark. It was mesmerised by something, her eyes glazed over as if she were sleepwalking. If she just raised a hand, Martha thought, then she could rub her hair – she was within touching distance now. Stay calm, she urged herself. Don't make any sudden moves, don't fall at the final hurdle . . .

"Mummy," said Ruby suddenly, as if it were the most natural thing in the world that her mother should be there, that she herself should be out in the blackness of the night, in the worst storm of her short life. "Look!"

Martha's body tingled as she watched Ruby's fat little hand rise up in the darkness, glowing white in contrast to the blackness of the night. She became aware again of the sound of the lake behind her, roaring and gushing and gurgling, making unnatural noises as the wind tossed the water from side to side. Ruby was pointing at something behind Martha. Something that she could see, but that her mother couldn't. Martha felt dizzy as she fixed her stare on the child's eyes, unable to see what she was pointing at.

"Look, Mummy," repeated Ruby, pointing out toward the water. "Kitty cat."

It was then that Martha felt the tug from behind. At first she thought it was the water itself, splashing up over the end of the pier, but in an instant she knew it wasn't. Knew she was being pulled, yanked over the edge of the wood like a ball of string. And there was nothing she could do to stop herself being pulled in. It was all happening in slow motion. Time slowed as her mouth opened, her eyes grew wide and her arms flailed helplessly, reaching out to steady herself. And failing. Martha's eyes fixed on Ruby's face as she fell backwards into the freezing cold belly of the lake. And as she fell, she watched the unnatural mist rise from nowhere and wrap itself around her child.

The last thing that Martha thought as she fell was: *"He's got her."*

Everything was somehow calm under the waves, still. It was pitch dark, of course. She didn't know if her eyes were open or closed, if she were conscious or not. After she fell – *was pulled* – she could feel nothing. Not the icy waves around her, nor could she feel any movement. It was as if she were cocooned by the lake itself. As if that under the water, the storm couldn't reach her.

Afterward, she had a vague memory – she must have dreamed it – of surfacing once again. She was far out now, too far to reach for the jetty, to try to get back to Ruby. But she could see her, which was odd as it was still so dark. She could see her still on the jetty, every one of her features as clear to Martha as if she held her in her arms. Her curls were dark from the rain, of course, but she looked as beautiful as she did after bath-time. Her skin was the colour of snow and drips of rain ran down it, her lips tinged with blue, but she was smiling. And she was completely still, and somehow she was *safe*. Because there was someone with her. Someone who had a light – no, someone who *was* a light. It was a young man, Martha saw. A skinny young man who was with Ruby, yet somehow *around* Ruby. Like a shield in some way. A boy with a smile who somehow made Martha know that Ruby was safe, that her baby was safe.

And in the distance she heard voices, shouting . . . someone calling her name, calling Ruby's name. So that was all right then. With that, she sank back under the waves, back to the calm of the lake.

That unnatural light was down here, too. It was far away just now, but growing closer, and brighter. Lighting up the water around her, the long reeds and the green and brown weeds, the dust and silt from the forming a strange cloud around her as she sank toward the bottom, everything green in the mysterious illumination. And suddenly she wasn't alone.

Martha felt the calmness leave her as she became suddenly aware of her body again, of the water which was seething, of the weeds that had curled around her foot. She tried to pull her leg away, tugged at them, succeeded in only tightening them and then she realised that the tightness in her chest was because she couldn't breathe and she was desperate, desperate for air. Her eyes . . . they were open . . . felt as though they would pop from her head, as if her neck was gripped by a vice. My God, but she needed to *breathe!*

She looked upward, tried to propel herself to the surface . . . but she couldn't, couldn't get away from the grip around her ankle. She twisted again, hungry with desire to take a gulp of air. And what she saw then made everything seem to stop, made time stand still. The body – the huge, bloated, grey body that floated into her line of vision simply hung there, suspended before her eyes. *Twenty stone if he were an ounce*, Claire Hibbert had said. His face was scrunched into a grimace, the eyes closed, the dark hair floating gracefully above his head.

In that instant, Martha felt the panic explode in her again. She tried to scream as the man's eyes suddenly opened and looked right at her, and the head turned slightly to reveal the scar in all its glory, the scar which slowly began to open before her eyes, filling the water with clouds of red as it did so, the gash coming apart from lip to temple, opening itself to reveal darkness underneath, spewing blood out into the turbulent water. And then in another instant the lake was plunged back into teeming darkness, the vision instantly gone, like it had been *sucked* away, somehow. Martha was surrounded once again by all-consuming darkness and the ice cold that pervaded every inch of her body. Without thinking, she finally opened her mouth and gave a great gasp, filling her lungs with the dark water of the lake.

CHAPTER 41

December 4th

Martha felt her limbs stir. At least she thought it was her own limbs. They didn't feel quite attached to her body. Then, she heard the noises, an occasional beep from what felt like very far away, coming closer to her.

Then the voice. "Hello, there," it said. It was a woman. She, too, sounded distant.

Martha stirred again, and opened her eyes very slowly. She was somewhere bright and warm. The room swam a little for a moment. She could make out the long strip light on the ceiling above her, then the curtains that hung either side of the bed.

A kindly face entered the picture, wearing a broad smile. "Well, good morning, Martha," it said. "Glad to see you've come back to join us."

The nurse bent over her, shining a small torch in each eye while holding her head steady with cold hands. The penlight stuffed back in her breast pocket, she reached over Martha's head and then placed a hard, cold object in her ear for a few moments, removing it when it gave a quiet beep. The woman was a study in efficiency as she unwound a blood-pressure strap from a mobile monitor nearby and attached it to Martha's arm. The sensation of the belt growing tight and then loosening again felt strange to Martha – her body still felt as though she were just a little outside it. The nurse's face, however, seemed to indicate that everything was normal.

The nurse stepped lightly to the end of the bed where she unhooked a chart and began to write on it. Martha watched her intently and tried to sit up a little, although her body betrayed her when she did. Her mouth too – when she attempted to speak it felt and sounded as though cotton wool was stuffed against her tongue. She tried to clear her throat, grimaced as it hurt fiercely, and then tried again. "Take it easy, love," the nurse said, her Scottish accent lilting but her tone serious. She replaced the chart and was at Martha's side in an instant, holding her elbow and guiding her into a sitting position, deftly arranging pillows at her head for support.

Martha tried again. "Where's Ruby? Where's my child?" she managed to croak and looked at the nurse hopefully, praying that she sounded more intelligible aloud than she did in her own head.

The nurse – Karen, her name-badge read – smiled softly. "Your wee girl is absolutely fine," she said. "She's gone home with her daddy. But we had to hold on to you for a little while longer."

Martha looked around her again, now that she had a better view of her surroundings. The curtains around the bed, bright green and decorated with rainbows, formed a small, private cubicle in what seemed to be a bigger ward. It was, of course, bright, clean and smelling of unmistakeable hospital odour.

The nurse picked up a plastic glass and jug from the locker beside the bed, and poured a little water before handing it to Martha, carefully maintaining a hold on it as she guided it to her lips. "Do you think you could drink this for me very slowly?" she asked.

Martha wasn't sure. Her arms didn't seem to be working very well. Nor did her lips come to think of it, but with Karen's help she managed, forcing the water down her jagged throat.

"Good girl," Karen crooned. "You've given us a wee bit of a fright, but everything's fine today and you've had a good sleep. Your cut is healing nicely too by the looks of things – we popped a couple of paper stitches into it . . .".

Martha watched her bend to get a closer look at her temple when suddenly it all flooded back in an instant. The cut on her head . . . the lake. Her body gave a start as the recollections flooded back in a rush. The lake . . . she had been in the lake . . . with that *thing* . . .

"There, there," said Karen, almost absent-mindedly, satisfied with the appearance of the stitches on Martha's temple. "Do you think you might be ready to see someone?"

Will must have brought Ruby back to see her, Martha thought, and nodded as enthusiastically as she was able. She longed suddenly to hold her, to smell her, to feel the comfort of having her child back with her.

Karen pushed the curtains back a little as she stepped from the room through a door at the end of the bed. Martha was almost disappointed when it re-opened moments later and only Sue stepped inside, carrying a cup with a hot drink in it.

"Christ, woman, I only went for a coffee – what did you have to wake up for?" she said, smiling, but with a tinge of concern in her voice. She sat down on the green padded chair beside the bed and placed the drink on the locker before reaching out and squeezing Martha's hand.

Martha squeezed back.

"How are you feeling?" Sue asked.

Martha saw that her skin was pale, her eyes bloodshot with tiredness. She wanted to make a quip, to pay Sue some joking insult, but she couldn't bring herself to do it. Instead, she rested back against the pillows that Karen had plumped for her and managed a weak smile.

"What happened?" she asked through her cotton mouth. "Drink," she said, moving her hand slightly to indicate that she needed help with some more water. Sue obliged.

"You're not fully operational just yet," Sue said. "We were a bit worried about you for a while. You've been under a honeycomb blanket for the last couple of days, trying to warm you up again. I warned you about swimming after the August Bank Holiday, didn't I?"

The joke was half-hearted, and Martha was struck by the sheen of tears in her friend's eyes.

"Ruby just needed a little bit of warming up – she's absolutely fine and she's dying to see you when you're able for her. But you need to rest a bit, they tell me."

"She's with Will?" mumbled Martha, seeking reassurance. She remembered suddenly the small, pale shape on the end of the wooden promontory, exposed to the wretched storm, yet unharmed.

Sue shook her head. "She's back at the castle – at Mrs Hibbert's – and no one is leaving her side for a second." She paused. "Em . . . Dan's there . . ."

"*Dan?*" said Martha. It was her clearest word yet.

Sue squeezed her hand hard. "You're not to get all worked up, okay? It's all *fine*. Will had to spend a bit of time in here too. He fished you out – proper Milk Tray Man stuff – jacket off, shoes off, into the drink with a great big dive. He was really brave. Found you in a couple of minutes – before it was . . . too late . . ." Sue swallowed before she could carry on. "And he got you back to shore. There were ambulances and all sorts – we were lucky that this place isn't too far from Dubhglas." She indicated her surroundings with a nod of her head. "It's just a little village hospital, but they're equipped for this sort of thing. I suppose lots of people get lost in the cold in the Highlands. Standard procedure, I expect."

She squeezed Martha's hand again and looked straight at her, before sitting back in the chair and taking a large swig of the drink she'd brought in. Martha could smell it was coffee after a moment and a craving hit her.

"Don't suppose I could have some of that?" she mumbled, managing a faint smile.

Sue beamed before pulling the plastic lid off the cup and waving the drink in her direction to ensure that the aroma filled the space around the bed. Then she snatched it back. "Nope," she grinned. "Hospital rations for you only, my dear. And lots and lots of lovely caffeine for me!"

Martha managed a grin. "How long have I been here?" she croaked. There was so much she needed to piece together – so many questions but she couldn't think of them all right now. She felt a wave of weakness wash over her limbs and her lids felt suddenly heavy. Ridiculous . . . she had only just woken up.

Sue leaned over toward the bed. "Three nights in total," she said quietly. "It was about three in the morning when we got you here and you've been pretty much out ever since – it's Tuesday by the way. And it's Will that we have to thank that you're here at all. Not only did he rescue you, he knows CPR – and you needed it."

Sue looked away from Martha, down at her hands where she held the cup, as if regaining her composure. She cleared her throat and paused a moment before feeling ready to look back into her friend's face.

"Your dress is *ruined*, by the way . . ." she began to quip but as she looked at Martha's face, she saw her eyes roll upward behind the heavy lids and her body relax against the pillow. She panicked for a moment, reached out a hand to press the 'call' button, but then looked again at Martha's peaceful face as natural sleep overtook her.

Sue closed her eyes for a moment, breathed deep with relief and exhaustion, before gathering together her belongings and leaving her friend to sleep.

CHAPTER 42

December 5th

Bright morning sunshine gleamed in through the ward window as Martha woke again, gently roused by the bustle of a nurse. A more matronly lady than Karen, called Deborah, checked her vital signs in silence and, as she did, a care assistant arrived with a tray of tea and toast. Deborah encouraged Martha to eat and drink small amounts at a time. Martha devoured the snack in seconds, looking eagerly around for more, but Deborah had vanished to tend to something else and Martha was left with more of an appetite than she had woken with. When she saw Gabriel's face peer through the glass panel on the door at her feet, her heart lifted, almost as much because she hoped he might have brought something to eat as anything else.

Sue followed close behind, a broad smile on her face and a cheery greeting of "Morning!" on her lips.

"Any food?" hissed Martha, pleased to hear that her voice sounded more like its usual self.

"Absolutely not!" retorted Gabriel sharply as he flounced on to the bedside chair. "We were warned you were nil by mouth, or whatever they call it."

Martha's eyes widened. "I've just had some tea and toast, for heaven's sakes!" she protested as strongly as she could, catching

Sue's eye and grinning. She couldn't help it. It felt so good to see the familiar, the people she loved. All she needed now were Will and Ruby.

Gabriel closed his eyes as if to block out the request and made a sweeping gesture with his palm. "Nothing," he said. "I'm giving you nothing. You've swallowed about a ton of pond sludge so it would be a complete waste of a Mars Bar to give you one. And if I *did*, and you were *sick* . . ." He wrinkled his face in horror at the thought, leaving the sentence unfinished. He glanced around the cubicle with distaste, as though something disgusting might manifest at any second.

Sue sat on the end of the bed and Martha pulled her feet toward herself to allow her space.

"Feeling better after your snooze?" asked Sue. "You slept most of yesterday and all last night too." Martha nodded. "Much. I'd feel better with a lot more grub, of course, but orders is orders." She smiled. "How's Ruby, can she come in yet?" she asked then, hopefully.

"All in good time," said Sue. "The doctors want to give you a once-over now and they want any exertion kept to a minimum."

Martha's face fell.

"But," added Sue sternly, "if you're a very good girl, and do everything the nice doctors say, then there's a chance they'll release you later on today, on the proviso that you promise to rest when they do."

Martha's face lit up. She could go home, to Calderwood, to Will, and close the door behind them on all of this. She smiled. "That's good news then, I suppose," she said.

Sue nodded vehemently.

Deborah bustled past again and Martha called her, enthused by the news of her imminent release. "Excuse me," she said. "but what time do you think the doctor might be here?"

"Soon, I'd imagine," came the response and the nurse strode quietly from the room in her thick-soled shoes. The door gave a long creak as it closed behind her on its spring. Martha sighed, frustrated.

"I'm impatient now," she muttered. "I hope the doctor's not off on an emergency or something."

Gabriel harrumphed. "A long emergency with a sand wedge," he grunted.

"What sort of sandwich?" Martha asked, keeping her face serious for a moment before breaking into a grin. She awaited a pithy response and her face fell as none came. For the first time since he'd entered the room, Martha noted that Gabriel seemed distracted and on edge.

"Where's Will today?" she asked, turning to Sue, who was staring into space. "I thought he might . . ."

Martha's voice trailed off as she saw Sue look directly at Gabriel. There was a pause as something passed between them. And then Sue sighed.

"What?" asked Martha, her heart falling slightly.

"You can walk now, can't you?" blurted Gabriel suddenly. "You've had a practice? Only I'm not nudging you out of here with my nose like you're a bloody newborn foal . . ."

"Gabriel!" snapped Martha. "Stop trying to change the subject. What's going on?"

He looked imploringly at Sue.

"Sue, will you tell me?" said Martha. "Will someone bloody tell me what all these *looks* are for?"

Sue gave Gabriel a slight nod and he pushed his bulk out of the chair.

"I'd best go get some coffees then," he mumbled and left, without so much as a second glance at Martha.

Martha turned an accusing glare on Sue. "You'd better tell me what all this is about," she warned.

Sue went and sat on the chair that Gabriel had just vacated. She leaned forward on the bed and fixed Martha with a serious stare. Martha felt very cold all of a sudden, even in the dull heat of the hospital room.

"Look," Sue said, "there have been some developments . . . some things that you need to know before we go get Ruby and go home."

Martha nodded, studying Sue's face intently. "Okay," she said. "Go on."

Sue took a deep breath. "Firstly, with Dan."

"What the hell was he doing here anyway?" demanded Martha,

having the energy for the first time to address the issue that had seemed to drift into her sphere of consciousness over the past days only as soon there was no one left to question. "Who told him what had happened? Was it you? Will?"

Sue drummed her fingers lightly on the bed. A sure sign that she was impatient. Martha stopped speaking.

"He's still here," Sue said simply.

"Why?" asked Martha.

Sue sat back in the chair and then immediately forward again, as though she couldn't get comfortable.

"It was Will's idea to call him. You know, the way he wanted to keep him happy while he's sniffing around for access? He just wanted to keep him informed, now that he's in the picture."

Martha nodded understandingly. "Of course. Will was right," she agreed. "It would never do to drop it all into conversation casually at a later point. 'By the way, Dan, your daughter spent last week on a rickety old jetty in a storm in freezing temperatures and was subsequently hospitalised with suspected hypothermia.' Best be upfront and all that."

"Something like that," responded Sue. She was still subdued in her answers.

Martha's heart fluttered a little as she realised that this wasn't all that Sue had to tell her. "Go on," she prompted.

"Well, all that stuff he told you about setting up by himself in business and breaking up with Paula and that . . ."

Martha took a moment to remind herself. Truth was, she hadn't thought one jot about anything that Dan had said since all of this had happened. Why should she? Best to bury it all in the cold light of day and, besides, she had enough on her plate.

"I took it upon myself to ring that awful Polly woman that you used to be friendly with in London – still had her number from your hen night, would you believe?" Sue paused to make sure that Martha was with her and was rewarded with Martha's puzzled face pulling itself into a deeper frown. "Why'd you do that?" she asked. She knew that Sue had little or no time for the London set. They were never real friends, Martha knew. Just acquaintances, work colleagues, wives of Dan's friends, always treating Martha like an outsider, making her feel even more isolated with them than without.

"Well," responded Sue, "it's *Dan*, for heaven's sake. I don't believe a word he says and I wanted to check up on him. Anyway, the thing is, as I suspected, a lot of what he told you isn't true . . ."

Martha wracked her brains in an attempt to remember exactly what he had told her. It was too much effort. She looked back at Sue for an explanation.

"Well, he's out of work – that bit is true. But he didn't resign. He got the sack from A&M . . ."

Martha's eyes widened in shock. Dan? Getting the sack? But he was their model employee – he loved it there.

"Because his recreational drug habit got a bit out of hand," Sue finished, pausing to let Martha take it in.

She gasped. "Dan? *Drugs?*" she spluttered. "*Drugs?*" she repeated, incredulous.

Sue nodded, with a grim expression on her face.

It did explain a couple of things though, thought Martha. He'd always liked to dabble a little behind her back – she knew that. And he'd looked so thin . . . and that cold he'd had when he'd called to Calderwood, the washed-out skin, the nervous disposition. "Of course," she muttered under her breath. But to get fired? That was lax, even for Dan.

"So Paula kicked him out, right?" she concluded.

Sue grimaced. "Not exactly," she said hesitantly. "Although he was, in Polly's words, 'totes unbearable', he actually walked."

Another shock. "He walked out on Paula? But she's the bloody love of his *life?*" hissed Martha. This was almost too much to take in. "Why would he do that?"

Sue eyed her suspiciously. "Martha, be straight with me," she stated. "I know you said you didn't but do you have *any* feelings left for Dan at all? That night in Edinburgh before we came here? When you kissed him?" She had lowered her voice, looking behind her to make sure they were alone.

Martha sank back against her pillows and looked at Sue in shock. "Sue," she protested, "I swear *on my life* that I don't have feelings for Dan. Jesus, I'd even forgotten I did that the other night –"

"Good," interrupted Sue bluntly. "Because if you did have feelings then what I'm going to tell you would hurt a lot. You're sure?"

Martha traced an X shape over her chest. "Promise," she said.

"Well, there's no easy way to say this, but Paula's pregnant. Due very soon. And Dan flitted when she was six months gone."

The world tilted a little on its axis. So he'd done the same to Paula as he'd done to her. And not only that, had left Paula to come to Edinburgh in search of her. Of some sort of reunion. The words were hazy but Martha remembered how he'd announced he'd fight for her, in that restaurant in Edinburgh. And for a weak moment she'd fallen for it.

What about Paula then? His perfect woman. *Babies weren't his bag*, he'd so memorably said. And there was no fear then of Queen Bitch deciding that she wanted any. But here she was, about to give birth to Dan's child. How had that come about? What would it be? Oh God . . .

Martha looked at Sue with dawning comprehension, tinged with sadness. She felt her eyes well up with tears.

Sue frowned. "You promised," she said sharply. "You promised you didn't feel anything!"

"I *don't*," whimpered Martha. "It's not Dan, it's Ruby. She's going to be a big sister, but that was something that *I* was going to make her. Me and Will. Not bloody Dan and Paula. He never wanted kids – neither did she. She used to call me a 'breeder' behind my back. She had such contempt for women who wanted children. Thought we were weak . . ."

Sue shrugged resignedly. "Well, she doesn't now, clearly," she said.

Martha blinked. She didn't know what she felt about this news. It was massive. Paula, expecting a baby. And now Dan back in her life. And the baby would have to be too, somehow. It had been easy to cut Dan out – in practical terms anyway – but now, there were two babies to consider. Both Ruby and his unborn child. Half-siblings . . .

Martha sat forward, impatient, glancing to the door in frustration. "Where is this bloody doctor?" she said. "I need to get out of here. I need to talk to Will . . ."

She felt a leap of optimism as the door squeaked and opened but it was short-lived as Gabriel reappeared carrying two coffee cups.

"Have I missed much?" he quipped half-heartedly. "I nipped to the caff in the village. Can't be doing with that hospital muck."

Sue glared at him. "Did you take the car?" she demanded.

He looked sheepish for a moment. "It was a latte you wanted, wasn't it?" he said, overriding the question.

"And where's Martha's?" Sue barked again as he held out one cup to her and kept the other for himself.

This time, his expression was genuinely blank. "Is she allowed one?" he shrieked in a high-pitched voice.

Both Martha and Sue hissed at him to be quiet.

He pulled his shoulders up to his ears and mouthed a 'sorry' before looking at Sue with a grave face. "Did you tell her?" he asked.

Martha coughed. "I am *here,* Gabriel," she said flatly.

Another sheepish face. "I'm sorry," he said.

Martha ignored him. Instead, she turned back to Sue. "I need to get out of here. I need to talk it all out with Will."

There was another glance between Gabriel and Sue.

"That's the thing," said Sue cautiously.

"What's the thing," said Martha.

"It's about Will," Sue continued. "Something else happened that you need to know about . . ."

"Will's gone," blurted Gabriel suddenly.

Sue jumped to her feet. "Gabriel, what the *fuck* did you have to go and say that for?" she shouted.

"*Gone?*" Martha said, her voice high-pitched. "What do you mean – 'gone'?"

Sue sank back on the edge of the chair and placed her hand on Martha's foot, curling it around her toes in a gesture of comfort.

"Martha, I don't know how else to say this but Dan told him."

For a moment, Martha was blank. Dan told him what?

And then it dawned on her. About that night. That they'd kissed. Worse, that they'd *talked.* That Martha hadn't batted him away when he suggested that they might be together again one day. That she'd flirted with him . . . Her cheeks suddenly burned a bright crimson, the heat spread to her chest, the tops of her arms and her back. She felt weak and looked at Sue with pleading eyes, begging to be told that it wasn't true. But it was.

Sue nodded, almost imperceptibly, a look of uncomfortable sympathy on her face. She squeezed Martha's foot again as Martha turned her stare to Gabriel who pursed his mouth in an attempt at empathy. But he offered no comfort this time.

"He's gone back to Edinburgh?"

Sue nodded.

"When? When did he go?"

"This morning," replied Sue. "He went out to see Ruby after breakfast – as I told you, she's been staying in Mrs Hibbert's while Will's stayed holed up in the castle. Dan was out there with Ruby and when Will came back he just stormed upstairs and packed his bags. He'd saved your life, Martha, at risk to his own and then he found all that stuff out."

"He rang me from the road," added Gabriel softly, genuine kindness in his voice. "He told me everything . . .what Dan had said to him . . ."

Martha put her hands to her ears. "Don't," she said. "Please don't tell me."

She squeezed her eyes shut as more and more flashbacks from the night in Gaudi's hit her. She couldn't cry – it hadn't sunk in enough for that. She couldn't think beyond the fact that he was gone. That he had left. Because she had been stupid, done something so idiotic, but completely out of character. That stupid wine, those stupid antibiotics.

"Stupid, stupid, stupid!" she said aloud, as Sue rubbed her arm and Gabriel silently sipped his coffee, glancing at the ward door to see if, indeed, the doctor would finally arrive.

It was only after she had been checked over and released an hour later, and had walked from the hospital with Gabriel carrying her bag, and sat into the back of the car that Martha began to cry. It the prospect of seeing Ruby that made it sink home. Will was gone. And where he should have been at her side to bring them home as a family, suddenly she was completely alone again.

CHAPTER 43

December 8th

Martha sneaked quietly down the stairs in her stocking feet. Sue had been already sound asleep by the time she'd made it back up to the bedroom with the painkillers and the water. Martha bit her lip, feeling guilty as she thought of how pale and hunched-over her friend had been when she'd arrived. "I think I've done my back in," she'd said, with a grimace, and pleaded to go to bed early. Martha couldn't have been sure but she thought that Sue might still even be in her clothes under the duvet.

It was all her fault, of course. If she'd just grown a backbone and not begged Sue to drive all the way back from London – having only returned there three days previously – then she wouldn't have hurt herself, hunched over the wheel trying to drive on icy treacherous roads. Martha could have kicked herself. She'd been wrong when she thought that she couldn't feel any worse than she already did.

The afternoon had been hellish. A stilted, heartbreaking meeting with Will at Gabriel's flat. It had been difficult enough to go back there after everything – after what had happened there and then at Dubhglas – without seeing Will's stuff around the place, knowing that he was sleeping in the spare room and that his toothbrush in Gabriel's bathroom wasn't just a temporary measure. Martha had left the apartment reeling. She'd thought she could talk him round, explain to him what happened. She sank onto the bottom step of the stairs and closed her eyes as the realisation hit her again. Will wasn't coming back.

It had been so odd to see him there in the first place, dressed in such familiar things – a checked shirt and jeans. But not once had he broken into a smile. Not for one second had he been anything but hard as nails with her. His words rang in her ears. "I don't think that we should be together any more." There was such a finality to them. Martha had pleaded and cried, begged, tried to explain herself over and over again, but Will had refused to listen to her. The tears came again at the bottom of the stairs in Calderwood as she remembered how the conversation had ended. Close to tears himself, he had asked her to leave. "There's nowhere else to take this conversation," he'd said. "You've hurt me so much, Martha. I'd have died for you and the whole thing was just a lie. I just can't be around you right now. Please leave."

She burned with shame as she'd made her way out the door without a goodbye. Dan had literally told him everything – and then some. Told him that she'd agreed to work with Dan again on whatever terms she chose, that she'd given him access to Ruby just like that, that she was thrilled he'd split up with Paula and that Dan's overriding feeling after their night together was that a reconciliation was on the cards. That the marriage was to pick up, tentatively, where it left off. That some bonds were too strong to be broken, like that between a man and his wife, and that between a father and a daughter. She'd tried to interrupt, to explain to Will that this was typical Dan-style embellishment but in the long run she stayed silent. What point was there? Will was hard as nails when he wanted to be. And right now he had every right and her excuses sounded feeble. She leaned her head against the bannisters as the tears streamed silently down her face.

The babble of Ruby's voice, engrossed in some game in the living room, did nothing to make Martha feel better, like it normally might. For a moment she sat there, feeling every ounce of energy and fight physically drain from her limbs. She couldn't get up, she felt. She stayed where she was for a moment, eyes shut, with no clue how she was going to even stand, much less get on with putting Ruby to bed and then following herself – though she longed to pull the duvet around her ears hoping for dark, protective sleep to envelop her and stay with her until the following day. A lively squeal from the living room, however, indicated to Martha that this was some time away.

She glanced at her watch. It was almost eight o'clock. Way past bedtime, but Martha hadn't had the energy to rouse her from a long snooze that afternoon when she returned from the bitter encounter with Will. And now she was paying the price, in every respect.

She was startled by the sound of the doorbell. Her heart leaped all the same. *Will*, she thought to herself, her chest starting to pound. Maybe he'd come to talk?

Martha somehow summoned the energy to stand up and padded across the hall in her stocking feet to the front door, fingers fumbling on the clasp of the lock. Her body thrilled as she pulled the door inwards, the thrill turning rapidly to anger as she saw who stood outside.

Dan looked exhausted, his skin grey, his face unshaven. His nose was red and his eyes watery.

A rage bubbled inside Martha as she looked at him, equipped now with an additional insight as to why he might look like that. "Dan," she barked, "what do you want?"

He shuffled a little from foot to foot before whipping his right hand out from behind his back. In it was clasped the familiar form of Hugo, Ruby's bear. Despite everything, Martha felt relieved. She hadn't been able to find it anywhere, and Ruby wasn't content with any substitutes. She'd resigned herself to the fact that Hugo would never be found – fuelling her sense that no good could happen to her.

"I picked this up by mistake when I was leaving the castle," Dan said politely, taking a step forward as if to come inside.

Martha suddenly felt herself begin to shake. A combination of rage, discomfort and the sheer disappointment of it not being Will overcame her. Without realising it, she squared her shoulders and filled the doorframe as best she could, blocking his passage. He paused for a moment, confused, before taking a small step backwards, moving nonchalantly, trying to look as if he hadn't intended coming in at all.

He was dressed in jeans and loafers and a black V-neck sweater which looked as if it had been washed at too high a temperature. Everything about him looked crumpled and dishevelled.

"You got back okay, then?" he said, casually.

A flash flood of rage coursed through Martha. *How dare he*, she thought.

"What have you done, Dan?" she asked, feeling the anger bubble up even more inside her as his smile diminished. "Are you so *thick*," she continued in an icy tone, "that you went and said what you did to Will and expect me to be glad to see you? To invite you in when you just turn up on my doorstep?"

Dan frowned in response, his expression flickering from contrived confusion to a cold stare at his ex-wife.

"'Thanks for going all the way up to the Highlands to look after *our* daughter'," he responded sarcastically, speaking as though he were Martha. "'*Our* daughter who *I* let fall in a freezing cold lake in the middle of December when *I* left her to party the night away with my *boyfriend*'."

Martha's face remained stony. "She didn't fall in a lake, Dan," she hissed. "She's fine. She –"

"Was left unsupervised so that she could escape into a storm and nearly drown!"

Martha was momentarily silenced.

"I think that this could do real damage to you as sole custodian," he hissed quietly, a sneer spreading over his features.

Martha squeezed her fists into a ball, dug her nails into her palms, and felt herself tremble all over.

"Why, Dan?" she replied in a low voice. "Do you want her, is that it? Do *you* want sole custody? Only it's going to be awfully busy round at yours being a single dad of two kids in that case." She watched for a reaction.

Dan blinked. "What do you mean?" he asked, trying to hold his combative tone.

Martha knew that she had him rattled. It was so easy to lapse into the old war games.

"When your baby comes along, Dan," she said. "Yours and Paula's. Only, that's the thing, isn't it? You don't actually want custody, sole or otherwise, of *anything*, do you? You've run away again. I know everything. You've done a runner on Paula. Your Queen Bitch turned out to be a breeder, just like everyone else who's let you down. So what do you do? Come running back to me? And you thought I'd *take* you? You thought some tapas and a trip down memory lane would solve everything?"

Martha's chest rose and fell as she glared at her ex-husband. She was oblivious to everything else, her rage growing minute by minute, fuelled by tiredness, fear and Will's desertion.

Dan's hard expression, his sneer, suddenly softened into something approaching a smile.

"You see, that's why I'm glad you're here," he responded. "I've just had a call from London. From the Portland, if you must know. Paula's gone into labour, so I've really got to make tracks if I'm going to make it to her." He paused for effect, watching Martha's face with cruel intent as the words began to sink in. "I couldn't leave Ruby without her bear for another night so I called here on my way – my car's at the end of the drive. Don't you see, Martha, I've got a second chance now. I got scared for a while, true. I ran away, as far as I could think to go which was here. But now I know Paula *needs* me. I know now, having taken care of Ruby over these last days, that this isn't something I should *run* from. I should run *to* it. To being a father. To doing it right. And don't think I'm going to leave Ruby out either – I'm going to be a proper dad to both my kids from now on. Take care of the two of them. Make sure they don't come to any . . . harm . . ."

Martha reeled at the words, his patronising tone, at his barefaced cheek. "You don't miss a bloody beat, do you?" she whispered as though winded.

"Look, I'm sorry if I got your hopes up," he said quietly.

Martha watched, incredulous, as he raised a hand and gently rubbed it down her cheek. She didn't flinch, was rendered immobile with shock. Her heart pounded so fiercely that she thought it might just stop altogether.

"*Leave . . . Ruby . . . alone!*" she wheezed, her eyes wide. For a second her concentration was disturbed as she thought she saw the hall light flicker on and off behind her but not for long. Dan's hateful face soon filled her vision again to the exclusion of everything else.

"I just want to make sure that she's safe," he said in a too-quiet voice, infused with warning.

"I'm sure she's safer here than with her druggy, deadbeat, unemployed dad," Martha retaliated. "If I am to allow anyone else take care of her, Dan," she said, the warning in her tone equalling his, "it certainly won't be you, do you hear me? Who fails to provide as it is and now has another mouth to feed . . ."

Electricity crackled between them.

"The Portland's pretty expensive, Dan, eh?" Martha continued, her voice barely audible. "You'd better hurry of course if you're going to get back to the birth. To be there, this time. Best of luck to Paula. And to your baby, of course . . ."

She left the words hang, allowed their implications to swirl in the air and settle on Dan's shoulders. Her arms and hands visibly shook. She tensed her body so that her knees didn't betray her and cave in. She felt so weak, standing there. To support herself, she leaned against the doorframe to her left. She lifted her head, however, at the distant crunch of car tyres on gravel, the familiar sound of a large engine growling up the drive. This time it was for real. Martha gasped. *It was Will.* Finally. The Volvo became visible at the turn in the drive, bathing herself and Dan in its headlights as it approached, and then it came to a halt.

Martha waited, her nerves alive with anticipation of the sound of the engine cutting out, the door slamming, his footsteps on the gravel. She was again distracted by something from within – by a sound from the living room, a clinking sound. Ruby, she thought. No doubt she was doing something she shouldn't. But it would be fine. In just moments, Will would be home to pick her up and cuddle her, to reassure her and calm her for bed.

Then the Volvo began to move again, to reverse awkwardly in the space at the top of the drive. Martha frowned. What was he doing? Was he going to reverse toward the front door? Maybe he wanted to bring equipment in?

She couldn't hide her dismay as the nose of the big red car turned slowly and clumsily and headed back down the drive.

Martha gazed in disbelief as the night air grew silent, the engine noise growing fainter and fainter until she could hear it no more. Her jaw dropped in shock and she straightened immediately. Why would he do that? She stared in disbelief at the space where she had just seen Will turn and leave. Where was he gone?

And then it struck her. Did he think . . .? She looked at Dan in horror. Of course. Will had seen something that he didn't want to see – Martha, casually leaning against the front door, deep in conversation with Dan of all people. Hugo being passed between them as if in some warped show of parental co-operation. Martha wanted to crumble. How could she explain now? She must call him. That was it, she had to phone him – had to get him to listen once and for all. She heard Ruby from inside – a sharp squeal followed by a longer note as she began to wail. *Not now, Ruby*, thought Martha, her irritation turning back to rage as she saw Dan shrug his shoulders and cough, a gesture that showed embarrassment, but not for himself. He was showing that he was embarrassed for *her*.

"Wow," he said quietly.

Ruby's wail grew louder and Martha half-turned to go back inside.

"That was awkward," Dan said, raising his eyebrows. "Look, thanks for everything – for giving me a go at being a dad. I mean, I feel I'm ready now . . . it was just a couple of days and in very odd circumstances, but rest assured you'll be hearing from me again." He smiled, confidently, before taking a step backward.

Ruby's wail turned to a scream just as Martha exploded. "Look, Dan, I wasn't here to provide you with a practice run at being a parent. Now just leave – you've done enough damage for one night. Just fuck right off, would you? Just get lost, get out of here . . ."

Her voice trailed as the crying from inside grew more and more distressed. There was so much she needed to say to him, so much that she wanted to hurl at him, but Ruby was hurt. Without another word, Martha slammed the door in Dan's face, her attention switching instantly to the persistent wailing from the living room, concern flooding through her. She heard his footsteps crunch away as she turned and paused to wipe a cobweb from her face before charging toward the living room and her distraught daughter.

CHAPTER 44

Martha's emotions were a jumble as she crossed the hall. Fury at Dan, heartache at what Will had just done, concern but also irritation that Ruby had managed to hurt herself somehow right at this particular moment. She didn't think that her tether had any give remaining.

Her irritation disappeared instantly, however, overtaken by concern, and then panic, as she stepped over the threshold of the living room onto the wooden floor and saw the blood.

Ruby's face was distorted with pain but, much worse than that, it was smeared red, like a finger-painting exercise but this time it was her bloody fingerprints that dotted her cheeks, and her clothes, and her hair . . . It was everywhere – on her hands, the rag-doll on her lap, the couch beside her . . . dear God, where was it coming from? There was so much of it! How had she cut herself? And where was the cut? Martha knelt and plucked her into her arms as quickly as she could and searched her small body frantically for the injury, praying that it wasn't somewhere that she couldn't make it stop. But where was it? Where was the source of the blood?

Ruby screamed in pain, looking at her mother with tear-stained eyes, desperate for comfort, yet Martha couldn't give it fully yet, couldn't stop searching until she found the source of the bleeding. Suddenly, she spotted something on the floor behind Ruby glint in the light. She stopped in her search for a moment as she identified, if not the location of the cut, the cause of it. Her own hands now stained red from her daughter, Martha held Ruby close to her with one arm while she reached out and picked up the small, sharp nail scissors that she concluded had been the weapon. The one she had used to cut the thread in her coat before meeting Dan, all that time ago. But how had it ended up on the floor? She was vigilant about keeping it in the dish on the mantelpiece, high above Ruby's reach, to avoid this exact scenario. Even if the toddler had climbed on something she couldn't have reached it. So how had it ended up within her grasp? Had Sue moved it?

Martha's mind raced to find a conclusion as she returned her attention back to the crying child. She tried soothing her this time, clucking and shushing and making soft noises which Ruby barely heard over her screams of shock and panic.

After a second, Martha suddenly recalled the noise she had heard when she'd stood at the front door. The metallic clink. *Exactly how the nail scissors would sound as it hit the wooden floor.* But that was ridiculous. How could it have hit the floor by itself? She knew for certain that she had left it in the pottery bowl – her eyes strayed to the mantel to check but the bowl was still where she had left it. The scissors couldn't have fallen of its own volition. It would have had to be lifted out and dropped on the ground. And thinking back, Sue hadn't even come in here on her arrival. She was in too much pain and after a brief exchange in the hallway had gone straight to bed.

It was impossible that the sharp implement could have got into Ruby's hands. *And yet it had.*

For a second Martha grew calmer as she looked at Ruby's wrists and neck, rubbing them with a spit-covered finger to ascertain that they were un-punctured, and they were. A second later, however, she froze completely, a sensation of prickling cold tracing its way along her cheeks. The overhead light flickered for a moment. And, at the same instant that she heard it 'pop' as it blew, she knew that she wasn't alone.

It wasn't just the living room lights either. She heard more distant 'pops' from the hallway, through to the kitchen. She had her back to the living-room door but knew by the darkness that engulfed her that they were all gone. All blown. Plunging the house into darkness.

Martha gripped Ruby tightly to her, the source of the bleeding now forgotten. It wasn't the gravest danger, Martha realised. That, she knew instinctively, was whatever stood behind her in the doorway.

She froze, couldn't have turned if she'd been paid a million pounds, knowing so clearly that there was something there.

Martha's blood ran cold as she clutched her child and tried to stand, but her legs wouldn't support her, her body was incapable of movement. It was no good. She had to see . . .

Slowly, Martha forced herself to turn around, her rational side trying to tell her that there was no one there, that she was overtired, an emotional wreck, and therefore just imagining things . . . it was nothing more than a tripped switch . . .

But no. She couldn't lie to herself. She knew that there was someone there. The low noise that she heard proved it wasn't her imagination. The breathing. In and out, in and out . . .

Martha trembled as she turned, still kneeling on the floor, her crying child encased in her arms, and forced her eyes to take in the doorway. To take in what stood there. A shadow. The shadow of a man. Martha's body jerked involuntarily, spasmed with terror, as she took in the huge shape of something she recognised. Something she had seen before, that had terrified her. She was unable to tear her eyes away from the shape that was blacker than the darkness itself. At what she realised, beyond any reason, was the ghost of Jack Ball.

He was here, somehow. At Calderwood. Not in the murky waters of a lake, or in the ancient stones of a nightmare castle, not even in the mists of her addled imagination. But physically here. In her house. Her sanctuary. She whimpered, pulling Ruby even tighter to her. Burying the child's head into the crook of her neck and shoulder so that she might not see it.

This was their home, where they were supposed to be safe, where Martha was supposed to keep Ruby safe. Her mouth attempted to form a word, to call Will's name, but she suddenly remembered – how could she have forgotten – that there was no point. That Will wasn't here. But Sue was . . . Sue was here. Martha opened her mouth to try to call her, but, like a scream in a nightmare, no sound came from her terrified throat. What little whisper she managed was instantly drowned by Ruby's screams. Martha gazed at the figure that filled the doorway and realised that there was no one to help.

Jack Ball's features were indistinguishable. Martha couldn't tear her eyes away from him. How could this happen? What was he made of? Was he really *there* or was he a by-product of her imagination, something to do with the painkillers the hospital gave her maybe? Did they cause hallucinations when they wore off, perhaps? But what about the lights . . .

In a flash, the vision was gone. Martha found herself frozen with fear, immobile, still staring at the door where she had seen him, willing herself to get to her feet and fill that vacant space and pass through it. If she could just get out of the room, she thought . . . but then, what good would that do? Surely if he were in the dark water at Dubhglas Castle, and then in her cosy, safe living room at Calderwood, he could be *anywhere?*

Martha squeezed Ruby even tighter and staggered to her feet. The toddler's tears had abated somewhat, but she was now struggling to be released, wriggling as hard as she could. Martha tried to restrain her. She couldn't allow her loose in the room – who knew what other dangers were there? It became suddenly clear to her how the baby had managed to get hold of the scissors in the first place. A fresh wave of terror washed over her as she replayed the clinking noise she had heard in her mind. *He* had done it. Just as he had unlocked the sliding door at Dubhglas and released Ruby into the storm. He had been in here with her all along. *Why was he here?*

Alone with her child. Martha's terror was replaced by desperation. What had he done, she wondered? And what else was he capable of doing?

Her answer came a second later as in the darkness she caught movement behind her, from the wall to the right of the fireplace. Was it a trick of the dark? Her tired, addled mind making the bookshelves look in the darkness like they were rocking back and forth somehow? Too late she realised that it was all too real.

Martha screamed and twisted her body to cover Ruby's as the shelves, floor to ceiling, packed tight with books, came crashing down on her, missing her head by inches but landing fully on her back. It wasn't heavy enough to crush her but as books spilled off the shelves over her body like an insect swarm, she felt blow after blow as they bounced against her, sliding over her head, burying her. Her back ached where the shelves had impacted on her body, hunched in this position with Ruby screaming underneath her, the wriggling worse now, the cries of pain turning to terror as she was smothered by her mother.

Martha stayed where she was, raising her head, feeling the last of the books slide off her and on to the floor. *Where was he gone?* she wondered frantically.

She looked around her, tried to take in as much of the room as she could. She could see no dark shape in front of her – outlined against the window that overlooked the garden, for instance. But she couldn't turn, couldn't see what was behind. There was silence for a moment, an unnatural stillness broken then by Martha's screams as crash after merciless crash came from around her. It was as if she were being shelled. Item after item, a glass dish here, a picture frame there, smashing around her head, each time missing, but getting closer and closer as her possessions, her trinkets rained down, flung by a force that she couldn't see, that she didn't want to see. She made herself as small as she could, curled into a tighter ball, folded her body as best she could around her daughter.

Finally, when Martha thought she could bear it no longer, it stopped as suddenly as it had begun. The room was filled by an eerie, electric silence. Martha squirmed in discomfort, still trapped under the bookcase. She stopped, feeling instinctively that she should lie still, like a hunted animal, like she was playing dead. She mustered every ounce of self-control that she could as the room was still, and stayed still for a long time. For too long. She had to get out.

With a sudden, adrenalin-fuelled roar she pushed as hard as she could and managed to crawl out from under the bookcase, Ruby still clutched to her, hearing it crash onto the floor behind her. She stood then, grappling to hold on to the squirming toddler. She tried to clutch Ruby closer to her again, stumbling in an attempt to regain her balance as she looked around, her eyes flickering frantically from one corner of the room to the next in case he was there, in case he was moving quickly, in case another missile would be launched at them. Ruby, terrified, with a final lurch half-wriggled, half-fell from Martha's arms. Grabbing and grappling at her clothing and then the air, Martha screamed as Ruby freed herself and bolted for the door. Martha howled her name, assaulted with fresh fright as she heard a voice from the hallway.

Then she realised it was Sue.

Martha was stumbling over her belongings, strewn all over the floor, when Sue was hit full-force with Ruby's fleeing body. The toddler howled in frustration as she was hoisted into her godmother's arms. Martha leaned against the arm of the couch for support, her relief that someone was holding Ruby, keeping her safe, enormous.

"Martha, what the hell is going on?" Sue cried, her voice filled with panic. "All the lights are blown – I was asleep, but I heard an almighty crash . . . are you okay? Ruby . . ."

Her voice trailed off as she made out the dark markings on the child's face, and she turned her to catch the faint light streaming in through the fanlight over the hall door. She gasped as she saw the streaks of blood, catching Ruby's head in the palm of her hand as the toddler arched her back in temper, in another attempt to writhe free.

"Jesus!" she exclaimed. "Is this . . .? Is it *blood?*"

Martha felt winded suddenly, closed her eyes for a moment to catch her breath. "She got hold of a nail scissors but I think she's okay," she managed. "But, Sue, it's Ball . . . he's here . . . in this room . . . he knocked over the shelves . . ."

Martha's sentence faded into silence as she opened her eyes again. Because she could see him again. In the hall behind Sue. This time, his silhouette framed in the same beam of light that shone faintly through the fanlight. She could make it out clearly, his hands on his hips, watching the scene play out, observing them so that he could make his next move. *Why?* But this time, somehow, Martha could see his face. It shouldn't have been possible – the shaft of light was too faint – but she could clearly make out his hideous sneer, the mottled skin streaked with greys and purples. The scar, closed this time, vivid against the paleness of the cheek through which it sliced. He stared at them, silent, cold, lifeless yet filled with danger.

Martha pointed. "There!" she screamed. "He's there, Sue!"

But of course by the time Sue turned to look he was gone. And at the same time Martha felt his breath close against her neck before she felt the sudden and painful smash of something hitting her full force at the base of her back.

Sue turned back just in time to see Martha's legs buckling underneath her and the fragments of what had been a small, wooden footstool lying on the floor. The whole thing had happened in an instant. Sue's instinct was to run to Martha but something stopped her and she reversed the decision in a split second. Instead she turned in the opposite direction and ran, gripping the wriggling child as hard as she could.

Through the agony and disbelief of what had just happened, Martha felt relief wash over her as she heard the jingle of keys from the hall table and then the front door slam. They were gone, at last. Safe. *He mustn't go after them,* she thought and, instead of sinking to the floor as her body urged her, she grabbed the couch for support and turned her body as best she could to see behind her, to watch for the next attack.

It came as an ornamental lamp was knocked to the ground, the glass globe and the bulb it contained smashing into hundreds of tiny pieces on the wooden floor, exploding upwards. Martha's hands flew to her face to defend her eyes and, in doing so, managed to unbalance herself. She instinctively took a step forward to regain her balance and in a second felt the sharp burning pain as the needles of broken bulb sank through her thin socks and into her foot. She cried out in pain, stepped backwards, was again unbalanced and instinctively brought the same foot down to prevent herself falling over but this time on yet more tiny pieces of glass. She screamed this time. As much in temper at the pain and frustration as anything else. Who did he think he was? Like Dan, how *dare* he invade the asylum that she had found in her home.

"What do you want from me?" she screamed at last.

An immediate, ominous stillness fell across the room.

Martha could feel her foot pulse as the blood continued to seep out. She could clearly detect the moist warmth spreading across the sole and it crossed her mind for a second to pray that the shards of glass could be removed easily. It was banished again as the stillness was broken by another shift in the darkness, this time in the alcove where her bookshelves had stood before falling, being knocked to the ground. *He's watching again*, she thought. A part of her still petrified, yet relieved that he was here, with her, and not with Ruby. She constantly warned Will about this, she remembered. *Don't bring anything home with you*, she remembered saying in the past. It was he who had told her that there was evidence of spirits attaching themselves to the living and travelling with them, covering great distances, going overseas, moving house. She hadn't believed him. Yet here she was, the one who had brought someone – something – home. A physical threat. She had no idea what to do next as she fixed her eyes on the now-still darkness of the corner of the room. Was he even still there?

"What do you want from me?" Martha growled in a low voice. It trembled, she knew, but somehow, confronting him, communicating with him as if he were just another person made her feel braver.

"Why are you here?" she said, louder now. She held her injured foot an inch off the ground, to avoid pushing the glass in any further. She felt the sock adhere to her foot, made sticky with the blood that flowed from God knew how many wounds on the soft sole. Martha hissed, suddenly aware of the pain, which drove an anger to rise within her again.

"*You have no right to be here*!" she shouted, bellowing the words as loud as she could in a primal reaction to everything – the fear, the pain, the uncertainty.

Enough was enough.

"This is *my* home and you should just get back to where you belong, do you hear me?" she roared, her rage gathering momentum. "I know what you did, you know. What you did to Martin Pine, what you wanted to do to Laurence McKenzie. We all do. We found your photographs – we know what kind of man you were!"

She fell silent, hearing the reverberation of her own words in her ears. It all felt so strange, suddenly. The surroundings. This room where she had always been so comfortable now felt cavernous and unwelcoming, filled with places where things could hide. She suppressed a shiver that ran the length of her body, bitterly cold all of a sudden. And all the time the silence, as if he were biding his time . . .

How *dare* he, she thought again.

"The police know too," she added, softer now.

For a brief moment she thought she felt the air grow thicker somehow. Her hair stood on end, as if some sort of electrical current had passed along the ground and up into her body. A reaction, she knew.

Keep him here.

"There are special places nowadays for people like you. You'd be on a list. And everyone would know exactly what you were capable of. Kids nowadays are warned about bullies and *perverts* like you!"

Her voice rang again around the room and she paused for breath, realising exactly what she was doing. *Provoking*, Will called it. Pushing spirit for a reaction. And not in a way that produced positive results either. Too late, she thought. She'd have to keep going, for Ruby's sake. To give her and Sue time to get away. Sue would know what to do, would know to call Gabriel and get Ruby to A&E. In the meantime, however, what sort of reaction would greet her provocation?

The darkness seethed again in the alcove and Martha suppressed a whimper. Her bravery evaporated suddenly at the sight of the movement. It was like some deadly animal in the corner, waiting to pounce. He was so strong, she acknowledged. He had really hurt her. He was truly evil.

She took a deep breath and opened her mouth to continue. Make it sound good, she thought to herself. Don't show him you're scared.

"I'm not frightened of you," she growled at the shape in the corner. "You think you're the big tough guy but you're not. You're nothing but scum who hurts little children. Does that make you feel big? Does it?"

In retrospect, what happened next was indescribable but Martha could somehow remember every split second with terrifying clarity. It wasn't any single thing but, as she provoked Jack Ball's spirit, it felt as though she had ignited a nuclear explosion. Unable to distinguish whether it was in her head, or happening outside her body, Martha was suddenly filled with colour and sound, overwhelmed by a vision of his hideous face pressed up against hers. She felt everything then – electricity, pain, sorrow, regret, hatred, evil – the purest terror imaginable. It was as if all of the dead were suddenly more alive than they had ever been and Martha felt – no, Martha *knew* that she was not alone with Jack Ball in that room. And she knew, beyond a shadow of a doubt, that it was all real. That the room had gradually filled with other presences.

Her body burned suddenly as she felt them all around her – her mother, her grandmother, Henry, Lily, Laurence McKenzie, Martin Pine . . . shielding her on all sides . . . dark shapes, there, yet not there . . . somehow working together to keep her safe.

And when it was over, when everything was still again and the space where she stood, so alone, covered in blood, her own and Ruby's, was nothing more than her own living room, Martha experienced a feeling like no other. The house around her was more empty than it had ever been but she herself felt somehow totally fulfilled. And safe.

There was no doubt in her mind that Jack Ball was finally gone. The atmosphere was completely empty of him, of anyone or anything. What's more, she knew that he hadn't gone of his own volition, but had been taken away forcibly. By spirits and souls who wanted to protect her. Shades that she herself had somehow summoned.

As Martha turned and limped from the room, her body aching and beyond exhaustion, she realised that she hadn't thought it possible to feel so fearless, yet she understood implicitly that she had never felt more protected in her life. And that something had changed forever.

CHAPTER 45

And at the precise moment that Calderwood grew suddenly empty, that Jack Ball's spirit was forcibly removed by those who wished to keep Martha safe, Gabriel McKenzie woke with a start in his apartment a couple of miles away. As before, he knew that he was not alone. That there was someone in his room with him. Yet this time, unlike the last, he felt no fear, just comfort, as he sat up in his bed and saw at the foot the vision of a boy. Gabriel smiled and sat completely upright, a sense of calm pervading every inch of his body. With the inner voice that was only heard by one other soul, Gabriel greeted his brother's spirit with relief.

CHAPTER 46

December 15th

For the second time in only a matter of weeks, Martha stood nervously in a room with Gabriel. She looked at her surroundings for the tenth time since entering. It was hard to believe that she had last been in this place only a fortnight before. It felt like a lifetime since that night at the lake. She had tried to block it from her mind and was still shaken at having had to relive it earlier that day for the Dubhglas police. They wanted a statement, they'd told her when they phoned, but needed to speak to her in person, to verify that what had happened involved no foul play. Martha was grateful to Gabriel for making the day trip with her, but hadn't expected him to suddenly announce a diversion to Dubhglas Castle while they were there.

Martha limped over to the window, her foot still throbbing from the procedure to remove all of the glass from the shattered lamp. She stood beside Gabriel and together they gazed out over the lawn, over the remaining stumps of the copse of apple trees and beyond – to the glimpses of the lake, now glinting in the winter sunshine between the trees.

"You're sure that you feel nothing here?" Gabriel asked again.

Martha sighed, and turned her back to the window, looking instead at the grim surroundings of the bedroom. "I told you, Gabriel, I can't feel anything here. Why would I? I never did before?"

Gabriel tutted impatiently, dismissing what she said with a wave of his hand. He was tired of her constant denials.

"You know damn well what I mean when I ask you if you can feel anything," he said flatly. "Now I've brought you here for a reason. And you bloody well agreed to come. Can you feel any spirits here now? Any evil? Any sense of discomfort?"

Martha shrugged and shook her head. She wished Gabriel would stop asking her these things. Not because she didn't know the answer, but because she did. As sure as she was standing there, she knew that there was no threat in that room. The same as now there was no threat – or presence – in Gabriel's apartment. Or in Calderwood.

"And you're sure that there's nothing at home either?" he continued.

Martha rolled her eyes. "Why do you keep asking me this, Gabriel? You brought me here but you've refused to explain *why*! Isn't it about time you told me what you're at?"

Gabriel cut her off with a black look. "Stop your nonsense!" he barked, and she did, closing her mouth suddenly and looking at him in shock. It was a tone that he hadn't used on her since they had first met. "You know as well I do that something's changed in you," he said. "Or something's emerged that might always have been there. Angeline saw it in you and once she pointed it out then so did I. You knew, Martha. You knew that Martin Pine's spirit was hanging round my flat, you knew exactly what was going on here the night of the storm but most of all you . . . you . . . were able to take care of yourself that night at Calderwood. The night that you say Jack Ball went away, that Laurence came back to me. You can deny it all you want, Martha, but I'm serious when I say that I think you've got the gift. And now, knowing what you managed to do when Ball invaded your home, who you managed to summon –"

"Shut *up,* Gabriel!" Martha snapped.

She'd had enough. All this talk of her having the same gift as he did, of being able to communicate with the dead. She didn't want to hear any more of it. Most of all, she didn't want to have it. She didn't want to see what Gabriel saw, be burdened with the responsibility he carried. She didn't want to have to attract more death into her life – into Ruby's life – than she already had. Attract even more danger . . .

"It was Dan, you know," said Gabriel quietly, interrupting her thoughts.

Martha decided to ignore him but then changed her mind. "What do you mean?" she asked.

"Dan," he replied. "Who brought Ball with him. To your door. It wasn't you. That's what you're worried about, isn't it? That it was you? You that put yourself and Ruby in danger, that lined her up for that hideous spirit to hurt?"

Martha avoided his gaze. He was absolutely right, of course.

"Dan had something – some quality – which Ball liked and to which he attached himself," said Gabriel. "Ball was a destructive spirit – he had no specific plan, no particular target, so get it out of your head that his sole aim was Ruby. He was, in death, as in life, a troublemaker. A violent, destructive . . . evil troublemaker. An opportunist."

Gabriel watched Martha closely as she flinched, shrugged her shoulders slightly as if to shake off what he was saying to her.

"He came back here because Martin came back here. Because the events of 1963 were being replayed after death, somehow. Martin came to find me but he was here as well to keep an eye on things, to make sure that Ball didn't get what he wanted – and what he wanted that night at the lake was to sort out some unfinished business. He wanted all the players back on set again. He needed to finish things off with Martin Pine and the only way to get Pine's spirit down to the lake that night was to use bait. To use a lure. Martin vowed that he'd never allow Ball to hurt another child. Ball knew that somehow. Unfortunately the bait he used to test this vow happened to be the only child who had visited that place in a very long time. Ball wanted to finish what he started back in 1963, but you stopped him . . ."

"Pine stopped him. It was Pine who protected Ruby on the jetty – I saw him," interjected Martha and regretted it instantly. Telling Gabriel that she had seen Martin Pine's spirit surround and protect Ruby was just adding more fuel to his fire. Next thing he'd have her attending his spiritualist church, engaging in séances with bloody Angeline Broadhead. She wanted none of it. She just wanted this to be over. It was maybe one benefit to having Will out of her life – no more ghosts. But then again she'd have fought an army of ghosts if it meant having Will back. She scowled, her temper growing more foul by the second, and checked her watch again with an angry sigh.

"He presented as a mist," Gabriel offered quietly. "Trying to summon attention. To get help, somehow. Laurence wanted help, too, but he couldn't ask it of me. That's why he went away. In case he brought Ball to my door." Gabriel smiled from the corner of his mouth, focusing on a shaft of sunlight which came through the window and fell on a perfect square of faded wood on the floor.

"That's where the filing cabinet was?" asked Martha tentatively.

Gabriel nodded, his expression one of disgust as he tapped the square of light with his foot. Sue had explained what she and Will had found in the room – the photographs, the camera marked with Ball's initials in the bottom drawer. It was the police who had lifted up the dirty pink eiderdown covered in cat hair and found the remaining pictures. They were nothing like the ones in the upper drawer. At least thirty of them, unbearable, proof enough that Ball was a predator. It seemed more likely than ever that Pine was to receive his posthumous pardon.

"At least he's gone now," murmured Gabriel softly. "We both feel now that he's not here any more . . ."

Martha tutted and shook her head. "We can't miss the train back, Gabriel. I've got to get home to Ruby. I'm going to go and wait for the taxi," she said and limped from the room without another word. She didn't want to talk about it any more, to be the subject of his probing questions. Heaven knew life was tough enough at the moment as it was. It was so difficult returning to an empty home, night after night, lit now with fairy lights and a tree which had been half-heartedly erected to please Ruby. Martha couldn't even think of Christmas, facing, as she was, into a future that didn't include Will. There had been times over the past weeks when she thought her heart might break with sadness at their separation and regret at her own stupidity.

She made for the stairs, intent on leaving, once and for all, and hopefully never returning again. In her haste, she completely missed a small figure emerging from one of the rooms further down the passage, and crossing the corridor into the room that she had just left.

Gabriel let her go and turned back to the window. He sighed and leaned his forehead against the pane of glass. It was so impossibly beautiful, he thought, with the low sun turning everything he could see before him to gold. And it had concealed such horror and unhappiness. He couldn't help, however, feel a frisson of gratitude and relief as he sensed Laurence once again nearby. He had missed his brother terribly.

What he wouldn't miss, of course, was Will. It had been almost two weeks now that he'd been cluttering up his space. Moping about with a face like a miserable fish. Cluttering up the apartment with his equipment and his papers, working all hours of the night, sleeping till lunchtime. Gabriel decided that his first task on returning to Edinburgh was to sit him down and talk some sense into him. He was sick of Martha's depressed state too. And he wanted his space back.

He was startled suddenly by the creak of the saddle-board behind him and he turned suddenly, a bolt of fear slicing through his body. The figure in the doorway was a shadow at first, but when she stepped into the light Claire Hibbert managed a weak smile.

"Sorry to startle you," she said in that ever so soft voice of hers.

Gabriel took a deep breath. "That's all right," he replied.

"Your taxi will be here in a minute," she said, nodding toward the open door of the bedroom. "I think it was wise of you to get the train up here today – I can feel frost in the air already. Such a cold night ahead. Too cold to be out on the roads."

Gabriel dug his hands deep into his pockets. "I don't suppose my godfather has come back yet?" he asked, tentatively.

Hibbert shook her head. "He's been in and out of that police station these past weeks like he's the sergeant," she said. "Answering questions about his uncle, about Martin. About what he said in court . . ."

"I'm sorry to have missed him," said Gabriel. "But I suppose if it means that Martin might achieve what he wanted to, then it can't all have been in vain, can it?"

He realised that they were speaking in hushed tones, in case they were overheard, even though there was no one to hear them.

Claire nodded in agreement, her breath catching. "I'll miss him," she said, simply.

Not 'I miss him' or 'I missed him'. Gabriel looked at her in surprise, although he knew, having spent weeks without Laurence, exactly what she meant.

"I'm glad I caught you – I wanted to give you this," she said, suddenly, reaching in her pocket and extending her hand toward Gabriel.

He couldn't make it out at first but after a moment recognised the item as something he had seen so many times. In particular, in the picture of his brother that looked down at him daily from his mantel in George's Street. The picture that had been disturbed so often by the ghostly fingerprints of his ghostly intruder.

He reached out his hand and took the cold metal of Laurence's swimming medal from Hibbert's hand. He stared at it, everything else in the room fading for a moment. He felt the heavy weight of it in his hand, looked at the engraving of a swimmer in a swimming cap and goggles, represented to show one arm forming an upside-down 'V' in the water as he swam through wiggly lines, indicating waves. He turned it slowly over and ran his thumb over the words *Laurence McKenzie, 1st place, Lifesaving* carved into the back and then with his other hand, ran the grubby red, white and blue striped ribbon through his fingers. He was silent for a moment, overcome by the irony of it all.

"He gave it to me to mind the night it all happened," explained Hibbert. "I put it in my pocket and then forgot about it. I've always had it with me, not as a keepsake, you understand, but it's somehow always been there. I want you to have it back now, for your mother to have it. She should have had it all these years. I hope that it will bring her some peace, perhaps."

Gabriel closed his hand over the medal and pocketed it with a sniff. "Thank you very much for that, Hibbert," he managed, dignified.

"I'd best be off then," she said suddenly. "We'll see you soon again, I hope?"

Gabriel nodded. "After Christmas, perhaps," he offered. He needed some space away from here, he knew.

"The very best of the season to you, then," said Claire. "We'll see you in the spring."

And before he could answer, she was gone, her small frame bustling out of the doorway and back to work.

The taxi was already there when he let himself out the front door, pulling it behind him and clutching his coat tight as he crossed over to the car.

The engine was running, the driver sitting patiently behind the wheel and a cloud of exhaust billowing out into the freezing air. Martha turned and smiled at Gabriel's approach, trying to show remorse for having stormed out earlier on. He grinned back and watched her climb in behind the driver's seat, then he turned and took a final look back at the building. Something about the moment seemed so significant, somehow. He wanted to memorise the place as it stood now, frozen in time, dark grey against the bluest of skies. His own breath came in clouds before him as he took it all in. He smelled the air, detected a hint of snow and shivered, regretting the absence of his gloves. He dug his hands deeper into his pockets instead, feeling again the cold metal and silk of Laurence's medal on its ribbon.

Gabriel turned then and looked out over the view – the manicured flowerbeds, the distant trees and purple mountains. He inhaled the air deeply, feeling the hit at the back of his throat, then that it was time to get into the taxi and leave.

Had he not, however, taken one last look back at the Castle, he'd never have seen him sitting there, on the bench that was positioned under the library window overlooking the front of the house. His skinny legs were spread wide before him, a plume of smoke rising up into the air from the cigarette between thumb and forefinger. Gabriel paused to take in the vision before him, one that was at once familiar and startling. He looked so out of place, he thought. A thin young man in his shirt sleeves on such a freezing a day, puffing away to himself, having a break.

Martin Pine's ghost raised its hand in a wave in Gabriel's direction and then suddenly was gone, leaving Gabriel with his own hand raised in response. There was nothing left but a faint trace of smoke in the air which then dissolved – so faint that it might not ever have been there. And Gabriel felt a familiar sense of completion. A wave of emotion washed over him and then was gone, replaced by a sense of satisfaction, of something achieved.

He muttered aloud, "Good luck, mate."

This time Martin Pine was truly gone for good.

CHAPTER 47

December 23rd

"So you didn't dispose of it then," said Gabriel, shutting the glove compartment with a bang.

Will didn't respond to his satisfaction so Gabriel made sure to snap it open and shut a second and third time, with a loud cough for effect on the last bang.

It did the trick. Will turned his gaze slowly away from Calderwood's front door and looked at Gabriel blankly. "What?" he asked in a voice that said he was still far away. Gabriel mimed slipping a ring onto the third finger of his left hand. Will looked back at the house, making a sound somewhere between a grunt and a cough. Gabriel leaned forward in the passenger seat to try to catch better sight of his face and also to try to regain his attention, but Will's gaze was firmly fixed on the door of what had been his home.

"The *ring*," Gabriel said loudly, giving the glove compartment door another loud bang for effect. Will swung his head around. "Ssssssh!" he hissed. "You'll wake Ruby."

Gabriel turned to look at the toddler asleep in her car-seat. She never stirred, her pacifier hanging limply, as always, from her lower lip and Hugo clutched loosely in her hands. Her cheeks were rosy red and her knitted hat was slightly askew from the struggle to get her into the seat in the first place. Gabriel rolled his eyes. "The

Trumpet Voluntary wouldn't wake that child," he observed, and returned his glance to Will, a provocative twinkle in his eyes. "Speaking of which, I'd thought you might walk down the aisle to that . . ."

"Drop it, Gabriel," said Will with a sigh. "It's not going to happen."

The radio, which Gabriel had tuned to a Christmas station, was the only sound in the car for a few moments as Will continued to stare at the facade of Calderwood. He blinked in surprise suddenly as his focus shifted and he noted the first flurries of snow finally begin to fall. It had threatened all day, another shower to top up the six inches that had fallen overnight.

Gabriel sat back in the passenger seat and looked straight ahead to the lamppost in the garden. "This is a lovely Christmas-card scene, William," he said, "but I can't feel my feet at the moment so any chance we could move it along a wee bit?"

Will sighed. "I suppose I should just take Ruby in," he said.

Gabriel stayed facing straight ahead. "Oh no, Will, let's hang on out here awhile staring into the freezing bushes, eh? I mean, my meeting at the *Ghosts R Us* offices is only in, oh, half an hour or so." He paused to look at his watch. "Plenty of time to get from here to the other side of town. No rush. Even if we have to dig ourselves out."

Will ignored the sarcasm and gave a sigh, turning the key to silence the ignition and removing it to pop it in his jacket pocket.

Gabriel gave him a sidelong glance. "Don't worry, William," he remarked drily. "I'm not going to drive off in the Volvo of all things. Wouldn't add anything to the street cred of the new permanent medium for *Ghosts Wanted* to be seen scooting down the road in a tractor now, would it?"

Will still didn't respond and Gabriel sat up in his seat, looking back again at Ruby.

"She loves you taking Ruby, you know," he said suddenly, his tone kinder. He realised he wasn't going to provoke Will into any banter today, despite his own happiness at being on his way to hand in his notice. The call had come by surprise the previous week and he'd needed little or no time to answer it. The new year would bring a new job and Gabriel relished the prospect.

"I always think it's going to be . . . you know . . . the last time I hand her back," said Will grimly, looking down at his hands.

"Jesus H, man," said Gabriel, alarm in his voice. "You've only taken her to see Santa in Jenners. Keep it together, for heaven's sake!" He waited for a response but got none. "The last time for what, though? The last time Martha lets you take Ruby or the last time you see *Martha*?" He left the thought hanging in the air, knowing that either and both scenarios were Will's concern. He'd sensed a change in him over the last few days, a softening.

Another silence fell between them while a shelf of snow formed quickly on the base of the windscreen.

Gabriel was patient for at least half a minute before he tutted and opened the glove compartment once more. "Oh, for heaven's sake, just go up to the door and give her this," he barked, thrusting the box containing the diamond and sapphire ring toward Will.

Batting Gabriel's hand away, Will turned and stepped from the car with a sigh. He closed his own door quietly and opened Ruby's, focusing on getting the little girl out of the car-seat as gently as he could without disturbing her. She'd loved seeing Santa, had refused to relinquish her gift, the copy of *Room on the Broom,* until it had fallen from her hand as she nodded off in the car on the way home. It was the third time that Martha had permitted him to take her out. And every time he handed her back he felt a physical pain of separation.

He hoisted Ruby up as gently as he could on his shoulder and she snuggled in there, a little arm still wrapped around Hugo, the pacifier sucked securely back into her mouth. He bent awkwardly to retrieve her book from the floor of the car and straightened himself. Now came the hard part. Crunching across the gravel, ringing the front doorbell on the home that he had thought would be his and Martha's to share. A home in which to start their own family . . .

Martha had been happy so far to let him take Ruby – it was Christmas after all – but as life went on who knew how long that would last? He was no blood relative of Ruby's – Calderwood was the only thing that bound them. As time went on, Martha was sure to meet someone else who would replace him. And then there was the issue of Dan, of course, and his baby – Ruby's half-brother – a boy called Alexander.

A pang of regret hit Will, then he pushed that away, reminding himself of how he had felt when Dan had blurted out what he had to say that day in Dubhglas. What a vile, vile individual, Will thought, remembering the relish with which he had told the tale. He was a creep, he knew. But a creep who Martha had been married to for a long time, had wanted to share the rest of her life with. And who she had said as much to only a few weeks ago.

He pressed his finger on the doorbell and heard it ring loudly inside. A moment later he heard a door open inside – the living-room door, he knew by the sound – and the click of the latch on the front door.

Martha's heart gave the little leap it always did when she saw him. The split second of first seeing his face, him and Ruby together, when everything was normal, before it was replaced by the dread, the regret, the guilt – the plain misery of living without him. She longed to get Christmas over, to get into the penance of January.

She saw her daughter asleep on his shoulder and looked awkwardly at them for a moment, and then up at the sky where the whirls of snow were coming down thick and fast. She looked back at Will, watched thick flakes land on his coat and stick there, wondered whether or not to invite him in.

In the long run, it was he who gave her the answer. "You'd better take her," he said. "I have to get Gabriel into town."

Silently, Martha slid her arms around Ruby, feeling a small electric charge as she touched against Will's hand as she took Ruby's book from him. A deep pang of longing hit her.

"Oh yes, he's finishing up with *Ghosts R Us* today, isn't he?" she said.

Whatever about herself and Will, she wasn't going to lose touch with Gabriel again. Then again, he was Will's friend of course. Over time . . . she blocked the thought from her mind and pulled Ruby toward her, taking her awkwardly, herself and Will close to each other as they made the exchange.

Will didn't answer, just made sure that Ruby was secure in Martha's arms and stepped back with a long step. Martha was wearing Jo Malone's Orange Blossom – her favourite perfume. He recoiled from the scent. In his mind's eye he saw the bottle on the dressing table in their bedroom. Such little familiar things, he thought to himself and felt the pain fresh again.

Martha settled Ruby in her arms. The little girl grizzled a little, made to wake up and then thought better of it, nuzzling into her mum's neck. That was it, thought Martha. Handover done, what next? She was always terrified at this point. Terrified that it would be the time that Will would say he couldn't see them again, that he didn't think it was a good idea for him to take Ruby. He didn't have to keep in touch with her, Martha knew. But if it was the only way that she could still see him . . .

She longed to apologise for the hundredth time, to protest that she hadn't been in her right mind, that Dan meant nothing to her and neither did anything she had told him. But she couldn't. Couldn't risk doing something that broke the fragile peace that had settled between them. She couldn't allow him out of her life. Couldn't risk that for a second.

"Would you –" she began.

"I'd like to see her again once Christmas is over –" he started at the same time.

Martha felt her stomach flutter faintly with habitual possibility and immediately quashed it. It didn't do to hope when there was none. "Fine," she said.

"I'll drop you a text to arrange," Will said in a businesslike fashion and without another word he turned his back and walked back across the gravel to the car.

In the passenger seat, she saw Gabriel crane his neck to catch her eye, frantically waving an envelope in his hand to which he pointed with exaggerated motion. His resignation letter, she knew, and allowed herself a smile. She'd helped him write it. No – she'd written it and emailed it to him to hand in. He made a gesture with his hand to indicate that he'd call her and turned away.

Martha stared at Will's tall figure as he opened the driver's door and climbed in. Please look back, she thought to herself. Please, just a glance, a wave – anything.

Nothing.

She saw him turn the key in the ignition, and leave without a backward glance. He drove slowly. The driveway was treacherous with the earlier snowfall and even in the few short moments of their exchange it had grown darker. Visibility was low with the thick snow that pelted down now. Taking a final look up into its mesmerising descent, Martha slowly and quietly went inside, closing the door behind her.

"Put it away, Gabriel," said Will to his friend as they turned around the corner in the drive and he could no longer see Martha and Ruby's shapes in the reflection of the rear-view mirror. He glanced back over his shoulder through the curtains of falling snow at the closed front door. His heart broke a little, as it always did. He turned on his headlamps and stared straight ahead.

Disappointed, Gabriel tossed the small box back into the glove compartment and had just managed to snap it shut again before he was flung forward in the seat. The car skidded slightly as the brakes were applied with force.

Martha laid Ruby in her cot, having first managed to extract her from her coat, hat and gloves. She sighed and made her way from the room back out onto the landing, turning to head into her own room and begin the nightly ritual of closing blinds and curtains, of blocking out the real world. Out there, she realised, people were finishing work for the Christmas holidays. Scores of merrymakers were filing into festive pubs, fathers and mothers were returning to their families to close their own blinds and curtains, to block out the world until the following morning. Christmas Eve, she thought with an inner groan. The day of the year that should most be filled with promise, yet here she was, alone, filled only with dread.

For a moment she thought she'd imagined it – the ring of the doorbell downstairs. She'd grown to hate the tone. That was one job to get done after Christmas, she thought. Get a new doorbell. Since that night it gave her the creeps, the only remnant of the encounter that still unnerved her. That in itself had been a huge source of surprise for her, the fact that Calderwood felt just as safe as it had beforehand. Once she'd tidied the living room, rearranged the furniture and given the walls a fresh colour as well as installing a brightly lit tree and some garlands, it had begun to feel like a sanctuary again. Martha felt safer here, in fact, than she had done beforehand. She wondered sometimes if there was a reason for that, if she had done something to incur protection?

She quickened her step down the stairs as the doorbell rang again. There was no mistaking it that time. Martha frowned. She wasn't expecting anyone – her father wouldn't arrive until the morning, weather permitting. The heavy snow made her nervous. If it stayed that heavy, then she and Ruby would spend Christmas alone and she wasn't sure if she could cope with that. Unless of course he had taken pre-emptive action and come a day early? But surely he would have phoned?

Martha heard music come from outside as she crossed the hallway and frowned again. Surely not carol singers? As she neared the door, she recognised the tune as 'Hark, the Herald Angels' – her favourite – and was stunned to feel tears prick her eyes. It should make her feel so joyous. Martha blinked back a tear as she opened the latch and pulled the door toward her.

She couldn't see him there at first. She peered out into the thick flakes of snow – like feathers drifting toward the ground. She looked out further to find the source of the music and was stunned by what she saw.

There, at the top of the driveway, Will's Volvo was parked again, the driver's door open, the engine still running, the radio blaring the carol. And out in the snow, a tall black shape becoming clearer as it stepped into the light spilling from the front door. It was Will.

He was before her in a single step, thrusting his hand in her direction, something clutched in his fist. Martha held out her hand to receive it.

"What did she forget now?" she asked, attempting a friendly smile. "Something vital, no doubt!"

She halted when whatever Will held in his hand wasn't forthcoming. She looked at his face directly and was surprised to see how serious it was. Her stomach sank. What had he come to tell her now?

They stared at each other for a few moments, Martha's eyes filled with fear and anxiety. Will's searching her face in an attempt to find the right words. Eventually, they came.

"I'm sorry," he said quietly.

Martha turned her head to one side to hear him better. She wasn't sure that he had said what she thought he did.

But she had.

"I'm sorry," he repeated, his voice growing more urgent now. "These last few weeks, Martha – they've been hell. Being without you . . . I can't . . . I've realised . . . I'm not made for that. Please listen to me when I say that I was all the way down that drive, in that snow . . . with Gabriel *nagging* me about being late for his bloody meeting and suddenly, it just felt . . . wrong . . ."

He paused for breath and Martha stared at him in confusion, straining her ears to hear what he was saying against the music coming from the car which seemed to have grown in volume since Will had started to speak. He had noticed it too, it seemed. When he spoke again, he found that he had to shout over the choir from King's College.

"If you'd seen Ruby's face today – in the store – when she saw Santa . . . Will you turn that *fucking* radio *down*!" he hollered suddenly in the direction of the car, turning his back on Martha as he did so.

The response was immediate. The swelling of the carol deflated instantly and a chunky arm poked from the passenger window as it did, waving in acknowledgement. Will turned back to face Martha who had started to laugh at the scene. It was preposterous.

"Look, when I saw her today, I had a wonderful time – I always do," Will went on. "She's such great company. But I find when I'm with her . . . I'm always lonely."

Martha tilted her head as he spoke, taking in his confused face, his flushed cheeks. He suddenly looked directly into her eyes.

"Because when I'm with her, I know that I should also be with you," he said and looked away again, momentarily embarrassed.

Martha gasped, her stomach lurching at his words. "Will," she began. She needed to stop him now. Whatever he was going to say would hurt her afresh, she realised. This was some sort of long goodbye. In the snow at Christmas time. She couldn't bear it, she realised. Couldn't listen to another word.

"I'm *sorry*, Martha," he said again.

"What have you got to be sorry for?" she replied. "It was me . . . it was all my fault. And *I'm* so sorry, Will. I never meant to hurt you – never meant to *do* what I did. Dan means absolutely nothing to me – even less now, if that's possible – you've *got* to believe me."

She was silenced by Will reaching out and taking her hands in his, the bulk of the small box which he still gripped awkward between them. Martha didn't even notice it. She was too anxious.

"I know," he replied firmly. "I know that now . . . in fact, I knew that *then* – when Dan told me – but I couldn't let myself believe it – it all hurt so much. I shouldn't have run off on you like that, but I was so *hurt*. I thought I'd lost you that night in the lake – I was still in shock from what had happened and I just couldn't deal with it, had to get away. But I've had so much time to think in Gabriel's spare room and I realise that, yes, we still have some things to work out but I don't want to be alone any more. Actually, that's wrong – I don't mind being alone – I can cope with that. What I can't cope with is being without *you.*"

He paused, looking directly into her eyes. A movement behind him caught Martha's eye and she saw Gabriel emerge from the car and stand to watch, silent, his black coat pulled around him and clouds of vapour dissipating into the air as he blew on his hands to keep warm.

And then she acknowledged the bulk of the small box being pushed into her hand as Will finally released it. She gasped slightly, unable to tear her eyes away from his face.

"I think I'm doing a really rubbish job of this," mumbled Will, "but I've started so I'll finish."

He paused for a breath, looking at the box and then back at her face. "Open it," he said, his voice barely more than a whisper.

And she did, her expression softening, then turning to shock as she saw what was inside. Her eyes grew wide as she looked from Will to the ring and back again.

"Will you wear it?" he managed. He rolled his eyes at his clumsy turn of phrase but it was as much as he could manage through the tears that were forming in them.

In turn, a drop trickled down Martha's face as she stared at him. Stared at his familiar features, at what she saw in his eyes –

everything that they had been through, already the stuff of life and death, and everything that was yet to come. All the hope, the dreams . . . she was stunned into silence for a moment.

And as the snow drifted silently around them, and their closest friend watched from a little way down the drive, Martha looked around her for a moment and saw everything with clarity. *This is how it's meant to be*, she said to herself all of a sudden as the scene before her, around her and ahead of her felt absolutely right.

Feeling the warmth as yet another tear trickled down her cheek, Martha looked back at Will and felt herself fill with love. And hope.

"I will," she said.

If you enjoyed
The Dark Water by Helen Moorhouse
why not try
The Dead Summer also published by Poolbeg?
Here's a sneak preview of Chapter One

The Dead Summer

HELEN MOORHOUSE

POOLBEG

CHAPTER 1

28th May

It was a balmy evening in Martha Armstrong's garden in London and she and five friends were drinking champagne.

"To Martha!" said Polly Humble and lifted her glass, insisting then in clinking it in turn against each of the five other glasses. It meant that she had to stand up out of her seat and lean over awkwardly to reach some of the others, but to Polly it had to be done this way or the toast hadn't been done correctly at all.

"To Martha!" chorused the other five.

"On her great country adventure!" added Polly, who thought the whole thing a great lark indeed.

All six took sips of champagne. Polly pretended to shudder with delight and rolled her eyes to the sky. Fiona smacked her lips loudly and Sarah said "Mmmm . . ." in an exaggerated fashion.

Standing behind Fiona, Sue Brice made a face at Martha and stuck out her tongue at each of the people at the table. Martha looked downwards, trying to suppress a giggle but also feeling sad at the sham of it all.

It took Claire Smith, one of Martha's ex-colleagues, to finally say what the others were thinking: "So, Martha, what does Dan think about all this?"

Sue opened her eyes wide at the question and cast a worried glance at Martha, who never flinched.

"Oh, I think he's actually quite pleased, to be honest," Martha said casually. "Me moving to the country gets the fly out of his ointment, the elephant out of his room so to speak."

There was silence for a moment.

"And is Ruby all excited about packing her case and moving away with Mummy?" chirped Polly in an exaggeratedly high-pitched voice, as if she were talking to a child or an idiot.

Sue rolled her eyes, unseen by the group.

Martha fixed Polly with a stare. "She's six months old," she replied drily. "She can't really tell the difference between moving to the country and next Tuesday fortnight."

Polly looked sideways under her lashes at Fiona and Sarah. Martha observed the glance, thinking that they couldn't wish to be gone any more than she wanted them to be.

"Are you sure that this is what you want to do?" asked Sue later when the others had gone and it was just the two of them left. She stood by the back door, smoking a cigarette out into the garden, while Martha shuffled about the kitchen making coffee for them both.

Martha stopped pouring milk into the two cups, picked up an envelope which had been tucked in beside the microwave and held it out to her friend.

"What's this?" said Sue, opening the envelope and drawing out a document. "Oh."

"Yup," said Martha. "Decree Absolute. Arrived this morning." She looked around her at the bare kitchen, all of the furniture sold or gone to Dan's new home, save the white goods which were remaining for the new owners. She sighed and handed Sue her coffee. "Oh, Sue, you know as well as I do that there's nothing left for me in the city."

"Your friends –" offered Sue.

"Who?" Martha cut in. "Polly Humble? Fiona Oldham? Sarah James? They're all wives and girlfriends of *Dan's* friends, not mine. They only turned up tonight to tick the box, as it were. I know for a fact that Sarah had Dan and Paula to dinner when I was five months pregnant!"

Sue blew out a cloud of smoke. "Oh yeah, forgot about that, sorry," she said apologetically.

"As for Claire . . ." continued Martha, sipping her own coffee and wandering over to join Sue in the doorway. "Well, she's been a good old sort but I know tomorrow she's just going to go into the office and get into a huddle with Liz and tell her that I'm storming off to the country and giving up my job because I'm all bitter and twisted about Dan. She'll make it sound all juicy and then by next week I'll be 'Remember Martha?' and pretty soon Claire will have moved on as well."

Sue dropped the cigarette butt and ground it with her foot. "And you're not at all bitter and twisted of course!" She picked up the butt between her forefinger and thumb. "What do you want me to do with this?"

"Oh, plant it somewhere and see if a ciggie-tree grows! I don't actually care any more – it's not my house, right?"

Sue smiled and flicked the butt out into the garden.

"Oh, sod this!" said Martha and turned back into the kitchen. She poured her coffee into the sink and opened the fridge. "This was for the new owners but, screw it, let's have a proper drink."

She took another chilled bottle of champagne out of the fridge and handed it to Sue who promptly ditched her own coffee and made her way back out into the dusky garden. Sue popped the cork and watched it bounce off the trellised wall and disappear into a flower-bed. She poured it into the two glasses Martha had set on the table.

"Of course I'm bitter and twisted!" said Martha. "I was with the same bloke for ten years for heaven's sake – had it all, I thought – the wedding in the country manor, the big house in the suburbs, baby coming along two years later, like I'd planned it. Shame it wasn't what Dan had planned in the slightest. His plans only extended to when he could next do the dirty with Paula Bloody Gooding!"

"Here," said Sue, familiar with the routine of letting Martha rant since she had discovered her husband's second relationship eight months previously. She topped up Martha's glass and lit herself another cigarette. "To keep the midges away, of course," she said, grinning at Martha.

Martha sipped her drink and inhaled Sue's second-hand smoke deeply, wishing at that moment she had never given up. "You know what bugs me the most, Sue? It's that he carried on with everything that we had planned and he'd have carried on forever if I hadn't found out. If Tom Oakes hadn't commiserated with me when he saw them at the Ad Awards, then I'd probably still be blissfully unaware my husband had a long-term girlfriend. It was only when he got caught that Dan actually grew the balls to admit that none of this was 'his bag'." She glanced back at the four-bedroomed terraced house that she had spent five years lovingly turning into a home for her family, then pointed at the window over the kitchen. "The only good thing that came out of that marriage is asleep in that room and her father doesn't even want to know her. And I think that he loves Paula Gooding more than he ever loved me, and more than he'll ever love Ruby, and that absolutely *kills* me. So yes – in answer to your question I think I am absolutely doing the right thing in selling up and getting out of Dodge. At least for six months or so to get my head straight, instead of just moping around here trying to . . . to catch a whiff of the nasty, leftover stink of my marriage." There were tears in Martha's eyes which she was trying her hardest to fight back. "You know what else kills me? That my little girl will never have a brother or sister who calls the same man 'Daddy', that she'll always feel left out at nursery or at school when kids talk about their dads – and what does she do if, say, they're making cards for Father's Day?"

"Relax," said Sue. "I don't think they do that any more – there are plenty of kids like Ruby with no dad, or kids with two dads, or twenty 'uncles' or two mummies."

"That's true," said Martha, comforted by this thought.

"Of course you're doing the right thing," said Sue reassuringly. "I'll just miss you both so much. We've never lived more than ten miles apart since we were at university." She rubbed Martha's hand lightly with her own.

Martha drained her glass. "That's another thing, Sue. I've got to do this writing thing as well, and everything in London is so tied up with the divorce that I can't get down to it with a clear head. I mean, I've left my job to finally write the book I've been promising myself I'd write since I was a kid. I've got to give it a proper go, now that I can finance it with this . . ." she indicated the house which she would leave forever the following morning, "and with the maintenance, provided Mr Lover can remember to pay it. I've brought Ruby into a broken home – I have to be able to offer her the best, be a mum who is trying her hardest to fulfil her own potential if I'm to be any example to her. I can't be someone who's face down in a bottle of wine every night because I'm trying to blot out the thought of going to work in the morning. You know I hate advertising with a passion and this is my chance to get away, start afresh. My life's just a great big bloody – *toilet* here in London."

Sue smirked, recognising that a combination of champagne and tiredness was beginning to speak instead of Martha. "Albeit a very nice toilet with a new Audi and lovely clothes and tons of handbags and shoes!"

Martha grinned, glad that her friend was there to bring her back down to earth. "Okay, so it's a gold-plated toilet with a thing that whirrs around to clean the seat for me!" she laughed. "But a toilet nonetheless, good madam! Seriously though, I've got to give this the best shot I can and if that means moving away then that's what I've got to do."

Sue nodded. "Pity Party over?"

Martha nodded. "Yes. Pity Party over. And please don't use that phrase around me again. It's going on the banned list along with 'twenty-four seven' and 'do the math'. Oh, and another one – 'so over it'!" She grinned. "I'm like totally so over that one!" she said, and the two laughed.

"To Martha and Ruby!" said Sue, raising her glass.

Martha followed suit.

"May your stint in the countryside be as fulfilling as you dream it can be," continued Sue, addressing the trees and shrubs in the darkening garden. "And may you bloody well cheer up soon!"

If you enjoyed this chapter from
The Dead Summer by Helen Moorhouse,
why not order the full book online
@ www.poolbeg.com

See also exclusive extract from Helen Moorhouse's
forthcoming book *Sing Me to Sleep*
coming October 2013

Enjoy!

HELEN MOORHOUSE

SING ME TO SLEEP

June 1998

Jenny

I'm sitting at my kitchen table. It's Saturday morning and it's raining outside, a steady downpour, noiseless, except for the steady drip-drip of water from the gutters just outside the back door. It's a nice rain. A stay-indoors rain. Even though it's June, the kitchen lights are on and it's cosy – there's a warm smell of coffee and toast and Ed has popped on the new Moby album. The washing machine is humming gently in the background – a gentle swish-swish sound. Adds to the atmosphere. Makes all this a moment.

I'm watching Ed do his usual Saturday-morning routine: standing at the countertop to go through the week's post in detail. He's always done it. Stood there with his diary to hand, filling in any appointments, filing the bank statements, making a neat pile of the bills, binning the junk mail.

Sitting beside him on the work surface, helping, is our daughter Bee. She'll be three in a couple of months. A fireball of energy at home, all ginger curls and green eyes and porcelain skin. Outside the front door of 17, Pilton Gardens, it's a different story: there she's a serene little thing, silent and angelic. She's ripping up the envelopes for Ed as he empties them of their contents.

I can't help but laugh as he wrestles a still-sealed A4 envelope from her hand.

"Bee!" he exclaims. "Give that back to Daddy! I haven't read it yet!"

Bee giggles and tries to tug it back. "But I'm helping Daddy!" she counters. "I'm the ripper – you said! I'm Bee the Ripper!"

Ed responds by tickling her exposed armpit, then nestling his head in her warm little neck and blowing a loud raspberry at which she shrieks with delight, relinquishing the envelope and grabbing his arm, making a scrabble-handed tickle gesture of her own.

Making sure she's secure, Ed withdraws from her, smiling, and returns his attention to the envelope.

It's then that Bee turns to the kitchen table and sees me. I'm sure of it. A smile plays on her lips. "Mummy," she says softly.

I smile back.

At the same moment Ed opens the envelope and groans softly before being momentarily distracted by Bee.

"Mummy," she says again, her eyes completely focused on me. Bee can see me.

Ed follows her stare to the kitchen table where I am sitting. He sees nothing of course. "Please, Bee . . ." he begins, and I see the start of tears in his eyes. Please don't, Ed. Not in front of her. Not again. But he can't seem to help it . . .

My name is Jenny Mycroft, née Adams, and my husband can't see me because I'm not there. Because I died in a car crash on the twenty-third of December 1997.

I watch as he takes my daughter, our only child, in his arms. He is crying silently into her hair while she struggles to look back at the table where I am sitting. Except I don't think she'll be able to see me now. Because the moment has gone. Because it's all broken.

I watch as my husband Ed slumps down to the floor where he sits with his arms wrapped so tightly around little Bee. A sob escapes him and he is helpless. And I am helpless too. I long to put my arms around both of them, to somehow touch them, but I can't because I'm not really there.

And then I see what has fallen to the ground from the envelope with which they struggled in their little game and I know why he's crying. It's a wet Saturday morning in June and my husband has found, among the week's post, his wife's death certificate.

"Jenny," I hear him whisper into Bee's neck. Her skinny little arms have snaked around his neck and she's hugging him back. It's not the first time that she's done this.

"Jenny," sobs Ed again, helplessly, into Bee's neck. "Why did you leave us? Why did you go?"

For all he knows, there is no one there to hear him. A louder sob escapes, his whole body surrendering to the tears, shuddering, convulsing with distress.

And there is nothing I can do. I didn't want to die, Ed. You have to believe that. But I'm here now and I'm not leaving. Please don't cry. I'm not going to leave you this time. Not ever.